THE RULES OF SEDUCTION

"Hunter is masterful at drawing readers in and creating realistic characters and powerful emotions so that each of her romances both satisfies readers and leaves them anxious for the next book."
—*Booklist*

"Rich in plot and characters, rich in wit and emotion, and rich in satisfaction for any reader." —*Romance Reviews Today*

"A carefully crafted, riveting romance showcasing Hunter's talent for both great storytelling and unforgettable romance. Her strong hero and equally fascinating heroine make this an irresistible read.... Hunter finds herself in the enviable position of being a writer whose novels every reader will adore."
—*Romantic Times*

LORD OF SIN

"Snappily paced and bone-deep satisfying, Hunter's books are so addictive they should come with a surgeon general's warning. [Hunter] doesn't neglect the absorbing historical details that set her apart from most of her counterparts, engaging the reader's mind even as she deftly captures the heart." —*Publishers Weekly*

THE ROMANTIC

"Every woman dreams of being the object of some man's secret passion, and readers will be swept away by Hunter's hero and her latest captivating romance." —*Booklist*

THE SINNER

"Packed with sensuality and foreboding undertones, this book boasts rich historical details and characters possessing unusual depth and vitality, traits that propel it beyond the standard historical romance fare." —*Publishers Weekly*

"Sensual, intriguing, and absorbing, prolific Hunter scores again." —*Booklist*

"There are books you finish with a sigh because they are so rich, so tender, so near to the heart that they will stay with you for a long, long time. Madeline Hunter's historical romance *The Sinner* is such a book." —*The Oakland Press*

THE CHARMER

"With its rich historical texture, steamy love scenes, and indelible protagonists, this book embodies the best of the genre."
—*Publishers Weekly* (starred review)

"In yet another excellent offering from Hunter, her intriguing characters elicit both fascination and sympathy." —*Booklist*

THE SAINT

"[An] unassuming, witty, and intriguing account of how love helps, not hinders, the achievement of dreams." —*Booklist*

THE SEDUCER

"Hunter . . . sweeps both her readers and her characters up in the embrace of history. Lush in detail and thrumming with sensuality, this offering will thrill those looking for a tale as rich and satisfying as a multi-course gourmet meal." —*Publishers Weekly*

BY DESIGN

"Realistic details that make the reader feel they are truly living in the 13th century enhance a story of love that knows no bounds: not social, political, or economic barriers. Ms. Hunter's knowledge of the period and her ability to create three-dimensional characters who interact with history make her an author medievalists will adore." —*Romantic Times*

"I'd heard a lot about the previous two books in this trilogy, *By Arrangement* and *By Possession,* but little did that prepare me for the experience that was reading this book. Whether you've already enjoyed Ms. Hunter's books or she is a new-to-you author, this is a wonderful, sensual, masterfully written tale of love overcoming odds, and one I heartily recommend." —*All About Romance*

"With each of the books in this series, Ms. Hunter's skill shines like a beacon." —*Rendezvous*

"Ms. Hunter has raised the bar, adding depth and texture to the medieval setting. With well-crafted characters and a delightful love story, *By Design* is well-plotted and well-timed without the contrived plot twists so often used in romances. I highly recommend *By Design* to not only lovers of medieval romance but to all readers." —*Romance Reviews Today*

BY POSSESSION

"With the release of this new volume, [Madeline Hunter] cements her position as one of the brightest new writers in the genre. Brimming with intelligent writing, historical detail, and passionate, complex protagonists . . . Hunter makes 14th-century England come alive—from the details of its sights, sounds, and smells to the political context of this rebellious and dangerous time, when alliances and treason went hand in hand. For all the historical richness of the story, the romantic aspect is never lost, and the poignancy of the characters' seemingly untamable love is truly touching." —*Publishers Weekly*

"Madeline Hunter's tale is a pleasant read with scenes that show the writer's brilliance. *By Possession* is rich in description and details that readers of romance will savor." —*The Oakland Press*

"Ms. Hunter skillfully weaves historical details into a captivating love story that resounds with sights, sounds, and more of the Middle Ages. This is another breathtaking romance from a talented storyteller." —*Romantic Times*

"With elegance and intelligence, Ms. Hunter consolidates her position as one of the best new voices in romantic fiction. I'm waiting on tenterhooks to see what is in store for readers in her next book, *By Design*." —*Romance Journal*

BY ARRANGEMENT

"Debut author Hunter begins this new series with a thoroughly satisfying launch that leaves the reader eager for the next episode in the lives of her engaging characters." —*Publishers Weekly*

"Romance author Madeline Hunter makes a dazzling debut into the genre with her medieval *By Arrangement,* a rich historical with unforgettable characters.... Layered with intrigue, history, passion, multidimensional characters, this book has it all. Quite simply, it's one of the best books I've read this year."
—*The Oakland Press*

"The first in a marvelous trilogy by a fresh voice in the genre, *By Arrangement* combines historical depth and riveting romance in a manner reminiscent of Roberta Gellis. Ms. Hunter has a true gift for bringing both history and her characters to life, making readers feel a part of the danger and pageantry of the era."
—*Romantic Times*

"*By Arrangement* is richly textured, historically fascinating, and filled with surprises." —*All About Romance*

"Splendid in every way." —*Rendezvous*

Also by Madeline Hunter

SECRETS
of
SURRENDER

Madeline Hunter

A DELL BOOK

SECRETS OF SURRENDER
A Dell Book / June 2008

Published by Bantam Dell
A Division of Random House, Inc.
New York, New York

This is a work of fiction. Names, characters, places, and incidents
either are the product of the author's imagination or are used fictitiously.
Any resemblance to actual persons, living or dead, events, or locales
is entirely coincidental.

Dell is a registered trademark of Random House, Inc., and
the colophon is a trademark of Random House, Inc.

ISBN 978-0-440-24395-3

Printed in the United States of America
Published simultaneously in Canada

www.bantamdell.com

OPM 10 9 8 7 6 5 4 3 2 1

SECRETS

of

SURRENDER

CHAPTER ONE

Roselyn Longworth contemplated her damnation.

Hell was not fire and brimstone, she realized. It consisted of merciless self-awareness. You learned the truth about yourself in hell. You faced the lies that you had told your soul in order to justify doing the wrong thing.

Hell was also eternal humiliation, such as she was suffering at this country house party.

All around her Lord Norbury's other guests laughed and played while they awaited the call to dinner. Upon arriving yesterday in Lord Norbury's coach, she had discovered that the guest list was not what she expected. The men were all members of polite society, but the women—

A loud screech interrupted her thoughts. A woman in a garish sapphire dinner dress playfully fought with a man who had grabbed her. The other men shouted encouragement to the fellow. Even Norbury urged him on. After a display of mock resistance, his captive surrendered to the kind of embrace and kiss that no one else should see.

Roselyn surveyed the painted faces and extreme attire of the other women. The men had not brought their wives with them. They had not even brought their refined mistresses. These women were common prostitutes imported from London's brothels. She suspected a few could not even claim that pedigree.

And here she sat among them.

She could not hide from the stark implications. The other men had brought their whores, and Lord Norbury had brought his.

How could she have misunderstood the events of the last month so badly? She tried to put her mind back to the day of Lord Norbury's first flatteries and overtures, but the memory was gone now, burned to ashes by the ruthless fire of reality during the last twenty-four hours.

The lover in question strolled among his guests, coming toward her. With each step the lights in his eyes brightened a bit more. She had thought those were the flames of love and passion. She now saw them as reflections off ice.

She had been pathetically stupid.

"You are very quiet, Rose. You have been all day." He sidled closely, looming beside her chair. A day ago she would have welcomed his closeness and found his attention romantic.

Stupid, stupid woman.

"I begged you to allow me to leave. I am in this drawing room only because you demanded that I come down for dinner, so do not complain that I do not engage in your party's games. I do not care for the company or the free behavior being shown." Over in the corner the embracing couple were lost to the world, but the world could watch their groping all the same.

"My, you are proud. Far more proud than you should be." His mutter carried a cruel edge. Her nape prickled.

He alluded to more than her disapproval of his house party. She had refused him things last night. She had not even understood what he wanted at first, and had not hidden her shock when he explained.

In the span of minutes the affectionate and generous lover had become the angry and spurned patron. Cold. Hard. Mean. He transformed into a man who had paid more than he ought for a possession, only to discover that he had been defrauded.

Her face warmed at the memory of the sordid scene in her bedchamber before he left. She had thought she was his beloved, his paramour. He had made it clear that he considered her a common whore. His scathing words had been so many slaps, wakening her from an illusion created out of her own hopelessness and loneliness.

"If I am too proud, call for the carriage and allow me to leave. Show the kindness of permitting me to retain what little of that pride remains."

"I would be alone without female company then. I will look a fool in my own home."

"We will say I became ill. We will say—"

His hand came to rest on her shoulder, silencing her. He grasped firmly, hurtfully. She tried to suppress a shiver of revulsion at the sensation of his palm on her skin.

"We will say nothing. You will go nowhere. I expect you to continue showing your gratitude for my generosity. If you please me, our arrangement can continue. You like the dresses and ensembles, Rose. You want the comforts and niceties that your family's fall denied you."

Her throat tightened. She blinked back the first tears of the day. "You misunderstood."

"You gave me your aging innocence and your favors. You took my gifts. I misunderstood nothing."

He bent down so his face was mere inches from hers. She fought the instinct to veer away from the ruddy complexion and pale eyes and tawny hair that once belonged to a man she respected. She had even convinced herself that he was handsome.

"We understand each other now at least, don't we?" He made it a demand. "There will be no more childish delicacy tonight."

Her stomach lurched. "There have been too many misunderstandings and I fear they continue. I have asked to leave all day because there will be nothing tonight."

His mouth formed a line so hard that she was grateful others were in the chamber. The hand on her shoulder gave a painful squeeze. "You do try a man's patience, Rose."

The prickling returned on her nape and scurried down her spine. She searched his expression for signs of the jovial man she had so recently thought loved her. She could find none. Of course not. That man had never existed.

A mild disturbance broke their silent battle of wills. The butler eased through the drawing room. Norbury took the card being borne on a silver salver. He read it and walked away.

He opened the doors that led into the library. Before the door closed she glimpsed a tall, dark-haired gentleman waiting in there.

Ill ease sloshed in her stomach. She fought to contain the panic that wanted to pour through her.

She had been stupid again. Ignorant and blind. What she endured now was nothing. Tonight would be the true descent into hell.

Norbury appeared angry when he entered the library. Kyle caught a glimpse of the drawing room before the doors closed.

"Bradwell. I expected you earlier."

"The surveyors took longer than expected." Kyle gestured toward the drawing room. "You are entertaining. I can return tomorrow."

"Nonsense. You are here now. Let us see what you have." Norbury's face creased into a smile intended to be reassuring.

Kyle surmised that the annoyance was not with the hour of his call, but something else. Like most men of his station, Viscount Norbury, son and heir to the Earl of Cottington, did not take disagreement well. He expected all but his peers to assume that whatever he did or said was correct. It looked as if someone in the drawing room had not conformed to those rules.

Kyle unfurled a large roll of paper on the desk. Norbury bent over it. He scanned the map closely, then stuck a finger on a blank section near a stream. "Why have you left this empty? We could fit another estate here. A good-sized one too."

"Your father does not want another house visible from the back of the manor house. With the stream, there is no way to use that land without positioning the new house—"

"He is of no mind or condition to make such decisions now. You know that. It is why he handed management of his affairs to me."

"It is still his land, and he spoke his wishes to me directly."

Norbury's anger was definitely directed at Kyle now. "How like him. He has agreed to carve up one of our properties into these small estates for the likes of your parvenu friends, but then he worries about the prospects from the old manor house. We never use it, so why should he care? I am telling you to put another one here. It will be the best of the lot and fetch the highest price."

Kyle had no interest in arguing and resented that he would now have to. Norbury knew nothing about land development. He did not know how to judge the best of the lot, let alone the prices that would be fetched. His family was providing the land alone and would profit handsomely. The real risk would be Kyle's own, along with the other investors who were joining the syndicate to build those houses and roads.

"You father's wishes may be ill-considered in your mind, but we lose nothing by accommodating them. The purchasers will not want to look up to the manor house any more than your family will want to look down and see them. Furthermore, to develop that section we will have to continue this road here, and that slices two other parcels inconveniently and lowers their value."

Norbury peered at Kyle's finger as it moved over the map. He did not like being wrong. No man did.

"Well, Kyle, I suppose it will do as it is," he finally said.

It sounded like acceptance, but Kyle knew every word had been chosen for a reason. "As it is" implied it could be better. "I suppose" was the lord giving his grudging approval. And calling him Kyle had been the most patronizing of all the deliberate words.

They knew each other very well. They had met often over the years, ever since they were boys. But even if they had liked each other, which they did not, their widely divergent births and some old bad blood between them meant they could never be friends. Norbury worked to avoid any presumptions on that count. His form of address was a way to put the upstart in his rightful place, which was far below Cottington and Norbury. It went without saying that Kyle could not return the informality.

"Let us see the plans for the houses," Norbury intoned. The "us" had become an imperious pronoun.

Kyle unrolled several of his architectural drawings. Considering Norbury's mood, he decided that his suspicion was right. Someone in the drawing room had pricked the host's pride.

It would not be hard to do. Norbury was jovial most of the time but could be temperamental at others. He also was not especially smart. Sometimes one had to point out the obvious to him, such as the problems with developing that land parcel. Unfortunately, Norbury could get mean when he realized that he had been caught being stupid or made to look a fool.

The mood turned friendlier while they discussed placements of rooms and how many servant chambers these homes needed. Kyle pretended to accept Norbury's judgment that everyone required a dozen servants to live at bare minimal levels of comfort.

"I envy you this skill." Norbury sighed and gestured to one of the drawings. "I would have liked to study such things. But for my birth, who knows, the world might have had another Wren. Duty calls, however, eh?"

Kyle smiled noncommittedly while he rolled the drawings. "I will see you in London, as scheduled. I will bring the final plans to our meeting."

"Expect a lengthy afternoon. We should have word from France about Longworth by then, and the group will meet first to decide our course."

"Hopefully we will be done with that soon. It is a distraction."

"Have no fear, justice will be served. We are all sworn to it." In a fit of bonhomie, such as he could display on occasion, Norbury helped tie the drawings.

Kyle made to leave, only to find his host examining him critically.

"Your coat is none the worse for wear considering you have been out in fields today."

"I was not planting hedgerows."

"Rather nice coat, actually. I'd say it is more than presentable."

"I do my best."

"I meant presentable enough to sit at dinner with us." He cocked his head toward the drawing room. "I told the butler to call them in and that I would join them when you and I were done. You must come too."

Norbury aimed for the door like a man who expected to be followed. "You will find the party very amusing."

As a man of affairs, Kyle never turned down the opportunity to mix with people of wealth and high station. Nor did gentlemen mind meeting him. Money was thicker than blood when you got down to it, and he had a talent for helping rich people get richer.

He trailed Norbury to the dining room. The muffled sounds of a merry party turned into a roar when the door opened.

Kyle took one look at the assembly and knew that no business connections would be made tonight. The men might be members of polite society, but the women were not. These were vulgar prostitutes, painted and flamboyant. They were already foxed beyond any hope of discretion.

Except one.

A blond woman of astonishing beauty and elegance sat silently at the far end of the table. She appeared not to notice the other guests. She gazed ahead at nothing and wore an expression of passivity.

Everything about her, from her discreetly plumed headdress to her blush dinner dress to the breeding that gave her such poise and dignity, set her apart from both the women and the men who had relinquished all reserve.

He recognized her. He had first seen her at a theater two years ago. He had barely noticed the play onstage after her lovely face caught his eye.

He glanced at Norbury. "What is Timothy Longworth's sister doing here?"

"I seduced her. I barely had to ask, actually. Bad

blood all around in that family, it seems. I've enjoyed a bit of justice already, while I wait to see that scoundrel swing."

Roselyn had hoped that the intruding gentleman had brought news of some disaster that would call Lord Norbury away for days.

She sickened when instead Norbury rejoined the party. A shiver of loathing claimed her while he walked down the table's length toward the empty chair beside her.

She saw two people notice her reaction. The tall, dark-haired gentleman from the library entered with Norbury. As he took a place at the other end of the table, he glanced her way. The vaguest alteration of his expression suggested that he saw something of the revulsion flexing through her.

Across the table, a woman named Katy also noticed. Her glistening eyes glanced at Norbury's approach, then met Rose's in comprehension.

Rose braced for smug satisfaction that the proud lady was being brought low. Instead, Katy smiled sympathetically. The men flanking her were engaged in other conversations, and she leaned forward confidentially.

"Not going good for you, is it?"

That was such an understatement that Rose almost laughed. "No, not well at all."

Katy shook her head in exasperation. "He should know better, and you should too. Didn't set the terms, did ye? Need to do that right at the beginning no matter where he found you, or things can get bad."

"So it appears." Norbury had paused to chat with a friend, but he would be in the chair beside her in a moment.

"They are like little boys, see. If mum says absolutely no sweets, then they know no sweets. 'Cept a few don't listen, of course. There's always them that like to make mum cry, but most know where else to go and get what they want. No need to hurt a girl if another will do it gladly enough for the same price, is there?"

Rose could not dispute Katy's expertise or logic. She felt Norbury nearing and braced herself.

Katy eyed her gown and headdress. "We can switch if you want. George here is easy, and I don't mind them like your lordship if the pay is right."

"Thank you, but I don't want George. I don't want any of them. I want to—"

"Finally deigning to speak, I see." Lord Norbury sat beside her. "Glad to see it. Won't do for you to cast such a pall over the party."

Katy's eyes still held her offer. Rose glanced to George. The corpulent brother of a baron noticed and smiled with delight.

Katy decided that was agreement enough. She commenced flirting shamelessly with Lord Norbury. Rose desperately tried to calculate a strategy if there really were a switch.

The new man who had entered with Norbury caught her eye. He appeared bigger and stronger than the besotted gentlemen, but perhaps his mere sobriety created an illusion. He sat down there beside one of these women, occasionally speaking to her and the man across the table. Mostly he just observed the others while he ate his meal.

There was nothing refined or soft about his face, but it was handsome enough. He was not in a dinner coat, but that made little difference in the raging informality in the room. The garments he did wear were unobjectionable in the extreme. He might have gone to his tailor and requested clothing that was expensive and of a cut and fabric to offend absolutely no one.

Katy appeared to be making progress in her seduction of Lord Norbury. Even while he parried shocking innuendoes with Katy, Lord Norbury kept turning his attention to Rose. She tried in vain to read his thoughts. He was calculating something, that was obvious.

He stood to address his guests. Silence slowly fell among them.

"It occurs to me that some of you may not know one of the guests here very well," he said. "I would like to enable you to make a better acquaintance."

Rose waited for him to introduce the new man at the end of the table. Instead he held out his hand to her.

"Stand, my dear."

There was nothing to do but rise. Every eye fixed on her. The only sober ones belonged to the new guest.

"You fair damsels may be wondering why this proud lady is among you," Norbury said. "Miss Longworth is the sister of a man who fled his debts, and considerable they were indeed. She is of good birth, but not good enough, of fortunes long gone and relations too distant to signify. Her final fall, into my bed as it happens, was perhaps too precipitous a one. She preferred gifts to money so that she could pretend it was other than it was. She inferred romantic notions when I merely suggested a good trading agreement."

Rose clenched her teeth to avoid crying or screaming. Everyone was watching, laughing. Even Katy. All the whores nodded. Yes, Miss Longworth was one of those ladies who like to pretend. These women who never pretended had little sympathy.

No, not everyone was watching. The new guest appeared not to hear. He drank his wine as if oblivious to this performance.

"Now, here is the thing," Norbury said. "I've this woman here, but I tire of her. I regret the indulgence and gifts that permit her to appear so lovely among you. Indeed, I've my eye on another." He leered at Katy, who tried to look coy and surprised. "George there seems to be thinking a simple trade is in order. Don't demur, George, I've been watching you flirt. I'm thinking, however, that maybe I can recoup my losses for this dress and whatnot. So, what do you say, gentlemen? Shall I auction off Miss Longworth?"

The party thought an auction would be wonderful fun. Laughter and calls rang off the ceiling as everyone prepared for a grand diversion.

Rose could not hide her appalled shock. She turned on Norbury and allowed him to see it. That only fed his satisfaction.

"I will not stand for this outrage." She moved her chair back and turned to leave. A hand on her arm stopped her.

"She has spirit and still needs taming, gentlemen. That alone should be worth a few shillings to some of you." He gripped tightly. Despite his laughter his glare contained a threat.

A few of the men sat up and took notice. She sickened at the evidence that an unwilling woman actually appealed to them.

"Let me see, I should hawk her a bit, shouldn't I?" Norbury made a display of thinking it over.

She wanted to hit him. No, she wanted to kill him. She tried to pull her arm away but his fingers only dug deeper. "You will *not* do this."

He ignored her. "Well, as all can see, she is very lovely. I have always thought she was among the most beautiful women in London."

"That beauty won't last much longer," a bawd warned. "She is older than me by a few years, I'd say."

"It is true that she is of maturing years, but the man who wins her will have shed her long before her delicious beauty dims." He scratched his head. "In the interests of fairness I need to describe the defects too, don't I? How do I put this delicately? No damned way, I guess. I am honor-bound to reveal that she is not an especially *warm* woman, if you gentlemen know what I mean."

She held on to the anger so she would not swoon. The faces seemed to multiply and move anyway, until she was on the block in front of a hundred leering masks.

"I am also bound to say that due to her late initiation, she still requires considerable training."

Dear God.

"I could give her a few lessons," a whore offered confidently.

Norbury bowed to her. "My dear, in the book of carnal knowledge you are writing chapter twenty and Miss Longworth has not yet studied chapter two. There are men who enjoy the role of schoolmaster, and it is they who should open their purses."

Rose refused to react. A few more of the men's interest suddenly piqued. Norbury's grip tightened yet more, almost numbing her arm.

"To her credit, however, I can offer several points," he said. "One, she is not greedy. Second, for those of you who, like me, were inconvenienced by her brother's ruin, her favors are one repayment—"

Shocked anew, she could not hold her pose of indifference. She turned and stared at him. She had no idea that he had been touched by that. No idea at all.

She had not misunderstood nearly as much as she was telling herself. He had deliberately pursued and seduced her for revenge.

The scoundrel.

"—and third, she has the most erotic dark nipples for one so fair."

They went wild. Amidst the shouts, a few called demands to see the charms that Norbury had just promised.

She spoke so only he could hear. "Do not even think to degrade me further by complying with that suggestion. If you dare to try it, I will do violence to you and gladly go to the gallows for it."

Lord Norbury's smirk wavered. He opened the bidding.

"Twenty-five pounds," George offered.

"Thirty!"

"Thirty-five," George countered after an ungallant pause.

"Fifty!"

"Sixty." A sly-eyed gentleman joined in. Rose recognized him as Sir Maurice Fenwick. His interest horrified her. It was unlikely that her willingness would matter much to this one.

"Sixty-five," George said in a tone of finality.

"Seventy."

"Seventy-five," Sir Maurice said immediately.

"Nine hundred and fifty pounds." The calm, even-toned bid seemed to come out of nowhere.

Shocked silence hung for a long moment, then a low buzz swarmed through the chamber. Everyone looked around to see which besotted gentleman had lost all sense.

Roselyn was as astonished as the rest. And very worried. It would be one thing to deny a man his seventy-five pounds' worth. A man who paid nine hundred and fifty would probably force a different accounting.

The party's attention found its way down the table to where the new guest drank some wine.

Lord Norbury aimed a frown at him. "Nine hundred and fifty, Bradwell? No doubt you misspoke."

The guest called over a footman and whispered something, then looked back very soberly. "Not at all. Feel free to continue the bidding."

Norbury's gaze darted around the table, but the high bid had taken the wind out of the auction's sails. Mr. Bradwell waited like a man in no hurry. He appeared to be more interested in admiring the candelabra on the table than on the progress of the game he had entered.

When the silence had stretched long enough, he rose and walked down the room.

Rose assessed his size and demeanor. Her instincts warned that she would have been better off with corpulent, happy George or even dangerous Sir Maurice. She might have even been better with Lord Norbury, who, she had just discovered, believed her capable of the violence she had threatened.

There was nothing visibly untoward about Mr. Bradwell. His very presentable garments and perfectly styled, wavy dark hair marked him as a man of wealth even more than his bid had. His face appeared rough-hewn in the candlelight. If people called him handsome, which he was, they would tend to add "in his way."

His skin had more color than the faces of the other men here, as if he spent time out-of-doors, and the fit of his coats revealed that he engaged in sport. Strength could be seen in his tall frame and in his confident, fluid movements.

There was nothing specifically threatening about him, but he alarmed her anyway. She sensed that the air parted to make room for him. The ripples of its retreat eddied over her, and she wanted to float away on them. The caution in her was similar to what one experiences when one meets unknown dogs on the road. Her instincts said it would be wise to give this particular animal wide berth.

He came up beside Norbury and the candlelight illuminated his face. She saw the bluest eyes she had ever seen. Those deep-set pools did not look at her at all. Instead they fixed on the man still holding her arm in a vise.

"Are we done?" Mr. Bradwell asked quietly. "Or do you feel obliged to knock her down?"

While "knock down" was an auction term, Lord Norbury seemed to think another *entendre* was intended. His face flushed. "You are a fool to spend such a sum."

"To be sure, but if a man can't be a fool about a beautiful woman, what good is money?"

"You just did it to—" Norbury caught himself before the petulant accusation was finished. The icy reflections lit his eyes. "See where your pride has gotten you, Rosie. From a viscount to a man born in the pits of Durham. Your fall may be the most rapid one in the history of whoring."

Mr. Bradwell did not react to the insult. "You can release her now. She is coming with me. The money will be delivered to your London house in two days."

Lord Norbury let her go. Rose saw the imprints of his fingers marking her. Mr. Bradwell did as well. Subtle anger flexed beneath his calm expression. The animal energy contained in this man leaked out. This was not someone who liked others to damage his property.

"Impatient are you, eh?" Norbury said loudly, to let the others enjoy the denouement.

"Absolutely," Mr. Bradwell said. "Come with me, Miss Longworth."

She did not want to go with him. She did not expect him to continue acting like a gentleman once they were alone. Her stomach turned violently at what might be waiting.

He leaned toward her. Dear heavens, he was going to kiss her! Right here in front of everyone.

The kiss was no more than a warm breath, but the dining room erupted into applause and hoots. While his face was close to hers, and his mouth near her ear, he spoke again. "Do not resist. They have had enough sport at your expense. I am sure that you do not want to give them more."

She had no choice but to accept his escort; otherwise, he would make good on his threat to give them more sport. Dragging the tattered rags of her dignity together as best she could, steeling herself to fight the battle soon to come, she accompanied the man who had bought her out of the dining room.

CHAPTER
TWO

Miss Longworth walked beside him like a queen. Kyle admired how well she hid her humiliation. No one else saw the moistness in her eyes.

She almost broke once the doors closed behind them. Almost. One long pause in her steps, one deep inhale, and she walked on.

She refused to acknowledge him. Of course. She was in a very vulnerable position now. They both knew she was at his mercy. The amount he had bid gave her good reason to worry.

Nine hundred and fifty pounds. He had been an idiot. The alternative had been to allow that sordid auction to take its own course, however. Fat, pliable George would not have won, either.

Sir Maurice Fenwick had been determined to have her, and the way he examined the property for sale did not speak well of his intentions. Sir Maurice's dark excesses were infamous.

"I called for my carriage," he said. "Go up with the

footman here and pack. He will carry your baggage down. Be quick about it."

Her posture straightened more. "I will not need to pack. Everything up there was ill-gotten and I want no reminder of the man who gave it."

"You have more than paid for every garment and jewel. You would be a fool to leave them behind."

Her exquisite face remained calm and perfect, but the glints in her eyes dared him to make a horrible night worse.

"As you wish." He shrugged off his frock coat and placed it around her shoulders. He beckoned her to follow him.

"I am not going with you."

"Trust me, you are. Now, before Norbury thinks twice about allowing it."

She kept her gaze skewed to the side of his head. She might have been looking past an obstructing piece of furniture.

He admired her pride. Right now, however, it was ill-timed and a nuisance. He wondered if she realized how perilous her position had been back there, and still was.

"I am sure that you know that I did not agree to that spectacle, Mr. Bradwell."

"You didn't? Well, damnation. How disappointing."

"You sound amused. You have a peculiar sense of humor."

"And you have chosen a bad time and place for this conversation."

She refused to budge. "If I go with you, where will you be taking me?"

"Perhaps to a brothel, so you can earn back what I

will be paying Lord Norbury. To be deprived of both the price and the prize doesn't seem fair, does it?"

Her attention abruptly shifted to his face. She tried to make her gaze disdainful, but fear showed enough to make him regret his cruel response.

"Miss Longworth, we must leave now. You will be safe, I promise." He forced the matter by placing his arm behind her shoulders and physically moving her out of the reception hall.

He got her as far as the carriage door before she resisted. She stopped cold and stared into the dark, enclosed space. He forced himself to be patient.

Suddenly his frock coat hit him in the face. He pulled it away and saw her striding down the lane, into the night. Her pale hair and dress made her appear like a fading dream.

He should probably let her go. Except there was no place for her *to* go, especially in those flimsy slippers women wore to fancy dinners. The closest town or manor was miles away. If something happened to her—

He threw the coat into the carriage, told the coachman to follow, and headed after her.

"Miss Longworth, I cannot allow you to go off on your own. It is dark, the way is dangerous, and it is cold." He barely raised his voice but she heard him well enough. Her head turned for a quick assessment of how close he was.

"You are safe with me, I promise." He walked more quickly but she did too. She angled toward a woods flanking the lane. "Forgive me my crude joke. Come back and get into the carriage."

She bolted, running for the woods. If she reached

them he'd be searching for her for hours. The dense trees allowed little moonlight to penetrate.

He ran after her, closing fast. She ran harder when she heard his boots nearing. The scent of her fear came to him on the cold breeze.

She cried out when he caught her. She turned wild, fighting and scratching. Her claws found his face.

He caught her hands, forced them behind her back, and held them there with his left hand. He imprisoned her body with his right arm and braced her against him.

She screamed in fury and indignation. The night swallowed the sounds. She squirmed and twisted like a madwoman. He held firmer.

"*Stop it,*" he commanded. "I am not going to hurt you. I said that you are safe with me."

"You are lying! You are a rogue just like them!"

All the same she suddenly stilled. She gazed up at him. The moonlight showed her anger and anguish, but determination entered her eyes.

She pressed her body closer to his. He felt her breasts against his chest. The willing contact startled him. He reacted like any man would, instantly. His erection prodded her stomach.

"See. Just like them," she said. "I would be a fool to trust you."

He barely heard her. Her face was beautiful in the moonlight. Mesmerizing. A moment stretched while he forgot what had led to this crude embrace. He only noticed every place where they touched and the softness of the body he held. Thunder rolled in his head.

Her expression softened. A lovely astonishment widened

her eyes. Her lips parted slightly. The fight completely left her and she became all pliant womanhood in his arms.

She stretched toward the kiss he wanted to give her, and the moonlight enhanced her perfection even more.

Suddenly it also revealed her bared teeth aiming up at his face.

He moved his head back just in time. She used the opportunity to try to break free again.

Cursing himself for being an idiot *again,* he bent down and rose with her slung over his shoulder. Her fists beat his back. She damned him to hell all the way to the carriage.

He dumped her into the carriage and settled across from her.

"Attack me again and I will turn you over my knee. I am no danger to you, and I'll be damned if I will let you claw and bite me after I paid a fortune to save you from men who are."

Whether his threat subdued her or she just gave up, he could not tell. The carriage moved. He found the frock coat buried amidst his rolls of drawings and handed it to her. "Put this on so you are not cold."

She obeyed. Her fear and wariness filled the air for several silent miles.

"Nine hundred and fifty was a high amount to pay for nothing," she finally said.

"The alternative was to let a man pay a lot less for something, wasn't it?"

She seemed to shrink inside the frock coat. "Thank you." Her gratitude came on a small, trembling voice.

She was not weeping, although she had good cause to. Her pride, so admirable thirty minutes ago, now irritated him. The burning scratches on his face probably had something to do with that.

He wondered if she understood the consequences of this night. She had dodged a man's misuse, but she would not escape the ruin coming when the world learned of that party and that auction. And the world *would* learn about it, he had no doubt.

Perhaps now, in the calm after the storm, she was assessing the costs, just as he was assessing his own. Norbury had been angered by his interference. He had not liked his fun spoiled and his revenge made less complete. The Earl of Cottington might be the benefactor, but his heir now held the purse strings and influence.

"I apologize for losing my head."

"It is understandable after your ordeal." It still impressed him, how well he had learned the lessons and syntax of polite discourse. They had become second nature, but sometimes the first nature still spoke in his head. *Damn right you should apologize.*

"I am so fortunate that you arrived. I am so glad there was one sober man there, who would be appalled at what Norbury was doing, and immune to his evil lures."

Oh, he had been appalled, but not nearly immune. He had paid a fortune, after all.

A few speculative images entered his head regarding what he would have been buying if he were not so damned decent. That embrace on the lane made the fleeting fantasy quite vivid.

He was glad for the dark so she could not see his thoughts. He could not see her face, either, which was for the best. She possessed the kind of beauty that left half of a man's soul in perpetual astonishment. He did not like that kind of disadvantage.

"May I ask you some questions?" She sounded very composed again. The lady had been rescued as was only her due. She would sleep contentedly tonight.

"You may ask anything you like."

"The amount of your bid was an odd one. A hundred would have been enough, I think."

"If I had bid a hundred, Sir Maurice would have bid two hundred, and by the time we were done the amount might have been much higher than I paid. Thousands, perhaps. I bid very high to shock the others into silence."

"If he would have bid thousands, why would he not bid one thousand?"

"It is one thing to jump from one hundred to two, then to four and then on up. It is another to jump from seventy-five to a thousand. It would have had to be a thousand, of course. Nine hundred seventy-five would sound small and mean."

"Yes, I see what you mean. Bidding a thousand so soon or right away would give anyone pause. It is such an undeniably foolish amount."

So was nine hundred and fifty, especially if you barely had it. A year ago he could cover it easily enough, although few men would not notice the depletion of their purses. A year hence he probably could too. Right now, however, paying Norbury would make somewhat shaky finances wobble all the more.

Miss Longworth had chosen a bad time to need res-cuing. It had been the only thing to do, however. He wanted to believe he would have done the same for any woman.

Of course, she was not just any woman. She was Roselyn Longworth. She had been vulnerable to Norbury's seduction because she had been impoverished by her brother's criminal acts. He did not miss the irony that Timothy Longworth had, in a manner of speaking, just managed to take yet more money from Kyle Bradwell's pocket.

"You are aware, I think, that I will never be able to pay you back nine hundred and fifty pounds. Do you hope that I will agree to do so in other ways? Perhaps you expect me to feel an obligation and thus remove the question of importuning."

Is that what she thought had just happened out on the lane? He had not been thinking about repayment, or anything much. Nor did he believe that she had felt any obligation to respond as she had. And she had re-sponded. Before she tried to bite him, of course.

"I have neither expectations nor delusions of enjoy-ing your favors in that way or for those reasons, Miss Longworth." *My, how noble you are, Kyle lad. Such an elegant idiot too.*

Those speculations kept having their way, however. The memory of that embrace remained fresh. He would probably indulge in a few dreams. Since he would pay dearly for them, he would not feel guilty.

"Perhaps instead you spoke of the brothel to make certain that I understood that tonight makes me fit for little else. I am all too aware of that. I know the high costs of what has occurred."

Yes, she probably did. Her poise had made him wonder, though. And the boy from the collier pits of Durham County had resented her reclaimed composure even while he admired it. A woman ruined irredeemably should not be so cool. She should weep the way the women of his mining village wept over loss.

"Miss Longworth, your accounting will have nothing to do with me. Forgive me for teasing you so unkindly. My annoyance at my own costs got the better of me."

She angled forward, as if peering to see if he was sincere. The vague moonlight leaking into the middle of the carriage gave form to her features—her large eyes and full mouth and perfect face. Even this dim view of her beauty made his breath catch.

"You have been kind and gallant, Mr. Bradwell. If you want to scold and remind me of my compliance in my final fall, I suppose that I should show the grace to listen."

He did not scold. He did not speak much at all. She wished that he would. Their brief conversation left her feeling less awkward. During the silences she could only sit there with her worry while his presence crowded her.

She could not really move farther away. A collection of large rolls of paper filled almost half the carriage. She wondered what they were.

An inner instinct remained alert for any movement from him. She knew that she was at the mercy of this man's honor. He knew it too, and that moment out on the lane had confused matters. There had been a second or two, no more she was sure, when that embrace had been less than adversarial.

She put the memory of it out of her mind. She did not want to dwell on how quickly her stupidity lured her to misunderstand a man again. She did not want to remember how she had stirred more easily than a decent woman ought.

He had spoken of his own costs. She wondered what they would be. His name would be attached to the gossip about that dinner party and to her "purchase," but as he was a man it would not destroy his reputation. Among some people it might even make him more interesting.

Maybe he referred to the bid itself. It was a huge amount for anyone. Perhaps he did not actually have the money to make good on this odd debt.

If he did not pay up he would be destroyed in the circles that mattered. In most circles, she suspected. Even the ones around the pits of Durham.

That reference had been an interesting comment. She wondered what Norbury had meant by it. Mr. Bradwell's speech and manner did not mark him as that common.

"If you are not taking me to a brothel in London, where are we going?"

"I am taking you to your cousin. The county paper noted that she is in residence at her husband's property here in Kent."

This man continued to surprise her. Not only with

this information, but also with his awareness of her cousin Alexia's movements.

"I had not realized that she had come down from town. I wish that I had known. I might have escaped this morning and walked there."

"It is at least an hour by carriage. You could not have walked. Nor, I suspect, could you have escaped."

"Is she alone, do you know?"

"The paper mentioned the family coming down."

That probably meant that Irene was with her. She would at least see her sister before . . . Her eyes stung and she bit her lip so hard that she tasted blood. The thought of seeing Alexia and Irene undid her as nothing else had.

"I assume that Lord Hayden is with her." She heard her own voice break. Mr. Bradwell's form blurred. "I pray, let us not intrude."

"I can hardly keep you with me at an inn."

"I do not see why not. My reputation is already totally ruined."

"Mine is not."

"Of course. Yes, I see. I am sorry. I do not want to bring more scandal to you. It is just that Lord Hayden has already been too kind, and I have been ungrateful in the past, and now to show up at his door with this horrible, hopeless—"

A sob snuck out, strangling her words. Then another. She bit her lip again, hard. It did not help this time.

He took her hand in his and pressed a handkerchief into her palm. His firm, dry hold branded her skin and mind. Not hurtful like Norbury. Not weak or grasping, either. Just careful and strong, and a little rough. Like that embrace on the lane.

It felt like the touch of a friend. Her wariness left her then. She finally knew for certain that she was safe.

Her composure left her too. Her rescuer made no effort to console her. He understood that nothing would change what was going to happen.

Her composure had annoyed him. Now her weeping dismayed him.

He resisted the impulse to gather her into his arms and offer comfort. He might frighten her. He knew that she still wondered about him. On the lane she had proven that he wanted her, which gave her good cause to suspect his motivations.

She continued crying. He could not take it anymore. He shoved aside the plans and moved to the place beside her. He carefully embraced her, ready to move away fast if she wanted to be alone in her misery.

She didn't. She cried into his shoulder while he held her. He tried to ignore how aware he was of the feel of her fragile form in his arms. He bit back the false words of reassurance that wanted to spring from him. She would reject them outright, he guessed. He suspected that she would never again lie to herself about much of anything.

The carriage turned off the road. She realized that the journey was ending. She valiantly tried to swallow her tears. He called to the coachman to slow down so she would have more time.

Her composure returned before they reached the

house. The embrace did not become awkward, however, and she made no attempt to break it. He held her until they rolled to a stop.

He climbed from the carriage and offered his hand.

She looked up at the house. The vertical forms of classical columns could be seen, and long blocks on either side of the central temple facade.

"It is the middle of the night. The whole household will be abed," she said.

"There will be a servant by the door. Come now."

She placed her hand in his. He felt a subtle roughness that surprised him, but the touch was mostly soft and warm. She stepped down. One pause, one deep inhale, and she walked with him to the door. She left her hand in his like a frightened child.

A servant eventually responded to the knock.

"This is Miss Longworth, Lady Alexia's cousin," Kyle explained. "Please ask Lord Hayden to receive us, if he is in residence."

The servant ushered them to the library. Kyle took in the room's perfect proportions. His practiced eye noted that even the wooden Doric engaged columns decorating the mahogany bookcases were true to the ancient system of measurements. Lord Hayden favored a pure classicism based on Greek rather than Roman models.

Miss Longworth refused to sit. She returned his frock coat, then paced the edges of the chamber, twisting his handkerchief in her hands.

"Will you stay while I explain, Mr. Bradwell? Please. Lord Hayden is a good man, but . . . I do not fear him, but after all the rest . . . He is not so stern as he appears, I think, but this story would strain the patience of a saint, and his love for my cousin may not spare me his worst reaction."

Kyle had met Lord Hayden only once, and agreed the man appeared stern. However, he also knew what she meant by "all the rest," and how it indicated that the man was not as hard as he looked. Or, as she suggested, Lord Hayden was so in love that he had put sternness aside in the case of his new wife's relatives.

Presumably "all the rest" would now include support of the relative in question today. Miss Longworth faced utter ruin, but Kyle assumed that Lord Hayden would make sure that she did not starve in her exile from family and decent society.

"I will remain until you have explained, if you wish."

Lord Hayden did not come down alone. His wife accompanied him. They arrived in dishabille, he in a dark blue brocade morning coat and she in a pale yellow undressing gown. A lace-edged cap covered most of her dark hair. Kyle had never met Lady Alexia but she appeared to be a kind woman of about Miss Longworth's age. Mid-twenties, he guessed. Right now her violet-gray eyes held noticeable worry for her cousin.

Lord Hayden appeared resigned, as if he expected nothing good if he was roused from his bed by a Longworth. His sharp gaze did not miss the way Miss Longworth's attempted escape had soiled the skirt of her dress. His attention lingered on Kyle's face, no doubt assessing the scratches so obviously made by a woman.

The ladies embraced and Miss Longworth made introductions. Lord Hayden nodded a silent acknowledgment that the introductions had been unnecessary since he and Kyle had met before.

"Mr. Bradwell helped me to escape from a house party of Lord Norbury's," Miss Longworth announced.

Lord Hayden caught his wife's eye in a meaningful glance. It was the look of a man who knew about that love affair and who had predicted the worst from the start.

"I fear," Miss Longworth added after an awkward pause, "I fear that something very scandalous happened at that house party that will be known to the world in a few days. Mr. Bradwell brought me here because there was nowhere else to go tonight, but come the morning I ask for transportation back to Oxfordshire."

"Exactly what happened?" Lord Hayden asked.

She told them. Bluntly. She spared herself not at all. She took full blame for her situation, which Kyle thought a bit hard. Her inclusion in a party of whores, her sale at the auction, her stupidity in misunderstanding Norbury's affection—it was all clear, specific, and honest. Ruthlessly so.

"So, I will return to Oxfordshire tomorrow," Miss Longworth concluded. "If I disappear completely and we cease any social connection, perhaps you will not be affected too much by the consequences of my behavior."

"Do not be so rash," Lady Alexia cried. "Surely it is not as bad as you say. Hayden, tell her she does not have to break with us completely. If we—"

"No, Alexia," Miss Longworth said. "I know how it must be, and so do you. Do not force your husband to command it."

Lady Alexia looked close to tears. Miss Longworth

held her poise. Kyle bowed to them both and eased away, to make his escape from this most private of family crises.

Miss Longworth looked in his eyes. "I am sorry that I did not trust you. I am very sorry for those scratches. Thank you for your kindness."

There was nothing to say in response, so he walked out of the library. He found Lord Hayden in his wake.

"Tell me, Bradwell—was it as sordid as she says? Or is there some hope that perhaps..." He shrugged, unable to think of what perhaps might be.

"Do you really want the truth, Lord Hayden?"

The man actually hesitated. "Yes, I suppose that I do."

"He publicly declared her a common whore, and treated her like one, in front of a dozen men whom you see daily at your clubs. I am sincerely sorry for her, but this is one Longworth that your money and protection cannot save."

Lord Hayden's dark eyes flashed anger at the allusion, but his ire passed quickly. Weary acceptance took its place.

"You have my gratitude that you stepped forward to take care of her and give her protection, Bradwell. In a dining room full of gentlemen, only you acted like one."

"Since I was the only man there who was *not* a gentleman, that should be the real scandal, don't you think?"

Kyle walked out of the house and away from the sad notes being played inside it. The melody would turn into a dirge of mourning soon.

He strode through the cold night to the carriage. Miss Longworth's scent lingered on his frock coat, filling his head.

After ensuring that a carriage would be ready in early morning, Lord Hayden took his leave and returned to his bed. Alexia drew Rose to a sofa and bade her to sit.

"I thank God that Mr. Bradwell stepped forward to protect you."

"It was very decent of him. I repaid him by scratching his face."

"You were distraught. I am sure that he understands. He appeared to."

Yes, he understood. All of it.

She pictured him walking toward her after the auction. No man there dared challenge him once he took the first step. Not even Lord Norbury. Those drunken fools had recognized a better man when they saw one.

She remembered his careful embrace in the carriage while she wept. His strength had soothed her. She regretted that she could never call on it again. The memory of his scent and the texture of his waistcoat and shirt came back to her vividly, giving her a few more moments of peace.

Mostly she thought about his confining embrace after she ran away. She should have been terrified by his rough handling, but instead his arms had seemed like a shelter. She had pressed close to throw him off his guard, only to be thrown off hers.

It had stirred her, their closeness. For a moment she forgot to fear him, even when she saw the desire in his face and felt it against her stomach. In truth she had reacted like the whore Norbury accused her of being. An undeniable excitement had flowed through her veins. That shocked her, and led to a last, desperate attempt to get free.

"What a horror you have endured. Norbury has behaved most dishonorably toward you, and—" A sob broke through Alexia's words. Rose's eyes burned and she gathered Alexia into her arms.

"Please calm yourself. Norbury is a scoundrel, but let us not pretend that I was other than a fool. I always knew a future earl could not marry me. Not after what Tim did. I allowed myself to think that I was more than a bought woman to him, but I realize now that his words of love were merely part of the game."

Alexia sniffed back her tears. "You spoke of breaking with us completely. Of being lost to me. You do not intend to—I cannot bear the thought of your being passed around, Rose. Please promise that you will at least take an allowance from us, so that you are never so desperate as to do that."

"Have no fear of that. I have discovered that I make a very bad mistress and would be a worse courtesan. I do not request enough jewels for one thing, and my lover does not get enough pleasure for another."

"Then will you take the money? *Finally?*"

This was an old argument. It had first been pride that made her refuse Lord Hayden's support after Timothy's ruin. Pride, and anger in her belief that Tim's fall was Lord Hayden's fault. Later, when she discovered that Lord Hayden had actually protected Timothy, pride had been replaced by chagrin and embarrassment.

"He has paid all the debts. He has protected our property in Oxfordshire. To accept more—"

"You *must*. Do not distress me so, Rose. It is bad enough that I will lose you, but must I picture you in that empty house hungry and sick?"

"I will not starve. The rents are not much, but they will keep me in bread and fuel. And I must ask your generosity on another matter instead. Irene—" The mention of her sister affected her so much that she could not go on.

"Of course she will stay with us," Alexia soothed. "She has enjoyed her visit this last month."

Rose had sent Irene to Alexia to keep her from knowing about the affair with Norbury. Now her sister would be the one most vulnerable to the scandal that affair would cause.

"Is she content with you?" she asked.

"Most content. She prefers town, but has also made some friends here in the county."

"They will say things and shun her. She will hear about it all. She will hate me for this."

"She is growing up, Rose. She is not so selfish anymore. She even apologized to Hayden for the things she said last spring. She will survive the gossip."

Rose pictured Irene trying to survive, and that distressed her more. "Do you think there is any hope for her future now, Alexia?"

"When Hayden and his brothers treat her as one of their own, she will be spared the worst. She also has that five thousand from your brother, although now I wish that you had not told Hayden to put it into a trust for her. You could use it better, I think."

"It is the spoils of a crime, Alexia. I could not touch it, but Irene will never know its source."

Alexia patted her hand like a mother reassuring a child. Rose suddenly felt exhausted and soiled and sad. Wiser than six months ago, but ignorance had been heaven in comparison.

"I will sleep with Irene tonight, if you do not mind, Alexia. I will leave soon after dawn, but I will explain everything to her first so that she knows why she will not be coming home to me." Not now and not ever. Saying good-bye to Irene would break her heart.

Alexia wrapped an arm around her shoulders. "If you want to do it that way, we will."

She leaned into Alexia's embrace and rested her head on her shoulder. "Hold me for a while, my dearest friend. I will be dead to both of you soon, and I cannot bear the thought of it."

CHAPTER
THREE

~

Jordan timed his steps to an inaudible fanfare of horns while he carried a letter across the chamber. His thin, pointed nose angled higher than normal, making his old-fashioned tail of graying hair dangle down his back.

"This was hand-delivered, sir. Just now. A messenger brought it. A *liveried* messenger."

When Kyle saw the letter he comprehended his manservant's performance. The paper must have cost five pounds a ream. An insignia further proclaimed the high station of its sender.

He recognized the crest. The Marquess of Easterbrook's. Well, well.

"Tell me, Jordan, can one just break the seal or am I supposed to perform some ritual first?"

Jordan's narrow face pinched into a frown. He prided himself on being an expert to whom the collier's son could turn for advice on the subtleties of navigating along the edges of polite society.

"Ritual? I do not think ... ah, you are joking, sir. Heh, heh, no, there is no ritual that I know of."

"Well, if you learn that there is one, don't tell anyone we skipped it."

Kyle broke the seal. Jordan's neck stretched in his hopes of spying a few words.

"I have been invited to call on the Marquess of Easterbrook," Kyle said. "At least I think it is an invitation. It reads more like a summons."

"What does it say?"

"That Easterbrook would be happy to receive me this afternoon."

"Of course that is an invitation."

"Good. That means that I can decline. I will write back and express my regrets that I am committed elsewhere."

"Oh, dear heavens, *no,* sir." Jordan stifled a horrified sigh. "When a marquess is happy to receive you, when he invites you to call, you must *go.*"

Kyle knew how it was done. He had been received by an earl often enough. He let Jordan fret while he eyed the letter.

It was said that Easterbrook did not receive much at all, let alone men like Kyle Bradwell. He was, however, Lord Hayden Rothwell's older brother, Christian Rothwell. No doubt Easterbrook had heard about that sad episode with Miss Longworth four nights ago. He probably wanted to make sure the rescuer would not try to dine on the story or take other advantage of this relative's ruin.

Kyle decided that he would answer the summons, but for his own reasons. In the course of their conversation he might learn how Miss Longworth was faring. He had thought about her these last days. He had indulged in a few of those dreams that he had promised himself, but a few concerns had also intruded on his mind.

"If you like, I will set out the appropriate garments," Jordan said.

"Fine, but do not overdo it. He isn't the King."

He set the "invitation" aside. The meeting with Easterbrook would no doubt be brief. It should not take the marquess long to threaten him.

Kyle had never been inside a house on Grosvenor Square. That made his call on Easterbrook interesting in itself. He studied the structure and furnishings while the servant brought him up to the drawing room.

That huge, towering chamber contained luxuries in the extreme. The decorating was a little out of style, but impressive in its restrained opulence. Every element, from the carpets to the ceiling moldings, from the sconces to the drapery tassels, was the best that money could buy.

He waited a long time for the reception so generously offered. He spent his time studying the paintings filling the walls, seeing if he could name the artists.

"That one has been attributed to both Ghirlandaio and Verrocchio. What do you think?"

Kyle pivoted at the question. A dark-haired man stood ten feet behind him. The marquess, he assumed, and not only because of the resemblance to Lord Hayden. No servant would dare dress like that, with no waistcoat or cravat, and with long hair streaming down past his shoulders.

"I would not know," Kyle said.

"You were examining the paintings as though you would."

Kyle shrugged. "It is before Raphael and not a Botticelli. I could get no closer than that."

"That is closer than most." He gestured to a grouping of chairs and a divan. "Let us sit over here. They will be bringing up ... something or other. Coffee, I suppose."

Kyle sat in a chair and Easterbrook on the divan. The marquess favored his guest with a thoughtful inspection. Kyle returned the examination. Time passed silently while they assessed each other.

"You strike me as an interesting man, Mr. Bradwell." A vague smile formed despite Easterbrook's critical gaze. "You are not ill at ease in the least. No doubt your patronage by Cottington has bred familiarity with the likes of me. Perhaps it has also bred contempt."

Easterbrook had made it his business to learn a thing or two before sending that letter, it seemed. "I have no contempt for the likes of you. If I did, I would not be here. I am merely waiting to learn why you wanted to meet me."

"You examine me very boldly while you wait. What are you thinking?"

"I am wondering how rich I have to be before I can stop strangling my neck with a cravat."

"Rich enough not to give a damn what the world thinks, I suppose."

They both knew that money actually had nothing to do with it. "And as *you* examine *me,* what do you think?"

Easterbrook gave one more long, careful scan. "I think that I am seeing the future."

The servants arrived with several trays loaded with

urns of coffee and tea, and decanters and cakes. It looked as if on receiving Easterbrook's order to provide "something," the kitchen servants had concluded it safest to provide almost everything.

Another quarter hour passed while servants offered various drink. Finally the marquess waved them all out of the room.

"I think that you were introduced to my brother several nights ago," he said.

They were finally getting down to it. "Actually, I had met Lord Hayden before. I did see him in Kent a few nights ago, however."

"He has come back up to town and brought Alexia with him. I am told that she is inconsolable in her grief over her cousin. I am very fond of my new sister. She is with child, and her distress is of concern to me."

"I am sorry to hear that she is distraught. Have you had any word on her cousin? Is she well?"

"I have learned nothing of Miss Longworth's health." His host found the question interesting, though. Kyle could not imagine why.

"My brother came to town to make sure that it is known that you delivered Miss Longworth to their home in Kent little more than an hour after removing her from Norbury's house party."

Kyle doubted that would help much. The scandal was breaking fast and hard, drawing more attention to him than he liked. Jordan had been approached on the street by some fellow from one of the scandal sheets, asking if Miss Longworth now resided in Mr. Bradwell's home.

Easterbrook rose to his feet. He strolled aimlessly, distracted by his contemplations.

No, not aimlessly. He more or less circled Kyle's chair.

"Your reputation will be spared by Hayden's efforts. You will probably be labeled so decent that you will never again be offered any fun in life," Easterbrook observed. "My question is whether anything might be done to spare Miss Longworth as well, so Alexia is not so unhappy."

"Miss Longworth's time with me was the least of it."

"Tell me about the rest. The servants bring me only bits and pieces, and my brother says only that she is lost."

Kyle described that night as he had seen it. Easterbrook paced his arcs while he listened. He asked some questions to clarify the details. He paced some more.

"It sounds as if Miss Longworth embarked on an affair with a man she thought loved her, and he in turn deliberately destroyed her. Did he have a reason for doing so, I ask myself. I have to assume that he did." Three more steps of contemplation. "This is about that damned brother of hers, I think."

Kyle let the conclusion lie there. He gave Easterbrook credit for understanding human motivations better than most people did.

Easterbrook's brooding ended abruptly. He sat on the divan again, closer to Kyle this time. Another long inspection ensued.

"You bid a very high amount. Shrewd of you, but it was an expensive ploy."

For the first time since he had set foot in this house, Kyle was uncomfortable. He did not like the hawkish way the marquess looked at him now. His instincts said a bald threat would be preferable to whatever this man intended.

"It must have taken a toll on your purse, paying all that at once."

"I managed." Barely. He had signed more mortgage papers two days ago than he wanted to think about.

Easterbrook relaxed back in the divan. "Miss Longworth is a very lovely woman. Don't you think so?"

"Very lovely." Why did he feel that he had just given ground in a battle by agreeing?

"I do not believe that Miss Longworth must be lost to my sister-in-law. I think that with very little effort we can blunt the worst so she can still have a future. There may always be whispers, but she is not irredeemable."

Who the hell did he mean by *we*? "It is said that you rarely leave this house, so maybe you forget how these things work. She will not survive this with even a shred of her reputation intact. Your brother knows it. Even Miss Longworth knows it."

"That is because my brother and Miss Longworth are accepting the play as Norbury staged it. However, in the hands of another director, all those scenes can affect the audience differently. One must merely change the denouement." The marquess gestured lazily, as if doing so was a small matter to achieve.

Kyle barely suppressed a laugh of derision. Easterbrook thought that he could alter history and fate.

"Let me tell you another way to view this story, Bradwell. In my play, a virtuous woman is lured by a libertine to a private house party. There she discovers his intentions are not honorable. When she resists him, he extracts his revenge by publicly humiliating her in a manner certain to ensure her ruin and degradation. It is a plausible story, no?"

Kyle shrugged. It was plausible, and even fairly accurate. However, it was not correct in the most important part. By the time she arrived at that house party, Miss Longworth had already relinquished her virtue. She had not resisted the seduction, no matter what its motives.

"No one in the audience knows that for certain." Easterbrook seemed to read his mind, which was damned irritating. "They only have the villain's word for it. Now, in my version, Norbury is thwarted unexpectedly by a chivalrous knight. The least likely man at that dinner risks his fortune to save this poor innocent from a fate worse than death."

"Now you are getting melodramatic."

"The audience loves melodrama, and it loves romance even more than scandal. Which brings us to my new denouement. The knight does not take advantage of the lovely lady's gratitude, as he could. Instead he protects her and delivers her safely to her family." Again that lazy gesture. "Then, he marries her."

He marries her.

Kyle peered into Easterbrook's eyes. Hell, the man was serious.

"You are mad."

"It is a perfect solution."

"Then you marry her."

"I was not the knight. Nor is she the wife for me. She is so lovely that I did briefly consider making her my mistress, but as the cousin of my brother's wife, well..."

Damnation, he was no better than Norbury. "You were right. There are times when I hold contempt for men such as you."

"I said it entered my mind. I did not say that I pursued her." The marquess was not in the least insulted. "I can see why my admission might offend your sense of fair play, however. Poor Miss Longworth, made so vulnerable by her family's ruin, her impoverishment, attracting these aristocratic vultures—"

"Yes, it offends me, *damn you.*"

His curse bit the air and hung there. He gritted his teeth and fought the unexpected surge of anger that had caused the outburst.

"As it stands, her future will probably be in the beds of such vultures, but if she marries she will have a chance for a decent life," Easterbrook said. "This morning I debated what it would cost me to get you to do it. Considering how offended you are, maybe not as much as I thought."

"Buy one of your own kind. A man more appropriate to her station. There's no doubt a fifth son of some baron for sale."

"That would not fit my story. If you marry her, that auction becomes a romantic beginning, not a sordid conclusion."

Easterbrook kept gazing over in that damned, arrogant way. Kyle wanted to punch him in his smug face. Instead he got up and walked away, heading to the door.

Easterbrook's voice followed him. "Marrying her will raise you up. You've the money and education. You have learned how to dress and talk, but on your own you will never get in the doors. On the other hand, I and my entire family will receive you if your wife is Roselyn Longworth. And if we do, others will."

Seething now, Kyle strode on. "I don't care if I get in the damned doors."

"I believe that, having met you now. But your children..."

Kyle halted a few feet from one of the doors in question. Easterbrook was a clever devil. Dangerously perceptive. He knew that it was one thing for a man to play the hand fate had dealt him and another to deny his children better cards.

A son or daughter born into this life that he had built would be painfully aware of what his background denied them. The hell of it was that one's blood mattered. There were more important doors than those to drawing rooms that would not open to his children.

A mother born to a gentry family would not fix that completely, but it would make a big difference. Especially if that mother was related by marriage to a marquess and received by him, and included in Lady Alexia's circle.

"You may not care about the social connections for yourself, but I think you would not mind the business ones. My brother Hayden manages the family's affairs, and is famously successful in his schemes. As a relative of sorts, you will be included." Easterbrook spoke to his back, but in a tone that assumed that they had opened negotiations.

He turned around. "There have not been any

schemes of late." He knew why, but he wondered if the marquess did.

"He has been distracted by his new wife. Trust me, you will grow richer than you ever dreamed. You have been successful with those syndicates, I have heard, but no one can surpass my brother in such matters."

Kyle suspected the marquess could, if he ever put his mind to it. As for Lord Hayden, he currently felt the pinch, but he was certain to recover.

"A lovely wife of gentry stock, the chance of wealth untold—now, what was the rest of the bribe that I worked out? Ah, yes. Five thousand to replenish the coffers."

"Ten."

Easterbrook smiled slowly. "I expected you to want twenty."

"If you were prepared to pay twenty you would have offered more to start."

Easterbrook appeared pleased with himself. "Can I assume that we have reached an agreement? I am sure that Alexia would be delighted to speak with Miss Longworth about it."

"You do not have my mark on the bill of sale yet." Kyle aimed for the door again. "And if I decide to do this, I will speak to Miss Longworth myself."

CHAPTER
FOUR

Roselyn folded the sheet of paper and sealed it. She picked up the letter that she had received the day before and copied the address it contained.

Her eyes rested on her brother's signature at the page's bottom. His pen had faltered at the end.

Poor Tim. She gently touched the spots on the letter where her tears had smeared the ink. He was so alone now. His words had been so sad. There were those who would say he deserved no better, and some who would insist he should receive far worse, but he was her brother. He might be weak and wrong, but she still loved him.

His letter had made her weep at her losses like nothing else had. Even saying good-bye to Irene had not left her so empty, and so aware of how their family was gone now, destroyed by its own mistakes. Tim's news about the death of his traveling companion had just been the most recent, horrible spin of a merciless downward spiral.

She stood and tied on her bonnet, lifted her basket,

and tucked her letter inside it. Tim would never manage on his own. He would be lost now. Sad and lost and alone in a strange country. He wrote that he wanted to come home, but of course he could not.

Her thoughts dwelled on him while she walked to the village. She would have to tell Alexia about the contents of Tim's letter. Alexia would need to know.

She stepped into the grocery near the edge of the village. Two women left the shop as soon as she entered. The grocer, Mr. Preston, was not pleased by the way her presence had interfered with his trade.

He filled her list silently, lining up the flour and salt and other items on the counter. A month ago they would have had some conversation while she shopped here. Mr. Preston would have laughed and smiled in his avuncular way. Now his mouth formed a hard line that said he would sell to her, but she deserved nothing more.

She plucked a few coins from her reticule to pay. Mr. Preston had never told her that he would no longer allow her any credit at his shop. Three days ago his wife had followed her out to the lane and explained it.

The scandal had made its way to Watlington a week ago. It seemed to float in on the wind. People who had been helpful and sympathetic after Tim fled, friends who had known her for years, managed not to see her anymore. She would live even more isolated than before from now on.

She handed Mr. Preston another coin and the letter. "Would you please see that this is sent for me? Here is the money to make it postpaid."

She packed her items in her basket and left the shop.

Once more, Mrs. Preston appeared out of nowhere and followed her out to the lane.

"There was a man looking for you," she said.

Rose stopped walking. "What man?"

"Didn't give his name. Gentleman from the looks of it. He came in about a half hour ago and asked where your house was." Mrs. Preston tried mightily to keep both censure and curiosity from her round face, without success.

Rose's heart sank. This was all she needed—a stranger asking for directions to Miss Longworth's house. The last gentleman who had called had been Lord Norbury, and now everyone knew what that had meant.

She could not bear the insult of a stranger at her door, introducing himself as if she were the whore that the scandal said she was.

"I am expecting no callers, Mrs. Preston. Nor do I wish to receive any. I ask that you and your husband not satisfy a passing stranger's curiosity regarding where I live."

"Oh, we didn't tell him anything. Not for us to aid the devil." Mrs. Preston's head lifted and her gaze shot down the lane. "Well, there he be, coming out of the tavern."

Rose snuck a quick look over her shoulder. She caught a bare glimpse of a man swinging onto a horse.

She decided that her visit to the butcher could wait until tomorrow. It wasn't as if she could afford to buy much meat anyway. She walked back up the lane toward the countryside and her home.

She heard nothing, but she *knew* that man had seen

her. She felt him following her. Eventually the subtle thuds of his horse's hooves approached behind her.

"Miss Longworth? Is that you?"

She knew that voice. She turned.

"Mr. Bradwell, what a surprise."

He gazed down at her, his remarkable blue eyes shadowed by the brim of his hat. Like the last time she had seen him, his garments showed not the slightest sartorial excess or individuality. The dark riding coat, fawn breeches, and high boots had been chosen to be unobjectionable.

"I was in the county and thought that I would see how you are faring, Miss Longworth." He glanced back at the diminished village, then ahead on the road. "May I walk with you?"

It would be rude to refuse, and in truth she would not mind the company. "Yes, you may."

He swung off his mount. They strolled down the road while he led the animal by its reins. He took the basket from her hand. "I wondered if I had misunderstood where you lived. No one back there seemed to know who you were."

"In their own way I think that they were protecting me. You are not known here."

"Of course. I understand."

That was something that she liked about this man. He understood. He had that night too. Understood that she had given herself to a man when she shouldn't. Understood that the auction would probably lead to her rape. Understood that he could spare her that horror, but not the rest of that night's consequences.

She looked over at him on occasion while they

walked. She had never seen him in daylight before. The strong bones and planes of his face did not appear so rough now, without lamps and moonlight chiseling them into harsh angles. It was a thoroughly masculine face, and its expression and his manner reflected the calm confidence that had led him to play the rescuer.

Her other impressions from that night were not much changed by the bright light of the sun. She still sensed a leashed energy in him despite his polite, almost quiet speech. His size and presence still seemed to force the air to roll away to make room. He even incited the same little buzzing caution.

That made no sense. There was no reason to fear this man. He had proven himself most trustworthy and more than decent. She actually experienced secure safety with him beside her. And yet she also experienced a physical alertness. That was not entirely unpleasant, but she was too aware of his size and of the manner in which her blood and instincts reacted to him.

"Has it been bad for you in town? The scandal, I mean." She asked to make conversation, not that he appeared to require any. The way he merely walked beside her had become a little awkward, however. For her, at least. Without words, all they shared was the road itself, like the strangers they practically were.

No, not like strangers. There existed a palpable, silent intimacy borne of that dreadful night's events. The awkwardness came from feeling such a stark familiarity with a person she hardly knew.

"It is already passing, and another man might have even enjoyed the attention." He gave her a sympathetic half-smile. "Such is the injustice in the world, Miss Longworth."

"I am relieved to hear it still exists. Your role was chivalrous, and I would not like to think that you paid with your reputation as well as your purse. I expect that I am goat enough for the wags to prod. Am I still the topic of choice in town, or will word of my sins be passed around only county drawing rooms now?"

His expression grew more serious. "Has your cousin not communicated with you? I think Lady Alexia would be a better ear for you."

"Alexia has written twice, even though she should not. Lord Hayden either does not know that she risks her own name in continuing such congress, or else he cannot deny her. I returned both letters unopened."

"No one would know if you read them."

"It is astonishing what people come to know. I will not risk Alexia being tainted by any of this. However . . ." She thought of Tim's letter, and how her resolve also created problems. "Will you be returning to London soon, Mr. Bradwell? If so, perhaps you would bring my cousin a message from me. There are times when one has to address the living even if one is essentially dead."

"I will begin back this afternoon. I will do it gladly."

She watched the slight swing of her basket along his slow stride. "Perhaps it would be better if you did not speak with her, but with Lord Hayden. He will then let her know. Yes, that would be best."

"I will do it however you prefer."

She steeled her composure to speak without emotion. "Please tell him that I have received news from

Timothy. Tell him that Tim writes that the companion who traveled with him died of a fever contracted in late summer."

"Nothing more? No news of how he fares or where he is?"

She looked over to find him watching her. His blue eyes appeared dark beneath his hat's brim. Dark and curious and . . . hard.

"He fares well enough for one alone and sad."

"You also appear alone and sad. I trust he does not fare better than you. That would be unjust."

She thought that a peculiar thing to say. It contained a good dose of truth, but this man would not know why.

"I do not mind being alone. The sadness you see is only today's spirit, made low by the letter from my brother. If you had chanced by tomorrow I would have been better company."

They reached the lane to her house. Mr. Bradwell turned down it with her.

"You avoided my question. I take that to mean the gossip about me still rages, and is as bad as I feared," she said.

"If it is any consolation, Lord Norbury is not escaping unscathed."

"For every criticism, he will receive two dinner invitations. Being a libertine has never damaged a man much."

The trees flanking the lane thinned and fell away as they arrived at the house. Mr. Bradwell removed his hat and surveyed the property with a slow, alert scan. He appeared to approve of what he saw.

She paused and looked at her house, seeing it anew

through this man's eyes. It had more charm than distinction in its stone block center and assortment of wings that did not really match. It rose only two stories, so it sprawled more than towered. It was big, while not especially grand, but the gardens crowding its walls sent wonderful fragrance into every chamber in spring and summer.

"My family has lived here for five generations. Our estate was once much larger, but there is still some land left, and six small farms."

He narrowed his gaze on the outbuildings barely visible beyond the eastern wing. "Is it a freehold?"

"There is no entailment. My grandfather did not approve of them, and my father neglected to arrange one before he passed away."

"Careless."

She opened the door. The house's gaping emptiness crackled with her arrival. It waited to echo with her solitary footsteps.

She thanked Mr. Bradwell as she took the basket from him.

To her surprise he stepped back and tied his horse's reins to a post.

"I have an interest in buildings, Miss Longworth. Perhaps you would be so kind as to let me see the inside of yours."

He waited patiently for her to respond. Tall. Imposing. Impressive. There was very little breeze today, but again she sensed the air churning in the space between them. That silly, almost exciting sense of caution pulsed through her more strongly.

She glanced around the empty yard and their isolation. "It would be comical for me to stand on ceremony now, wouldn't it? Inviting you inside is a small impropriety in light of the big ones attached to my name."

"If you prefer to avoid this small one, I understand."

Of course he did. But it would still be ludicrous, and he understood that too. This man would probably not ask such a thing of a woman with a shred of reputation left to be risked. Like his garments, his behavior would be unexceptionable in the extreme.

She did not make her decision on that basis, however. The cruel truth was that she hungered to hear a voice other than the one in her own head. His unexpected visit had lightened her mood and helped relieve her sorrow about Tim's letter.

"Please come in and study the house to your content, sir."

He had not lied. He had been in the county and came to see how she was faring. But he had ridden far out of his way, and Easterbrook's offer had occupied his mind for days during those spells when that mind was not occupied by other things.

He had recognized her on the road even at a distance. From the back all he could see was her bonnet and cloak, but she had drawn his eye at once. The pride with which she walked had identified her more clearly than any portrait ever could.

He stepped across her threshold, accepting the invitation that a good woman should not give. He was glad that she had not stood on ceremony. There might yet be games between them, but she was too sensible to try to play the cards of virtue, propriety, or safety with him.

He was curious about this house, and her. As he looked over the former, he knew at once how she was faring. Not well. The chambers were all but empty. Whatever furniture had once graced this home had been sold.

It went without saying that there were no servants. The yard had been empty and no sounds had come from the stables or gardens. Now the house quaked with a silence that their presence only seemed to amplify.

She noticed him taking it all in. She removed her cloak and turned away to untie her bonnet. "My brother Timothy suffered financial reversals. Severe ones. You may have heard about it last spring."

"Yes, I am aware of that." Financial reversals, hell. The scoundrel dared not return to England. "How did this property survive unsold?"

"Lord Hayden made sure that my sister and I would not be put out. He protected us and this holding. That is what I meant that night when I spoke of his generosity. He covered all my brother's debts. Of course, I can never repay him."

Actually, Lord Hayden had not covered all of the debts, much as he had tried to. At least one person had refused to be made whole by other than Longworth himself. Nor had that restitution satisfied everyone who accepted it.

She led him into the drawing room. Three wooden chairs remained there, and one small table and a worn carpet. The windows had been stripped of their silks and left with only a thin, white translucent draping.

"Please sit, Mr. Bradwell. Allow me to arrange some refreshment for you."

She was gone before he could decline. He did not sit, but instead paced the room, taking its measurements by foot and eye. He examined the sills and ceiling, then moved to the dining room and did the same.

He examined the library, then wandered to the back of the house. Slight sounds drew him to the kitchen.

Miss Longworth stood at a worktable near a window. The afternoon sun glistened off her blond hair and bathed her profile in a glaring light that permitted no hiding of imperfections. Even from the doorway he could trace the delicate line of that profile and count the long, golden lashes that hovered above the lovely curve of her porcelain cheek.

She is not for the likes of you, boy. That was what he had thought that night he admired her in the theater. The warning had been repeated often during the last few days, while Easterbrook's mad scheme cast its lures in his head.

She was beautiful and elegant and proud. She was from a family that had been among the best in this county for five generations. Definitely not for him.

She carefully sliced a pie, or what remained of one. Beyond the window he could see fruit trees growing. She had picked the apples herself and made this pie herself. He glanced over the meager stores on the kitchen shelving. That pie was probably intended to last her for a week.

Two glasses of cider waited on the table. She slid the pie pieces onto two plates.

"Allow me to help you," he said.

She twirled on her feet like a dancer at the sound of his voice. He ignored her blush and lifted the glasses and walked back to the chairs in the drawing room.

"I see that you do for yourself," he said after a few bites of the pie. It was almost inedible. It tasted like she had scrimped on both sugar and salt.

"My father left debts, so we lived modestly here afterward. Only when my brother bought a partnership in a London bank did our situation improve. For a while, that is."

"That would be your older brother, Benjamin? The one who died in Greece?"

Her expression fell at his mention of that old grief, so much that he regretted bringing it up. Her lids lowered in a poignant acknowledgment of his reference.

She nibbled a bit of her pie. "Due to those earlier years of scrimping, I have long experience with doing for myself. I do not mind. It is good to be occupied."

"I would have expected Lord Hayden to ensure that you did not live alone in an empty house."

"I have refused his generosity for myself. I cannot for my younger sister. She lives with them now. Alexia says that I am too proud, but it is not pride that makes me refuse. Her husband is paying dearly for matters not of his doing. I am grateful, but I feel guilty enough without taking an allowance too."

She blushed on the word guilty. He did not know if she referred to her recent sins or those of her brother Timothy. If the latter, the guilt was misplaced.

She was just one more of Timothy Longworth's many victims. No doubt the bastard had counted on that allowance from Lord Hayden keeping his sisters in modest style at least. If so, one Longworth had mis-judged another one's sense of fair play.

"The pie is very good," he said after finishing the last mouthful.

"You are just being kind." The flattery pleased her, though.

"Not at all. I eat a lot of fruit pies and know a good one. I even eat them for breakfast some days because I enjoy them so much. Do you have an apple tree in your garden?"

"Yes. Would you like to see it? We might take a walk. I'll show you the garden and the property if you like."

"I am always interested in such things."

It was not until they were out in that garden that she spoke again. He had paced well into it so he could see the back of the house from a good perspective.

"I notice that you do not indulge your interest in buildings and land with a casual eye, Mr. Bradwell."

"That is because I do not have a casual interest, but rather a professional one."

"Are you an estate agent?"

"On occasion. I build houses, and I am stealing ideas from yours."

"You are an architect, then?"

"On occasion."

He turned his attention from the house just in time to see her working it out. Her mouth pursed and her lids lowered a fraction.

"You are one of those men who take estates and divide them up, aren't you? As they have been doing in Middlesex so much."

He could tell that she found the notion distasteful.

Many did. "People who own land often want to develop it. There would be no Mayfair without men like me, decades ago. No London squares." He knew all the objections. He answered the ones that he suspected formed in her head. "I assure you that when I design the houses for those small estates, you would never know they had not been there for generations. As I said, I am stealing ideas from yours and to that purpose."

"Can they require that? Do the people who lease or sell their land get to demand that the new homes do not ruin the countryside?"

"Since there is never enough land to satisfy the demand, they can require whatever they choose."

Without further comment, she strolled down the garden. He followed her along a path that revealed squared sections of worked ground, indicating that vegetables and flowers grew here in summer.

"How well do you know land, Mr. Bradwell? Can you only assess its value to your building, or are you familiar with agricultural matters?"

"I know a bit about the latter."

"Then I will ask your advice about something."

They passed out a rear garden gate and she led him across a field of grass and weeds. It had probably been a pasture in better times. A place for her family's horses to graze.

She strode up a rise in the land until they reached the crest of a hill. A handsome prospect waited there, giving a view of the rolling countryside. The roofs of farmhouses dotted the closest acreage. Her tenants, no doubt. He sized up the holding very quickly. In the far distance he could make out the buildings of Oxford, maybe twenty miles away.

"Have you ever thought of selling it?" he asked.

"It is not mine to sell. A man like you has written to inquire about that, however. Perhaps you know him. Mr. Harrison."

"I know him. The proximity of this property to Oxford would appeal to him."

"He spoke of a handsome offer, but there was no point in encouraging him. This is our family home, and it belongs to my brother, not to me. It will never be sold if I have a say."

They walked down the hill and entered a field of perhaps five acres. The remnants of a harvest littered its dark furrows.

"This is part of one of the farms," she explained. "The tenant is leaving. He told me two months ago."

Not because of the scandal, then. If she depended on the rents, losing a tenant would be disheartening.

"Another will take his place."

"Perhaps not." She toed at the dirt beneath her half-boot. "He said his harvest had been poor and that it has been getting worse every year. He said the soil has gotten weak. If that is true, there may not be another. Even if there is, the rent cannot be the same."

He crouched and filled his hand with the soil. "In your memory, has this field ever lain fallow?"

"I do not recall that it has ever been left unworked." She bent over his shoulder to see what he was doing. Since he was not really doing anything, he was aware of her hovering face and body. Too aware.

He dug his fingers down further, bringing up earth.

He scooped a good amount of it into his hat. Jordan would not be amused. "I know a man in town who conducts experiments to see if soil is worn out. I will bring him this soil and find out if the problem is in the land itself. If not, perhaps your tenant was just a bad farmer."

He stood. She had moved close to watch, and on his rising her body was no more than six inches from his. She startled as if he had suddenly appeared out of thin air.

Her femininity flowed to him and around him, conjuring up memories of that crude embrace the night of the auction. The hat filled with dirt, even the landscape itself, ceased to exist while he looked down on her lovely face. Details from those stolen dreams entered his head.

She gazed back with a wariness that made her appear very young. She did not seem afraid or insulted, just curious. And expectant, as if she assumed he would step back to a more proper distance.

His inclinations were to do the opposite. Her eyes were incredibly expressive. He wondered if she knew how much they revealed. The sorrow that she carried today showed in them, and her worry about this land, and the loneliness that she now endured. There was something else too. A frankness. An acknowledgment of the intimacy forged between them on a night that had permitted no dissembling.

She turned her head, blushing, to break their connected gaze. He reached out and ran two fingers down the side of her unbearably soft cheek until he cupped her chin. He turned her face back to his.

Her pride dissolved while they looked at each other.

They were back in the moonlight on the lane at Norbury's house, only now it was day and the bright sun revealed her reactions more clearly. Caution. Surprise. Confusion. They mesmerized him as much as her beauty did, and only fed the pulse pounding through him and into the hand's length of space that separated them.

He barely touched her, but he felt her subtle tremble anyway.

She is not for the likes of you, boy.

Undoubtedly true. He kissed her anyway.

It was a very brief kiss, although he wanted much more. So much that he did not trust himself. The softness of her lips, their pliable, accepting warmth, reminded him of his first kiss many years ago.

She flushed. She stepped away awkwardly, seeking some distance.

She leveled a direct gaze at him and this time there was no confusion. It was almost sad, just how knowing her eyes were.

"You told me that you had no expectations of that kind."

"I told you that I had no illusions regarding your favors because of that night. You are a beautiful woman, and I would not be a man if I did not notice."

Her resurrected poise visibly wobbled. "Under my current circumstances, being noticed in that way carries some insult now. I will always wonder if my admirer is wondering if I am what that scandal says I am."

"I am the one man in England who will not wonder, because he knows everything. But to spare *you* from wondering whether I wonder, and from feeling any insult, I will try to be indifferent to your beauty. I doubt that I will succeed."

She laughed at his wordplay, or maybe at herself. She turned toward her house. She gestured to his hat while she began walking. "It is so kind of you to help me, again. I fear your hat will be ruined."

"The hat is of no account."

Bearing his dirt, he fell into step beside her. She strode back to her house with purpose. Her expression grew a little vexed due to whatever she contemplated.

Once in her garden she paused under the branches of the apple tree. He guessed that she was hesitant to let him back in the house now. She was not an innocent, and she had seen and sensed what was in him back there in the field.

"What is your given name, Mr. Bradwell? If a man has stolen a kiss, I think that I should know."

He had stolen nothing, and she knew it. "Kyle."

"Kyle. I like that name. Lord Norbury said that you were from the pits of Durham. What did he mean?"

"He meant that I was born into a collier's family in a mining village up north."

"And now you are an architect on occasion, and an estate agent on occasion, and you have a professional interest in buildings and land. It is an unusual history."

"I received the attention of a benefactor, and was educated. He sent me to France to study engineering and architecture."

"France! Your history is even more unusual than I thought. I trust this benefactor is pleased with his investment in you. The evidence is that the education was quite complete."

She glanced over him, taking in the results of those years of improvement. She meant her assessment as a flattery, so he accepted it in that spirit.

"I like to think that he is pleased. His good opinion is important to me."

Her smile changed. She offered it now in reassurance, which made it patronizing. The warmth in her eyes dazzled him so he did not care very much about that. She had been subdued today. The smile brought some vitality back to her.

"I will go now, Miss Longworth. Thank you for the pie, and for the tour of your property." He held up his hat. "I will let you know what I learn about the soil on your farms."

He found his way to the garden's side gate. One of its hinges was broken so he had to kick it aside to get through. He walked around to his horse and calculated how to carry the hat full of dirt while he sat in the saddle.

He did not want to lose that soil. It was his excuse to see Miss Longworth again.

CHAPTER FIVE

❦

You do not need to wait. I am not going to do anything now. By week's end, perhaps I can find time."

Jean Pierre spoke distractedly, dismissing Kyle with a shooing gesture. His attention remained on the array of tubes and beakers that formed a city of glass on a long table between them.

He crouched down and peered at a contraption distilling liquid. The bulbous vessel magnified Kyle's view of Jean Pierre's fine-boned, heavy-lidded face, distorting the French countenance that so easily made fools out of sensible women.

Miss Longworth's soil, now in a small wooden box, rested on Jean Pierre's worktable in this cluttered, garret study, waiting to be analyzed when the young chemist deigned to give it his time.

Kyle knew the various matters that might delay that experiment. Jean Pierre Lacroix had been taught his science by some of France's great minds, and he dropped their names freely. Those references brought him enough employment in London to support his research and his sins.

Kyle walked around the table and sat on a chair where he would get in Jean Pierre's way.

"I do not want to wait for week's end. You will forget about it entirely by then. The flower whom you currently cultivate is sure to get plucked in a day or so, and there will be no experiments for a fortnight."

Jean Pierre tisked his tongue in exasperation. He stretched past Kyle to reach a dish holding some green grains of metal. Kyle shifted enough to interfere.

"*Mon dieu,* you are the nuisance. Go away."

Kyle gestured to the wooden box. "The soil. Now."

"The soil, the soil—what do you care about soil? You do not till dirt. You move it to build."

"It is for a friend of mine. A lady."

"A *lady.* This is not a word you English use lightly. This is the soil of that woman who showed no discretion when we gamed last week, no? She drinks hard spirits, *mon ami,* and that is most unpleasant. And if she bores you with her worries about *soil*—" He shrugged.

Kyle knew that shrug. Ever since he met Jean Pierre when they were students in Paris, that casual movement had meant this Frenchman had much more to say but assumed he would be wasting his breath.

"It is not the bold, foxed, gambling lady, but another."

A merry gleam entered Jean Pierre's eyes. He adjusted the flame below his distillation, then gave Kyle his attention.

"Another?"

"Another."

"I feared that you did not understand your good fortune these last weeks, but eh, *c'est bon,* you are not so

blind. I am like an old uncle, thinking you are too bour-
geois to appreciate the opportunities in these big scan-
dals you English make over little things." He smiled
slyly and wagged his finger. "I should have known that
you are too smart to miss the *bonne chance* and—"

"What the hell are you talking about?"

"This soil lady. Other ladies, and many more who
are less than ladies. So many women look for you now.
They want to know about this man who paid a fortune to
protect a whore. All my feminine friends ask what you
are like." He sighed. "Their questions are a burden, I
will tell you."

"I have not dined on this scandal, but it sounds as if
you have been well fed."

"They hear I know you, and like flies they stick to
me. True, there are some who think you were a stupid
fool or a self-righteous peasant, but many others have
fallen in love, as you surely know."

Jean Pierre had assumed the role of the knight's
squire. No wonder he was so busy today. He probably
had not been at this chemist's table in days.

Jean Pierre peered at him. "You appear so blank.
So . . . English. Do not tell me that you have squandered
this scandal. Do not say that you have refused the invitations that come your way. I will throw you out and never
drink wine with you again."

Jean Pierre's exhortations were often like this one,
urging Kyle to cut a wide swath through available women
while he was still young, rich, and free.

Kyle ignored the lessons. He managed that part of
his life his own way. He was not a monk, but to Jean
Pierre's dismay he was not a rake, either. There had in-

deed been many invitations to dine of late. He simply was not interested in any dinners that might come his way because of that night, whether they were offered at a table or in a bed.

Unless Miss Longworth served the meal.

"The soil," he said, pointing. "If you have had your pleasure due to my fame, you can deal with it at once."

Jean Pierre rolled his eyes. He grabbed the box and slammed it down. He began collecting little vials of liquids. "Do not tell me that you are buying land now to work. Do not tell me that you have decided to become a good, dull English farmer."

"You have a long list of things that I cannot say and cannot tell you. So long that I am left without words. I will just sit here and watch."

"Do that." Jean Pierre scooped little bits of soil into a series of long glass tubes. He began dripping liquids from the vials on top. "This is only a theory, you understand? A good one, though, and I think it is correct. We know what chemicals the soil must hold in order to grow plants. Now we try to see if it lacks those things."

The last of the liquid dribbled into its tube. Jean Pierre corked each one and shook it, then set it in a rack.

"Now we wait." He opened a cupboard, grabbed a wine bottle and two glasses, and led the way to a table at a window overlooking the Cheapside street below his chambers.

The December sky hung low and gray. A pleasant fire crackled nearby. The wrought-iron chairs were similar to those found on terraces and balconies in France. Jean Pierre had reconstructed a bit of his homeland at this window, one that always evoked Kyle's memories of his years there.

The education at the École had been rigorous and il-luminating, but other lessons had been learned in Paris as well. There had been a sexual curriculum, of course. Jean Pierre had seen to that. More interesting had been witnessing a changing view of society. Napoleon was dead, the Revolution was long over, and a king reigned again, but a generation of cries of *égalité* had altered the French perspective forever.

Not completely, of course. Even in France, when it came to marriage blood was blood. The difference was that the entire country did not accept that blood should rule every area of life.

Was that why Cottington had sent him there? The earl was no radical. More likely he had chosen France because of Norbury, who had begun to chafe back then at his father's continuing role of benefactor.

"I am thinking of getting married." Kyle stretched out his legs and tried to get comfortable. He was much taller than Jean Pierre, and the iron chairs, while pictur-esque, left something to be desired. "I have not decided whether to offer, but I am considering it."

"The soil lady?"

"Yes."

"Is she truly a lady?"

"Yes, but like your mam'selle Janette that first year I knew you."

"Ah, *oui*. High birth, corrupt relatives, no money." Jean Pierre raised his glass. "And, from the looks of those tubes over there, weak soil. Congratulations."

"You do not approve."

"She will remind you every day of your life that you are not good enough for her. You will empty your purse in the vain attempt to make her happy. Your own children will see you as their inferior. No, I do not approve."

He could always count on Jean Pierre to be blunt. He knew from his experience with French that subtlety was the last thing learned in a new language, and often never achieved.

So there it was, a damned good reason to decline Easterbrook's grand plan. The marquess might see this as a minor concern, but since he lived at the top of the heap he would not comprehend just how big an objection it could be.

"Who is this lady?" Jean Pierre's eyes narrowed on him.

"Miss Longworth."

"I wondered if not. It is so like you English." He sat forward with his arms on the table. "Because of your chivalry you now feel responsible. She is beautiful and flatters you with her gratitude. So now you feel obligated to save her from the rest."

Jean Pierre was filling in the marquess's play quite nicely, and touching on more truths than Kyle wanted to admit.

"Let me tell you how it really was with those damsels in peril, *mon ami*. We have the old songs and *romans* still in my country, so we know the truth. The knight saved the lovely lady, who was very grateful. Then he took her into the field beside the road, stripped her, fucked her good, then got back on his horse and rode away."

Kyle had to laugh. "That is damned close to a dream I had last night."

"Your dreams know that you do not have to marry her if you are sympathetic and want her. She will be glad for anything now. Why would you marry such a woman, about whom your whole country talks?"

Why indeed? Mostly because he did want her, and he liked to think himself better than those vultures like Norbury. Maybe because fate had created the rare situation in which she might actually accept.

That was not to say that he had not considered the alternative. She had been seduced once, and his visit had convinced him that she could probably be seduced again. Especially by the knight.

"There would be a settlement," he said.

"From whom? It is said that her brother fled due to his debts. Another thing that will stand between you."

"Not from her family. Someone else has offered one."

"Then it will not be big enough, this settlement. Good-hearted souls are never generous with their purses. They would rather say masses for you and promise a reward in heaven."

"Actually, it is a handsome settlement."

"*Vraiment?* Handsome even for you?"

"Even for me."

Jean Pierre was impressed. He poured more wine. "Why did you not say so? That changes everything, of course."

Roselyn strode up the hill past the field behind her home. She did not care about the raw, overcast day or the wind biting her face. She did not notice the dead leaves flying around her legs. In her mind she walked in sunshine and warmth through a world blooming with flowers that never die.

She pulled her cloak around her and sat on the hill. She set her back to the wind and faced the direction that allowed her to see the farthest. She slipped two letters from under her cloak. Each in its own way promised a reprieve from her relentless loneliness.

The letters had been waiting in the village for her yesterday when she walked there to buy some thread. Light had reentered her dull world upon reading them.

One came from London, from a woman she had never met. Phaedra Blair, newly married to Lord Hayden's brother Elliot, was famously *outré* in her ideas, behavior, and appearance. Now Lady Phaedra had written to introduce herself and to declare that Roselyn's exile was barbaric and unjust.

Not a woman to complain and not act, Lady Phaedra had also written that she owned a small house near Aldgate that Roselyn could use, should she ever want to come to London. She also made it clear that Roselyn would be received by Lord Elliot and herself, both of whom refused to accommodate the world's hypocrisy.

The firmly penned, somewhat strident words made Rose chuckle. Lord Elliot would have a very interesting life.

The sensation of laughing almost startled her. It felt so strange. So foreign. When had she last laughed? She gazed to the horizon and tried to calculate it. Weeks, certainly. Perhaps months. She was so out of practice at being happy that her joy today made her light-headed.

She looked down at the other letter that had caused this unexpected mood.

Tim had written again. She had been stunned to see his handwriting. It was impossible for her own letter to have reached him in time for this one to be sent. As soon as she tore it open, she had realized he was not responding to her, but sending more news.

He would never see her letter because he was leaving the French city from where he wrote. However, he had read her mind and now proposed what she had broached with him. He wanted her to join him, and would write again once he had resettled in Italy.

She read his pleas. Tim did not know that he need not cajole. He had not yet learned that there was no life left for her in England.

He described travel and adventure. He promised mountains and the sea, Florence and Rome and beyond. She had not been able to sleep last night because the images excited her so much. She had been without hope for so long, but now she felt drunk on it.

She lay back in the grass and looked up at the sky. It was said that there was more sunshine on the Continent. She already felt its warmth. It incited a happiness that created an exhilarating sense of freedom.

She was glad Tim had written before her letter reached him. That meant he really wanted her with him and was not just being kind. They were both alone now, both disgraced. There would be freedom abroad, and they would form a family again.

She pushed herself up and began the walk to the house. She would examine her wardrobe this afternoon, the one that she had saved when the family left London in ruin. It would be some time before she actually went to Tim, but she could fill her days with dreams and plans at least.

She entered the garden through the back portal. As she passed the apple tree, a vague sound penetrated her thoughts. More curious than cautious, she followed the series of little thuds and scrapes around to the side gate.

A white shirt, stark in the gray day, obscured her view of the gate. It covered a strong back and broad shoulders, and gathered at the top of fawn breeches. Arms that were far from pale, exposed below rolls of shirtsleeve, held the gate by its sides. A dark head turned, revealing a strong profile.

Mr. Bradwell did not hear her while he lifted the gate and carefully set it right on its hinges. One of those hinges gleamed shiny and new.

The soft linen of his shirt and the snug fabric of his breeches revealed his form while he moved. The wind blew his dark locks, mussing them in a most appealing way. Despite his cravat and collar he appeared rakish and romantic and very competent.

One sound push, one heavy thump, and the gate swung easily. He tested it, then began fixing his sleeves.

He saw her then. It bothered him not at all that she witnessed him working like this. He greeted her while he dressed himself.

She walked over and examined the gate. It had been broken for years.

"I noticed that it needed repair when last I visited," he said, reaching for the coats lying in the grass.

"Thank you." She seemed to say that to him a lot. "Were you in the county again, Mr. Bradwell? Just riding by?"

He slid on his frock coat and set himself right. He looked very proper now. She had rather preferred him active and half undressed.

"I rode down from London just to see you, Miss Longworth. I have information about your soil, and a message from your cousin."

He could have written with both. She suspected that he had really come about that kiss. Before this visit was over he would probably try to kiss her again.

It was obvious now that he wanted her. Oh, he did not leer or stare. Desire only increased the directness of his gaze and slightly darkened the vitality he exuded. This man was well practiced in hiding his hungers, but he could not control the tension his interest created and how it affected the air. And her. She was too happy today to lie to herself about that.

She should probably be insulted. Today it did not matter. Not his interest and not her response.

Maybe she would let him have that kiss. She would not even be hurt when he offered the special arrangement that she expected another kiss to presage. It would taint the memory of that night. It would show him to be less than chivalrous in the end, but that would not matter now, either.

She would be gone soon. In a few weeks Roselyn Longworth would disappear completely.

"Please come in and give me this news." She led the way into the house.

She appeared much happier today. And very beautiful. Always beautiful.

Kyle spied sprigs of grass on her cloak as he followed her. She had laid the cloak down out there in the hills. Since it was cold, he suspected that she had been inside it when she did.

He pictured her in her isolation, a solitary figure stretched on the grass under the sky. He could understand why she might look up to the boundless expanse above. This was a nice house, but it was still a prison.

"I fear that I do not have any pie to offer you today." She slid off the cloak and shook the grass away. "In truth I have nothing to offer you."

"Your cousin sent some things. The basket is outside the front door. If you will permit me . . ."

She nodded while she added a little fuel to the fireplace in the drawing room. He fetched the basket. She sat on one of the wooden chairs and poked through the gifts, lifting each in turn while she smiled with delight.

She set the boxes of tea and biscuits on the little table. She lined up the bag of coffee, the bottle of wine, and the jar of honey.

"What is this down at the bottom?" She poked at the broad, wrapped form there.

"I think that is some cooked fowl. Duck or goose, I believe."

She laughed. He had never heard her do so before. Not outright like this. It was a lovely laugh. Melodic. Angelic.

Watch yourself, Kyle lad. You'll be writing bad poetry soon.

"How like Alexia. Luxuries, but practical ones. You must join me in eating the fowl and drinking the wine, Mr. Bradwell. We will share a feast."

"It might be best if you saved it all for yourself."

"Nonsense." She set the basket on the floor beside her. "Now, what news have you about my soil?"

He sat on another chair with the little table between them and the fire warming their shoulders. "The experiments done are theoretical. However, they appear to show that the soil is depleted. Did your brothers never require the tenants to rotate their crops? It is recognized now as useful. In the least, the old system of leaving fields fallow every third year should have been required."

"My father collected rents, nothing more. His interests were in town, not here. After his death no one truly managed the property. We assumed, wrongly it appears, that farmers would know how to farm and would not do so in ways that made the land less productive."

"An extra field of crops is tempting. There are those who will exhaust the land and move on."

She shrugged. "Apparently so."

That shrug was her entire reaction. He had brought very bad news that would affect her meager income, but she appeared not to care.

Her eyes sparkled while she ran her elegantly tapered finger down the edge of the box of tea. He watched that distracted caress and imagined it on himself, sliding slowly down his side. He clenched his teeth to control what the little fantasy did to him.

He was glad that she was not sad today, but she appeared almost drunk instead. He did not flatter himself that her big smiles and bright eyes were due to his visit.

"You are a bad liar, Mr. Bradwell. Alexia did not give you this basket. I think that you bought these items yourself."

"What makes you think so?"

"Alexia would have sent a different company's tea, and a different kind of biscuit. She also would have included soaps and hairpins and other practical luxuries that a woman cannot eat."

She grinned mischievously. She was definitely in high spirits today. Vivacious. Almost flirtatious.

"You have found me out, Miss Longworth. I hoped to avoid awkwardness by saying it came from your cousin."

"Is this gift because of that kiss? There must be at least ten shillings' worth of goods here, and that kiss was barely worth one. Then again, perhaps you hope for nine more."

Now she was getting reckless. "The basket has nothing to do with the kiss, but with my concern for your health and lack of comforts. And perhaps to help you feel less sad about the implications of what I learned about your land."

"Of course. My apologies for impugning your motives." Her eyes mocked her serious words. She began setting the items back in the basket. "Let us sit to a proper meal. If you share it with me, the reasons that you brought it will not signify. Although, in a manner of speaking, nothing does anymore."

He took the basket from her arms when she rose. He followed her into the kitchen. Her manner flattered him. It also stirred him. His desire had flared like oil touched by a torch.

However, her demeanor disturbed him too, and not because she spoke too frankly and had lost her cool grace. She acted like someone who had made a decision, one that rendered all proprieties irrelevant.

He wondered what she had been thinking out there while she lay in the grass under the gray sky.

He stood near the worktable watching her while she gathered and unwrapped food. He was a handsome man, really. As the "in his way" became more familiar, he grew even more attractive. His eyes in particular demanded attention. Intelligent eyes. Intense sometimes, like now while they followed her movements. Too intense, perhaps, considering that she did nothing special to deserve such thoughtful scrutiny.

His perfect garments struck her as less than appropriate now. The effect that he sought to create, of a reserved and unnotable man of wealth, worked only if one never saw him dressed otherwise.

She had seen him without those coats, however. She had seen him in shirtsleeves, his strength stretching beneath white linen and his arms straining from the weight of that gate. The coats held in a tightly coiled spirit that became palpable when they were removed. One might as well put a cravat and waistcoat on a stallion.

His attention caused that odd excitement that he always provoked in her to hum merrily. She rather enjoyed its lively stimulation. The caution it contained struck her as unnecessary today. She was too happy to be afraid, or insulted, or worried.

She boiled water for tea. The fowl turned out to be a goose and was still warm. He must have bought it in a town or village nearby.

"You appeared very composed on hearing my news about the soil," he said. "I am relieved that it did not distress you."

She set a crude table on the planks of the kitchen's work surface and laid out some cheese and bread alongside the goose. "Very soon that land and those rents will not matter. I will no longer need them. I thank you for learning what you could for me, however."

He frowned slightly while they sat to their meal. "You did not ask about the message from your cousin, either."

"Goodness, you are correct. How remiss of me. Pray, what does Alexia say?"

"She said that her heart breaks about your brother's letter, and she is pained that she cannot be with you. She said that you will be receiving a letter from Lord Elliot's wife, and that she hopes that you will avail yourself of Lady Phaedra's offer of a residence in town."

"I received that letter. Alexia thinks to sneak away and see me if I make use of that house. However, perhaps for one last visit . . . Yes, I may do that."

He retreated into his thoughts while they ate their dinner. He was her guest and she did not ignore him. That would be impossible with this man anyway. However, his silence permitted half of her mind to visit the sunny adventures she anticipated enjoying in a few months.

"You are much happier today, Miss Lo

"I trust that is good to see."

"Of course. However, your indiffe
ture, your dismissal of the proble
your lack of curiosity about your

have no right to be concerned, but your mood today worries me more than your sorrow did the last time I visited."

"You should not worry. If I am a little giddy, or indifferent to the details of my life, it is because I expect to be done with this life and this scandal and this loneliness very soon. I have made a decision, Mr. Bradwell. I will be going far away forever."

His expression fell. He viewed her with alarm, then crisp determination slid over his expression. He sat back, folded his arms, and pinned her in place with a direct gaze.

"No, you will not. I will stop you."

"You can not *stop* me. It is my decision."

"It is the devil's decision." His restrained power rushed out. It blew around her like a gale. "I should have seen your melancholy for what it was. I will speak with your cousin and Lord Hayden and we will find a place for you to go and rest, away from this village and the damned gossip. In a few weeks you will realize that—"

"Mr. Bradwell, please." She held up a hand, stopping him. He had misunderstood, terribly.

"Mr. Bradwell, your conclusions are far too dark, and in error. I am not melancholic. I am not going to do myself harm, if that is how it sounded. I am just going away. To the Continent. I am merely waiting for a letter from a friend before I leave."

He went very still. He looked out the window beside the table, contemplating she knew not what.

"To the Continent, you say."

"Italy."

"is friend?"

"That is no concern to you, surely."

He did not care for that response. "You will leave your sister? Your cousin?"

"They are lost to me already, and I to them."

"How will you keep yourself?"

"I will be fine. Be happy for me, that I have this chance at another life. It is far better than being buried alive in this house. It is the right decision. It is the only choice that offers a future."

He turned his gaze on her. The odd intimacy that they shared drenched his intensity. It was not just the familiarity of friends. He was a man and she was a woman and he knew far too much about her.

Suddenly that excitement that he could provoke flowed. Her blood warmed. She felt the same as she had out in the field before he kissed her—expectant and vulnerable and at a disadvantage.

"Two women traveling alone? In Italy? It is neither safe nor wise. Who will protect the two of you? Does your friend have servants, at least?"

She refused to answer. His help that night did not give him the right to quiz her like this.

"This friend is not a woman, is it?" He hid most of his disapproval. What showed carried more concern than censure. "Whoever he is, he will eventually leave you. What if that happens while you are abroad? What if this man's intentions are even worse than the last's? On the Continent you will not even have your cousin to turn to."

"He is not a lover. He is not that kind of friend."

"So he says now."

"I know this man very well. I know that I will be safe. It is not what you assume."

His protracted attention made her uncomfortable. His disapproval crackled in the air.

"It is not the only choice," he said. "If you do not travel to a secure home, and to a secure future, it is not even the right one."

"It is better than *this*." It came out close to a hiss. His persistent disagreement annoyed her. She had been so happy today, and now he was ruining it with a litany of practicalities.

"*This* is not your only other choice."

"Indeed? Perhaps you brought other news too? Absolutions from Canterbury, the Queen, and the patronesses of Almack's? Maybe Alexia sent word of a legacy bequeathed to me by an unknown rich relative of mine?"

"If I were a magician I would conjure up all of that for you. However, you can have half measures at least, without magic. You can have security and safety. You can have your sister and your cousin again, and take a long step toward retrieving your reputation."

He had not offered her false hope the night of the auction. It disappointed her that he did now. "What you describe will definitely take magic, sir. Do not paint pretty, sentimental landscapes in an attempt to discourage me from my plan. Your reassurances are patronizing and cruel."

"I never paint pretty landscapes, Miss Longworth. I am a man who draws maps of roads where carts will roll, and plans of houses where people must live. What I describe can all be yours. You just need to marry a respectable, established man." A half-smile formed. "A man like me, for example."

CHAPTER SIX

Roselyn stared at him. He had thrown out the idea of marriage with incredible calm and absolutely no ceremony. It had almost been an aside, a mere sentence to prove that his argument had merit.

It took her a few dazed moments to realize that he was serious. He had just proposed.

"You have a reckless streak in you, Mr. Bradwell. Twice now you have spoken too quickly on my account. I would think that the last time cost you dearly enough."

"I would never make this offer if I had not considered it very carefully."

The shock sunk in, evoking an inner agitation. Sitting under his gaze put her at a disadvantage, so she stood. Since he had to as well, it did not help at all.

"You are just being kind."

He barely shook his head. "I am not that good."

"The world will mock you. I am winter's scandal."

"The world will rethink that scandal if we marry. It will take time to reclaim whatever place you had in society a year ago, but your cousin and her husband's family will immediately receive you."

They would receive him too. He had calculated that, while he weighed what he would risk and what he might gain.

Her confusion cleared. She pictured the accounting. She knew what had happened.

"Mr. Bradwell, I am well past the normal age for marriage. Have you never wondered why I am on the shelf?"

"I assumed that you never met a man who suited you. Or that you did not favor the wedded state and could afford to indulge your preferences."

Which you no longer can. He was wrong if he thought that. She could wait to hear from Timothy. She could go away.

"There were no offers when I was a girl. We lived here and our fortunes were bad. Later, after the investment in the bank, after my brothers grew wealthy, there were many offers. Addresses were paid by men of all stripes, but always, *always,* their interest in a settlement exceeded their interest in me. I preferred not to marry just to enhance a man's purse."

"I see. You had to be impoverished before you believed a man's addresses were the result of affection and not avarice. That is understandable, I suppose. It would also explain why you gave yourself to Norbury, when you had declined more honorable offers before."

Her face warmed. He regarded her with a gentle firmness that suggested he comprehended more than she wanted.

"Miss Longworth, you are not the sister of a rich banker now."

"That is true. I am nobody now. There are so many reasons to discourage you from such a rash proposal that I must wonder why you spoke. Not out of pity, I hope."

She needed to move, to relieve the nervous pattering in her heart. She began wrapping and storing the remains of their meal. She carried the plates to the washbasin on the other side of the kitchen.

He remained standing near the table and window, but he intruded on every inch of the room.

"Not out of pity," he finally said. "I will admit some concern for you, but not pity."

She set the plates in the basin. She was not handling this well. It would be better to clear the air and speak honestly. He deserved that much.

She turned to face him. She realized at once that was a mistake.

His attention acted like a tether, tugging her back across the chamber. Warmth and soft amusement showed in his eyes and vague smile. Those same qualities implied he expected a challenge and did not mind one.

"Lord Hayden put you up to this, didn't he? Alexia asked him to approach you, no doubt, but he made the overture. How big is the settlement that he promised?"

"Lord Hayden has no knowledge of this. He offered nothing."

His tone almost made her believe him. Almost. If he was being truthful, which she doubted, he was a fool. "So you propose to a woman scorned because you feel some concern and because you will be received by her cousin's relatives? For a successful man of affairs, you make bad bargains when you carefully consider your actions."

His expression firmed just enough to reflect displeasure at the criticism. "You are very sure that you have guessed my calculations. However, you neglect the most important one. I get something else besides the small benefits that you list."

"I do not see what it might be."

"You, Miss Longworth. I get you, as the mother of my children and as the wife in my bed."

He walked toward her. The coats no longer obscured the man they draped. He might have been free of them, with his dark hair and loose shirt blowing in the wind. His expression stunned her. Knowing. Confident. Devastating.

Each step created a stronger pull on that tether. She gripped the edge of the table behind her. As he neared she angled back in alarm until her back hit the washbasin's rim.

She found her voice. She had less success locating her composure. "Most men would not think me fit to be the mother of their children."

"Other men do not know your true character the way I do."

"Most men would not want a wife whose virtue has so infamously been lost. They would demand that their brides be untouched."

"This man demands only that his bride be touched by him alone from this day forward."

He stood so close that she could not straighten without inviting that touch. His presence pressed on her in less physical ways. The depths of his blue eyes drew her in. Her thoughts scattered.

I get you, as the wife in my bed. She had sensed the desire in him. She had anticipated an overture today. Just not this one.

"It is still a bad bargain," she stammered. "You were warned that night that I am not warm in the ways that men want. It would be wrong for me to let you think he lied about that."

"What an honest woman you are. I am not inclined to take another man's judgment in such a thing. I think I will form my own opinion, especially since I already have cause to believe he erred badly."

He cupped her neck in his hand. The contact made her jump. He caressed around her neck until that firm, gentle hold cradled her nape.

She could not speak. She could not object. He eased her forward, toward him.

His kiss bore little resemblance to the one in the field. This one was sweet enough and careful too, but it was designed to conquer objections. It enkindled a deep warmth that seduced her soul to sigh. *This is so pleasant and enlivening. Perhaps, just a little more, a little longer.*

Innumerable tiny thrills slithered through her body, many of their prickling paths warming her far from the place he actually kissed. *Yes, just a little longer . . .*

She melted into it, unaccustomed as she was to the mastery of this quiet assault. There was nothing hesitant in this long kiss, but she felt the care and the deliberate attempt to give her pleasure. *Yes, this part at least can be good. So good . . .*

His mouth manipulated her astonishment. His gentle hold on her nape commanded her to accept him. He lured her lips to part.

The small invasion seemed inevitable when it came. She considered rebelling but surrendered instead. The sensations overwhelmed defenses that had lost their foundations long ago. Instead of shock, she reacted with wonderment at the way this kiss resonated with erotic intimacy.

You are lost and he knows it. He can take you now if he wants and he knows it. In falling you lost your best weapon and your best reason to resist, and he knows it.

She did not heed her mind's warning. She did not want the sweetness to end. This pleasure took her to a place far away from the sad world she now knew.

The kisses stopped anyway. She opened her eyes to see him looking at her seriously, as if he weighed whatever her lack of resistance meant. Then his eyes closed and his head dipped until his brow rested on hers. His hand still cradled her neck, holding her to the contact. She almost heard the argument that his desire gave him.

"You are warm enough for me." His fingertips caressed her lips while a small smile played on his own. "Although the claim that you lack training has some merit."

His allusion to that night, to Norbury, surprised her. This man of all men could never forget her shame. "How can you speak so calmly of it? You know that I... you *know*."

"I know what I have in you. I am not saying that scandal does not matter. I am not claiming that I do not care. It does not matter enough, however."

Still, he *did* care and it *did* matter. Of course it did. He had been honorable toward her, but he was not a saint. No man was.

She did not believe that he had come here to offer marriage today. She still suspected that he had chosen a different way to have her in his bed. He had only diverted to this path because he thought she was going to give herself to someone else.

Those impressions flew through her heart, but they anchored there no better than any other right now. Her mind proved incapable of being sensible while he touched her and while that kiss still stirred her so powerfully.

"I expect no answer today. I only ask that you consider my offer of this other choice. I realize that you have much to weigh. I know that you never expected to marry a man like me when you were a girl, but much has changed since then." His fingers lightly caressed her face in that careful, thoughtful touch he had used in the field. "Tell me that you will think about it."

It was not really a request. Nor did she possess enough of a will to disagree.

He removed a paper from his frock coat. "This is where I live in London. When you decide, send for me. Or write if you prefer. If I do not hear from you in ten days, I will return."

He set the paper beside the washbasin. His bootsteps sounded loud in the barren house as he strode to the door.

A few drops of water smeared the address on the paper while she washed the dishes. Bending awkwardly, she pushed the paper aside with her dry elbow so the writing would not get ruined.

Mr. Bradwell had been gone a long while before she even moved. An hour had passed before she retrieved something of her normal composure. She guessed it would be days before she could think clearly about what had transpired today.

She had capitulated with shocking quickness—so shocking that she would not blame him if he rethought her character now. She had not expected to actually like that deep kiss, however. His artistry had been a revelation that put her at a disadvantage.

Her lack of virtue probably had too, she suspected. Evidently it was very easy to fall if one had already fallen. Didn't the older women warn as much?

Warm enough for me. He did not know that. The intimacies in marriage involved more than kisses in a kitchen.

She had not liked that part of being Norbury's mistress. The kisses were somewhat fun, but the rest—she made a face at memories of embarrassment and discomfort and awkwardness. She knew that some women did not receive much pleasure, but no one had warned her how distasteful it was to remain unmoved while her lover lost all reserve.

Finished with her chore, she dried her hands on a towel. The low sun revealed the roughness of their skin. She had slathered her hands in creams when she was a girl, and still did when she could afford the lotions. She had washed and scrubbed enough in her life, however, that she no longer had a lady's hands.

Much has changed since then. Heavens, but that was the truth.

Her inclination was to reject this proposal. All the ways in which such a marriage could be horrible clamored for attention with their warnings.

He had probably been offered money, but soon that money would be spent or forgotten, and they would still be bound forever.

At best he had offered only out of an impulse to save her again. He thought she meant to go abroad with another scoundrel, so he felt obligated to sacrifice himself.

Still, the offer had been made. It *was* another choice. She would be a fool to decline it outright. She doubted that she could sort through the resentments and worries and prejudices that already were lining up to discourage her, however.

She wished Alexia were here. Alexia was so sensible and wise. Alexia could help her to think clearly about this unexpected development.

CHAPTER
SEVEN

T he summons to Norbury's house came four days after Kyle had visited Miss Longworth. Since Norbury's note did not indicate the subject of this meeting, Kyle wondered if the viscount had somehow heard about the proposal.

He rode his horse from his chambers in Piccadilly to Mayfair. He had not seen Norbury since the night of the auction, and the events at that party were enough to cause a strain of their own today. He did not expect his presumption in now offering marriage to pass without a few scathing words.

Of course, Miss Longworth had not accepted. She had not even written. Perhaps she never would.

She had been less than amenable to this new denouement for her drama. He doubted that she would become more so while she debated her choices. Being tied to a man of low birth whom she hardly knew would probably pale compared to the adventures being dangled by that other man.

A series of protectors was the common fate of women

who fell in such a public manner. Easterbrook's sure confidence about that had been infuriating mostly because it was well founded. Having seen how Miss Longworth lived, having seen her bleak future and sad isolation, only the hardest soul would not comprehend the temptation.

Italy. Hell.

She thought his marriage proposal was impulsive and reckless. Instead it appeared that he had pondered it too long. Long enough for Miss Longworth to be found, pursued, cajoled, and tempted by another vulture.

So long that a liveried servant had delivered another letter from the marquess the morning after the visit to Jean Pierre's laboratory. This time the expensive paper had borne no words, just a large, elegantly penned question mark.

Grooms populated the street in front of Norbury's house. One was leading away a horse. It appeared this would not be a private confrontation about matters concerning Miss Longworth after all.

As soon as Kyle entered the library, he realized that the men gathered there did have a connection to her. They had all been defrauded by her brother Timothy.

The meeting served as a reminder that even while he had pondered that proposal too long, he had not resolved the biggest debate in his head. Her brother was a thief and a criminal, but she would probably be angered by this gathering of victims in Norbury's house.

On the other hand, this meeting also pointed up that the day would come when Miss Longworth's current scandal would pale compared to another waiting to embroil her. In her vulnerable situation, it would devastate what little pride and dignity she retained.

Norbury barely acknowledged Kyle's arrival. The viscount continued a conversation with another man while Kyle found a chair and accepted coffee from a servant.

Norbury disengaged from his guest and addressed the room at large. "Gentlemen, we have a decision to make and I thought it best to bring you all together so we could settle it quickly."

Conversations quieted. Eyes turned to the host.

"I have received a letter from Royds. It arrived yesterday and he writes from Dijon."

"Does he have the rogue in hand?" the deep voice of Sir Robert Lillingston queried. "I don't know why it is taking him so long."

A low chorus of muttered agreements backed up the observation.

"Unfortunately, he does not. However—"

The mutters got louder.

"Gentlemen, allow me to continue. Mr. Royds writes that he has discovered why tracking his quarry proved so difficult. Longworth was not traveling alone as we told him. He had a companion the whole way. Nevertheless, Royds followed the trail to Dijon, where Longworth was in residence, using the last name Goddard. The companion, a man named Pennilot, caught fever and died there, and Longworth was forced to dally as a result of that illness."

"So where is he now?" Lillingston demanded. "Not Dijon, from the sounds of things."

"Not Dijon," Norbury said. "Royds just missed him. He has good reason to believe that Longworth aimed south, with Italy as his destination."

No one liked hearing that. The news of a near miss caused a good deal of complaining.

Kyle did not say a word. His attention locked on the last detail from the letter.

Italy. Roselyn spoke of traveling there with her friend. No, now that he parsed the conversation in his mind, she had never indicated that she would actually travel to the continent with that man. She could be planning to meet him there.

He cursed his own stupidity. She was not being deceptive or naive when she insisted her friend had no ulterior motives. She did not envision this new life as a kept woman at all. She intended to join that rogue brother of hers.

The implications of that, to her and to him and to his offer and her choices, distracted most of his mind. A small part continued to follow the discussion in the library.

"Mr. Royds has followed, but anticipates considerable cost if he must continue the search in Italy," Norbury explained. "With all the little sovereign states on the peninsula, many bribes will be required. I must write to him at an address in Milan with authorization to incur the costs on expectation of repayment from us."

"He could be poking through Italy for years," Mr. Barston, a wealthy importer, insisted. "I've a mind to say we end this. Thanks to Lord Hayden Rothwell, we are not badly burned. I want to see the bastard himself pay as much as the rest of you, but it is sounding like this hunt may go on forever. I've no interest in perfect justice if it costs me hundreds."

Norbury's face turned red. "He made fools of you.

Of all of us. Insinuated himself into our circles and lured us to use his bank. He played us like idiots, then ran with the plunder. Have some pride, for God's sake."

"It doesn't sound as if Royds even knows where he is going," Barston countered.

"He'll find him. He'll use the same methods he used to get to Dijon."

"It took him months to locate Longworth there. It could be months before Royds or anyone else learns where Longworth lands now."

That was not true, Kyle realized. Someone in England would know very soon where Timothy Longworth's new lair would be. Roselyn waited for a letter before she embarked on her new life.

He gazed at the men around him. Some were gentlemen and some were merchants like Barston. One was a noted financier. All that bound them was the hunger for revenge.

Not because of big losses. They all had been repaid by Lord Hayden. That restitution was designed to salve the victims' anger and abort their laying down information. They had learned how Longworth had forged names and documents to sell out the securities that his bank held for them, but a man made whole forgets much quickly.

With most of the victims, Lord Hayden's plan had worked. Except these men here had not been satisfied. Restitution had not been enough for them in the end.

Slowly they had found each other. They joined together in the cause of finding Longworth and bringing him back. In the months since there had been scant news.

Norbury sniffed the air for more objections. "He will be found soon, I am confident. However, even if Royds goes to every town in Italy, it is money well spent. No doubt Longworth dines in high style and laughs at the fools he robbed while he does so. Some of you may be willing to live with that image, but no man of honor can do so."

That insinuation ended all discussion. An informal vote was taken. They charged Norbury to write to Royds and promise the necessary payments.

Bodies rose and farewells flew. Kyle held back while the others departed. It was time to test the water in the shallow pond named Norbury and see just what the temperature might be.

His host pretended to ignore him for a few minutes while he shuffled papers. Eventually the tawny head rose and the pale eyes acknowledged him.

"You were silent today, Kyle. That was wise."

"I had nothing to say."

"You used to. I remember the fine speeches about the why and the why not, about the poor men hung every week for much less because they have no rich friend to buy their lives from the victims. You preached moral re-solve like a vicar or a damned philosopher, except you are neither and your opinions do not signify." His lids lowered and brittle lights blazed in his eyes. "You think to imitate the high-grounded ideas taught you by those books and tutors, but you forget it is impertinent for such as you to dare lecture your betters."

"I lecture no one."

"The hell you don't. Your performance at my dinner party spoke loudly enough." Norbury's expression pulsed petulantly. "Lord Hayden has gone out of his way to let it be known you did not enjoy the prize you bought that night. You did it only to—"

"What do you care why I did it? You made tenfold what you would have otherwise, and you are free of her. As you said, the opinions of such as me do not signify to such as you."

Norbury averted his gaze. He appeared to achieve some calm. Kyle took his leave. He had reached the door when Norbury spoke again.

"I tire of your presumptions, Kyle. Your simple ideas are better suited to the ignorant miners of your village." His voice rose to a snarl. "Do not cross me again."

"I lived here for almost ten years. It is very modest, but the street is safer than it looks."

Lady Phaedra swept up to the door of the house in question. Her billowing black dress and cape flapped in the wind, revealing the unexpected Apollo gold lining of the latter. Her rippling red hair hung like a curtain of fire along one side of her face while she bent to poke her key in the lock.

Rose waited, valise in hand. Lady Phaedra's last sentence reassured her a little. This street, not far from Aldgate, did not appear especially safe. Lord Elliot's coachman must have agreed, because he sat at attention with whip at the ready.

The houses were old and the lane narrow. A beggar woman sat not fifteen feet away from Phaedra's door. Another woman at the open window across the way called with suspicious familiarity to passing men.

Lady Phaedra noticed and laughed. "Elliot warned

that you would be shocked. He said that we should let a better place and present it as mine and you would be none the wiser. Alexia, however, said that you are too proud to accept such charity, and I am not good at living a lie."

"I am glad that you did not do that. If you lived here for almost ten years, I think I will be very happy for several days."

Phaedra threw open the door. "You will need to air it. It has been closed for over a month."

The house was as unusual as the woman who owned it. The sitting room also served as a library. Tall bookcases filled one wall, and odd paintings and engravings the others. An old divan stood in front of the windows, covered in an array of colorful shawls that did not entirely hide its worn upholstery.

"I will send a servant to stay here with you, so you will be more comfortable," Lady Phaedra said.

"Please do not. You have already been too generous, and very gracious to display no surprise when I showed up at your door. You do not even know me."

"I know all about you, though, and I know that Alexia loves you dearly. I also know what it means to be the object of whispers and scorn. It matters only if you allow it to, Roselyn. There are many people who do not abide by society's dictates and who will accept you without prejudice."

Rose understood the lesson that Lady Phaedra tried to give. She knew that there were circles that held to different rules. Phaedra Blair had not conformed and according to Alexia had led an interesting, colorful life prior to agreeing to marry Lord Elliot. From the looks of things, her benefactress was one lady who would never completely fit into polite society, because she chose not to.

However, Rose also knew that she was no Phaedra Blair. She had not been raised in radical, artistic circles and would feel silly trying to join them. Lady Phaedra tried to show that there was yet one more choice for her future, but it was not one that Rose considered practicable.

"It is easy to find hackney cabs on the next street," Phaedra explained while she gave a tour of the kitchen and dining room. "The shops are there as well."

Up above, Rose left her valise in one of the two small bedrooms. It looked out over a tiny garden in the back that needed some tending.

"I will leave you to rest," Lady Phaedra said when they went back downstairs. "You have been in the carriage too long and that always takes a toll. I will come tomorrow to see how you fare."

Rose watched the black drapery billow out to the street and into the carriage. The coach would take Phaedra back to that nice house in Mayfair that she now shared with Lord Elliot. It was not far from the one on Hill Street where Alexia lived.

She pictured Alexia walking through that house. It was not hard to conjure up images of her cousin in every chamber. They had both lived there a mere year ago. It had been the Longworths' home then, where they had all gathered as a family.

Much has changed since then.

Everything had changed since then.

Rose heard the carriage stop outside the next morning. She jumped up to look out the front window.

She recognized the carriage. As she anticipated, Alexia

had learned from Phaedra about this visit and had come to see her.

Her heart dropped a little when the carriage door opened. A tall, stern man stepped out of its shadows, then turned and handed down her cousin. Lord Hayden Rothwell had accompanied his wife.

Perhaps that was just as well. She had questions for him and it would be best to ask them directly.

She opened the front door as they approached. Alexia beamed delight at seeing her. Lord Hayden was too busy frowning at the beggar and whore to smile.

"You used to visit Phaedra here?" she heard him ask. "Alone, before we wed? Even after?"

"On occasion," Alexia said, ignoring her husband's dismay. She stepped over the threshold and embraced Rose. "Do not scold me, Rose. When you returned my letters unopened you made it clear that you would not allow any risks, but even Hayden agrees that it is unlikely that this meeting will be reported to the harpies. The denizens of this neighborhood do not know us, and do not gossip in polite drawing rooms in any event."

Rose brought them into the odd sitting room. Lord Hayden occupied his attention with the bizarre engravings hanging on the wall.

"I am glad that you came, Alexia. And you too, Lord Hayden. I was hoping that you would. I do not intend to stay long, so your prompt visit is most welcome."

Alexia's face fell. "There is no need to rush back to Oxfordshire. You can surely remain in town until after Christmas. I had hoped we could dine together then, if not before."

"That would not be wise. If not for your sake, then

for my sister's we must accept the penalty of my fall."
She took her cousin's hand and squeezed it. "Please sit,
Alexia. I have need of your advice."

Alexia perched on the divan. Lord Hayden moved
his examination of Phaedra's possessions to the book-
case.

Rose sat in a chair where she could see his profile.
No matter how carefully he read those spines, she
doubted that he would miss one word of her conversation with her cousin.

"Alexia, a most unexpected thing happened four
days ago. Mr. Bradwell proposed marriage."

Alexia's astonishment was honest. Lord Hayden's
lids merely lowered a fraction.

"Did you accept?" Alexia asked.

"I was so startled that I begged off making a decision
at once. My inclination was to turn him down immediately. I fear that he does not comprehend the consequences of such a match. Indeed, I cannot imagine why
he would speak so rashly. Unless, of course . . ."

"Unless what?"

"Unless he had been encouraged to do so by someone's promise of a settlement." She glanced at Lord
Hayden but saw no reaction to her insinuation.

Alexia turned her attention to her husband too.
"Hayden, did you have a hand in this?"

He faced them. "I did not bribe Mr. Bradwell."

"To be sure," Rose said. "However, a settlement is
not normally thought of as a bribe."

"Why do you assume that this offer is dependent on
my meddling? It could be that Mr. Bradwell comprehended the consequences very well, perhaps better than

you do. Such a marriage is of mutual advantage. In your case, Miss Longworth, marriage will transform this scandal into one much less damaging."

Rose granted Lord Hayden his brilliance, but his little speech did not speak well of his strict honesty. It sounded as if he had thought it out at leisure, not in the last half minute. Nor had he explicitly said he that he had not offered a settlement.

Husband and wife exchanged an eloquent gaze. Lord Hayden bowed and strolled toward the doorway. "If this is the reason for your visit to town, Miss Longworth, I expect that there will be much feminine talk now, and confidences that no man should hear. I will say good day to you and return to the carriage."

Rose waited until the door closed behind him. "I am not sure that I believe him."

"If he speaks so plainly, you should believe him. He can be very clever but he is rarely sly." Alexia unpinned her mantlet and let it fall off her shoulders. "I assume that you do not want to accept this offer and are looking for an excuse to refuse."

"Why do you think that?"

"I know how you loathed proposals in the past that had financial incentives. You found the best excuse to convince your heart to decline Mr. Bradwell. Only you are wrong about the settlement, so now what reason will you use instead?"

Alexia waited for an answer, as if Rose had one.

"Must I enumerate the benefits of this match?" Alexia asked. "Hayden is correct, and I saw it immediately too. If you marry Mr. Bradwell it will transform this scandal. He is not a gentleman, but his honor toward you will make Norbury appear an ass and a rogue all the more. The assumptions that people have made will be rethought. I daresay many will even believe there was no affair with Norbury prior to that scandalous night."

That transformation played out in Rose's mind. Mr. Bradwell had alluded to this, but it took Alexia's firm gaze to make it plausible.

"It is brilliant, actually," Alexia said, indicating all the nuances were lining up in her mind too.

"And in return he gets what?"

"Your blood and your connections, Roselyn. You are a gentleman's daughter. You have a cousin related by marriage to a marquess. And, of course, he gets a most beautiful wife."

"The beauty will dim soon, and the blood is badly tainted. Nor do I think he cares much about social connections. Can you see why I am suspicious of your husband's frankness? No doubt he fears I will reject it outright if I know the truth, since it is one more debt to him that I can never repay."

"If you are right, then the debt is mine and there are no accounts to be balanced between Hayden and me. We do not play such childish games." Alexia stood and crossed her arms. Her expression grew strict while she began pacing out her thoughts. "Do you dislike this man, Rose?"

"Not at all. Although, in truth I do not know him very well."

"I would say you know the most important things about him. Does he repulse you?" A little pink spotted her cheeks. "You know what I mean."

"No." At least not as far as she knew. She would not admit to Alexia that the notion of the carnal side of marriage left her chilled, however. Alexia was so passionately in love that she would not comprehend that problem at all.

"Do you hope for better? Another rescuer, but this time one more appropriate to your birth?"

"Hardly."

"Then I do not understand. Perhaps you think me too practical, but if the choice is between poverty and ruin or security and salvation—"

"There is another offer."

Alexia halted in mid stride. Astonishment widened her eyes. "Another offer? Not another rescuer, though. Pray, do not tell me that you are being pursued by another Norbury, and have received an offer to be some gentleman's bought possession."

"It is not that kind of offer. I received another letter from Timothy. He begs me to join him, to live with him."

Alexia's face fell into a mask of sorrow. She closed her eyes to hold in a private pain. Rose said nothing, but her heart joined Alexia's in experiencing the poignant grief that mention of her brother evoked.

"And you are considering going to him?" Alexia asked.

"Yes. I had made my decision before Mr. Bradwell spoke to me."

Alexia sat on the divan again. Her violet eyes misted. "You worry for him now, of course. Now that he is alone. He was always the weakest among you, and now—I want you to know that I understand, Rose. And

I understand how tempting that must be, to have travel and a new life dangled in front of you. But—"

"Yes, it is tempting. Very tempting. I will take a new name. No one will know about me, about Norbury, about Tim. No one will know about *anything*."

She heard the force and bitterness in her own voice. Alexia bowed her head and allowed the vehemence to roll over her.

"*You* will know, Rose," she said gently. "You would not take that five thousand. You would not accept Hayden's support. Will you now live off the fruits of that crime?"

"It need not be that way. I can find employment. Tim can serve as a secretary and support us both. I can convince him to return the money—"

"He never will. It is probably mostly gone already, to drink and gambling. You have been in constant sorrow since his ruin, and not yourself. I understand why you want to run away, but you are not thinking clearly."

"I doubt that you do understand."

"Doubt that if you want, but do not doubt my love, Rose, or my sympathy for why you seek escape. You admitted that you lied to yourself about Norbury. Do not lie to yourself about this now, I beg you."

Every word that Alexia spoke added stones to a wall that gradually enclosed a very small place from which there was no escape. Rose wanted to scream that Alexia was wrong and arrogant. A bitter corner of her heart snarled that Alexia was too smug in her own happiness to be capable of all the knowing and understanding that she professed.

Seeing that wall looming, she yearned to run home

and back up that hill. She wanted to lie beneath the sky and again know the hopeful joy that had filled her that day.

A sound broke through her furious distraction. A small voice intruded on her anger and resentment.

"It is cold in the carriage and Lord Hayden said that I might come in now. Should I have waited longer, Alexia?"

A surge of emotion crested Roselyn's composure. She looked at the doorway through pools of brimming tears.

Irene stood there. Her sister appeared fashionable and fresh. Her long blond hair hung below a lovely bonnet, and her apple green carriage ensemble enhanced her youth and beauty. The garments were all new ones, gifts from Alexia.

"Do not look so angry, Rose," Irene pleaded. "I have been so unhappy since you left, and grieving that we would never speak again. Alexia said I could see you today, and even Hayden agreed that no one would know."

"I am not angry, darling. I am surprised and grateful and moved beyond words." She stood and held open her arms. Irene rushed to her embrace.

She held Irene close. She looked over her sister's shoulder at Alexia. It was clear that Alexia considered their argument over.

CHAPTER
EIGHT

~~

He saw her at once, standing beside the canal in her blue cloak. Her letter had given detailed instructions on where to meet her in Regent's Park. No more than five other bodies could be seen at this hour.

He had not known what to expect when she finally contacted him, but he had not anticipated the brief letter requesting a meeting here in London. There had been nothing encouraging about those few sentences.

As he walked toward her, he debated whether to plead his case further. He doubted it would make a difference. If she had decided to decline his offer, her reasons would be ones he had no answer for.

She noticed his approach. The sun caught the golden rim of her hair visible beneath the blue bonnet. Her smile could at best be called polite, but it still blotted out half of his mind.

He would probably be better off if she made short work of this mad idea.

"Thank you for coming, Mr. Bradwell. Especially at such an early hour."

"I always visit the parks at nine in the morning, Miss Longworth, so we have something in common."

He did not think she had ever been in one of London's parks this early before. She sought public privacy with him, however, and there were few other locations and times that would do.

He looked down the deserted paths and saw no conveyance but his own. "How did you get here?"

"I walked. A friend of Alexia's gave me use of her house and I came up for a few days."

"Have you walked enough, or shall we take a turn along the canal?"

She agreed to that. He offered a few pleasantries while he waited for her to address the reason for this meeting.

"Mr. Bradwell, I was hoping we could have another conversation about your generous offer. I believe that if two people are going to even consider such an irrevocable step, absolute honesty is best."

"Absolute honesty is never a good idea, to my thinking. I do not believe the world could survive it."

She looked at him, aghast.

He laughed. "I shock you. Will you settle for circumspect honesty? Some truths change, after all, and others are not even known."

"I only require sufficient honesty so that if we do this we have a right understanding."

She had just revealed more than all the absolute honesty ever would. Whatever she had been debating these last days, the scales had somehow tipped in his favor.

It is only yours to lose now, Kyle lad.

"Speak frankly, Miss Longworth, and I will try to do so as well."

"I understand what you are offering. I want you to know that I comprehend its value. The security and protection are important, but the chance for redemption—I have realized the fullness of that now. If I appear skeptical, please forgive me. Please know that I am truly grateful. However, I think it best if we both know what we are getting in such a match, in real and practical terms."

"How sensible."

She blushed. "I sound like a heartless and cold merchant, don't I? I do not mean to. It is just that I find myself incapable of creating romantic illusions. I am well done with those girlish ideas."

Despite her request for absolutes, she did prefer some circumspection. He heard the hard truth anyway. *If we do this, I do not expect love. Nor should you.*

"Mr. Bradwell, I need to know if you understand that whatever redemption I achieve will not be complete. I will never entirely live down that disastrous affair with Lord Norbury. When you are old and gray there will still be those who whisper as you walk by, if we are wed. Since you are not a gentleman, there are those who will speak of it right to your face."

"I am the son of a collier. I am accustomed to whispers, and rudeness spoken right to my face."

"The day may come when some malicious person claims that I have begun another affair. I would like to know if you will be inclined to believe that."

"You have weighed every eventuality, haven't you? I

do not know what I will believe. I promise to ask you if it is true before I kill the man, however."

She stopped walking near a tree. The sun's crisp light reflected in a ribbon down the canal. "You must think me small and mean to parse your offer so thoroughly."

"I think that all smart women scrutinize marriage offers. It is only unusual that I am hearing every point of debate."

She gazed up at him with disconcerting directness. Her brow puckered, as if she sought to see his soul and regretted that she could not.

"You were at Norbury's house for a reason that day. Are you friends with him?"

"I have known him for years. Our connection goes far back. At the moment we are involved in some business together."

"So you will see this man. You will know, and he will know, and—"

"Women are not the only ones who scrutinize marriage offers, Miss Longworth. I have considered how that might be awkward. I promise you that he will not mention it to me. At least not more than once. I will not allow any man to insult my wife." He took her hand in both of his. Since she allowed it, he regretted that they both wore gloves. "Nor will I ever speak of it to you. You made a mistake with a dishonorable man, but it is over."

She searched his eyes as if trying to see if he meant it. He let her look as long as she wanted.

"It is unlikely that you will conjure up an objection for me that I have not already considered, Miss Longworth."

"Actually, there is one, and it would be wrong not to speak of it." She forced poise on her posture, much as she had that night. "Mr. Bradwell, I am one whisper away from being involved in a scandal that will make the current one child's play in comparison."

She appeared so adorably earnest and brave. The martyrs of old probably looked like this before entering the arena. "What scandal is that?"

"You know about my brother, you said. You do not know the whole of it. He stole money from people who had trusts and three percenters at his bank. And they know he did. He promised to repay them so no one laid down information, but then he fled and Lord Hayden made good on his debts." It came out fast, in a torrent of confession that clearly pained her to admit. "There are dozens of victims and it will take only one of them to speak of it, you see. Just one, and it will be known what he did and my relationship to him will bring his disgrace on me. And on my husband, if I am married."

He lifted her hand and dipped his head to kiss it. "I already know about your brother."

"You do? How—oh, dear, were you one of the ones—"

"Someone I know was."

"And yet you proposed marriage?"

"It was his crime. His sin. You are innocent. You are also one of the victims. You and your sister have suffered much due to him, have you not?"

The mention of her sister made her eyes glisten. He was not too good to press his advantage.

"That one whisper is another reason to marry me. It will make it clear that you are separate from him, and

he from you. You will not be piling one fall upon another, the way it would be if you lived your exile in
Oxfordshire."

"I do not think anyone will see me as separate. I am
his sister."

"You will be my wife in the world's eyes before you
are his sister. In this scandal even more than the other,
marriage offers protection."

Her resistance was palpable. So was her vulnerabil-
ity. "You said Lord Hayden was not paying you a settlement to do this. I assume the payment will come in
other ways."

"I never denied that there would be benefits."

"They must be bigger than the ones I can imagine, if
you are willing to tie yourself to so much disgrace."

"Weigh your own gain and costs, Miss Longworth,
and leave me to weigh mine. If I did not want you, nothing could lure me to this match no matter what the status of your fortune, family, or virtue."

She stopped walking and faced him. She eyed him
critically, as if deciding if that want of his would be tolerable. There were no words to convince her of that. For
this woman, however, her conclusion would be a heavy
weight no matter which side of the scales it rested on.

"Perhaps now is not the moment to make your decision, Miss Longworth. There is no hurry, and it is a decision that requires much thought on a woman's part."

Her expression relaxed. "Thank you, Mr. Bradwell. I
confess that the mere permanence of it makes my
courage falter. You are, as always, very kind and considerate."

Hardly.

His carriage had been following along the lane. He gestured for his man to wait. "Allow me to escort you back to your residence. I think that you have walked too far today already."

Relieved of the worry of his proposal for another day, she accepted gladly. Innocently. She even smiled while they walked to the carriage.

He handed her in. It was time to close the negotiations.

She should have known that nice Mr. Bradwell would not press her for a decision. He was not that kind of man. He had understood, as always. He knew that such a step should not be taken lightly.

She settled in the carriage and he sat across from her. The carriage rolled toward the park's entrance.

He was tall and imposing, and he seemed to crowd her, just as he had that horrible night. Once more she experienced the odd combination of danger and safety.

"You need not make a decision today, but I hope that you will soon," he said.

"Of course. Tomorrow, I promise. I would never be so heartless as to leave an offer dangling. I am embarrassed that I have done so this long."

"That is of no account. I understand why."

Did he? She wondered for the first time if his comprehension was correct. She doubted any man would really know the terror that a woman could feel when faced with a proposal, as she imagined both the good and the bad it might bring to her life.

"It might be best if I explained some things, so that

you can assess the situation most fully." His gaze sharpened ever so slightly, but enough to raise a small, almost thrilling caution in her.

"Please speak freely, Mr. Bradwell."

"I still have family up north. I will never deny them, or hide them, or pretend I am other than I am. Not for anyone. Not even for you."

"Do you think me so hard as to want that?"

"I do not know what you will want, so I am making it clear how it will be. Also, as you begin returning to society, there will be those who want to receive you, but who will hesitate due to me. I want you to let it be known that you will accept invitations and that I will decline them when necessary. I will leave it to you to decide when those situations arise."

She wished she could say that they never would. She thought it noble of him not to want to hold her back. Since he offered redemption he wanted it to be as complete as possible.

"You have expressed interest in any settlement that I will receive," he continued. "However, you have neglected to ask about yours. Should you accept me, I will discuss your jointure with Lord Hayden, if that is acceptable to you."

"Yes, that would be acceptable." She *had* been neglectful. That more than anything reflected her ambivalence about this proposal. Had he guessed as much? Probably so.

"There is also the matter of your brother."

"You said in the park that it did not matter to you."

"I said that his crime does not taint you. However, it is very important, for your sake and for that of the family you will be able to reclaim, that you accept him as dead to you."

Dead to you. Rather suddenly, nice Mr. Bradwell had become strict and dire and a little presumptuous in his demands regarding a marriage he might not even have.

His command raised the devil in her, and fed her impractical resistance to the stark "forever" that she contemplated with him.

"He is my brother. It is unfair for you to ask this."

"I do not ask, but demand."

A demand now. "You are offering to give me half of my family back even as you insist that I relinquish the other half."

"If that is how you see it, yes. I demand this more easily of you than I would of most women. I saw you the night of that auction, explaining to Lady Alexia how you must be dead to her and your sister. When she wrote, you returned her letters unopened, to make sure you would not taint her. It is how it must be, you said. If you saw that reality, you surely see this one."

She felt her face warming. She resented the way he cornered her with her own words and actions.

"I will not think of him as dead. I cannot. In fact, if there is a chance that I can see him, I must *demand* that you promise now that you will permit it."

The ultimatum hung in the air. The man who might become her husband let it dangle while he considered her. She half expected him to withdraw his proposal on the spot.

Instead of relief, the notion panicked her.

It was the escape that she wanted, for reasons she could not explain to Alexia or even herself. And yet, facing it now, she saw that if it happened she would have no decent life to honestly choose.

She almost retracted her words. A small, lonely, confused voice clamored to surrender. *Yes, I will do as you want. I will do anything if you feed me and flatter me and pretend to care. I will forget who I am and relinquish all my dreams and be obedient if you buy fuel for my hearth so I am not cold.*

She gritted her teeth so that voice would not actually speak. The last time she had heeded that pitiful part of her soul, she had found herself with a scoundrel.

Still, the desperation increased while she waited for him to speak. She hated that. She hated how it proved she really did not have any other choice but this marriage. She even hated Tim, and that he had once more left her teetering on the line between utter ruin and abject dependency.

"If he returns to England, you can see him," he finally said. "However, you will not go to him where he now hides. Whether you marry me or not, you will not go to him, so you can remove that from any weighing that you are doing. Do not think that I cannot stop you. I can and I will."

Her face burned. He had guessed her plan, and who the man was.

Nor was his compromise generous. Tim would never return to England. He dared not. Mr. Bradwell won even as he retreated.

The carriage seemed to be moving very slowly through town. She wished it would hurry. This conversation vexed her. She worried that he had seen the spiking desperation in her as she waited for him to speak. If so, he might continue these "explanations" until she was little better than a dutiful child in this marriage he proposed.

Her pique got the better of her. "I think I will need more than the single day that I assumed to make my decision, since you saved so many conditions for the end. Pray tell me, is there more?"

"Just one detail."

"Enlighten me."

"I do not hold with the loose morals so easily accepted in polite society. I do not mind sharing what is mine if I agree to it, but I will never agree to share you."

"You will, however, still ask me for the truth before you kill a man over a rumor? That assurance was not false, I trust."

He smiled. "It was not false."

"Is there anything else? I hope not. As it is, I may forget some of this litany of increasingly disconcerting terms. I should have brought paper and pencil this morning so I could write it all down."

He leaned forward and took her hand in his. The gesture implied he had a right to both comfort and claim her.

His thumb gently caressed her palm. She felt it through her glove very plainly. The touch made her arm tingle all the way up to her shoulder.

"I do not think that any of these terms truly disconcerts you," he said. "If you require more time for a decision, it is not due to matters such as we have addressed today. If you want a right understanding, as you say, we must speak as honestly of the true reason."

They had discussed everything that mattered, and a

good deal that she had not expected. "You are omniscient today, as well as demanding."

"Not omniscient. You spoke of this last concern when I proposed." He looked in her eyes. "You are trying to decide if you can bear the duties of a wife. You are trying to decide if you will loathe the sexual part of this marriage."

She felt her face flaming. "I told you that I am beyond romantic illusions. In truth I have no concerns at all because that implies an open question. I was giving you fair warning about how I know it will be."

"If I believed that were true, I would find a way to make you reject the offer. Romantic feelings and illusions are not required to make those duties tolerable, Miss Longworth. Believing that they are may even make matters worse. Instead of an expression of undying romantic love, you might better think of that congress as a good meal that satisfies a hunger."

She could not believe that he spoke of this so bluntly. A gentleman would not. But then he was not a gentleman. Worse, he expected some response from her besides the flustered dismay this indelicate turn in the conversation evoked.

A meal to satisfy a hunger. That was a rather novel if bawdy way to think about it. It certainly demolished the notion of romance, but at least it implied something more satisfying than what she had known.

"This meal—would it be porridge, or pheasant?" she blurted.

He laughed quietly and appeared a little dismayed himself now.

"You see, I do not much care for porridge. I have had my fill of that," she said.

"There are many courses, and a whole menu from which to choose. I am sure that we can find something to your taste. We will only discover what it is if you agree to sit at the table, however."

They had arrived at another term by an indirect route. He was saying that he expected her to accept him in this way, without dramatics and excuses.

She pictured that. She imagined lying in bed, and this man joining her there. She braced herself for the unpleasant resignation that she had experienced in her brief affair.

Instead, the picture stirred her. The waiting contained an alluring anticipation that physically affected her. Any fear carried a delicious overtone.

He watched her, his expression one of dangerous charm, as if he too saw her in that bed and knew how the waiting excited more than imposed.

He still held her hand. Now his own tightened just enough to control and confine. He gently pulled. The scene outside the window slid past as her whole body floated across to him. With elegant smoothness he settled her on his lap.

Surprise gave way to alarm. The light surrounding them dimmed. She twisted to see him pulling the curtains.

"What are you doing?" She could feel his thighs beneath her, despite her dress. She began to scramble off her perch.

The arm with which he supported her back held her

in place so she did not fall on the floor. Or get free. She
straightened her back to achieve some independence.

"*What* are you doing?" she repeated.

His gaze followed his fingertips while they traced
the side of her face in that familiar way. Only this time
his touch did not end, but gently held her chin while he
gave her a kiss. A light kiss, like that first one in the
field, but her lip trembled and a shudder slid down to her
chest.

"I am making sure that you judge my offer fairly, and
without prejudice." He kissed her again. "I am pleading
my case on your final concern with the only argument
that matters."

"Final concern—?" His meaning shocked her. She
pressed her hands against his shoulder and reared back.

He smiled slowly while he eased her back to him. A
polite, slow, careful wrestling match ensued. She did
not truly fight and he did not really restrain. She merely
kept trying to position herself out of an intimate embrace and he kept managing to encompass her in one
anyway.

Somehow he arranged her to where she definitely
had lost. If he thought to seduce her, he was badly mistaken. She pushed against his shoulders again. "Good
heavens. You can not think to—not here, in a carriage."

"I will not. Unless you beg it of me, of course."

Beg it? She swallowed her mirth as best she could.

He saw it anyway. "You are right. It would be best to
leave that for another day."

She would have laughed outright at his confidence,
except he kissed her then. Suddenly his insinuation
ceased being a lark.

The kiss in the field had surprised her. The one in the kitchen had defeated her. This one frightened her.

The excitement did not trickle through her this time. It flooded her in a rush. His firm kiss demolished whatever barrier held physical composure in. Her body responded fast, as if it knew the happy pleasure that waited now, and longed to experience it again.

Warm kisses led her to a mindless, breathless place. Kisses on her lips and neck lured and titillated. Tense, small bites on her ear sent trembles into her blood. If marriage meant this and only this, she was very sure she would accept his offer.

Only it did not, and his passion darkened even as hers increased. She felt it in him, the restraint that he put on his desire, but it still reminded her of that desire's goal. She did not relinquish the little pleasures in seeing that, but she was not inexperienced. She knew how pleasure could abruptly end.

He did not have to cajole her mouth open this time. She submitted to that invasion because she already knew it would not be unpleasant. He ravished her mouth, carefully and deliberately, as if he knew how to provoke every thrilling response that streaked and pulsed down her body. Soon she noticed nothing except their lively paths and the way she wanted to feel more of them.

He caressed her and the spring breeze of her pleasure turned to summer's hot wind. She felt his hand under her cloak, through fabric and stays, warm and firm and very sure of its path. Her body moved into it even as the possessive touch shocked her. Soon she resented the cloth that inhibited the warmth. A storm of madness threatened to break in her head.

He kissed her hard and called the lightning forth with a caress on her breast. Her body responded as if it had been waiting for that touch.

His fingers submerged her in a pleasure so luscious that she could not bear it. He found the hard tip and teased until her body whimpered. Images entered her mind of other intimacies and touches.

He was making her crazed. Insane. She understood what he meant by hunger now. She understood his allusion to begging, because pleas chanted in her mind.

She clutched his arms to try to hold on to her sense of the world. Still his hand devastated her. She clenched her teeth to keep from crying out or moaning. She wanted relief. She wanted more.

Her pleasure peaked to an intensity both painfully needful and wonderfully delirious. It was then—while her body screamed and her control shattered and she ached to rip off her clothes and feel him touch her whole body and fill the aching voids trembling in her—it was then that he stopped.

She could not breathe. She could not think. The sweet kiss with which he ended the passion seemed a cruel joke. She blinked back to awareness and saw the carriage wall and ceiling, and him.

He gazed down, no more content than she. Perhaps he waited for her to beg as he had said she would have to.

She almost did, God help her. His fingers came to rest on her lips, stopping any such impulse.

"Agree to marry me now, Roselyn."

The desire still stimulated her. The sweet torture had not ceased. But a peaceful mood of beauty and freedom settled on her while the storm slowly calmed. She floated in a lively, carefree stupor drenched with the intimacy of his kisses and touch.

The mood reminded her of how she had felt while she lay on the hill that day and gazed up at the boundless sky.

"Yes. I will marry you."

CHAPTER
NINE

⌀

The clerk ushered Kyle into a spartan sitting room in the City, part of a suite of chambers such as a bachelor solicitor might use. Kyle guessed that a bedchamber could be found behind the closed door at the far end, opposite the Venetian window with its compass pane at the top.

His letter to Lord Hayden had produced the invitation to call at these chambers. It appeared that his host used this apartment for business and other things. Women, perhaps, in the days before he married. Private pursuits, like whatever was being written on the pages piled on the standing desk near the window.

Lord Hayden greeted him. They sat in two deep red upholstered chairs near the fireplace.

The memory of their last private meeting cast a shadow on this one. Lord Hayden Rothwell had come to Kyle's chambers that time, seeking him out after an invitation like this one had been declined.

"Miss Longworth has asked me to speak for her,"

Lord Hayden said. "She indicated that you suggested this."

"In considering my offer she had been impractical in neglecting the financial terms."

Lord Hayden lounged in his chair as if a friendly chat were part of the settlement ritual. "I did not know her before her brother's ruin. She blamed me for it, and although she now knows the truth there is still much formality between us. I knew her older brother very well, but not his sisters."

"That would be her brother Benjamin. The one who died some years back."

Lord Hayden's face turned stern, taking on the mask this man usually showed the world. "My wife tells me that her cousin has not been herself the last year. She says that affair with Norbury was the bad judgment of a woman in a deep melancholy. Her neglect regarding your offer's financial terms no doubt reflects her state of mind as well."

"Then it is well that we address the matter for her. Although her state of mind, while affected, is not melancholic. I am not taking advantage of a woman unable to make sound decisions."

"I did not mean to imply that you were. Even if you did, the chance this will give her—I will not be sorry to see her restored to my wife."

For a man not sorry to see this marriage, Lord Hayden was taking his time about settling the details.

"To now play the father in marriage discussions for her is unexpected and a little unwelcome, Bradwell. Regrettably, I know more than I would like and I am compelled to address more than pin money."

"I trust that you believe that my intentions are honorable."

"That is not the matter on my mind, and I think that you know it."

Of course Kyle knew it. He just did not know what tack Lord Hayden would take.

"Has she told you about Timothy's crimes? I cannot blame her if she has not," Lord Hayden said.

"She was very honest and insisted that I hear all."

"Brave of her."

"I think that she assumed that I would retract the offer when I heard, so it was very brave." Actually, he suspected that she *hoped* he would retract, and spare her making a decision herself. She no longer trusted her own mind even if she still knew it.

"Were you as honest with her as she was with you?"

"I told her that I already knew what her brother had done, and that I am familiar with one of his victims."

"Hell, you *were* one of his victims. As trustee, that loss was yours too."

"Only because I made it mine. I had other choices." Only one, in truth. The one talking to him now. The other alternative to replenishing that trust with his own money had been to allow the trust to lie empty and useless. He could not do that.

"Does she know that you refused to be made whole?"

"No. Do you think I should tell her?"

"I do not know what the hell I think." Lord Hayden shot to his feet. Mouth hard, frown deep, he paced away, deliberating the same conundrum that had vexed Kyle often enough the last few weeks.

"She was thinking of going to her brother," Kyle said. "She received another letter and he asked her to join him."

"Damn." Lord Hayden shook his head. "Still, while you are not deceiving her, you are being less than completely honest."

Another call for complete honesty, as if such a thing were not only possible, but normal.

He would have dealings with this man in the future. He did not want Lord Hayden thinking him a liar or scoundrel. He would attempt to explain, even though he almost never did with anyone.

He stood too, and strolled through the chamber while he decided what to say and what to avoid. His walk took him near the standing desk. He spied the jotting on the pages. Numbers and notations filled the sheets. This was where Lord Hayden pursued those mathematical investigations for which he was rumored to have a passion.

"Tell me, Lord Hayden, what would the world assume if it knew of Longworth's crime and his sister fled in his wake?"

"The world does not know of his crime."

"It will. Someday. It is inevitable. Too many were burned for it to remain a secret."

His confidence in that alarmed Lord Hayden. "They have all had their losses restored, damn it." He glared the rest—*except you.*

"The loss to their purses, yes. To their pride, no. You may have miscalculated."

Lord Hayden did not like that idea. A sigh of frustration signaled how weary this talk of Longworth made him. "If she were with him when it all came out, she would probably be seen as an accomplice."

"I think so too. So, should I tell her everything? If I do, if she knows how I was touched by that, she might change her mind on this marriage. She might run to her brother, to save him or help him or to escape the pending shame to herself. She assumes time is short for that secret, even if you do not."

Lord Hayden's lids lowered while he subjected Kyle to an examination much like the one Easterbrook had given that day.

"Is that why you refused the money? Pride, like the others you mention?"

"It was not your crime. Why should you pay? You have paid dearly too. An astonishing sum for a crime of which you are innocent. If I took your money I would have made myself whole at the expense of another victim, that is all."

"A willing victim, so it was not the same. I think it was pride after all."

Lord Hayden's arrogance annoyed Kyle. He gestured to the chamber. "No financial schemes have been concocted here of late. No syndicates formed. You remain in that house, which is modest by Mayfair standards. Even you have felt the bite of laying out all that money. Should I have bled you for another twenty thousand? Agreed to the blackmail that you proposed I take?"

"Blackmail, hell. Your purse would have been spared the ravage of his crime, that is all."

"You did not only make them whole. You required that they forget the fraud. Silence for money, that was part of the deal. Would that every sinner had an angel like you pleading his case."

He expected an argument, even anger. Instead Lord Hayden rubbed his brow and spoke with resignation. "And when time runs out the way you expect, Bradwell? Justice will require that he pay with his life. If that day comes, what will you say to her?"

"That pain waits for her whether she marries me or not. If that day comes, I will protect and comfort her as best I can."

Lord Hayden considered that a good while. Then he walked to his desk and gestured for Kyle to join him.

"Let us prepare for the solicitors. This marriage would sit better with me if you had let me pay that blackmail. However, that sorry episode has shadowed the Longworth sisters too much. Perhaps after this marriage it will weigh less heavily in Roselyn's future."

"Don't you look all grown up, Miss Irene," Mr. Preston said with a grin. "The women in the village will be talking about that bonnet for days."

Irene beamed while Mr. Preston counted out Rose's money and wrapped the groceries she had bought.

She did look all grown up, Rose thought. Alexia had raised the idea of launching Irene next season. It was definitely time in terms of Irene's age, but probably too early in light of other things. Even this marriage would not blunt the scandal quickly enough for Irene to be received this season.

The mere idea that Irene might have a better future calmed Rose's nervousness about the pending wedding.

That constant agitation had not been helped by Kyle's absence the last week. He had gone north for Christmas, to the aunt and uncle who had raised him.

His absence meant that she could prepare without distraction, but the conviction that she knew the man she was marrying dimmed a bit with each day.

"We are all looking forward to the big day, Miss Longworth," Mr. Preston said with a wide smile. "May I say that those who met Mr. Bradwell last month when he was in the village all extol his fine manner and good nature."

"Thank you. I trust that you and Mrs. Preston will honor us with your attendance."

"My wife would not miss it. She said all along that some people are too fast to assume the worst. It grieved her, it did, the way some others—" He stopped abruptly and gave Irene a meaningful glance. His eyes communicated apology for referring to the scandal in front of her.

"It moves me that your wife defended me, Mr. Preston. Good day to you now."

She and Irene stepped out of the shop. Irene's impressive bonnet, made of Terre d'Egypte gros de Naples, dipped close. "Do you think the whole village is of Mr. Preston's mind?"

"It is unlikely that Mrs. Preston would allow her husband to be so friendly unless most of the village is."

"Then it appears to be working the way Alexia hoped."

"Here, yes. However, Watlington is one thing. London will be another."

"I think it will not be bad in London. Easterbrook is

coming to your wedding. When the notices report that, it will make quick work of wagging tongues."

"Since tongues wag plenty about him, I would not put too much faith in his powers on that count."

It had been Kyle's idea, not Alexia's, that they hold the wedding here in the country. Lord Hayden had then offered his brother's nearby estate, Aylesbury Abbey, but Kyle had said the Longworth house would be preferable. Even though he had procured a special license, they would marry in her girlhood parish church amidst the people who had known her all her life.

Rose now realized the wisdom in that. Kyle knew villagers better than a marquess's brother ever would. The money the family would spend on preparations in the village, and the celebration open to everyone, would do more to encourage a generous view of that scandal than ten years of honest living.

She and Irene strolled down the village lane, exchanging greetings with neighbors and stopping so some girls could admire Irene's fine bonnet. They bought some ribbons and fabric before making the walk back to the house.

Commotion waited for them there. Three large wagons laden with furniture crowded the drive. An army of servants carted items past Alexia, who stood sentry at the front door with a long sheet of paper in her hand.

"That goes to the library," she said to two men carrying a big rug.

"What are you doing?" Rose asked, ducking aside as a large wardrobe traveled past her.

"To the south bedchamber," Alexia commanded three men straining with the wardrobe's weight. She glanced at Rose. "You cannot hold a wedding in a house with no chairs."

"That was not a chair."

"Do not get proud on me. Do not dare. Hayden said that you would and I will not allow you to make him right. I am vexed enough that he convinced me to wait so long to do this. If bad weather had set in, you would be hosting a party in a barren house next week." A fellow with a chest on his back staggered past. She rapped his shoulder with her paper. "Get help in the future, my good man. You cannot even see where you are going."

"I'm strong, Madam. It'll take more than this to hurt me."

"To be sure. However, one bad turn and the walls will be gouged. We do not have time to start with new plaster. Now, Rose, Aylesbury Abbey has attics full of furniture that is never used. It is sinful to see such waste. Nor is this a gift from Hayden. That house and its contents are not his."

Irene nodded. "That is true, Rose. It is all Easterbrook's."

A line of chairs marched past Rose. "Alexia, did the marquess give permission for you to raid Aylesbury's attics?"

Alexia counted the chairs, then consulted her paper. "I had not discovered the riches in them until we came down this time. However, the last I saw him the conversation turned to your wedding. I mentioned that I planned to help you prepare, and he said that I could make free with Aylesbury's servants and such if I needed to." She grinned. "This is the 'and such.'"

Rose pictured the marquess in her house, sardonic

when he was not silent, eyeing furniture that looked sus-
piciously familiar. She had met him only twice since
Alexia wed, and she found him an enigmatic, rather
darkly humored man who would benefit from more
country air than he ever sought.

"Of course, he may change his mind about attending," she muttered, rather wishing he might even if his
presence would help redeem her. The villagers' fawning
and scraping would be so thick on her wedding day that
no one would have any fun.

"Oh, he will be here," Alexia said. "His aunt
Henrietta was making sounds about not attending and
he ordered her to accompany him. He will drag himself
out of London now if only to discomfort her."

Irene made a face. "*She* is coming?"

Rose stepped into the line of human pack horses. "I
wonder if *she* has ever examined the contents of those
attics."

"I daresay Henrietta has inventoried Easterbrook's
possessions down to the last pillow since she took residence with him last spring," Alexia said.

"Then I can see her at my wedding party. Her eye-
brows will rise with every chair and table she passes until they merge with her hairline."

Alexia and Irene scooted in beside her. They let the
river of furniture carry them inside.

They left the men to set the furniture in the rooms
according to drawings that Alexia had made. Rose
brought her sister and cousin up to the sanctuary of her
bedchamber.

The door to her own attic stood open. She peered in

and saw some of the house's old furniture stacked inside. The presence of a few items surprised her.

Instead of going to her room she entered the south bedchamber. It was the biggest one. All of its old furniture had been replaced by objects brought by Alexia. A large bed awaited its hangings, and the newly delivered wardrobe gleamed against one wall. A man's dressing table stood ready for someone's brushes and private objects.

She looked at Alexia, whose face reflected her stoic practicality.

"It is time, Rose. Ben has been gone for years now," Alexia said. "This house will have a new master and a new life soon, and this chamber should be his."

Rose gazed around the room, transformed now by foreign objects, soon to be owned by a foreign presence. Her heart clenched at the finality of Alexia's action.

Irene bit her lower lip. "She is right, Rose. I do not think you will mind so much in a few days."

Rose embraced Irene's shoulders with one arm. "I do not mind now, darling. Alexia is correct. It is time to move on."

She guided Irene from the chamber. Alexia caught her eye as they passed. They exchanged a look much as they had in Phaedra's house.

Sometimes there really weren't any choices. Sometimes there was only one thing to do and one decision to make if you wanted a chance at contentment.

CHAPTER
TEN

Jordan insisted on dressing his master the morning of the wedding. He commandeered the staff of the Knight's Lily in Watlington and issued orders like a field marshal. He called for breakfast and coffee, for a bath and more towels, for yet more hot water, and for an assistant while he wielded the razor.

Kyle submitted, and surmised that the inn's servants did not mind the impositions. It allowed them to participate in the wedding that had the whole village excited.

All the while, Jordan gave reports on the progress he had made in preparing the house in London for the future Mrs. Bradwell.

Finally all was done. Jordan twitched a collar, smoothed a sleeve, and stood back to give an inspection.

"Finished, and an hour to spare. The waistcoat was a superb choice, sir. That faint touch of deep rose in the gray is perfect with the blue superfine of the frock coat."

"Since the waistcoat was your choice, I am relieved that you approve. I still think the simpler gray would have been better."

"It is your wedding, sir. A touch of sartorial festivity—an extremely minor touch, I might add—is not only appropriate but expected." Jordan packed away the last of his battery of weapons. He bowed to take his leave. "If I may say, sir, you look as fine a gentleman as I have ever seen. It was a privilege to serve you on this most felicitous day."

Kyle glanced in the looking glass at the fine image time and practice and Jordan had wrought. He certainly felt more pressed and clean and presentable than he had in years. It reminded him of the day his aunt had scrubbed him raw prior to sending him to Kirtonlow Hall for the first time, at the Earl of Cottington's summons. He had been ready an hour too early that day too, and left alone to try not to ruin the effect while he sweated.

He looked out the window at the village lane below. Few people could be seen. They all prepared as he did, for a ceremony and party to surpass anything that they had enjoyed in years.

He had assumed that the earl intended to scold at best and whip at worst that day. Instead, Cottington had changed his life.

For the better, to be sure. Only a fool or ingrate would not admit it. Only now, as he gazed out the window at Watlington, he experienced unanticipated nostalgia for his own village of Teeslow.

It would have been nice to have some faces he knew at his wedding, only they were far away, in time as well as place. Cottington's generosity had plucked him from that world, but there had been no other world in which to set him down.

He had cobbled together something resembling a circle out of his friends and associates, but it was not the same. He did not really belong anywhere anymore, and had not for some time. His life was like a vine rambling farther and farther from the roots that had given it birth.

Nor would this marriage change matters. He would stand on the edge of Rose's world, not in it. He had made his choice of wife fully aware of that. He knew what he gained and what he would never have in ways even Rose did not comprehend.

His gaze fell on his valise. Tucked inside it was a letter brought down from London by Jordan. The earl had been too ill to receive him when he was up north, but had rallied enough to write advice and congratulations on this marriage, and indicate that his solicitor had been instructed on arranging a gift.

The earl would not be here. Nor would Aunt Prudence and Uncle Harold, who had not been able to hide their shock at his choice of wife when he informed them during his Christmas visit. Harold was too ill to travel, but they would never have undertaken such a journey anyway in January. The other people of his youth would not celebrate with him, either, and only one person from his current, vague world was in Watlington.

Kyle went in search of him.

He entered Jean Pierre's chamber to find him tying his cravat at the looking glass. After a few studied twists and turns of the linen, Jean Pierre's fine profile nodded with contentment. He turned and examined Kyle's face.

"*Mon dieu,* why do men always look like they go to the guillotine on their wedding day?" He grabbed a flask off the dressing table and threw it. "One swallow, no more. It would be rude to be drunk, although it might be more painless."

Kyle laughed, but he took a swallow anyway.

Jean Pierre fussed with his cravat a bit more. "I am not impressed by this Easterbrook, but, *oui,* I am being a fool anyway. I tell myself my care with my dress is not for him and his great title. The servants say your bride is very lovely and I want to impress her, not him."

"Why? She is *my* bride."

A laugh. A sigh. "It is good that you marry. You have never enjoyed the game. Some of your views are . . . simple."

"Very simple." His voice sounded more dangerous than he intended. Stupidly so.

"I hope that you will not be one of those boring men who get angry if someone flatters your wife. A man does not pluck every flower that he sniffs."

"Flatter all you want, but I know all about your way with those flowers. I am sure that you know better than to play in my garden."

"Truly, *mon ami,* you must accept that among her circle there will be flirting and not be stupid—"

"I do not need lessons from you. I know all that. I am just mentioning to *you* that *you* will not be plucking, smelling, or even strolling by any hedgerows."

"The day's strain is already affecting your mind. It is good I am here to help you. Another sip of those spirits is needed, I think. Then we will play cards until the wedding so you find some calm and do not talk like an idiot."

"I am very calm. Not a ripple. Hell, I've never been more placid."

"Of course you are. Now, one more swallow. Ah, *bon*."

"The coach from Aylesbury had passed."

The information came from a footman who had been stationed as sentry down on the road. Alexia stood and smiled expectantly at Rose. "We can go now."

Rose looked down on her ensemble. It was not truly new. This dress had been stored away a year ago, when Tim had been selling everything in sight. Angrily and selfishly, she had hidden some of her best garments in the hope she might have cause to wear them again. Alexia had helped her remake the dress so its history was not apparent.

Rose was glad that she wore her own clothes today. Very little else in the house now belonged to her. Even the food being cooked in the kitchen by Aylesbury's servants was not hers, and Kyle had sent the ale and wine. She would have felt even more strange if she stood in one of Alexia's gowns.

They all filed out to the waiting carriages. Lady Phaedra and Lord Elliot had come for this procession instead of joining Easterbrook's. The full attendance of Lord Hayden's family moved her. They announced their protection of her, motivated by their love for Alexia.

Alexia, Irene, and Lord Hayden rode with her in an open phaeton. No one was to be seen on the lanes when they arrived at the village. Instead, everyone waited at the church. Quite a few milled outside because the old medieval stones could not contain them all.

When Rose entered the church, the change in light

and temperature affected her. She became light-headed. The scene turned unreal, like images from a dream.

Her blood pounded in her head and impressions flashed to its beat. Smiles and mumbles and women pointing to the ladies' fine ensembles—faces from her whole life turning to watch—a walk, long and dark, toward the priest.

Kyle waited for her, looking so handsome in his way. His small smile of reassurance made the world right itself some, but not entirely. She spoke words that sounded very far away. Important words, vows and promises, that bound her irrevocably.

Exhilaration filled her unexpectedly when she realized it was over. She soared, amazed by her courage, but she also feared that unless angels appeared to hold her in flight, she might crash to the ground in the valley below.

She found herself in the phaeton again, with Kyle beside her this time. The village followed on foot or in carriages as they all made their way back to her house.

Kyle took her hand in his. His physical gesture snapped her out of her daze. The meaning of what had occurred pressed on her with a reality so absolute that she could barely accommodate it.

She looked at the profile of the man who was now her husband and master. Of the whole of him she knew only two parts, that of rescuer and suitor. The rest, almost everything, remained a stranger.

Kyle watched the gay party crowding Rose's home. The most honored guests had sat to a wedding breakfast even while the villagers made free with the drawing room and library and spilled out into the garden and property. Now everyone mixed in the crush, and pressed good wishes on Rose who stood ten feet away.

Kyle did not look at her too often. He dared not. When he did he saw details that made his body tighten. The nape of her neck, elegantly bowed toward a conversation, was feathered by errant hairs that looked like silk. Her lips, like velvet to kiss, curved in a serene smile.

Her dress was of a soft ivory-hued material that fitted her closely enough for him to again feel in his mind the breasts he had caressed. He imagined that dress gone soon, and the rest, and her perfect skin all along his body.

She noticed his gaze. She must have known the general direction of his thoughts even though he doubted she could guess their erotic details. She blushed and returned to the guest who occupied her.

He forced his attention on the party in order to distract himself. He watched Easterbrook holding court in front of the mantel. Villagers approached him with deference and trepidation, and not only because he was a marquess.

The man's manner did not encourage anything else. His eccentric appearance had been tamed somewhat. His garments were surprisingly conservative in fashion and his long hair had been gathered in a tail. But he watched from on high, content in the results of his capricious meddling.

A feminine giggle averted Kyle's attention. In a nearby corner of the drawing room, Jean Pierre charmed

Easterbrook's young cousin Caroline. The pretty girl flushed under his attention.

Her mother, Lady Wallingford—Aunt Henrietta to her family—encouraged Jean Pierre to flirt some more. Pale like her daughter, and adorned by a hat extraordinary in its excessive plumage, Lady Wallingford communicated a somewhat dotty vacancy with her blank, ethereal expressions. According to Rose, that guileless face masked the sharp, calculating mind of a woman determined to remain forever in Easterbrook's household after she finally gained entry last year. Rumor had it that the reclusive marquess met the continued intrusion of his aunt and cousin with increasingly strained forbearance.

Jean Pierre shortly excused himself from both ladies and wandered amidst bumping shoulders and rumps to where Kyle stood.

"Jean Pierre, about those flowers—Lord Hayden is guardian of the one you recently sniffed. Look at him. Do you want that man as an enemy?"

Jean Pierre's gaze sought Lord Hayden. "I do not think he will care."

"He will have no choice but to care. She is an innocent."

"I do not sniff innocents." He looked at Henrietta and Caroline. "The child does not interest me. Lady Wallingford cannot be more than middle thirties. You see a matron who wears ugly hats. I see a woman with a hidden, ethereal beauty who, my nose is happy to report, would not mind a little seduction."

It was no use to try to dissuade Jean Pierre from such

a pursuit. Kyle trusted that Lord Hayden would not consider his aunt's virtue a matter for a duel.

The tone in the party suddenly changed. Quieted. Bodies shifted to create an aisle. The marquess strolled down it, vaguely smiling his condescension left and right as he went.

"Finally," Jean Pierre muttered. "Now you must hide the ale and wine and everyone else will leave too."

Yes, finally.

Rose curtsied as Easterbrook took his leave of her. Kyle bowed and hoped nothing would distract the man from his course. Until Easterbrook left, no one else would.

The marquess's aunt felt obligated to follow him. In short order his brothers did too. The end of the festivities had begun.

Kyle mentally urged them out the door. The villagers and servants, all of them. It took effort to control his impatience.

Wanting Rose before was one thing. Wanting her now, today, when he knew he could have her, was proving to be torture.

It had been so long since Rose had a servant that she did not know what to do with the woman. Fortunately, the lady's maid arranged by Alexia did not require any direction. With efficient movements and downcast eyes she prepared Rose for her wedding night.

The house was almost empty now. No one remained except husband and wife, maid and valet. Soon the latter would make themselves scarce, disappearing to whatever chambers above they had chosen.

The last few hours had been excruciating. This moment had affected every second and minute. Neither she nor Kyle had said anything, not even on the long walk they had taken while Aylesbury's servants cleared the house of kegs and dishes. The coming night had just been an invisible cloak surrounding every instant and transforming every look and touch.

She sent the woman away and steadied herself. She was not afraid. Not at all. Nervous and worried and curious, but not really afraid.

She felt her hair, brushed out and hanging free. She checked her nightdress, almost demure in its long sleeves and ruffled collar. She looked at the bed, turned down and waiting. It had stood in the very same spot her entire life.

She was not sure that she wanted this to happen in that bed. She was not even sure that she wanted it to happen in this chamber.

This was where she had lived as a happy child and hopeful girl. This was where she had grieved her parents' deaths, and Benjamin's, and where she had suffered through her brother's ruin and then her own. This chamber held her whole history, good and bad, and it still echoed with girlhood dreams never realized.

If Kyle came here tonight she would never be able to enter this room again without his presence affecting all the memories.

Altering them. Maybe obliterating them. Her life would change in so many ways now. She should be able to at least keep this corner of her old world the same.

She threw a shawl around her shoulders. She lifted a candle and slipped from her chamber. She listened for sounds coming from the south bedroom, to hear if Jordan still served his master.

No voices or movements came to her. She pushed open the door a little and looked in.

Jordan was not there. Only Kyle. He stood by the fireplace, distracted by thoughts that hardened his expression. The contemplation had stopped his own preparations, it appeared. He had stripped to the waist, but still wore trousers.

Seeing him like this stunned her. The man submerged in those fine coats now stood fully exposed to her eyes, in ways not only physical. A gentleman could box and fence for months and not achieve the restrained, raw strength exuded by this man right now. It was not so much his size and physique, although his lean and taut muscularity hardly diminished the effect. Rather it came from within and needed no explanation.

She knew that she was seeing something that he hid from the world. He buried it from view beneath the educated speech and polite manners, but it was probably always alive in him. She had sensed it from the start, however. She had felt its effects in ways both subtle and strong. This was the power that excited her, and made her feel both safe and afraid.

He turned to her as if a sound had come from the doorway, when actually she had not even breathed. His gaze took her in—the shawl and the nightdress, the candle and her hair.

"I was just going to come to you," he said.

"I thought that I would come to you instead. Do you mind?"

"Of course not."

She walked over and set her candle on the dressing table. "You were deep in thought. What distracted you so?"

"A memory from long ago. So long ago that I had forgotten it completely until now."

"An unpleasant one?"

"Yes."

"Then I am glad that I intruded."

She grew awkward under his attention. Perhaps if she came here instead of him coming to her, she was expected to do something.

"Did he hurt you?"

He asked so calmly that it took a moment for her to realize what he meant. It saddened her that he would refer to Norbury now, on this night of all nights.

"I thought that you were never going to speak—"

"Did he? I ask only because of tonight and what we will soon share. It just occurred to me now, that perhaps he did. That maybe I had assumed he was better than he was, even though I knew he was far less than most people believe."

She was not sure what he meant. She only knew that he alluded to something darker than she had experienced. Although, that last night, Norbury had asked for something that, if one thought about it, could have been not only shocking but hurtful.

She looked at the man now sworn to protect her. There was danger in his intensity, and it showed in his eyes. She did not think he would take well the possibility that had just entered her head, even if she assured him it had never actually happened.

"No, he did not hurt me. Not the way that I think you mean."

"I am glad." He did seem glad. Relieved.

His vague smile did much to lighten the mood and banish whatever anger had built in him as he contemplated that old memory. The ghost of Norbury, and anyone else from the past who had entered the chamber, disappeared like so much thin smoke floating out a window.

His thoughts were for her alone now, she could tell. His attention was too. It made her nervous and flustered to stand there while he looked at her. She looked too, at his shoulders and torso washed in the hot glow from the fire. Her body reacted to the anticipation saturating the air.

"Come here, Roselyn."

Of course she obeyed. This was part of what she had promised today. She was not an innocent girl, and she would not reveal how much she felt like one.

She stood right in front of him. His naked chest was mere inches from her nose. An alluring chest. Their closeness alone stirred her, and the impulse entered her to kiss the body captivating her.

He kissed her first. He held her head in both his hands and kissed her more carefully than he ever had. It was as if he sought to reassure her, which she thought very good of him. Only he had already done that in the carriage the day they met in the park. She knew that part of this duty might still be unpleasant, but she also knew that some of it would be very nice.

Her body agreed. It responded to the kiss more than the care requested. The nervousness dimmed and the excitement grew.

He drew her to the bed. He sat on its edge so he did not loom above her. He could kiss her more easily now. More intimately. Less carefully. While he kissed, his hand came to rest on her breast. His caresses aroused her so quickly it astonished her. She let the hunger have its way and noticed how it centered low and deep, creating scandalous pulses of need right *there*.

He watched how his hand molded the cloth of the nightdress around her breast, making its shape visible. She inwardly gasped every time he grazed the nipple, so sharp was the sensation that caused.

"You are very beautiful, Roselyn."

That beauty had not served her so well, through her own fault. His flattery still charmed her.

He looked in her eyes so deeply that she feared he would be disappointed by what he saw. "You have heard that often before. Since you were a child, I'd guess."

"If you find me beautiful tonight, I am glad."

"I always have. I saw you once years ago. In a theater. I did not know who you were, only that I had never seen a woman so lovely. Then I noticed your brother in the box too, and I realized you must be the beautiful Longworth sister whom so many admired."

His slow touch created so much joy, so much pleasure, that she almost chided him for not seeking her out once he knew who she was. She caught herself in time. She knew why he had not.

Was that why he had proposed? Her mind could barely consider the question and did so in a lazy, indifferent way.

Had he been unable to resist the chance to possess something that the world forbade the coalminer's son to covet?

The idea saddened her. It raised the impulse to kiss him again. This time she did, on the hard swell of his shoulder.

She might have lit a torch, so clearly did it affect him despite the restraints that he immediately threw around his desire. His eyes darkened to where she thought she might drown in them if she gazed too long.

He pulled the end of the bow on the ribbons holding her gown at the neck. She looked down at his hand and the ribbon, while the glossy strips slid and unwound and parted. It took forever, it seemed. Deep in her body a spot tingled and tensed in reaction, as if an invisible tongue flicked her flesh.

She realized he was going to undress her. Right here, in full view, with that candle glowing on the table near her side. She was very sure this was not how it was done. But then, he might not know that. Still—

The nightdress slid down her shoulders even as surprise brought these thoughts to her mind. His expression acknowledged her astonishment, but he did not stop. He eased the dress lower until her breasts showed, heavy now and with tight dark nipples. Lower over her hips and down her legs until she stood naked above a pool of white fabric.

Shyness assaulted her. It should be dark, or almost so, if she was like this. It should be dark and they should be beneath a sheet and almost anonymous in the acts to come. She moved to cover herself with her arms.

"No." He caught her arms before she managed it. He

pulled her closer. His tongue barely touched the very tip of one nipple.

A streak of pleasure shot through her—intense, direct, and determined. Then another, and another, burying her embarrassment, making her only want him to do this forever so the wonderful pleasure would not stop.

His tongue and mouth sent her to heaven. He caressed her whole body and she was glad now that the nightdress was gone. The feel of his hands on her body, on her hips and bottom, her thighs and back, seemed right and necessary and perfect. She spun in a stupor of increasingly intense sensuality and need, where pleasure incited more pleasure in a rising crescendo.

So lost was she in that daze that she did not realize she grasped his shoulder until he pried her hand loose. She barely noticed how he stood and laid her down. She regained some sense in the pause that followed, and saw him stripping in the light from the candle that still burned.

She reached over and extinguished it before she saw his body as completely as he had seen hers. He became a silhouette then, a dark figure backlit and vague. He came to her in the bed.

A kiss, so deep and intimate she would never forget it. A caress, so firm and possessive that she could only surrender to its mastery. A touch, so direct and knowing in its effect that her entire body shouted from the high-pitched pleasure it created.

He did not stop. She remained in that soundless scream full of nothing except need and excruciating sensation. She lost control of every part of herself except the small consciousness that demanded more, anything, everything.

His voice, quiet and deep. "Surrender to it. You will see what I mean. Let it happen. Choose it."

She barely heard him. She did not understand. Her body unclenched slightly, however. Just enough for a profound shudder to begin, then increase and rise in waves of pleasure that pitched higher and higher. It burst through her body and obliterated her mind in an ethereal moment of awe.

He was in her embrace then, in her arms and over her body. She felt him pressing into her, carefully. Too carefully. She held him and shifted her hips so he would be there, so he would fill her before this incredible experience leached away.

His patience cracked. His power flowed. She did not mind. It was not horrible or even unpleasant. She surrendered to the way he took her just as she had to the release, still floating in a perfection that his thrusts only prolonged.

He woke near dawn to find Roselyn gone. Sometime during the night, soon after he fell asleep perhaps, she had returned to her own chamber and bed.

If he had gone to her, she would have expected him to leave quickly too. That was how it was done among her sort. They did not live in cottages with five chambers, where husband and wife shared a bed all night, every night.

Memories came to him, of quiet mumbles and intimate laughter in the chamber beneath his own as a boy. Those private sounds gave the cottage its life. He had no place in those conversations, but their mumbles brought peace to the night.

Odd that the memory should emerge now, so vividly that if he closed his eyes he was on his boyhood bed again. Strange that this wedding had opened so many doors to the past in his mind. Only he looked through them as a man now, and saw things that the boy had never understood.

One door would be difficult to close again. But for Roselyn's arrival last night, he might have pondered for hours what he had glimpsed again across that threshold.

The images wanted to occupy his mind. He forced them away for now. Maybe forever. The complete truth, like complete honesty, was not always a good thing.

He drowsed, then woke again with a start. The day was far gone. He had more than nodded off.

Water waited. Clothes had been laid out. Jordan had visited but left the bridegroom to sleep. He did not call for his valet, but prepared himself to meet the day.

He went below and followed the sound of voices to the kitchen far in the back of the house. Rose was there with Jordan. She wore a simple gray dress that would be fitting for a cottage wife. She still looked beautiful.

He could not look at her without seeing her body in the candlelight, and her shyness, and the trembles of her arousal. Snuffing the candle had probably been wise, even if he had wanted to look at her all night. She had found some freedom in the dark, and he had found enough restraint to keep from ravishing her.

Her first look in his direction carried an acknowledgment of the night. Then she lowered her gaze.

Jordan set out a breakfast. "It is rustic in here, sir,

but the garden view and the light are pleasant. I will move things to the dining room if you prefer."

"This will be fine." He sat at the table where he and Rose had eaten the dinner the day he proposed. With efficient movements Jordan served up a very late breakfast.

When he was done, Roselyn came over and put the final course on the table.

"It is an apple pie," she said. "You told me that you like it so much that you eat it for breakfast some days."

"Good man, Jordan."

"He did not make it. I did."

In the background Jordan quickly finished drying a pot. He reached for his coat. "I want to study the garden, Madam. With your permission I think that I can recommend some improvements."

"Certainly, Jordan."

Rose cut a big piece of pie and slid it on a plate. She stood back and waited for her husband to taste it.

He took a big bite.

The last pie had not been good. This one was horrible. He glanced to the shelf and its abundant stores. He had credited the last one's bad taste to lack of sugar and salt. Apparently that was not the problem. Roselyn just made terrible pies.

She took pleasure in watching him eat it. He made a few appreciative sounds and expressions.

"Wonderful." He swallowed the last bite.

"I am relieved that you liked it. Jordan kept clucking his tongue while I baked, but I think it just annoyed him that I was in the way."

He reached for her and drew her to him. "You do not

need to cook anymore. You do not need to make your own pies."

"I know that. Only this morning I remembered how I served you pie the first time you visited and how you seemed to like it. I thought that I would like to make you another one."

He realized that he had just been complimented for last night.

He gave her a kiss and released her. He was not hungry now, at least not for food. Least of all for this pie.

He cut himself another slice anyway.

CHAPTER
ELEVEN

~~~

Kyle placed the rolled drawings in a large canvas bag.

The matter could not be delayed any longer. Too much had already been invested. He had no choice but to keep this long-agreed meeting with Norbury.

He listened for sounds from Roselyn's chamber. She usually started her day early. She did not have the habit of lying abed until noon like some ladies. Today, however, this level of the house remained starkly silent. Since he had kept her up most of the night, he was not surprised.

She did not seem to mind. She did not act as if she was eating porridge. And unlike in Oxfordshire, where she always came to him as if to prove she would not shirk her marital duties, here in London he went to her. That meant sometimes, like last night, he did not leave very soon at all.

She did not mind, but she had also gently arranged the nightly ritual so she would not be embarrassed. The lights were always snuffed early after that first night. He knew her body better than she thought, despite the dark. Touch revealed everything, and moonlight even more. She might prefer the obscuring shadows, she might even forget the face of the man who took her, but he never forgot it was Roselyn whom he caressed.

He smiled to himself as he acknowledged the little war his body fought every night. Roselyn Longworth incited a desire so intense, so shattering, that ferocity beckoned too often. But because it was Roselyn, a lady who could still be shy and shocked by nakedness, relinquishing control was out of the question.

It did not matter. The end was always good. Her sweet ecstacies and his own thunderous climaxes amazed him. Afterward he relinquished the total contentment that he experienced in her embrace with regret. Sometimes, like last night, he refused to leave her for hours, which meant imposing more than once.

He walked down the stairs. This house still felt new and strange to him. Roselyn had appeared very happy with it when he brought her here. She occupied herself now with rearranging it to her preference, and with making her first careful sorties back into society.

He spent his time on his business affairs, like this meeting. He rode his horse to Norbury's with the canvas satchel slung from the saddle. The day was more fair than his mood. He would not speak of Norbury to Rose, but last night's repeated hunger to possess her had been tied to the unpleasant anticipation of today's meeting.

In truth the man intruded on his thoughts too much now. Not only because of Rose, although Kyle had to work hard to keep away images of that affair. Those thoughts only provoked anger, and the unholy desire to hurt the scoundrel badly.

The memory that had emerged on his wedding night kept beckoning too, demanding reassessment. He kept seeing the face of a woman, beaten and bruised. That woman's eyes haunted him. The humiliation that they reflected was much like Rose's expression that night of the auction.

When he came upon his aunt that day, battered from fending off the young bloods making sport of her, he had fought like a soul possessed. It had been three against one and he had only been twelve, but his enemies had not already spent four years carrying baskets of coal out of a pit.

He thought he had saved her. Only now, as the details continued their relentless resurrection in his head, he wondered. He might not have intruded at the beginning of her misuse, but at the end.

Thoughts of Rose had raised that memory on their wedding night. As he weighed how to handle her, how to make sure it was not porridge but also not frightening, the shadow of her previous lover had loomed. Then the memory came, and with it the unexpected thought that porridge might have been the least of the reasons for Rose's distaste for physical intimacy.

He stopped his horse in front of Norbury's house. He gazed up the facade at the perfectly wrought Palladian style that gave this building such elegance. He thought it was one of London's best homes, with an excellence most would not notice in a sea of Classical derivations. It was wasted on Norbury, who had little sensibility for such things.

The aesthetics could not distract his mind the way they normally did. The new question mark about that long-ago fight affected much more than his boyhood history. It made him wonder more than he wanted about Rose's affair. It even bore on his meeting today, because Norbury had been one of those boys he had thrashed.

His aunt said he had come in time, and he had believed her. But those mumbles below in the cottage had been silent for a long while after that day, and his uncle had never viewed Cottington's patronage with grace.

Take the money but don't be his lackey, Kyle lad. Use them good the ways they use others, but don't ever turn into one of 'em.

The footman smiled while he took the calling card. The familiarity was not disrespectful. The servants of this house, like those at many other fine London addresses, had quickly warmed to the poor boy made good, to the man who straddled the two worlds they knew.

"My lord is occupied, but will receive you within the hour," the footman reported on his return. Kyle followed him to the library, assuming "within the hour" meant a wait of at least fifty-nine minutes.

No sooner had the library door closed than Kyle opened it again. He headed below stairs to the kitchen. Norbury probably was not occupied with anything at all. This delay was merely the viscount's tedious way of declaring his own importance. The time Norbury had just granted would be useful, however.

The pastry cook turned in surprise when she heard his step on the stairs. "Mr. Bradwell! Now this is an honor. My, don't you look handsome. Your new marital situation seems to suit you."

"Hello, Lizzy. You are looking well yourself. A bit more flour than normal."

She brushed her gray hair and a cloud rose. Lizzy was one of several servants in this house who had family in Teeslow. She had taken service with Cottington when she was a girl, and moved to London when Norbury established his own household here.

The cook, a dour man, nodded his acknowledgment to Kyle and muttered congratulations on his marriage. He moved a large pot off the worktable, kicked a stool to the spot, and went back to scolding a scullery maid. Kyle sat on the stool.

"Here to see his lordship, are you?" Lizzy halved and quartered a huge pile of bread dough. "Here for one of those money things you do that no one understands?"

"Yes."

"Like gambling, some say."

"A bit like gambling, except I get to decide where most of the cards will be in the deck."

"Still, one wrong deal and—"

"That is possible."

"Not so much for you, I'll say. You have always been smarter than most, so you probably stack the deck better than most."

Usually. Normally. The risk was still there. The thing about any gambling was you couldn't care overmuch if you won or lost. A nervous or desperate man always played wrong.

His own success depended on his firm belief that if it all went to hell, he could always come back, and that a few years' setback would not make much difference in his life.

Marriage changed that. He had realized it as soon as he spoke the vows. His responsibility for Rose meant that he might never be fearless again, and others would sense that no matter how he tried to mask the truth.

That was why two days ago he had established a trust for his new wife.

Two bank drafts had been waiting upon their return to London. One, from Cottington, was a wedding gift.

The other draft had been much larger. Easterbrook's ten thousand had come with no note, no letter.

If Rose learned about that money, she would think it meant someone had paid him to marry her, which in a manner of speaking someone had. Looking at the draft, he had realized he did not want her believing that. She refused to lie to herself and build any romantic illusions about this match, but it would not be good for her to have no illusions at all.

Cottington's gift alone pulled him back from the brink, so he took enough of Easterbrook's settlement to pay for Rose's jointure, then put the rest of it in trust for her. She would be provided for, should the deck ever play against him in the future.

"Any word from Teeslow, Lizzy?"

She was not above gossip, which was one reason Kyle liked to visit. She learned all about Teeslow from her family's letters, in much more detail than he ever received from his aunt.

"Well, that Hazlett girl got herself with child and the father is nowhere to be found. Peter Jenkins passed away. It was a mercy, he was so ill. And there is talk of reopening that tunnel in the mine. You know the one."

He knew the one. He had heard that rumor when he visited in December. Now it seemed it had not died the way an untrue rumor would. "How is Cottington faring?"

"Not well, I fear. That household will mourn the earl bad when he goes, I tell you. Too much will change with his passing."

"More than the household will mourn. All will regret his heir taking his place."

Lizzy checked the cook's proximity before allowing her expression to concur with the part about the heir. She turned her strength to kneading the dough. "I don't suppose the viscount was at your wedding."

"Hardly."

Her glance spoke volumes. That of course Norbury would not inconvenience himself even if he had been invited. That of course Kyle's bride would not want her past lover at her wedding anyway.

"It was good of you, Mr. Bradwell. How you helped that poor woman, and what you now do for her. That is what everyone says."

"Unfortunately I could not thrash him again like I did the last time, much as I wanted."

He watched for her reaction. Lizzy had been in service with Cottington back then. In such a household the servants often knew everything.

She appeared surprised by the allusion. Her gaze locked on his, then fell to her bread dough. She kneaded with vigor.

She acted as if the entire event had been shocking, and its details understood to be a secret.

Mere bad behavior by some youths—the story that he knew—would not be either.

"I still say the houses do not have enough servant chambers." Norbury issued the complaint after ten minutes of perusing the drawings.

Up until now, things had been going well. Norbury's reception had been coolly indifferent and the project had occupied their attention. Norbury appeared to be making an effort to act like a gentleman, but Kyle sensed the viscount constantly swallowing a fellow far less civilized.

"These will be bought by families with incomes of several thousand a year. Five servant chambers, plus those in the stable yard for the groom and coachman, should be more than adequate."

"Several thousand. It is a wonder how they do it."

It was a stupid statement by a stupid man, intended to emphasize how he was above such petty concerns as a thousand more or less. Norbury bent his tawny head over the drawings some more.

"My solicitor says that my father intends to sign the papers on the land." Norbury's lower lip pulsed. "He is out of it all, and has not seen these drawings, but he sent word anyway."

Fine, we will go forward, but it is the old man's choice, not mine. I will see a fine profit off you, but I will not be choosing this association.

Kyle did not care how it happened. He resented this

project now, and how it required that he accept Norbury's company. If the earl did not recover and take up the reins of his affairs again, this would be the last partnership with this family.

"I will call on your solicitor tomorrow." He collected the drawings. "Work on the roads will begin soon, and the timber and supplies ordered. The first estates will be available by midsummer, I think."

His host examined his preparations for departure. An icy gleam entered his eyes. "Felicitations are due."

"Thank you."

"I was not invited."

"It was a village wedding, not in London."

"I read that Easterbrook attended." The idea annoyed him. Kyle did not know if it was because *that* lord had been invited, or because Easterbrook's attendance made Norbury's absence irrelevant.

"His county seat is nearby, and my wife is related to him through marriage, of course."

Norbury's eyes narrowed. "You have done well for yourself, Kyle, in marrying my whore."

Kyle forced himself to continue with the drawings but he barely controlled the urge to strangle Norbury. This was how duels got fought. Stupid men said stupid things because pride or pique got the better of them. They said things that another man cannot allow to stand.

"Call her that once more, or anything like it, to me or anyone else, and I will thrash you. If I hear that you even hint at your dishonorable behavior toward her, I will not finish with you until you cannot move for a fortnight."

Norbury flushed so red that Kyle expected him to

throw the first punch right then. He sorely wished he would.

"Thrash me, hell. I box twice weekly."

"That only helps if your opponent uses Queensberry's rules. You will be fighting a collier's son, and your soft, useless hands can't stand against me."

Kyle walked to the door. Norbury's snarl followed him. "My solicitor said that my father sent you a wedding gift."

"He did. He was very generous."

"How generous? How much was it?" Animosity poured off Norbury, as if this were all that really mattered.

Maybe it was. Maybe Cottington's patronage had never been swallowed by Norbury. Bad enough the ignoble beating had happened. Worse that it meant his father had learned of his dishonorable behavior that day, however bad it had been.

"How much? An astonishing amount, just fifty shy of a thousand."

Kyle took satisfaction in Norbury's expression as he left. The man was stupid, but not too stupid. In a few minutes Norbury would realize that Cottington's gift came out of the estate that his heir would soon own.

Which meant that Norbury had indirectly paid back the auction price, and that his father had learned about the auction itself.

Henrietta looked different today. Roselyn sat in the drawing room at Grosvenor Square and tried to determine why.

The hat's effect could not be discounted. An Arcadian bonnet over a lace cornet, it looked much more restrained and tasteful than her usual millinery. And now that Rose noticed, her pale hair had been dressed differently and in a manner more suited to her fine-boned face.

Mostly, however, the change lay in Hen's expression. Her airy vagueness made her appear youthful instead of dotty this afternoon. Nor had disdain crimped those features that, unexpectedly, appeared almost girlish in this light.

They talked about fashion and society and speculated on the upcoming season. Alexia was with them. So were three other ladies, all of good social standing and generous disposition. Alexia had dragged Rose on calls to these ladies the last week, with their permission presumably. Now they in turn had called on Henrietta on a day that Alexia had designated so that Rose would be present too.

It was all part of a little campaign in which, wonder of wonders, Henrietta had agreed to participate. If Hen were not acting her part so well, were not being so gracious and helpful, Rose would wonder if Alexia had found a way to blackmail her husband's aunt.

Their callers did not stay long, but they stayed long enough. They might never call on Rose herself, but by the time they left she had taken another stride toward some level of acceptance.

That road would be a circuitous one. Her choice of husband would create detours and blocked lanes. Her own scandal would provide others. Alexia's campaign, however, looked to be succeeding more quickly than anyone could hope.

"That went well," Hen confided when the three of them were alone again. "I think that Mrs. Vaughn will be inviting you to join her at the theater soon, Roselyn. It sounded that way when she conversed with you about favorite plays and such. Since her aunt did marry that importer, she is probably not too particular about a man being in trade and may even welcome your husband too."

Rose bit her tongue. Hen did not intend to be provocative with that comment. There was no point in resenting the truth, either.

She did resent it, though. Much more than she expected. Kyle accepted how things were, but increasingly she rebelled against them.

She did not understand how anyone who saw him, who met him, could object to his presence in their drawing room. Even his trade was not the normal sort, but one that combined finance and art and investment. When her brothers became bankers some doors had closed to them, but most had not.

It came down to blood, of course. To family and ancestors. To the family Kyle would never deny. He had warned her about that.

While they strolled to the library, Alexia explained the next phase of the war, one that involved a dinner party at her house. These three ladies would be invited, along with two others who were their friends. She counted on their callers to convince the others to attend. All five had husbands known to be pliable. Once a few husbands allowed their wives to associate with Rose, other husbands would be more likely to as well.

While they discussed strategy, Easterbrook entered the library. He excused his interference and took a position near the cases, examining bindings. His presence kept distracting Henrietta, whose curiosity got the better of her.

"Are you intending to go abroad, Easterbrook? That is the case with travel memoirs and such."

He pulled out a book and flipped through it. "I am not going anywhere. I am doing some research for my young cousin."

"Oh, my, are you going to send Caroline on a Grand Tour? I had so hoped—she must go to Paris, of course, and—"

"No, not a Grand Tour," he muttered. "I am looking for information on very specific kinds of places where young girls sometimes visit, but it appears that none of these writers report on them with any particulars."

Hen frowned. "What sorts of places?"

He returned that book to the case and pulled out another. "Convents."

"Convents!"

Rose thought Hen would need salts. Alexia soothed her, then addressed the marquess. "That is a joke, I am sure. Please tell your aunt that you are teasing her again."

"I wish that I were. In fact, I wish Hayden would take up his role as guardian again instead of leaving me to fumble along with matters not of my interest or expertise."

"*See,* he still has not forgiven her that flirtation with

Suttonly last summer," Hen cried. "She has accepted your authority on the matter, Easterbrook. She has not uttered his name in weeks."

"Henrietta, last summer was bad enough, but I regret to say that we have another one of those dramatic disasters that young girls cause. Anticipating one duel a year would be more than enough, thank you. To prepare for two tries my patience." He frowned at the books, and slid another one out. "I will make short work of this annoying duty. I will fight the fellow, wound him good, send Caroline to a convent, and be left in peace for a few years at least."

Hen wept. Easterbrook calmly perused the books. Alexia tried diplomacy. "Neither your aunt nor I know of any current suitor who addresses Caroline. I think that you are mistaken."

He snapped the book shut. "This man is not a proper suitor. He is a seducer. I am not mistaken, Alexia. I regret to say that I am convinced Caroline's virtue is lost already."

That caused alarm all around. Hen's shock left her breathless and openmouthed. Then she wailed.

"Pray, who is this man?" Alexia demanded.

"That French chemist. Bradwell's friend."

Henrietta stopped crying. Her eyes grew large. She glanced to the side to see the proximity of the man behind her at the cases.

"I am sure that you are wrong," Alexia said.

"I saw him just this morning. As dawn broke I was at my window overlooking the garden, and he was there. Leaving this house." He shot an annoyed glare at his aunt. "Must I now play nursemaid too, Aunt Hen? That you would be so careless with her appalls even me, and I don't much give a damn about such things."

Hen had gone very still. Easterbrook stood behind her, so he did not see what Rose and Alexia saw. Her face kept getting more red.

Rose looked at Alexia just as Alexia looked her way too. They both stared at Henrietta.

"Easterbrook, I still think that you are mistaken," Alexia said. "If it was the break of dawn, you could not be sure what you saw, or whom. Perhaps one of the gardeners was up and about."

"No, Alexia. It was he." He gave up on the books. "Unfortunately, there are no references to convents. I will ask the solicitor to make some discreet inquiries. One in France, I think, so Hen can visit her once a year."

As Easterbrook walked to the door, Alexia blocked his path. "Even if you are correct and he was in the garden, that is no proof that he was in the house. Nor that he sought Caroline. It could have been one of the servants, after all."

He looked on her kindly, as he always did. "I saw him flirting with her at your cousin's wedding. I was remiss in not issuing warnings, but Hen was with them and I assumed—"

They all froze in a *tableau vivant* while his memory hung in the air. Rose could almost hear the marquess reviewing, wondering, rejecting . . . reconsidering.

Easterbrook turned and looked at his aunt. He angled his head and studied her. She squirmed while he eyed her new hat, her new hair, and her new youthful glow.

"Alexia, your estimable good sense spares me from

unwelcome obligations. I have probably been too rash in assuming the worst about Caroline. Perhaps it was not M'sieur Lacroix in the garden."

He excused himself. From the door, before he departed, he spoke again. "However, in the event it was—Henrietta, please speak with the servants. If one of them is entertaining a man I wish them both nothing but pleasure. However, it might be better if he left while it was still dark so no one else misunderstands."

Rose padded through her dressing room to the door that connected with Kyle's chambers. He would not come to her tonight. She had her flux. Finding a delicate way to inform him of that today had taken considerable ingenuity. He had appeared amused by her euphemisms, but he had understood.

She heard the sounds of undressing, and Jordan's low mumbles. Then all fell silent. She opened the door. The dressing rooms were not elaborate and large, and the doorway to his bedchamber was only eight feet away. The lamp in there had not been extinguished and she could make out the shadows of his dressing table and brushes and looking glass.

She went across and peered in. The bed drapes had not been closed. He lay on his bed, in a nightshirt open enough to reveal his strong chest.

Her gaze lingered. She had not seen him undressed since their wedding night. She always snuffed the candles and lamps, even when she went to him in Oxfordshire. The dark made that bed mysterious and otherworldly and negated a lot of awkwardness. It helped her to surrender to the abandon.

His arms were bent so his head rested on his hands. He appeared very serious, as if his gaze perceived some pattern on the canopy that required analysis. Then again, he lay so still that perhaps he was not even awake.

"Kyle, are you asleep?" she whispered.

He sat up. His gaze swept her, taking in her nightcap and undressing gown, neither of which was especially new or pretty.

"Did I wake you?" she asked.

"No. I was thinking about some matters that I dealt with today."

"Land and syndicates and such?"

"Yes."

She ventured into the room. "Alexia arranged for some ladies to call on me. Well, not me, but Henrietta. They knew I would be there, however, and they did call."

"Come and tell me about it."

She climbed up on the bed and described her little victory.

He seemed very interested. "Lady Alexia is moving fast."

"She still believes there is a chance for Irene this season, I think." Irene had not left Hill Street. Everyone agreed that the only hope was if Alexia launched her.

"When she has this dinner, you must have a new dress," he said. "I will send you off as the most fashionable woman to sit at that table."

"Perhaps you will not be sending me off, but escorting me."

"That is unlikely. Lady Alexia is too smart to fight on two fronts at the same time."

"I am not sure that I will enjoy going, then."

His expression altered slightly, enough to become unreadable.

"Do you want to hear some gossip?" she asked. "It is about someone you know."

"Everyone wants to hear gossip, especially about someone they know."

"This is very good gossip. The evidence indicates that your friend, Mr. Lacroix, is having an affair with... Henrietta!"

"Evidence?"

"None other than Easterbrook saw him leaving the house. Can you believe it?"

"How indiscreet of Jean Pierre. Should I warn him off?"

"As long as he does not seduce Caroline, I do not think Easterbrook cares if he has his way with every other woman in that house. As for Henrietta, the marquess appeared fascinated, and delighted that he can goad her about it for the next few years."

They laughed about that. It was very pleasant, sitting here in the night talking about everyday things. When the gossip was done, however, she sensed the distraction reclaiming him. It entered his eyes, turning them deep the way she had seen when she entered.

"Well, good night." She began sliding off the bed.

He caught her hand. "Stay."

Perhaps her euphemisms had been too vague after all. "I... that is, today I... it is that time when..."

"Stay anyway."

The oddest sensation entered her heart as she clumsily found her way under the bedclothes. He gutted the lamp and darkness shrouded their chaste intimacy. He drew her into an embrace.

She did not sleep right away. The novelty of this different kind of warmth preoccupied her.

"I need to go north again." His voice did not startle her, so quietly it came in the night. "In a fortnight, perhaps. I will not be gone more than a week."

"Can I come with you? You said we would go in the spring, but if you return there now I would like to go too."

"The journey will be cold. You have that dinner party."

"Alexia will plan it around any journey. Nor do I fear a little cold."

Two weeks ago she would not have argued to go. Even a few days ago she might have let it pass. Right now, however, the desire to see this old life of his compelled her. Their embrace tonight moved her, but it also made it too clear that for all the pleasure there was a vacancy in this marriage that she could not explain.

She did not know if it would ever be filled. Maybe he would forever be part stranger. Perhaps he preferred it that way. She was not even certain that she would like what filled it, if anything did. She only knew that the empty spot loomed large tonight, perhaps because a new emotion served as its foil. Her soul almost ached from reaching for something too far out of grasp.

"We shall see," he said. "Tomorrow I will go to Kent for several days as well. You cannot come since I will be starting some new estates and it will only be me, some workers, and a lot of winter mud."

Some new estates. In Kent. This must be the business he had visited Norbury about that day of the auction.

She suddenly understood Kyle's intense thoughts when she entered this chamber tonight. He must have met with Norbury recently. Perhaps even today.

He would never let her know if Norbury had been insulting. He would never reveal if he thought about that affair. She was sure that he did, however. Maybe right now, as his mind roamed through the night.

She might learn more about him and start filling that vacancy. They might have many nights like this one, where they talked as friends and not lovers.

No matter what happened, however, no matter how long they were married, Norbury would be an ugly shadow between them, affecting everything, even the good things, without either of them ever mentioning the man's name.

That thought came close to ruining this pleasant night. Norbury had entered her mind. She practically heard him speaking in Kyle's head. His malevolent influence grew so oppressive that she sought a way to leave this bed.

Kyle turned on his side as he fell asleep. His arm crossed her body in a casual embrace. His hand cupped her breast in a gesture both comforting and possessive. It stayed there through the night, preventing her from slipping away.

CHAPTER
TWELVE

〜

K yle had been in Kent for two days when Roselyn
received the letter. It had been redirected from
Watlington. She knew at once from the penmanship that
Timothy had written again, even though it bore the
name of Mr. Goddard.

Timothy did not write from Dijon this time, but from
an Italian town called Prato.

> I am finally across the Alps, and residing here
> because it is less expensive than Florence. I am
> also less likely to be recognized. The journey
> was strenuous and the climate miserable. I
> feared I would die and was ill most of the way.
> Now I walk among strangers whose language I
> do not know, and suffer from a melancholy too
> deep to bear.
> It is my intention to remain here until you
> join me. Please write at once and say that you
> will. I will not see the sunshine out my window
> until you arrive. I need you to write to me and

tell me your plans so that I have something to
look forward to.

Rose, my purse has suffered from the long
stay in Dijon, and from the fees to the physicians
who proved useless but expensive. I want you to
sell the house and property in Oxfordshire and
bring the proceeds with you. This letter gives
you permission to do so in my name. Take it to
Yardley, our old solicitor. He will recognize my
hand and advise you. I hereby authorize him to
act as my proxy in such a sale if as a woman
your proxy will not be acceptable. If there are
further requirements from me, you must write
immediately and tell me so that we can effect
this business as soon as possible.

I know that it will be months yet, but I will
count the days and trust that as ever you are my
loving sister, upon whose strength and good
heart I have so miserably depended for most of
my life. I promise that everything will be better
once we are together again.
Timothy

He still sounded lost and alone. The reference to his
illness did not help matters. She did not know whether
to hope he meant too much drink, as that was Tim's
great weakness, or another malady.

Nor could she go to him now, no matter how ill he
became. He would never know that she had briefly intended to, during a few hours of reckless happiness on a
hillside one day.

She could not deny the truth of her choice, either. In

accepting Kyle's proposal she had rejected her brother's need in order to try to salvage a life in England for Irene and herself.

A desperate need, perhaps. If not now, then eventually.

He spoke of his purse getting lighter fast. A little anger stirred at that sentence. She had scrimped along on almost nothing all these months. He might have been more frugal while he spent all that money he had stolen.

A sigh came out of her, one so deep that her whole body sank in on itself. Timothy was just being Timothy. Without her influence he would go on being Timothy in the worst way. She could not save him. Not now, not after Kyle had so pointedly said she would never go to him. However, she could not abandon him the way that Kyle expected, either.

She called for her abigail and changed from her morning dress into a carriage ensemble. She was supposed to meet Alexia today at a modiste's to commission some new items for her wardrobe. She would go to the City first, however. She needed to find out if it were possible to still help her brother.

Kyle watched his engineer twist a borer down through the hard earth, to double-check the ground before foundations were begun.

Two hundred yards away another man marked which trees to cut and which to save when the new lane was brought through. Kyle pictured the house that should soon rise next to that copse.

If all went as planned, in two years' time families

would inhabit these fields and carriages would roll on new roads. Cottington's estate would grow in wealth and a syndicate of partners would see their profits.

As would he. Kyle still walked a fine line. His balance was practiced and good. The risks did not keep him up nights. Still, like any man he preferred to have his feet firmly planted on the solvent side of that divide.

The fellow at the trees called and gestured south. Kyle turned his attention to the road that ran there. A carriage was pulling up behind the wagon that had hauled the tools to be used today.

He recognized the new conveyance. He walked down to the road. He arrived just as Norbury stepped out.

"I trust that you did not come down from town just to see our progress," Kyle said. "There is not much to inspect yet."

Norbury peered at the rise in the land from beneath the brim of his tall hat. "I am holding a house party at my manor. I decided to come by before the guests arrive."

He glanced over to see Kyle's reaction. Kyle let him look to his heart's content. He did not need Norbury's references to the last house party to be reminded of it. The image of Rose's humiliation came to him often enough without anyone's help.

That picture provoked the devil in him, and a low, cold urge to beat this viscount bloody. He had carried that impulse away from their last meeting and it tensed through him again now.

"I trust that this party will be more discreet than the last. If word gets out that orgies are held nearby, these estates will never sell."

"I daresay they might sell all the faster." Norbury

gestured for Kyle to walk with him. "I came to speak with you about some matters of mutual interest besides these estates. I have had word from Kirtonlow Hall. My father had another mild apoplexy. The physician says it will not be long now."

"He is stronger than most. It could be longer than the physician expects."

Longer than you hope. The son was so unlike the father that there had never been much warmth between them. The earl let his heir know in many ways what a disappointment he had been.

It was not only that Norbury lacked Cottington's intellectual depth. Something essential was missing in the son besides brilliance. The natural sympathy that a human being felt for others seemed absent or malformed. Norbury just lacked the moral core that served most people as a guide in matters big and small.

"We can but hope he lives forever, but no one ever does." Norbury spoke with dramatic sobriety. "Now the other matter is one which the living can influence. I have been thinking about your marriage."

Kyle paced along, encouraging his companion farther down the road. He glanced back to judge the distance of the workers. What would they see or hear if his fist broke Norbury's jaw?

"You can stop looking like a pugilist preparing for a round in the ring," Norbury said. "Your decision to marry such a woman is your own folly. I am more interested in her brother and how this marriage changes our plans for him. Once I recovered from my shock that you had tied yourself to her so permanently, I saw the silver lining."

"There is no silver lining aside from my happiness in

my choice of wife. Timothy Longworth is gone. Neither she nor I am tied to him."

"Does he write to her? I think it likely that he does."

"He has no reason to."

"She is his sister. You must check her mail for letters from him, either under his own name or that of Goddard. Hell, look for any letters from the continent, especially from Italy."

"No."

"It will save much time. If he writes to her we will have—"

"No. I am out of that whole business now. I want no part in it and I will not help you."

A grasp on his arm. A demand to stop walking. Kyle looked down at Norbury, whose expression had lost all gentility.

"My, how quickly the pure knight is seduced and sullied. You forget fast your fine ideas about justice, Kyle."

"I am not going to spy on my wife."

"Then don't spy. Make her tell you."

"She will not volunteer her brother's neck to our noose. Nor will I demand it of her."

"The hell you say! There is no dishonor in it. Damn, you will be protecting her." Norbury's outburst provoked insight. His eyes turned sly. "Indeed, if you do not do it, you may actually *endanger* her."

Norbury's mind could be sluggish, but it worked when it had to. Kyle watched new thoughts lining up, turning Norbury's expression into a mask of smugness.

"She probably was an accomplice from the start," Norbury said.

"Of course she wasn't."

"Damnation, I should have seen it before. It explains Rothwell's restitution. He was not sparing a man who had already skipped out of our grasp, but the accomplice left behind. She may even have most of the money right here in England. All that humble frugality no doubt was a feint to throw off suspicion. Hell, Longworth wasn't even very clever. It may have been her idea from the start—"

"You are speaking nonsense."

"Even that business with me. I thought I was seducing her, but she may have wanted to stay near me so she could discover if the victims were on to her. That would be ironic, no? If all the time she had—"

"Pursue that thought and I will kill you."

"Are you so drunk on her beauty that you would risk everything? I doubt it. In a few months you will cease being so besotted by your great prize. Then you will see what is beneath the gilding. Her brother is a thief and her own character is proven to be weak and immoral."

Kyle grabbed Norbury's coats near his neck. He pulled the man close and lifted him to his toes. "I warned you."

Norbury's eyes bulged and his head angled back. "Dare one blow and I'll not stay my own hand. I think a judge would listen closely and think hard before assuming that I am wrong. I believe a good case can be made for my point of view. With a little effort, even some evidence might be found."

The threat was unmistakable. Justice perverted was even worse than justice denied, and a lord had more ways to do the former than the latter.

Kyle barely contained his fury. He released his hold. Norbury set himself to rights, smoothing his garments and checking his cravat. He drew himself straight and gazed over with the placid delight of a man who had suddenly discovered an ace in his hand while playing whist.

"Find out where the bastard is, Kyle." Norbury began strolling back to his carriage. "With all the honor that you think you have, sacrificing a small amount will be a little thing."

As soon as Kyle returned from Kent, Rose knew that he had seen Norbury again. He carried the shadow into the house with him. It affected his expression, making it harder than usual.

He treated her no differently when he sat to dinner with her that night. He even listened generously to her descriptions of her days while they were apart. Norbury might have sat in the room with them, however, so clearly did she sense his presence in Kyle's thoughts.

When he sent the footman away, she braced herself. It might be best to clear the air of whatever darkened his mood. That did not mean that she welcomed the storm breaking, however.

"Rose, when you were in Oxfordshire, did your brother write to you? I mean besides the letter that you had received the first time I called on you."

She had not expected *this* question or topic. If not for the way his intensity coiled, she would have blurted the truth. Instead she held her tongue while her mind tried to weigh why he asked, and whether her answer actually mattered in some way.

"I think that he did, at least one more time," he added.

"Yes. Once." It was the truth, just not the total truth. She *had* only received one more letter while she was *in* Oxfordshire.

"I was correct, then. When you spoke of leaving forever, you meant to go to him."

She nodded.

Being correct did nothing for his mood. "I do not want you to have any communication with him in the future, Rose. If he writes again, you are to burn his letters without reading them. Do not save them. Do not even note the city from which he writes."

Shock blocked her thoughts for a long count. Then anger replaced it. "You said before we married that I could never go to him, even to visit. You did not say I could not write to him or receive his letters."

"I did say it. However, if you misunderstood, I am saying it again now."

"I told you that I would not think of him as dead, but now you demand that I treat him as if he is."

"Yes." His gaze carried the command more than his voice.

She rose from her chair and left the dining room. She sought some privacy in the library. To her astonishment he followed.

"You would do better to leave me alone to accommodate what you require regarding him," she said.

"I need to know that you do accommodate it. I want your word that you do."

"My word? What about your word? If my word can be changed as quickly as yours, I will gladly give it. You allowed me to believe that you had retreated from this demand that day."

She thought guilt might soften him. Instead his anger flared.

"I require this for a reason. I would like you to believe that but if you do not, it changes nothing. You know what he is. You told me yourself the danger that he presents to you. You must have no contact with him."

"He is *my brother.*"

"He is a cowardly thief. A criminal."

The force of Kyle's response took her back. She stared, astonished by the power pouring out of him, seeing it and feeling it totally unleashed.

He calmed the storm but it hovered, waiting.

"Rose, do you fully understand what he did? How many people he stole from?"

"Lord Hayden—"

"Lord Hayden kept untold misery from falling on the victims. How much do you think he laid out to do so?"

She felt like a schoolgirl groping for an answer to a cipher. "A good deal. Twenty thousand at least."

Anger even colored his low, brief laugh. "Twenty thousand would not even make Rothwell blink. Consider the house in which your cousin still lives. What new jewels has she shown you? Even her new garments—see them in your head, and the choice of fabrics and embellishments."

A knot lodged low in her stomach. She had never calculated the evidence, in part because she noticed enough to suspect she would hate the final sum.

"How much?" she whispered.

"When all came out and all was told, at least one hundred thousand. Probably much more."

She gasped. Such a sum!

Kyle approached her. One small light of sympathy showed amidst the many hot ones in his eyes. "Your brother did not know Rothwell would repay even a single pound. Your brother assumed that the victims would just have to suffer. So would the depositors when the bank went under. He did not only steal from the rich, but from old women and vulnerable orphans and retainers who depended on those funds to survive."

"I am sure he did not fully understand—he could not have deliberately—"

"*Of course* he understood. Fully. He most surely did it *deliberately.*" He again leashed the fury. He visibly collected himself. "Is it any wonder that I command you to break all relations with such a scoundrel?"

Her vision of Kyle blurred. She turned away and tried to hold in the sobs paining her as they sought release. One hundred thousand. Dear God. And Alexia and Hayden—

She wiped her eyes and found her breath. "You said that you knew people who lost funds because of it. Who were they?"

For an instant she thought he would not reply.

"My aunt and uncle."

Shock slapped her again. Not friends, but family. "But they were made whole, weren't they?"

"Yes, they were made whole. Is that what you keep saying to yourself, when you think about him? At least they were made whole? At least there was only one victim who paid dearly instead of dozens who lost everything? Is that your excuse for him?"

"I do not excuse him."

"I think that you do. He is your brother and you want to find reasons to lessen his guilt. But he is not my brother, Rose."

No, and there would be no excuses from Kyle. No sympathy or desire to save. If Tim had been caught, Kyle would have thought it just when he went to the gallows.

She had no words to argue with that. Nothing to offer except her love for a brother who once had been a much better person as a boy than he proved on becoming a man.

She thought that at least Kyle would understand, even if he did not approve. Only he remained implacable, unmoving, and determined to make her condemn Tim the way everyone else would.

"You must cease any contact," he said again. "If you have letters, burn them. If you receive another, destroy it immediately."

He strode from the library. He had not asked for her promise again. He had commanded, and she was supposed to obey.

Rose considered locking her dressing room door that night.

She never had before in this brief marriage. She did not mind that he came to her every night. She was his wife and it was his due, and he never left without ensuring that she experienced the holy freedom that pleasure could create.

This night was different. She was not sure she would respond to his touch. A brittle silence had fallen on the house after they argued. It still affected the air, and her.

A small part of Kyle that had remained a stranger was revealed to her tonight. His force of will had stunned her. She had sensed it in him, but seeing it, feeling it directed at her, frightened her a little.

She should have guessed just how much inner conviction he contained. In himself, and in his decisions. He could have never survived on the path he walked without it. Not many men traveled from a coal mining village to the drawing rooms of London in little more than a decade.

Not many men born in such a village would propose to Roselyn Longworth, no matter what the status of her family, finances, or reputation.

She stood in front of her door, gazing at the latch. Not for the first time with this man she suspected that she should not act capriciously. She did not think he would break down the door if she locked it. She did not even believe it would anger him.

Instead she guessed that one of two things would happen. They might have another conversation like today's, where he explained what he would or would not accept in her behavior. Or, possibly, a chilling formality would enter her bed the next time he came to her, and maybe remain between them for a long while. It might even stay forever.

She turned away from the door and returned to her bed. She snuffed out the lamps as she did each night and darkness shrouded her.

Perhaps he would not come, even though with her

flux and his time in Kent it had been some days now. Surely he felt the way their argument still rang through the house. He had retreated to his study and his work afterward, but maybe their words repeated in his head like they did in hers.

Her heart still pounded when she remembered the way he laid out Tim's guilt. One hundred thousand pounds. She often dreamed of repaying Alexia and Hayden, but such a sum could never be repaid. Never. No wonder Alexia had so mercilessly discouraged that plan to join Tim in Italy.

Only now instead she was married to a man who would gladly hang Tim with his own hands, she suspected. She could not defend her brother. She could not say Kyle was wrong. But right and wrong and justice were not the bases by which a sister judges.

One hundred thousand. How could it almost be gone? Tim claimed he needed more, and she believed him.

The most subtle movement of air pulled her out of her thoughts. She opened her eyes to the dark. Kyle stood beside the bed, no more than a darker presence in a room without light.

He had come after all. That surprised her. So did her reaction. Her heart flipped with relief before her mind caught up with her instincts.

He appeared to be waiting for something, or making some decision. She could not imagine what. She shifted over on the bed, her body making the bed ropes sound against the boards.

His body made sounds too, and movements barely visible. Of the robe dropping. Of warmth lowering. Of limbs stretching and skin touching. She inhaled and all of him was in bed with her, that total presence that transformed the night.

He untied her nightdress and began sliding it down her shoulders and body. "Thank you for not locking your door."

Had he heard her there, debating? How like him to speak of it, to not allow it to be a silent choice. She trusted they would not also speak of why she considered the choice in the first place.

His caress and kiss said they would not.

"And if I had locked it?" Already she did not much care what his answer might be. The luscious trembles of arousal had begun distracting her.

"I do not know. I had not yet decided when I tried the latch."

She did not contemplate his answer, other than noting that the ambiguity contained some danger. Already the pleasure diverted her. Seduced her. That was dangerous too. The pleasure blunted clear thought and lured one to put the best light on everything, even during the day.

Kyle made sure she was pleased. With his confident, masterful caresses and kisses, he commanded her to the abandon that had become so familiar now, so captivating. The pleasure forced a kind of surrender, she realized. Loss of will and loss of self existed within it. She had never fully understood that before.

Soon she understood nothing, not even the argument. The blur of sensations obscured everything except the desire for him to lick her breasts and kiss her stomach and touch the flesh that ached to be filled by him.

He lifted her and set her down so she straddled his

hips. He eased her hips forward and entered her so deeply that she moaned from the welcome sensation of completeness.

His palms brushed her nipples and she came alive where their bodies joined. Directly. Wonderfully. The excitement shot straight down and pooled around his fullness.

"Come here."

He eased her body forward in the dark until she had to brace her weight on her arms. Her breasts hovered above him. His mouth replaced his hands. The pleasure increased in intensity so much that she gasped. The way he aroused her was too good, too compelling, too overwhelming to maintain even tenuous control.

She dissolved into madness, crying and moaning and moving so she felt him more, better, harder. He grabbed her hips and thrust hard and long toward his completion. Her entire being submitted to the way he took her.

She was still aroused when he finished. Despite the repeated waves of pleasure and release, her body still hungered. He seemed to know. He flipped her on her back and caressed again, this time on folds of sensitive and pulsing flesh.

She almost died. She clawed at him to escape the almost painful pleasure. She heard him as she had the first night, telling her to surrender to it.

The sweetest ecstasy waited this time. It crashed through her with violence first, then subsided in undulating eddies that astonished her entire body. She wondered at it, and held her breath to make it last forever.

It didn't, of course, even if her stunned body took a long time to accept it would not.

The night's prior events came back with the reemergence of her awareness of time and place. Perhaps they had retreated from his thoughts too, banished by delirium.

He did not stay long after she reclaimed her senses. In that brief aftermath so sated with peace, she sensed the shadow in him.

She suspected he had never forgotten that argument, not even at the moment of his release. He had come tonight in part because of their confrontation. He had made it clear that such things would not stand between them in this most basic part of marriage. He had also made very sure that she would not mind that too much.

That cold calculation did not change the truth of how he treated her, though. If he carried any anger into this bed he had not shown it. As always, he had been considerate and asked little of her except her own pleasure.

An insight came to her. A startling one. Who she was and who he was, the way they had met and the scandal and redemption, affected everything. Especially what occurred in this bed on the best and worst of nights.

CHAPTER
THIRTEEN

~

K yle had not lied. The way north was cold in late
January. As they crossed into Durham County the
sky hung low with damp clouds.

The land became hilly farther north, and also increasingly bleak. They rolled through villages large and
small. Rose came to recognize the ones where colliers
lived. The residue from the nearby pits, carried out on
the clothes and bodies of the workers, left its mark in
ways big and small.

As they neared Teeslow, she grew nervous. Kyle had
discouraged her coming, but relented when she pressed
the matter. She wanted to see this home of his and meet
his aunt and uncle, but there was the chance she would
not be welcomed.

"Are there other relatives and family besides them?"
she asked.

"Not living. They had two daughters, younger than I
am. Both died of cholera when I was in Paris."

"Did you always live with them?"

He did not mind the conversation, but he did not

welcome it, either. "My father died in a mining accident when I was nine. My mother had passed away a few years before. Her brother took me in."

Soon their carriage entered the village. Rose examined the few lanes and stores, the clusters of cottages. Coal dust marked the sills and jambs of some buildings, and the faces and garments of some residents.

They did not stop in the village, but continued down the road to another lane that aimed north. A nice stone house waited at its end. Two levels high, it looked similar to the smaller homes that could be found on southern estates, the ones in which a steward or tenant might live.

"It is not what I expected," she said.

"You thought it would be a tiny cottage of five chambers at most? They lived for years in one, back in the village. I built this for them five years ago."

He alighted from the carriage. "I will go in while you wait here. I am not expected, and you will be a complete surprise."

He walked to the door, opened it, and disappeared. Rose watched the house. She saw a woman's face briefly at a window. No doubt his aunt was peeking to see the complete surprise.

He was being very careful. When she met them, their faces would mask their thoughts much as his often did. If they disapproved of her, or thought her a bad match for their nephew, they would not reveal that in a moment of surprise.

Kyle returned and handed her down. A woman appeared in the doorway, smiling a welcome.

"Rose, this is my aunt, Prudence Miller."

Prudence was ready with kind words and friendly expressions. "We are so pleased that you have come."

A slender woman with dark hair and sparkling eyes, Prudence had reached her middle years with much of her beauty intact. Rose pictured her at twenty and thirty, pale-skinned and dark-eyed.

Since Prudence had greeted her alone, Rose assumed that Kyle's uncle was at the mine. As soon as they brought her to the sitting room, she learned differently.

His uncle Harold sat in a chair near the fire, as dark-haired as his wife and almost as thin. Despite his haggard face, Rose could see a resemblance to Kyle in his vivid blue eyes and the hard planes of his countenance.

He examined her closely during introductions. She noted his pallor and the blanket covering his lap and legs. A spittoon stood at the ready on a low table near his right leg. Uncle Harold was a very sick man.

Welcoming her made him cough. He turned his head and spit into the spittoon. "You'll be having to make a pie, Pru. Can't have Kyle visit without his fill of pies."

"We'll have one with dinner," she said. "Now you visit for a spell while I go above and air the chamber a bit."

It appeared they would be staying here. Kyle went out and returned with the coachman and the baggage. The house had a carriage house and he sent the driver there.

He carried the baggage above himself, following his aunt up the stairs. Rose sat in a chair not far from Harold, who continued to examine her.

"You are a very beautiful woman, Mrs. Bradwell. I'm understanding this marriage a bit better now."

"I am hoping that you will address me as Rose."

He chuckled. "Well now, that will be a rare experience, addressing a lady like yourself with such familiarity."

Did she imagine the disapproving note in his tone? Considering the circumstances of this marriage, the "lady like yourself" could have several meanings.

She did not think that scandal would have reached Teeslow, but perhaps it had. Or maybe Kyle had explained things in detail when he visited in December.

I've a chance to marry a lady because she ruined herself enough that she will never do better. I am stuck with her taint, but in a generation no one will much remember.

She groped to find friendly conversation. The need to do so disappeared when Harold began coughing. It racked his body something terrible. She got up to try to aid him, although she had no idea how. He held up a hand, stopping her. Eventually the coughs subsided and he again used the spittoon.

"I am not a well man, as you can see. T'is the miners' disease. I thought I'd have another good ten years before it felled me like this."

"I am sorry."

He shrugged. "Can't get the coal out without raising the dust."

Kyle returned then, saving her from having to find a reply to that. "I must steal her from you, Uncle. The chamber has been made ready and Rose should rest and warm herself after the journey."

Rose removed her carriage mantle and positioned herself close to the fire. "You uncle is very ill, isn't he?"

"He is dying."

She nodded, as if that had been obvious to her. "He said it was the miners' disease. From the dust."

"Many of them get sick in their lungs. It is expected, and they are a frugal lot as a result. The pay must provide later for the families they leave behind."

"That is sad. You speak of it without passion, however."

"It is the way the life is, Rose. It is as common for these men as the gout is among lords. A collier goes into the pit knowing how it might be, much as a sailor knows he might drown."

He set about unpacking his baggage. He never brought Jordan here, for the same reasons he hesitated bringing Rose. There was nothing wrong with this house, but his aunt and uncle would not begin to know what to do with servants about.

He was glad that he knew that Rose could do for herself. If not, he would have insisted on staying at an inn, and the nearest one was not convenient to his purposes. His aunt also would have been hurt if this marriage so quickly changed their habits with one another.

Still...

"Will you be comfortable here? Tell me if you will not be."

She gazed around the chamber, at its bed that lacked drapes and the curtains of which Aunt Pru was so proud. "It is far nicer than an inn. We will be sharing it?"

"Yes."

She did not appear to mind that. She sat on the bed, then lay down. "I think that I will rest a short while. I never realized that being in a carriage for several days could tire one so much."

When she woke, Kyle was gone. She ventured down the stairs in search of him.

Harold dozed in his chair by the sitting room fire. She followed sounds into the kitchen in the back of the house.

Prudence worked there, rolling out pastry dough. She smiled, and angled her head toward the hearth.

"There's some warm cider in that pot on the stones, and a cup on the table, if you want."

Rose helped herself, and looked out a back window at a little grove of young fruit trees, barren now in winter's cold. A large garden flanked the western edge of it, waiting a spring planting.

"This is a very pleasant house," she said. "The prospects from all the windows are lovely."

"Kyle built it for us. Came back from France he did. Went to London to find his fortune, then he had this built. Harold did not want to take it, of course, but I could already see he was getting sick. You'll see him goad Kyle a bit about his fine clothes and lordly ways, but he is proud to bursting with what his sister's son has become."

Rose ambled closer to watch Prudence work on the pastry. "I make pies too."

"Do you now? I didn't think ladies baked much."

"Most don't. I like to, though. I could help, if you like."

Prudence moved some apples and a bowl to one side. "You can pare and slice them into this."

Rose set to work. "Where is Kyle?"

"He walked down to the village. I expect he will visit with the vicar, then have a pint with the men at the tavern. He would have taken Harold in the carriage, but Harold was asleep. Tomorrow maybe. Harold misses his pints with the lads."

Rose pictured Kyle, walking the half mile or so back into Teeslow. Walking back into his old life. Would he shed his coats as he went? Remove the layers of education and change he had accepted in order to find his fortune in London? Lapse back into the accent that marked Harold's speech?

It would not be the Kyle she knew in that tavern. It would be the Kyle who remained a stranger to her.

"Is he good friends with the vicar?"

Prudence laughed. "Well, now, friends is not the word. The earl charged the vicar with teaching Kyle his letters and numbers and Latin and French. A hard taskmaster he was. Warmed his students' bums with a rod on occasion. Kyle didn't like that, but he knew the lessons might mean a different life so he kept going back."

"The earl? Do you mean the Earl of Cottington? He was Kyle's benefactor?"

"None other."

He had never told her. Not outright. She just assumed the benefactor had been—someone. Not an earl. Not Cottington. Not Norbury's father.

It explained so much. The partnership with those new estates. His presence at that dinner party.

"Why would the earl do that?"

Prudence fixed her attention on scraping sugar off a cone. "The earl came to know Kyle by accident. Saw at once what was in him. Saw he wasn't no ordinary boy, but smart and brave. He knew my nephew would be wasted in the mine, even though as a boy he could already do the work of a man. So he told the vicar to teach him so he could go to schools and such when he grew." She gathered the sugar into a cup. "A good and just man, the earl is. Such as they ever are."

The little story made questions jump in Rose's mind. Too many to ask Prudence without quizzing her as if she was in the dock.

She knew very little about her husband's life. She was very curious, but she had never asked him for the information even though he was the most likely source of it.

She had never asked, but neither had he explained. She did not believe it was because Kyle was embarrassed about his past or even because he was not a man who spoke much about himself.

They both avoided all of that because talking about his past would mean talking about Norbury.

The shadow of that affair affected even their knowledge of each other.

"Goin' to be trouble. No two ways about it," Jon said. He gulped some ale for emphasis.

Kyle drank in agreement. Jonathan was a miner of about his own age. They had entered the pit about the same time when they were boys, and carried baskets up the ladder together.

Now Jon was a radical, which made him indiscreet with the fellow in fine coats who had lived here long ago.

The rest of the miners were friendly enough, even jovial. They had raised pints in salute when Kyle entered the tavern and peppered him with questions about London. They had been unwilling to talk about the real happenings in this town, however. A misspoken word might affect their livelihoods.

"Three times now the committee has gone to the owners and objected to reopening that tunnel and explained the danger," Jon said. "Cheaper to lose a few men than to do what needs doing, though. We seen it before, and it will happen again."

Kyle had certainly seen it before. His father's bones still lay in that sealed off tunnel. It had been too dangerous to dig those men out. The first attempt had only caused another cave-in.

"Have you gone to Cottington?" he asked. "He sold most of it to others long ago, but he still has influence. The surrounding land is still his."

"Two of us tried. He is so sick they won't let anyone near him. Even you could not get in last time you were here. As for petitioning his heir..." Jon's expression conveyed his opinion of that, and of the son in question.

Jon glanced over his shoulder. He ran his hand through his blond curls, then leaned across the table to speak in confidence. "We are organizing to speak and act as one. Not just here. We've had meetings with other groups in other towns, and them that work for other owners. If we all stand shoulder to shoulder and talk as one, we will be heard."

"Be careful, Jon."

"Careful, hell. The Combination Act is dead now, finally, and we've a right to join together. What can they do? Kill me? They can't kill us all. They can't put us all out. You talked about this yourself years back, before—" He looked away, then gulped more ale.

Before you went away and became one of them.

"When you stand shoulder to shoulder, every man must be in that line. Every man must be willing to go hungry. There's always those who will break."

"If we walk out, no man will go back in. We'll see to that."

"There are always others who need the work."

"If those lines are in front of the pits, it won't matter."

"They will call out the yeomanry. It will be another Peterloo."

Jon slammed down his fist. "Stop talking like my wife. Have you forgotten what is down there? Go back to that fine house you built for Harold and borrow his boots and clothes. Come in with me tomorrow if you are forgetting why the danger doesn't matter to such as us."

That "such as us" did not include Kyle. He was one of them, but also no longer one of them. This was his home, but he had traveled so far from it in so many ways that each time he returned he was less a part of this world.

He felt it. Nor could he stop it. His ties here were like sand that ran through his fingers no matter how closely he pressed them together.

How long before few even recognized him when he walked these lanes? The day would come when he would enter this tavern and the voices would fall silent while eyes examined the intruding gentleman.

"I am going up to Kirtonlow while I am here," he said. "I will speak to Cottington about that tunnel."

Jon's shrug communicated his lack of faith in that making any difference. He called for more ale and set the conversation aside along with his empty glass.

Kyle returned to the house in time for dinner. Rose helped Prudence set out the food. The conversation revolved around small things the way talk among strangers often did. Finally Uncle Harold could not stand it. He demanded to know what had been learned at the tavern.

"They don't come here much. Too far to walk after a day's work," he explained.

Aunt Pru weakly smiled her apologies for what sounded like lack of gratitude for the house. Kyle let it pass. Harold knew they would not visit much even if he still lived in the village. A man too weak to get to the tavern was a man isolated.

"There is talk of reopening the tunnel," he said. "I heard of it in December, but it sounds like it will happen for certain."

"The fools. The greedy fools." The news agitated Harold so much that he lapsed into a coughing fit.

"At least maybe your father and the others can have a Christian burial," Pru quietly said.

Rose looked over in surprise. An expression entered her eyes that Kyle had seen several times tonight.

Curiosity. Maybe reevaluation. Something was on her mind and this reference to that tunnel piqued it.

Aunt Pru brought out one of her pies. Its aroma was enough to lighten everyone's mood. Pru had a famous hand at pasties of all sorts. It did not matter if the fruit had been in a root cellar all winter, she still managed to conjure excellence.

He felt like a boy again, anticipating a treat only available then on paydays, when some sugar could be bought.

Prudence sliced. "Rose helped me make it."

"Did she now?"

"Nothing like cooking together for women to get to know each other," Harold said. "I'm glad to see your wife likes to bake, Kyle lad. It is good to know you won't be deprived down there in London now."

"Rose is an excellent pastry cook," he said. She beamed at the compliment. He eyed the piece of pie in front of him. "So, I've you to thank for this, dear?"

"I did not do much. I only cut the apples."

He dug in. No, she had not helped much. It tasted wonderful.

Rose watched him swallow every bite. Again that look entered her eyes. Something had her thinking again.

CHAPTER FOURTEEN

~

R ose wanted some conversation with her husband. It annoyed her when he did not retire with her, but allowed her to go up to the bedchamber alone.

As soon as she got there she realized why he had not accompanied her. Sharing this room meant having no privacy. Preparations normally done separately would now be performed with him right there.

She wondered about that while she removed her dress and stays and chemise and hose. She slid her nightdress on and sat on the bed to take down her hair. She imagined him here, undressing too.

She looked at the bed. Prudence and Harold had shared one all night, every night, for years. They did not go their separate ways after the marital duties were performed. What must it be like, to have one's life so completely intertwined with another's?

Quite nice if there were love, she guessed. Horrible if there were hatred. Intrusive if there were indifference.

She heard his boots on the stairs soon enough to

know he had indeed delayed in respect for her delicacy. There was a lot of that in this marriage.

She left the lamp burning and climbed into the bed. It was not an overly large one. All kinds of intimacies would be forced on them during this visit.

He knocked before he entered. She doubted Harold had ever knocked to make sure Prudence would allow him in.

She fought the impulse to turn on her side so he too would have privacy. But *he* wasn't a delicate flower and she wanted to talk.

He removed his coats and hung them in the wardrobe.

"Did you enjoy the pie?" she asked.

He sat on the chair and pulled off his boots. "Yes, very much. It was almost as good as yours."

She found herself unable to speak. Her heart filled with an emotion sweet and poignant.

The truth was that she made mediocre pies. No one had ever taught her how to do it. As a girl, out of necessity she had experimented until she came up with something deemed more or less edible by her brothers. The result in no way compared with Prudence's magic.

She had watched Prudence today, and seen what had been missing all those years from her own baking. She had tasted the difference too.

Yet here Kyle was, lying so she would not feel bad. He could have just not mentioned her pies at all. Just like he could have eaten only one small piece the morning after their wedding.

He probably choked on every mouthful that day.

"Prudence said you would probably visit the vicar

today. She told me how he had taught you your first
school lessons." She debated whether to go on. They
could live their entire lives without broaching the questions that had risen in her mind today. It might be best to
do that.

Only she would not sleep if she did not ask them.
The answers affected not only her knowledge of the
stranger, but her understanding of the Kyle she knew.

"She said that it was Cottington who had the vicar
give you lessons. That the earl was your benefactor. You
never told me that."

He pulled off his cravat. "You never asked."

"That is true. I never asked. I am asking now. I want
to know about this."

"You want to know for the wrong reasons."

What was that supposed to mean? "I want to know
because you are my husband, and this extraordinary oc-
currence changed your life and made you the man I
married."

He sat back in the chair and looked at her. "Fine. I
came to the earl's attention when I was twelve. He decided that I had abilities that should be nurtured. He
arranged for the vicar to give me lessons, then paid my
fees to learn from an engineer in Durham for two years.
He arranged that I take entrance examinations to the
École des Beaux-Arts in Paris, then sent me there to
study architecture. When I returned he handed me one
hundred pounds and the largesse ended, although he
continued as a friend and as an occasional business
partner."

And that one hundred had been turned into one thousand, then more and more. "It is an amazing story. That

you astonish is a given, but I find the earl astonishing too. Why did he extend this patronage to you? Because of your father's death in the tunnel?"

"He had no idea that I was the son of one of those men. That had happened three years before." He went to work on his cuffs. "I am not sure why he did it. I think it was because I had thrashed his son. Maybe he admired my audacity. Perhaps he just believed the son needed thrashing and was glad another boy dared to do it for him."

"You thrashed Norbury? How delicious. It is unfortunate, however, that this story touches on him."

"Unfortunate but inevitable, Rose. Do not pretend that you did not know where the story would lead when you first asked the question."

He stripped off his shirt. He poured water in the basin and began washing.

She had never seen him this unclothed since their wedding night. After that he had been no more than a silhouette in the dark. She had felt those shoulders and embraced his nakedness, but not seen it.

The low light flattered him, but his strength would have impressed even in the glaring summer sun. Nothing soft could be seen. No threatening corpulence due to easy living. His muscles did not appear bulky, but just the size and tautness required for his height. Like his face, his body appeared roughly sculpted, and it managed to imply contained energy that waited to burst forth. She wondered if that tension ever disappeared. Maybe when he slept it went dormant.

He so captivated her attention that she almost abandoned the conversation. Her silence drew his attention, and he caught her watching him. He returned to his washing.

"I suppose that I did know where the story would lead," she said. "That you know Norbury so well has always been a surprise. That you now continue in a partnership with him, and use his family lands—"

"My business is with Cottington. It always has been. Norbury is involved now only because the earl is very ill."

This conversation was leading onto dangerous ground. She saw the space between them suddenly full of crevices and holes. His tone said it would be unwise to try to walk there.

"If the earl is so ill, Norbury may be in your life a very long time," she said. "He already has been, from the sounds of things. He is in both our lives now, Kyle."

He threw down the towel. "When I must see him, I see him. Then he is gone from my thoughts along with his presence. He is not in our lives."

"How can he not be, with how we met? I feel him; he is like a specter. I do not think that he leaves your thoughts at all where I am concerned. I think that you try hard to forget my affair, but—"

"Yes, damn it, I try hard. The alternative is to want to kill him. For the shameful way he treated you at that dinner. For the way I suspect he treated you before it. I picture him with you and—" His fist clenched and unclenched. He tensed hard, and forced a dark calm on himself. "It is not in my mind when I am with you, however. It does not reflect on you."

"How can it not? He affects everything. That night affects everything, even how you treat me as a wife."

"If you are talking about my command about your brother—"

"My brother? Goodness, my brother is one thing we share that Norbury does not touch. I did not like that argument, but at least for once I spoke with the man I married. The whole man. The real man. Not the careful, polite creation who dresses so perfectly and talks so perfectly and gives me pleasure so correctly and with such perfect respect."

She doubted she would ever see him so surprised again in her life. It only lasted a few seconds. Then his gaze focused on her in a way that made her heart rise to her throat.

"I treat you with respect, like a lady, and you are *complaining*?"

"I am not complaining. I know that I am fortunate to have such a considerate lover. I just think that you are so careful with that respect for reasons that sadden me."

He did not like the criticism. No man would. "It sounds like you know my mind and my reasons better than I do, Rose."

She should retreat, apologize, be silent and grateful. Only if she did, all he would remember was an insult that she had not intended to give.

"Perhaps I do, Kyle. Or maybe the little that I know of your mind has me misunderstanding. Just tell me this. If not for that terrible night, if not for my affair, would you feel that you needed to be so carefully respectful? If you had married an innocent girl from this village, or a woman who had never been called a whore, would you even think of such a thing all the time? If you had not been born in this village, but in a manor house, and offered me marriage under other circumstances, would you believe it so important to treat me like a lady?"

At least he did not look even more angered by her outpouring. Intense and serious, but not furious. The time pulsed by so slowly, so silently, that she regretted her words anyway.

"I am sorry. I should not have—" She picked at a loose thread on the coverlet. "I just sense, when we are together—you are almost always wearing your perfectly tailored coats, Kyle. Even in bed when you have nothing on in reality."

She had made a bad situation worse. She flopped onto her back and pulled the coverlet high, to hide from the flotsam of the shipwreck she had no doubt just made of this marriage.

She wished that she were a writer or poet and could explain what she meant. She wished there were words to express how she felt the way his birth and hers, his redemption and her scandal, his awareness of her affair and her need to *not* be treated like a whore, had built these invisible barriers of formality.

Impossible to explain. Unlikely to change. She should accept how it was. She should scold her heart so it did not keep stretching toward something unknown in that aching, restless way. She should—

"The coats do not fit well when I am here, Rose. For all the tailor's skill, they become too tight when I come home."

His quiet voice flowed to her through the tense silence.

"I expect that is uncomfortable."

"Damnably so."

"Then again, perhaps they are always too tight, and you only notice when you come home."

"I think that you may be correct about that."

She sat up again. His attention had turned to the low fire, and his own thoughts. He stood with one forearm resting on the mantel while he gazed at the flames. Their light illuminated him beautifully.

The sight mesmerized her. The whole chamber seemed to fill with the glow from the hearth. Its warmth entered her.

"Actually, I have also noticed that my garments seem tight since I came here, Kyle. Perhaps it is the air. Or the pies."

He smiled. "Then you should remove them."

"I have no practice in taking off these garments. I was trussed in this corset the day I was born."

He looked at her. Her heart skipped and began a rapid patter. Even the day he proposed he had not allowed her to see his desire so boldly.

He strode toward her. "I'll be taking that as an invitation, Rose."

He grabbed her in an embrace so strong, so supportive, that her knees left the mattress. He kissed her possessively, hard, asking for nothing and everything. He put no restraints on his desire this time. He pulled her into its whirlwind of untamed power.

The kisses claimed, commanded, and aroused her fast. She could not have stood against the way he took control of her even if she wanted to. She had asked for this, and she allowed her own savage reactions to have free rein. They overwhelmed her initial fear and surprise.

Hot kisses. Hard and deep and biting and devouring. Arms of steel held her up to the fury scorching her neck and mouth. Shock upon wonderful shock slashed through her body like arrows of fire. He called forth her primitive self until she moaned from the glorious assault and lost all restraint.

He set her down so she knelt again, on the edge of the bed. He caressed up her thighs beneath her night-dress. His hand smoothed over her hips and her bottom. A sly, erotic touch traced down her cleft. A stunning quiver followed that path to where his fingers teased at her.

She moved one knee to encourage him to continue that delicious torture. He did, but broke the long kiss. With his other hand he swept her nightdress up to her shoulders and over her head. It fell down her arms, onto the floor at his feet.

He looked down on her nakedness with an expression made severe by desire. His caress glossed over her breasts while his other hand flicked and teased below. The dual sensations left her trembling, weakened by pleasure and wobbling on her stance. She leaned into him for support until her face smoothed against his chest.

A hand on her nape pressed her closer until her cheek rested on taut skin. "I can remove the nightdress, Rose, but the rest of the garments you will have to shed yourself."

She understood. His encouragement emboldened her. She placed her palms on his chest, feeling and seeing at the same time. Her mere touch raised his desire even more and made a new tightness flex through him.

She caressed more purposefully. She watched her hands smooth over his chest, sliding down and over the hard ridges of his muscles and ribs. He looked at her just as she did him, his own caresses and touches on her body mimicking her strokes on his. Their hot breaths met and merged in increasingly frantic kisses while the sensations pushed them both further into madness.

His hand left her thighs and began unbuttoning his breeches. A petulant moan snuck out of her before she could stop it. She pushed his hands away and worked on the buttons herself. She swooned from the feel of his touch stroking her again.

She fumbled with his garment while he touched her more deliberately. His head bent to her neck and her ear. His finger probed carefully. "Do you want it like that, Rose?"

She could not respond. She could not speak. It was all she could do to stay upright. She grabbed at his garments clumsily, blindly, pushing them down his hips while the light touches on her breast and between her thighs left her whimpering.

"Or like this?" His hand slipped around her hip to touch her from the front. One long, slow, incredible stroke caused a quake of pleasure to shake through her.

She knew that he could see how helpless he made her. She clung to his shoulders, hanging on him for support.

He released one of her hands, kissed it, then moved it lower on his body. A small slice of rationality returned, enough for her to comprehend what he was do-

ing, what he wanted. Too lost to care, too far gone to
know embarrassment, she let him close her fingers
around his phallus.

Another devilish stroke with his other hand made it
easier for her. Pleasure streaked up through her body in
a rippling tide, and in response she caressed him as he
did her.

Whatever restraint he still maintained cracked then.
He kissed her with new savagery. She felt the tension all
through him, in his stance and his kiss and even in the
way he touched her. Deliberate now. Determined to
command her total surrender.

Pride lost its meaning. She swayed on her knees,
arching into his dominating kisses, moaning from the
want.

He moved her, but not the way she expected. He
turned her so her back faced him and his hands caressed
her breasts freely. She leaned into him, arching her
back. Her nipples rose high, tight and hard, begging for
more, for anything, for everything.

He moved her again, bending her body until she
knelt low on the edge of the bed with her legs bent beneath her body. A stunning erotic shiver trembled low in
her loins.

He lifted her hips. She waited, breathless, so excited
that she could not bear it. Her body throbbed, waiting,
expecting. She pictured what he saw, her bottom rising
to him and that hidden flesh exposed. The scandalous
image only excited her more.

He did not take her at once. He let her wait, hovering
on that point of madness. He caressed her bottom,
firmly kneading the swells of her flesh, looking at her,

she was sure. He watched her submissive surrender and her desperation.

He touched her again and she cried out. It was different this time. She was exposed and open and she knew that he watched, knew that he saw her naked body. She dipped her back lower and raised her bottom more.

She was begging soon. Begging and moaning and smothering her cries in the bedclothes. Finally he entered her in a long, deliberate, slow thrust. Beneath her moan of relief she thought that she heard his as well.

She lost herself after that. She experienced only the torturous pleasure of need and the violent crescendo of fulfillment.

"Did you come here to see Cottington before he dies?" Rose rested in Kyle's arms beneath the bedclothes. It had been some while since he lifted her limp body and moved her here, situating her so that she lay tight against him while he sat with his body resting on the headboard. The candle still cast a glow over their mutual contentment.

"That was one reason. I will try tomorrow."

"Try? Does he not receive you now?"

"He does not know that I have called. His secretary and physician do not tell him about visitors, unless they choose to. That is how it is now with him."

She thought that it was probably how it had always been. An earl usually had people who made sure he was not disturbed unless he wanted to be. Now that Cottington was ill, someone else was deciding when he wanted to be, not him. That was all that had changed.

"If he cannot see you now, perhaps in the spring, when you had planned to come, he can."

"I do not think that he will be alive in the spring."

She realized that he had heard the earl was dying. That was why he had come north right now.

"It will be very sad if you cannot say good-bye, after all he has done for you. Surely his secretary knows that."

"To his secretary I am the boy from Teeslow." His mouth pressed her hair in a distracted kiss. "It is not only saying good-bye. I need to see if he still has his mind about him. I would like to ask one final favor, for the miners."

"Is it about reopening that tunnel?"

"Yes. Some think to stop it, in ways that will only get their heads broken."

"It could work, if they all—"

"It won't be all of them. There are families who lost men in that cave-in who will want the tunnel opened again, so they can bury their dead."

"You said that your father died in an accident. It was that one, wasn't it?"

He nodded. "I would like to bury him too. But I know that tunnel will never be safe unless things are done differently. Its walls move."

"It is solid rock. Rock does not move."

"The earth is a living thing, Rose. Before I build I have to make sure the ground is stable. That mine is not in stable ground, and that tunnel was the worst. I knew it as a boy. I could see it."

She sat up and faced him. An echo of the night's earlier trembles fluttered in her when she looked at him. A woman cannot allow a man to do such things without accepting a certain disadvantage with him in the future. She sensed that she had ceded him mastery of her in other ways too, ways that were between them now, encouraging those flutters.

"How long did you work in the mine, Kyle?"

"I first went down when I was eight. Children carry coal out in baskets. Usually they are nine or ten when they start, but I was big for my age. But not as big as a man. So I could see what the men never saw because it was right above their bowed heads. There were cracks above and near the top of the walls. I could see them shift over the months. I told my father. He and the others saw no danger because they had not been watching and had not seen the changes. Then one day—it all came down. Ten men were buried alive on the other side of a new wall."

"And they were just left there?"

"They are never left if it can be helped. Men began digging. More rock fell and another man was gone. There was no more digging after that. A service was held. Prayers were said. And two days later the men went back into the pit. Except the families of the men lost. They waited a week. By then the men would be dead for certain. Lack of air or water would do it by then."

She pictured him, holding vigil with his aunt and uncle. She saw the child imagining the father behind that wall of rock, maybe still alive but beyond help.

"I told the men we should dig from above. Bore a hole down so there would be air until we figured out how to get them out. No one listened to a child, least of all the men who supervised for the owners. I know now it could work. An engineer could do it. I could do it now, if ever such a cave-in occurs in a lateral tunnel."

Yes, he probably could, even if the ground would not permit it. He would do it with his bare hands, she guessed, if that was what it took. If he set his mind to it, rock and ground would not stop him.

He had told her the story and answered her questions. She could tell that his mind had moved on to other things. He had left that candle burning for a reason.

He took her arm and drew her toward him. He sat up and positioned her so she faced him, with her legs wrapping his hips.

He watched his hands curve around her breasts and his thumbs brush their large dark nipples. "I saw you well enough in the dark, or my mind did at least. I like this better."

In other words, he did not want any more ladylike snuffing of lamps and candles at night. She did not mind. She could see him too this way. However, it would take some time before she did not experience some shyness when he looked at her body like this.

He lifted her and moved his leg so she sat on it, bringing her higher. His tongue and teeth began arousing her breast with leisurely, devastating flicks and nips.

Their position allowed her to caress him freely too. She stroked over his shoulders. "I think that you should take me with you when you go to Kirtonlow to try to see Cottington."

His fingers replaced his mouth, freeing the latter to reply. "No."

She wondered if he did not want her to see him turned away.

"If I come with you, the secretary will not refuse us."

"Yes, he will, and I'll not have you insulted."

"It is much harder to dismiss a lady, Kyle. We will let him know that he dare not do so, that the earl will be most displeased if he tries."

"No."

Her hand wandered low between their bodies in a quest to open his mind. She closed her fingers around his hard shaft and teased the tip with her thumb. "You married me for my blood, Kyle. You should let me open doors if I can."

His smile could not hide the sensual storm her caresses created. "Rose, are you using feminine wiles to make me pliable?"

She glanced down at what her hand was doing. "I appear to be having the opposite effect. There is nothing pliable about you right now. Except ever so slightly, right here." She gave a gentle squeeze at the tip.

His hands cupped her bottom and lifted her slightly. She knew what to do without instruction because it seemed natural and necessary. She shifted and settled so that she could guide him into her.

The first touch of penetration caused a shock of pleasure through her whole body. The sensation captivated her and stole her breath. She did not move to take him in farther but remained like that, barely joined, so that the delicious shudders would not stop.

He allowed it even though desire tensed through him so violently that his jaw clenched and his teeth bared. She lowered a little so that she felt him a bit more.

"You are going to kill me, Rose." He grasped her hips. "You can torture me for hours another night, but now—" He drew her closer, lowering her until they were snugly together.

He guided her after that, his strong hands easing her hips into a rhythm of absorption and release that she controlled. She discovered new pleasures with subtle shifts and pressures on her body. She closed her eyes and tensed around him again and again.

Then he filled her more, and so deeply that she gasped. She opened her eyes and looked into his and could not look away again. She did not see him move, but she felt him filling her, thrusting and claiming while the depths of his gaze invited her to drown in sapphire fathoms. He held her hips firmly immobile at the end. No longer free, she surrendered to the way he ravished her body and soul.

Her violent climax was almost painful in its intensity. She collapsed on him. Her face pressed to his chest, bound to him by his strong embrace while her body slowly relinquished the last shivers of bliss.

"When will you leave for Kirtonlow Hall tomorrow?" she asked when their breaths and hearts had calmed.

A stretching arm. A billowing sheet. He drew the bedclothes up and tucked them around her. "Noon, I think."

"I want to go with you. I will be ready at noon."

She waited for his "no." It did not come. Instead, his embrace adjusted around her, wrapping her closely. His breath warmed her temple with a kiss.

CHAPTER FIFTEEN

≈

The bleakness of the hills disappeared five miles away from Kirtonlow Hall and the landscape became more lush by the minute. The house loomed tall and broad, overlooking a large pond that reflected its gray stone in silver water.

As their carriage turned along the drive, Rose examined Kyle and herself. His cravat creased perfectly. His coat sat perfectly on his shoulders. Even the chain of his watch glowed in a perfect arc of links. A fashion plate would not be more precise in its correctness.

She had worn the best garments she had brought, a newly commissioned lavender carriage ensemble with a mantlet lined and trimmed in gray squirrel. It had joined her wardrobe on this journey for the most practical of reasons, but its current style and discreet luxury would serve a different purpose today. This officious secretary would never know the fur had been salvaged from one of her old garments that had gone hopelessly out of style.

Kyle's card was taken away. Eventually steps were

heard, this time two sets. The servant clicked his way down the staircase with a short, bald man in tow.

"Well, well. At least Conway will turn me away himself this time," Kyle muttered. "You were correct. He dare not dismiss a lady without explanation."

Mr. Conway approached with an ingratiating smile. "Mr. Bradwell. Mrs. Bradwell. I regret that the earl is too ill to have visitors. His condition is far worse, it saddens me to say, than when you called the last time, Mr. Bradwell. I will, of course, bring him any message that you may have, although it is not clear that he understands all that is said to him."

"My message is for his ears alone, competent or not, however they be now," Kyle said. "Since he is failing, I must insist on seeing him."

Mr. Conway's smile thinned.

"I also have a message that must be given directly," Rose said. "Lord Easterbrook charged me quite specifically with personally communicating his exact words to Lord Cottington."

"Lord Easterbrook!"

"He is my relative through marriage. I visit his London house regularly and he condescends to include my husband and myself in his circle."

Mr. Conway frowned unhappily at this news.

"I fear Easterbrook's anger if I return to London and report that I failed him. You appear a faithful servant, Mr. Conway, and I know that you seek only to ensure your master's comfort, but I doubt that I will be able to keep your name out of my sad story. As you may have heard, Easterbrook is somewhat eccentric. One never

knows what he will do if he favors or disfavors someone."

Conway's eyes blinked hard at the implied threat.
Rose smiled as sweetly as she could. Kyle remained
passive, but she detected deep sparks in his eyes that
said he found her speech stunning.

Conway chewed his lip while he masticated his
thoughts. "Madam, forgive me. I was unaware of your
relationship to the marquess. However, Lord Norbury
has insisted his father not be agitated by visitors."

"Agitated? Does your presence agitate him, my good
man?"

"Of course not. He knows me so well that—"

"Then Mr. Bradwell's presence will not, either. He
knows my husband as well as he knows you. Better, I
daresay. I will pay Easterbrook's respects and leave
them alone at once, so as to avoid any agitation. As for
Lord Norbury, if he is not in residence he need never
know of this visit unless you inform him, and need
never waste his time judging whether we qualified as
agitating visitors under the terms of his command."

She let her expression and pose show that she
assumed she would be accommodated. Mr. Conway
seemed relieved by the excuses her performance gave
him.

"Under the circumstances—yes, I will bring you to
him. In the case of visitors like yourselves, the issue of
agitation is negligible. Please follow me, Madam. Sir."

They paraded after Mr. Conway as he led the way to
the grand staircase. Kyle took her arm and angled his
head close to hers.

"I had no idea that you carried a message from Easterbrook," he muttered. "You should have told me."

"I am certain he would want me to give this fellow peer his greetings and express his hope that Cottington recovers."

"In Easterbrook's closest circle, are we?"

"It is not clear he has any circle besides his family. I do visit Henrietta. He does have great affection for Alexia. I do not think I was exactly untruthful."

"You were not exactly untruthful. And you were magnificent."

"You should receive some benefits from this marriage. My relations are the only dowry that I brought to you."

He squeezed her hand. "Your beneficial relations are the last things on my mind this morning."

The insinuation warmed her. Echoes of the night's soul-shaking trembles spoke in their quiet, devastating ways. She focused on Mr. Conway's back to maintain her bearings, but she noticed nothing else except the masculine mystery at her side. Images flashed, wonderful, shocking ones, of the various ways he had eased her into erotic intimacy.

Her last few paces to the earl's chamber proved unsteady. Suddenly Mr. Conway's face appeared in her eyes.

"Please wait here. I must announce you and ensure that he feels capable of the visit. If he does not, we must try again tomorrow."

Conway entered the chamber alone, but returned quickly. He opened the white paneled door and stood aside.

The earl sat in a large, green-patterned chair next to a roaring fire. Blankets covered legs propped on a footrest. Age and illness had diminished any resemblance he might have to his son, except perhaps a similar vanity.

The earl's white hair had been perfectly groomed and his face cleanly shaven. Despite his infirmity his valet had turned him out in an expertly creased cravat and a colorful silk waistcoat. Rose expected that the parts hidden by the blanket were equally presentable on a day when this man had no expectations of leaving this chair.

Eyes far more shrewd than Norbury's examined them. A smile broke on his pallid face. It formed only on one side of his mouth. The rest remained flaccid, a victim of his apoplexies.

"Well, come forward, Bradwell. Bring that wife of yours here so I can see her." Illness had not affected the tone of command, even if it slurred the words' pronunciations.

Kyle guided Rose forward and made formal introductions. The earl eyed her from head to toe.

"Conway there says that you have a message for me, Mrs. Bradwell. From Easterbrook."

"Indeed I do. The marquess sends his best wishes to you, and his fervent hope for your quick recovery."

"Does he now? I haven't seen Easterbrook in some years. Not since shortly after he returned from that journey to God knows where, so odd and different. I have not visited London much. How generous of him to remember me and send this kind regard."

His tone was sardonic, and his eyes too knowing.

She tried not to flush at the evidence that he had so easily seen through her ruse.

"You can carry my message back to the marquess in turn, Mrs. Bradwell. Will you do that for an old, dying man?"

"Certainly, sir."

"Tell him that he shirks his duties most shamefully. Tell him I said it is time he got out in the world and stopped indulging his bent for eccentricity. Tell him he must marry and sire an heir, and take his place in the government. That family has too much intelligence to waste it, and his life is not his own to live as he likes and that is the damned truth of it."

"I will communicate your sentiments, I promise."

"Sentiments, hell. Word for word, that is how you will do it, not prettied up the way women speak." A strangled chuckle snuck out. "Wait until I'm dead, though. If he is angry he can take it out on my son, not me."

"If I am to wait until you are gone, I am sure it will be a long while before I must take up this duty. If you will excuse me now, I will leave my husband to speak with you alone."

Cottington watched Rose leave the chamber. Then he gestured to his secretary. "Go now. If you are needed, Mr. Bradwell here will come for you."

As soon as Conway left, the earl gave another order. "There's brandy in that cupboard over there. Pour me some, Kyle, and for yourself too, if you want. They won't let me have any. I'm supposed to face death stone sober, to their way of thinking."

Kyle found the brandy and glasses and poured them each a finger. The earl sipped his like it was nectar. "Hell of a thing, to be treated like a child. It is better now than a fortnight ago. For a week I needed servants to deal with even matters of the most basic hygiene."

"It sounds as if you are recovering, then."

"I'll be dead by summer, if not long before. I don't need a physician to tell me. I can feel it. It is strange, how one just *knows.*" He set down the glass and used a handkerchief to wipe the spirits that had leaked out the bad side of his mouth. "She is beautiful, your wife. Pretty enough to make the rest not matter so much, I suppose. Her brother and whatnot."

"As for the whatnot, thank you for the wedding gift."

The earl chortled. "My son will be furious about that. Better if you had not been in the middle this time. Bad luck that. Better if it had not been you who two times now forced him to face his dishonorable behavior."

Despite the laugh, a deep sorrow showed in the earl's eyes. He blinked it away. Norbury was only one more disappointment in a life that, like all lives, probably held many.

"So, you came all the way up here to say good-bye, did you? I am glad that you did."

"That is why I came, but I find that I also bear a petition, one I did not know I would hold until I arrived in Teeslow."

"There is nought that I can do for anyone much anymore."

Kyle told him about the mine. The earl listened with a sober expression.

"It was a rich deposit there," he said. "They wanted to go back in a few years ago but I told them no. I had already sold most of it to the others, but my voice still carried. Being an earl is useful sometimes. My son will not stop it like I did. I will write anyway, and use my influence, but once I die . . ."

Once he died the hunger for profit would win in a weighing where men's lives were cheaply valued.

"Even if it is delayed some months, it may give everyone time to calm," Kyle said. "Tempers are high among the colliers. One strong voice, one leader, and there will be trouble."

The earl sighed and closed his eyes. His lids remained down so long that it appeared he had drifted to sleep. Kyle had just decided to slip away when the earl spoke again.

"We'll not see each other again, Mr. Bradwell. If you have any questions to ask, now is the time for them." The eyes opened and pierced in his direction. "You do have questions, don't you?"

Kyle had several questions. The most recent one could not be asked, however. No matter that it sat in a corner of his mind. He could not ask this dying man if his only son had been even more dishonorable as a boy than as a man.

"I do have a question."

"Out with it then."

"Why?"

"Why? Why what?"

"All of it. Why?"

"Ah. *That* why." The earl thought it over. "Part impulse. Part instinct." That smile, half-formed. "For one thing, I knew that if you stayed in Teeslow, the colliers would have their one voice and one leader in a few years, after you reached manhood."

Kyle studied him, wondering if he was serious. In all the years they had exchanged generosity and gratitude, it had never entered his mind that the earl had ulterior motives. That was mostly because he could not conceive of any way the largesse could ever benefit an earl.

"Hell, it wasn't just that. You were wasted there. I saw it at once. Saw it in your eyes and determination. You came here that day, all polished and cleaned up, and I saw the man you would be. I'd heard about you before, see. I'd been told about this child who said we should bore down to that tunnel when it caved."

"It would have worked."

"Damned if I believe if it would or not. That a child had thought of it and dared to propose it—you were presented to me that day after you thrashed my son, and the memory of the manager laughing about that child's boldness entered my head from God knows where. I knew that child had been you. Just knew it, but I checked anyway."

He wiped his mouth of the drool that formed with talking. "Then, that business with my son. There you were again, daring what most grown men would not. So, in part I did it so you would not be wasted. And in part so you would not grow into a man who might lead them." He paused. "And, I admit, in part to punish my son by favoring the boy who had beat him. Not that it helped much. As you know better than most, his disgraceful behavior toward women continues to this day."

So there it was. Most of it Kyle had already known. The generosity had not been entirely charitable in its motivations, but then few human acts or decisions ever were.

The earl's whole face sagged. The damage appeared to invade the good side from the bad.

"You are tired and should rest. I will go now. Thank you for agreeing to see me."

Before Kyle could walk away, the earl stretched one hand in his direction. Kyle took it in his own, feeling for the first time the grasp of this man as a friend.

"You are none the worse for it, no matter the why," the earl said, his speech slurring badly. "Although I expect there are times when you wish I'd not interfered."

"In the tally of gains and losses, I come out far ahead. Whatever your reasons, I am grateful. I will never forget you. Nor will my children, or their children in turn."

The grasp tightened. The old man's eyes filmed. His lids closed. His hand fell away, then rose in a sovereign's gesture of blessing and farewell.

Kyle appeared sober when he emerged from Cottington's chamber. Rose left him to his thoughts while they walked down the staircase and out into the cold.

He did not enter the carriage at once, but instead walked around it and gazed out over the pond. She followed and waited. He was saying good-bye to more than a man today. An entire period of his life would end with Cottington's death.

"Have you been here often?" she asked.

"Not often. When I went away to school, however, he would send for me when I returned between terms. The first time, his messenger found half the town following him to my uncle's cottage to see what was happening."

"He received you regularly then."

"Yes. Perhaps it was part of the lessons."

"More likely he wanted to hear of your progress. You also brought him news of Durham, then Paris and London. I daresay your conversation was more interesting than most that he heard in this county."

"Perhaps." He let the carriage wait while he began strolling along the drive.

She fell into step. "Did you speak to him about the mine?"

He nodded. "He will do what he can, but at best it will be delayed. That may give them time to ensure it is more safe. There are ways to do that."

He did not sound optimistic that those ways would be employed.

"You have done all that you can, I suppose."

"Have I?"

They turned and aimed back to the carriage. "You are quiet, Kyle. Was it not a good meeting? Were you not free to speak as you wanted?"

"It was a very good meeting. He invited questions, and answered all that I could in good conscience ask of him."

"Were there some you could not ask?"

"Only one. I had planned to ask it, because I think he

may be the only person who would answer honestly. However, seeing him—the topic would only bring him sorrow, and the answer only satisfy my curiosity."

"If only one question remains between you, it was a very good meeting. I do not think there are many people who know another with whom they have only one unanswered question."

He looked down at her. Suddenly they were not speaking of Cottington, but of each other.

"He is a dying man, Rose. There is nothing left to lose in answering the questions. No consequences to the future and no loss of pride. Either to the person who asks the question, or the one who answers it."

They reached the carriage. His self-absorption waned once they began their journey back to Teeslow.

"You appear thoughtful too, Rose. Do you contemplate a question of your own?"

"I have many, but that is not the cause of any frown you may see. I am wondering whether I am going to survive the meeting with Easterbrook when I give him Cottington's scold."

The carriage was almost out of Teeslow before Kyle noticed the silence. He had been so lost in his thoughts that the unnatural quiet did not penetrate his awareness at first.

He called for the carriage to stop. He looked out the window.

Rose did too. "What is it? All appears calm to me."

"Too calm. The lane should be busier this time of day. Women should be about."

He cocked his ear and listened. He eyed the roofs of buildings and cottages. Where could they all be? At the mine? It was too soon for such an action. That left the tavern or the church.

He opened the door and stepped out. Rose gathered her skirt and held out her hand.

"No, Rose. The carriage will take you back to Pru. I will return shortly."

"Do you anticipate trouble? Danger?"

"No, but I—"

"If there is no danger, you have no reason to send me back. I am curious about this village. If you are going to visit, I am going to accompany you."

He braced his arm against the carriage jamb, blocking her descent. "You are curious about a lot of things lately."

"It is a woman's nature. Nor have I found that satisfying my curiosity is unpleasant."

She alluded to last night. Which made him hard. Memories filled his head, of her begging cries and shy but sure touch, of her back dipping and her bottom rising. Of her legs wrapping him while her tight warmth absorbed him and they rocked together in an embrace with bodies and gazes locked.

The thoughts made him want to kiss her and take her right here on the lane. They made him forget all the reasons she should go back.

With one bold look she turned him into an idiot.

"Do you think to command me to go back, Kyle? If so I should inform you that any husband has a limited number of commands per marriage, and it is foolish to waste them on insignificant matters."

So much for his sweet, pliable wife. Last night had changed more than the heat and intensity of their passion. The subtle formality that had imbued this marriage was eroding fast.

Her eyes held an explicit challenge.

"You may come, Rose, but only if you leave at once if I say so. I do not expect trouble, but I could be wrong. It would be better if you just returned—"

Her lids lowered.

Hell.

He told the coachman where to wait. He handed Rose down.

The village had gathered in the church. He could hear the voices as he and Rose approached the old stone structure with its single tower over the front portal. It had been part of a priory centuries ago, on land given over to a long-ago ancestor of Cottington. Before coal was found nearby, Teeslow had been a simple farming village.

"Shouldn't the men be in the mine now?" Rose asked.

"The men, and the older children, and even some of the women." He opened the ancient wooden door and the roar of an argument poured over them both.

They slipped in and stood along the back wall of the nave. Few noticed their arrival. All attention centered on the men standing in front of the altar. Jon was there, his blond curls wild, trying to force his will on the gathering.

That proved impossible. Voices crossed and interrupted. Emotions ran high and tones rang sharply. Cheers and jeers competed.

"I cannot even understand what is being discussed," Rose whispered.

"They were ordered to start clearing away that rock from the cave-in today. The men walked out instead. Now they must decide what to do tomorrow."

"I thought that you said that it caved even more when that was tried the last time."

"The owners sent in an engineer who says that will not happen this time."

Jon was making some headway gathering voices to his call to stay out. Not enough, though, which meant it would solve nothing.

Kyle let the voices pour over him. He recognized most of them. He knew these men and had played in the lanes with some of them as a boy.

His gaze swept the families and lit on a pale, pretty woman with red hair, holding two children by their hands. He had shared his first kiss with her when he was fourteen.

A far prettier woman stood by his side. No one had noticed her yet, but they would soon. The carriage ensemble that had impressed Conway looked all the richer here, with its fur and expensive needlework. Her bonnet contrasted with the kerchiefs worn by the other women. All of the light in the old, dim building seemed to seek her, making her blond beauty radiant.

"We should go," he said.

"If I were not here, would you go?"

He did not know. It was not his world anymore. Not his battle.

"If my presence will compromise your voice, if I only symbolize to them how far you have journeyed from this village, I will leave," she said. "However, if I only remind you of what you might lose if you speak, then one more question has been answered, and not in a way I had hoped." She turned to face him. "You are not a stranger to them yet, even if they increasingly become strangers to you."

Her understanding moved him. That she even tried to comprehend touched him profoundly.

He left her side and walked toward Jon. Since his head rose above the others in the nave, his voice carried. "You are not ready for this action, Jon, and you know it. Shoulder to shoulder, you said. It sounds like there are shoulders here that will not be with you."

The roar dimmed. Jon spotted him. "We've a gentleman here to advise us. Brought his fine wife too. How lucky we are for his counsel."

Kyle did not look back but he could tell from the buzz of mutters and exclamations that Rose had been sought and located. "I brought my wife to meet my old friends, Jon. Imagine my surprise to find a political meeting in this church. What do you think to gain by staying out except a lot of hungry women and children?"

"Fewer bodies to bury."

"I spoke with Cottington today. He will write to his partners. The tunnel will not open while he lives."

"You have bought us a few days, maybe a few weeks, that is all."

"It is long enough to make sure that when it opens it is safe."

Jon hooted. "Safe! We were told today to move that

rock. They found an engineer who says it is already safe."

"Then you must find one who can prove it is not. One who does not owe his living to the owners. One who has the education to back up his findings." Kyle reached the front of the nave. "One like me."

Jon consulted with the four other men arrayed around him. The church held a tense silence while they debated.

"You'll go down there?" The eldest of them spoke with a subtle sneer. His name was Peter MacLaran and he was the radical of yesterday, now passing the crown to Jon. "It will get your fine coats all dirty, m'lord. It might take a few days too. You'll be missing some of those dinner parties in London."

Peter got a few snickers for his sarcasm.

"I'll go right now. It won't be the first time I've been in that pit. The coats can stay here. Find a man to loan me his boots, find five of your best to join me, and we will begin it today. I will not leave Teeslow until I know what I need to know. If it is unsafe, I will explain why in a report. If it can be made safe, I will describe how. If they proceed anyway, and another cave-in happens, that report will hang them."

"They won't let you in to do it."

"Cottington's name will get me in. He isn't dead yet."

He did not wait for Jon and Peter to agree. The shouts sounding around him said that he had won.

He walked back to Rose. "You should go back to Pru now. I will walk you to the carriage."

"I will manage on my own. Do what you must do."

He unbuttoned his coats, shrugged them off, and handed them to her. A boy came over with some boots. Kyle sat down and pulled them on. Five of the most experienced miners waited at the church door with lamps.

Rose hugged the coats and watched the preparations. She might have been observing some ritual in an exotic land, she appeared so interested.

"Tell Pru I'll be needing a lot of hot water when I get back to the house," he said.

She stretched up to speak in his ear. "I expect that you will need a whole bath. Perhaps you will be so tired that I will have to help."

He hardened at once. Images of last night, of future nights, of that bath, made it worse.

He gritted his teeth, stared at the stone floor and forced the urges under control.

"Rose. Darling. I am facing hours in a black pit. That was very naughty of you."

She did not even pretend chagrin. She looked very pleased with herself as he left her.

CHAPTER
SIXTEEN

T he men followed Kyle out of the church. The colliers had decided that their engineer would definitely get into that pit today, and God help the manager
who tried to stop him.

The children ran off, but many of the women dallied
in the church. A lot of attention came Rose's way while
she folded Kyle's coats. Finally a woman of middle
years, wearing a full-skirted simple dress and a white
cotton kerchief, approached her.

"They'll be gone until night, most likely. We'll send
one of the little 'uns for that carriage of yours."

"I think that I will leave the carriage for Kyle and
walk back. It would be good if someone would tell the
coachman that, so he can deal with the horses properly."

The woman called over a little boy of about six years
and sent him off with the message. Then she gave
Rose's ensemble a good look. "You should be warm
enough in that, so he won't be scolding us for letting
you walk. All fur inside there, is it?"

Rose lifted the edge of the mantlet and showed the

fur lining. "I took it off an older one and had it put here."

A few other women ventured closer to listen and watch. One of them reached out to stroke the fur. "I didn't think ladies did that. Turned skirts and such."

"There are lots of ladies who do it. They just don't tell anyone."

The women laughed at that. The ensemble received attention from more of them.

Rose stayed and chatted for a while. The women of Teeslow were much like the women of London, or women anywhere. They wanted to know about the latest fashions even if they could not buy them, and the gossip about society too.

When she began her walk back to Harold's house, the first woman, whose name was Ellie, fell into step to accompany her. "I'll walk with you, if you don't mind. I've a mind to see Prudence. Been some days now since she came to the village. We are old friends. Our homes were side by side when we were girls."

Rose was glad for the company. As they passed the outskirts of Teeslow, Ellie spoke again.

"She was surprised by Kyle's marriage, Prudence was. Concerned too. She told me, but no one else."

"I hope that she is not so concerned now that she has met me."

"T'weren't you that concerned her." Ellie's white kerchief bobbed along with her heavy gait. "She wants the best for him, of course. She understood why marrying you would be good for his future."

"Then what concerned her?"

Ellie frowned, as if making a decision whether to

answer. "I did not know at first. Then the rumor started in the village. About you and Norbury."

Rose's heart sank. The whole village knew. They might be interested in her as Kyle's lady wife, but they were also curious about Norbury's whore.

Would something be said to him, even while he tried to help? Would some man who disliked compromise make a comment that alluded to her past?

Rose had never regretted her foolishness with Norbury more than at this moment, while she walked beside solid, honest Ellie on this lane so often traversed by the people Kyle had known since birth.

"I did not think that story would find its way to Teeslow," she said. "I did not think that my presence by his side today would embarrass him. I wish now that I had heeded his request that I return to Prudence at once."

"He married you, didn't he? He can't be too embarrassed by you. As for that story coming here, well, it began being told after the earl's son visited a few weeks ago. No one missed the coincidence of that. We aren't stupid, and we know there's bad blood between those two and some of us know why."

"You mean that thrashing he gave Norbury when they were young. Yes, I can see how that would leave things bad between them." It sounded like Norbury was still a boy, spreading stories to get back at the one who had beat him.

Ellie looked at her with a peculiar expression. "It wasn't the thrashing itself. Even if Kyle had lost that fight, he'd'a won. He'd'a proven that there's things no one should do, no matter what their birth. That there is right and wrong for all of us, and it doesn't change if you are from the manor. Humiliating to have your inferior remind you of that, I expect. Twice now, from the sounds of it."

"Was the first time about a woman too?"

They were at the point where the lane to Harold's house branched off. Ellie squinted in that direction, as if she could see the people who lived there.

"He didn't tell you why he took on an earl's son and those other boys? I guess I'm not surprised. It was so long ago." Her chin rose in the direction of the house. "Pru never speaks of it, as if silence makes it go away. She did once, though, to me and a few others. So we know what we'll have nearby when the earl dies and his son gets Kirtonlow Hall. Let's just say the son ain't the father, and has a bad way with women. Always has."

They walked up the lane together. Prudence was delighted to see her old friend. Rose left them together in the kitchen and went above to hang Kyle's coats.

Ellie had not been very clear in her condemnation of Norbury, but she had said enough that it troubled Rose. It seemed that Kyle had a history of challenging Norbury's sense of rights and prerogatives. In a way he was doing it again today in investigating that tunnel.

That was the least of it, however. According to Ellie, only a few people knew the real reason Kyle had thrashed Norbury all those years ago. And Prudence had been the one to tell them.

Which meant it was all about Prudence to begin with.

Kyle dragged himself out of the carriage and into the dark. He reached for the sky and stretched his whole body.

He had forgotten how low that tunnel was. Even men shorter than he had to bend over to make their way. He had just spent the last five hours twisting his body into unnatural positions in order to examine that stone.

He was grateful that Rose had left the carriage, but he dared not move inside it. Dirt covered his shirt, his hair, his . . . everything. Dirt and black dust. Even in the moonlight he could see the large smudges on his arms.

The house appeared dark. Everyone had gone to sleep. Just as well. He did not want Rose seeing him like this. Sending him off to do a good deed was one thing. Having him return looking like the collier he was born to be was another.

Light leaked from the kitchen, etching a few shapes in the front rooms. A dwindling fire cast a faint glow in the sitting room. A figure curled itself in Harold's chair, but it was not his uncle. Rose slept there in her night-dress and a big shawl, her legs drawn up on the cushion and her bare feet rosy from the fire's heat.

She had taken down her hair and brushed it until it flowed like a golden, glossy river. Her lips and eye-lashes appeared very dark in the faint illumination.

He needed food and hot water and was so tired that he could barely stand, but she dazzled him into dumb astonishment. Like she always had. Like she always would. *Not for you, boy.*

Her effect on him was even stronger now. She was no longer a stunning face viewed across a theater or seen in the moonlight. She was not even just the passionate woman he had possessed in soul-shattering fulfillment. He was coming to know her so well, so thoroughly, that his knowing of her changed his knowing of himself.

The shawl had fallen off the shoulder turned toward the fire. He carefully lifted it back in place so she would not be cold. He left her sleeping and went to the kitchen.

The bath that Rose had promised waited, with the tin tub half filled with water. Buckets of more water warmed by the hearth. A crockery bowl inverted over a plate stood on the table.

He lifted the bowl to find cold fowl and cheese and bread. He took a cup into the storeroom and helped himself from the small keg of ale that Harold had tapped there. He carried it back and sat down to eat.

The food helped, but sitting only reminded him of his sore body. He got up and poured one of the buckets into the tub. As he reached for another, a white sleeve and feminine hand took the third.

Rose poured her bucket, then faced him. He did not miss how her gaze took in all the dirt and dust. She was too good to show distaste, but not so practiced as to totally hide her surprise.

"I was correct. You will need this bath." She reached for another bucket.

He took it from her. "I will do it."

"I have prepared many in my time, Kyle."

"Now that you are married to me you are not supposed to have to perform such tasks anymore."

"I do not remember that part of the settlement. If Prudence allowed a servant in her home I would gladly hand the duty over, but you would better spend your time getting out of those clothes and having a good soak."

She did not wait for agreement, but set to lifting and pouring the rest of the buckets. He stripped off his clothes, stepped into the tub, and sank low in the steaming water.

She picked up his shirt and breeches. "Can they be cleaned?"

"Not pristine clean, if that is what you mean. Put them outside the back door. Pru will know what to do."

She did as he said, then knelt behind him and started scrubbing his back. Her matter-of-fact service charmed him with its calm domesticity. She had probably done this when she was younger, before her brothers became bankers. There had been some bad years then. She probably had a lot of experience in keeping men clean.

There was no insinuation of seduction in the way this bath progressed. She no doubt had taken one look at him covered in coal dust, his eyes red from bad light and bad air, and lost interest in that. Or realized that he certainly had.

"Did you accomplish much today? Do you think you can help them?" she asked.

"Not much was done today, but enough to know what I need to do tomorrow. And the next day. I need some tools. I told the manager that if he did not loan them to me that I would go to the earl and come back with written permission."

He had dropped the earl's name so often today that the man would turn in his grave if he were not still alive. He was pushing that relationship to its limit even as it entered its final days. He hoped and trusted that Cottington would understand if he ever learned of it.

Rose rinsed her rag, soaped it again, and handed it to

him to use. She scooted to the tub's side and sat cross-legged on the floor. "I met some of the village women today after you left. We spoke for a while."

"What did you talk about?"

She shrugged. "Women things."

She dipped her finger into a little pool of water on the worn floor planks near her foot. She drew a water sketch with it.

"They all know. About me. He made sure everyone knew that you had married his whore. Norbury did."

"Who told you this?"

"A woman named Ellie. She is one of Pru's friends from girlhood. She walked me back and they visited for an hour or so."

"It was unkind of her to tell you that. However, you are not the first woman to make a mistake about a man, Rose. If I remember correctly, Ellie had her first child a mere seven months after she wed. A big, strapping babe it was too."

She smiled while she elaborated her water drawing. "You are very sweet to try to make me feel less awkward about it. Ellie said something else that was interesting. She told me that when you were a boy and you thrashed Norbury, it was about how he treated a woman. I think it was your aunt, from what Ellie said."

"That is true. He and some of his friends were interfering with her, making sport of her the way bad boys do sometimes." He continued washing. "What else did Ellie say?"

"A lot of nice things about you. She was a little mysterious about that thrashing. She said a few of them knew the truth of it because Prudence had told them.

Something about Pru saying it should be known what they had in Norbury and would have in the future when he inherited."

Kyle kept his attention on the rag and the soap. He listened for sounds from above, from the chamber where Pru and Harold slept. He guessed Pru had kept her silence about that day for a long time. Years maybe. He thought he knew what she had finally confided in Ellie and a few others, and why.

He felt less tired now. Food and washing the day off had given him back some energy. The bath's heat had served like a long sleep.

Anger revitalized him too. Anger at his own ignorance all these years. A convenient ignorance. If he had known the truth he doubted he could have seen the earl's gifts as anything other than bribery for silence.

Rose got up. "It is very late. You will have another hard day tomorrow. You should get some sleep now."

She padded over to the hearth. The flames sent hot light through her nightdress, revealing the shape of her body in an alluring silhouette. He watched the swells of her bottom and breasts move while she picked up a large towel warming on the hearthstone.

She carried the towel back to him. He stood and dried himself. She watched, much as she had watched last night while she sat in that bed so determined to have a conversation that could have been avoided for a lifetime.

Her gaze drifted lower. "It appears that you are recovered from the day's exertions. Rather decidedly." She reached out and lightly stroked the prominent evidence of that. "It is amazing what some ale and food will do. I trust that you can walk up the stairs?"

"To hell with that." He cast aside the towel and grabbed her. Desire cracked through him with unholy fury and he claimed her mouth with a hard kiss. That was the anger having its way, even if it was not directed at her.

He needed to have her. Now. He needed to bury himself in her warmth and softness. He turned her to the plaster wall and lifted her nightdress so her legs and bottom were bare.

He kissed her neck and nape and stepped closely so he covered her. He slid his cock between her legs until it nestled in her damp warmth. The feel of her only made him harder, more impatient. He pressed so the pressure caressed her, and reached around her body to tease her breasts. She began caressing him too, through the subtle sway of her hips and the pulses of her lower lips.

Madness descended. Fire and desire owned him. He turned her and lifted her even as he thrust into her. She wrapped her legs around his hips and clung to him and absorbed his reckless hunger.

Kyle scratched out the third copy of his report. There would be four in all, lengthy and detailed and complete, with drawings to show how to make that tunnel safe. He intended to give one to the manager and one to the workers, but he would also send one each to Cottington and to the owners. The original would return to London with him, to be copied yet again if he thought it needed to be.

Rose slept above. He checked his pocket watch. Dawn would come soon. He would deliver these documents, and he and Rose would start for London by noon.

Five days he had descended into that mine, often enough for it to become familiar again. He would not even need the lamps to know his way today. And while he had studied cracks and supports near the tunnel, the sound of pickaxes chipping away earth and lives had echoed toward him.

"Have you been up all night, Kyle? That is not healthy."

He looked to the doorway. Prudence stood there, wrapping on an apron.

"I am almost finished. I can sleep in the carriage."

She came over and stood near him, gazing down at the stacks of papers. "Thank you for doing this. They are all grateful. I am too."

She lifted a bucket and went outside to draw water at the well he'd had dug in the garden. He finished the last page and set aside his pen.

Pru returned and began moving pots near the hearth. She did not have to begin her day so early now, but the habit of a lifetime was not easily set aside.

"Aunt Pru, before I leave I want to talk to you about something. Since no one else is about, now would be a good time."

Her hand stilled on a pot handle. Perhaps it had been his tone. Maybe she just knew, the way some people can sense a summer storm approaching.

She continued her work. "Of course, Kyle."

"Ellie told Rose that you explained to some women

the truth about Norbury. I would like to know that truth as well."

"I would say that you know the truth about him better than most."

"But not better than you, Pru. I am almost sure of it."

She knelt and built up the fire. She remained so impassive she might not have heard him.

"What did you tell Ellie and the other women, Pru?"

"If it was something for your ears, I would have told you too," she snapped. Her face flushed. "Ellie is an old gossip and I will burn her ears when I see her next. To tell your wife—"

"She told Rose very little, and only to reassure her about the village's view of Rose's own history with Norbury. Another woman would have taken the kindness at face worth, but Rose is...curious." Oddly so. She had been picking through the details of his life here.

"I said he is a scoundrel and not to be trusted around women. No news there, to you or Rose." She spoke with finality.

He did not blame her for not wanting to speak of it. He debated leaving it alone. Leaving her alone too.

He walked over to the fireplace. He leaned against the hearth wall so he could see her while she worked. She acknowledged him with a quick glance but kept her gaze on the water she had set to boil.

"I have been thinking about that day, Pru, when I found you with him and his two friends, in the trees near the road to Kirtonlow Hall. I have been thinking about the cries and jeers that led me there, and what I saw. I was a boy, and I wonder if I misunderstood. Maybe I wanted to misunderstand."

She looked at him with sad eyes. Angry eyes. She glanced above her, to the chamber where Harold slept. Abruptly she walked to the door and out to the garden.

He followed. She strode through the barren fruit trees to the far edge of the orchard. She faced him with her arms crossed.

"Why do you speak of this now, after all these years?"

"I do not know. Maybe what happened to Rose caused me to start wondering."

"Better if you did not wonder, Kyle. It was long ago. The father will be dead soon, and you'll be dealing with the son."

"Let me worry about the dealing. Am I right? Did I get there too late, Pru?"

"What's the good of knowing? There's nothing to be done now."

"I'll know what I have in him in that dealing. If you broke your silence so the women would know, you can understand why I might need to as well."

She gazed at the fruit trees now taking form in the gray light seeping through the air. He barely saw her nod.

"The earl knew," she said. "The son lied to him, but the friends were too afraid to lie too. So the earl knew. Offered me good money, he did. I refused. I said I would see his son in the dock and even if he went free the whole world would learn he was only a well-born pig."

"When did he make this offer?"

"The day before he sent for you. I knew while I scrubbed you that day how it would be. That he'd thought of another way to make it worth my while to keep silent. He never said a word about it. Never threatened to send you back to the mine if I spoke, but I knew."

And Cottington had known she would know. The earl had seen this angry woman and recognized her intelligence and realized he would never have to mention his motives for her to see the largesse in those terms.

So there was probably one more why, other than the ones the earl had given. On the other hand, Cottington was not stupid. He knew that for some crimes there could be no restitution, no making whole again.

"I don't mind," she said. "He'd'a never been convicted, of course. Better this way, and that you became the man you are. I imagine he sees you in London, and he knows you are only there because of that day. He sees that his father made a better man out of a boy from Teeslow than he himself will ever be. There's some satisfaction in that. A lot more than pointing at him in court, I tell myself."

"I am sorry that you never had the satisfaction of pointing to him in court, Pru."

"It is not an easy thing for a woman to do. There's always them that will say she asked for it, isn't there? It is what he would of said, and many would of believed it. Women know how it will be if they accuse a man of that." She reached up and patted his face like he was a boy. "So now you know, for all the good it will do. Better if you just wondered, seems to me."

"Does Harold know?"

"He never asked outright and I never said. But he guessed; I could tell. It took a few years to put it behind us. If I had told him he would of had to kill Norbury, wouldn't he? Then he would have swung. So I held my tongue in the end. But now, with the earl dying—Norbury will be in these parts more. He hasn't changed, as you know. So I told some of the older women in the village, so they could keep an eye on things and warn off the young ones."

She began walking to the house and he fell in step with her. "As I know? If you mean Rose, it was not the same."

"From what I hear, it was close enough except that you interfered." Pru shook her head. "Poor thing, to believe he loved her only to find he just wanted his way with her. Then she refuses him and what happens? He tries to sell her to another, who would of only taken her against her will instead of him. All of a piece, most of those highborn men are."

He almost corrected her. Against all odds, amazingly enough, Easterbrook's staging and new denouement of that auction had made its way all the way to Teeslow and circulated in the village after Norbury's version.

Kyle followed his aunt back into the kitchen. He had wondered, and now he knew. Hopefully the spiking impulse to find Norbury and kill him would pass in a day or so.

CHAPTER
SEVENTEEN

❧

"They have all accepted. The dinner party promises to be a success." Alexia shared the news while she and Rose left her house on Hill Street. "You will look perfect in that geranium dinner dress you ordered. We are on our way to another small but important victory."

Rose squeezed Alexia's hand in a gesture of gratitude. Glove in glove they strolled toward Hyde Park.

The prospect of another pending social advance could not raise Rose's spirits. She had been back in London for three days now. Three happy days and three glorious nights.

Her fear that the new warmth in her marriage might end with the return to town had not been justified. The first night back, she and Kyle had been so eager to continue the explorations that they had each gone to the other and bumped into each other in her dark dressing room.

She would never open her wardrobe again without thinking of how he made her embrace it, naked and spread-legged, while he covered her body with his and took her from behind.

Unfortunately, this morning a cloud had marred the sated, joyful aftermath of the night. A letter had arrived from the family solicitor, asking for a meeting about the property in Oxfordshire.

She had not thought about Timothy's plight at all while she was up north. There had been freedom in the absence of worry over her brother. Now his demands harped on her conscience again.

The pending meeting with the solicitor unsettled her. She had drawn Alexia out on this walk in part to delay it a few hours at least.

"You were up north longer than I expected," Alexia said. "I feared Mrs. Vaughn would think I had decided not to go forward with the dinner, or had chosen not to invite her. Such a misunderstanding would have been unfortunate. Is all well with your husband's family?"

"Well enough. I liked them, Alexia. They are both honest, good people. I would like to think that they think better of me now too."

"No one who meets you would think badly of you. That is why we are seeing such progress in our plans. That and the evidence that a revised interpretation of that scandalous auction is being whispered. One in which you are an innocent damsel and Norbury is the worst rake. I confess that I have not felt obligated to disabuse anyone of this other version of events."

"Normally people are inclined to think the worst, not stretch their minds to find excuses for a woman in such a scandal."

"The world knows the viscount, and does not like him much. He is not a very pleasant man, and there have been rumors about his excesses for years. You, in turn, have led an exemplary life. Let the error stand. Norbury's behavior toward you was vile enough to deserve this misunderstanding."

They entered the park, barren now of fresh growth and people. A few bodies dotted the walks, but the weather, the month, and the time of day ensured vast privacy.

"I appreciate all that you are doing for me, Alexia. And yet I wish that Kyle could attend this party too. He says that you should not fight a war on two fronts at once. I just think it odd that Mrs. Vaughn and her husband are willing to overlook that I have been labeled a whore, but not that my husband was born in a mining village."

"That you chafe at the injustice speaks well for your marriage. It shows that a mutual sympathy is growing."

Rose doubted Alexia guessed the half of it. She wanted to tell her cousin about this man she had married. She sought the words to describe how safe and alive and defenseless she felt in his embrace.

In the least she would announce that the world be damned, she would not attend any dinner parties from which he was deliberately excluded.

Alexia spoke first. "Now, about Irene, I have a proposal to suggest. A most astonishing one."

The mention of Irene stopped the words forming on Rose's tongue. This war was about her sister more than herself. Even her marriage had mostly been for Irene's sake.

"I think this season will be too early for her," Rose said. "You are too optimistic if you believe otherwise."

"Hear me out before you discard the notion. I have

been aware all along that this child will interfere as surely as your scandal." Alexia instinctively placed her hand on the large swell beneath her aurora blue pelisse. "I mentioned that when Hayden and I were dining over at his brother's house a fortnight ago. Hayden is sympathetic to Irene's plight, but he has been most firm that I not take on more than he thinks my frail strength can endure."

"Your husband is correct. The timing of your child's pending arrival is the strongest argument. Irene can wait one more year."

"That appears to be the thinking, and after that dinner I was swayed myself. Imagine my surprise when Henrietta came to me a few days ago and proposed that she hold a ball in April and that it be the event at which Irene comes out."

"Henrietta? You amaze me."

"I amaze myself. She amazes me even more. If a love affair can bring about such a change in a woman, I pray that every harpy in society finds a lover before the season."

"Perhaps arranging such affairs should be our real strategy. Happiness in that area of life tends to influence one's view of most things."

Alexia arched an eyebrow. "And what is your view of most things these days, Roselyn? You proposed this turn in the park despite the bite in the air and the heavy clouds overhead. Perchance you did not notice the weather this morning, but saw a fair day despite winter's chill."

Rose felt her face warming. Alexia laughed, leaned over, and kissed her hot cheek. "Since I argued for you to make this match, I am relieved if one part of it suits you. I think there would be nothing more tiresome than viewing the marriage bed as a place for nothing but duty."

Not duty. Never just that. Kyle had always been a considerate lover, one who knew that their marriage would be more contented if she experienced pleasure too.

And now, since that night in Teeslow, their time together in bed was the best time. In some ways it was the only time when she was completely at ease with him, and sure that she had not made a mistake.

It could be enough. His words in her ear, his breath on her hair and breast, even the masterful way he moved her body and demanded surrenders that she never questioned. The pleasure alone could make it enough, but the scorching brands he left on her spirit made her more his and less her own with every encounter.

Like a good meal, that was how he described carnal pleasure that day she accepted his proposal. They were dining very well of late. Most likely that was all it remained to him. A varied menu with many delights.

So why was she feeling less practical every day in this practical marriage? Kyle would probably say that she was making the same mistake in pleasure that she had made in the lack of it, confusing the physical side of life with the emotional. The new familiarity that came with these explorations was inevitable, most likely. Men probably reacted the same way to the sensual artists in brothels.

All the same, ties were forming that complicated certain things. Like this meeting that she would have today with that solicitor.

"Alexia, have you ever deceived Hayden? Disobeyed him?"

Alexia paced on while she contemplated the question. "Once or twice. I told myself I did not, but of course that was only so I could justify doing it." She smiled to herself while a private memory seemed to play out in her head. "He caught me in the worst deception. I doubt that I will try another one soon, or need to."

"Did you feel guilty?"

"In passing I did. However, there are some things husbands do not need to know. I committed a few sins of omission in the tally of total honesty because the matter was important to me in ways he would never have understood at the time." She considered her own answer. "He would understand now, but such comprehension takes a good while to achieve in a marriage made even under the best of circumstances, which ours was not."

Typical of Alexia, it was a forthright, measured answer to a difficult and intrusive question. Rose guessed what her cousin did not explain. Those important deceptions had been about Rose herself, and Irene and Tim, and about Alexia's determination to preserve the family that hated the man she had married.

"Why do you ask, Rose? Circumstances left me alone while I made my choice, but you need not be."

Rose considered confiding. Alexia would be discreet. She would not even tell Hayden if asked to keep a secret.

However, Alexia had not been agreeable that Tim needed help. She had argued firmly against that idea of joining him.

Tim was dead to Alexia. She had learned the worst firsthand. She had watched Tim flee and leave Hayden to risk his own fortune to save the remnants of the Longworth family and reputation. And Alexia had probably known for a long time just how much money had been stolen.

Alexia would never condone the small deception that Rose now faced. Not for Tim's benefit. Nor would it be fair to distress her again by the sordid consequences of the Longworths' bad behavior.

"I love you, Alexia, and I am grateful for the offer of a sympathetic ear. I fear that circumstances leave me to decide on my own, just as you did."

Mr. Yardley managed to communicate precise professionalism in every way possible. He greeted Rose in his law chambers near Lincoln's Inn with the sort of bland, polite words that a business meeting called for. He settled her into a chair and faced her with his stack of documents. He smiled to put her at ease. A clerk sat at a desk nearby, silent and inconspicuous, pen poised to make notes.

Mr. Yardley's high collar points squeezed his pudgy jaws and his cravat hugged his double chin. His fashionably cut locks did not tousle much because his graying hair had thinned too much to allow it. An experienced solicitor who had long served the Longworth family, first their father and then the sons, he had not seen any respectable business from them for a year now.

Rose waited for her inquiry to be addressed. The solicitor appeared cautious. No doubt his own reputation had been stained by her brother's spectacular ruin. To now serve Timothy might be so distasteful that Mr. Yardley had concluded that he wanted no part of the disposal of the property. This meeting could be a dismissal and final farewell.

He cleared his throat. "Mrs. Bradwell, I researched the law and concluded that your brother's proxy would withstand scrutiny. On the basis of this letter, I could sell the property in his name."

"That is good news, sir. When can we do this? How long will it take to effect such a sale?"

He cleared his throat again. "There is a complication. I regret to say that the property cannot be sold."

She cocked her head in question. "You are confusing me. Please explain why it cannot be sold."

"Perhaps if I met with your husband..."

"The property is not mine, but my brother's, and my husband has no authority in the matter. I think that I can understand the situation if you endeavor to make it comprehensible."

His mouth puffed. Mr. Yardley was not comfortable explaining financial matters to women, it appeared.

"Mrs. Bradwell, when your brother fled his debts the property became vulnerable to his debtors." He put a meaningful emphasis on the word debts, indicating that he was one person at least who knew about the crimes behind those debts. "Lord Hayden Rothwell placed a lien on the property at that time. I have the document here. It was only that lien that kept other creditors from taking it in payment for their own losses."

"I was aware that Lord Hayden had done something to protect the property. I am grateful that he did. I did not realize that his lien was still on it."

She should have anticipated this. She could hardly blame Lord Hayden if the lien remained now, even after all those debtors had been repaid. He had been the one to repay them, after all. Even if he took the property in return, she could not object.

"Actually, his lien was removed late last summer."

"If this lien was removed and the property is a freehold and the proxy will stand, what stops the sale?"

"Another lien."

"So there were two? I do not believe that Lord Hayden would remove his, which was intended to protect our family estate, and leave it vulnerable to a second creditor."

"This second one was not on it when Lord Hayden removed his. It is newer. It was entered against the property just a few months ago."

"This is most alarming, Mr. Yardley. Why did you not inform me when it happened?"

"My service was to your brother, who appeared to no longer need it, considering the developments in the last year regarding his fortune, his debts, and his new residence abroad. In short, Madam, I assumed that our relationship had ended so I no longer addressed matters of your family's concern. Your inquiry regarding this proxy surprised me as much as my report today surprises you."

She stood and paced away. The chamber window overlooked the street where a fine rain drizzled down on people and carriages. Her own coachman was leading her carriage out so as to walk and warm the pair that drew it.

A new lien. It appeared that Lord Hayden has missed

one or two of those debts. Finding all of the victims might have been impossible within the tangled web that fraud had made.

"How far has this claim on the property gone, Mr. Yardley?"

The land might be taken soon. She and Irene could lose the home they had known all their lives. They would be uprooted from that soil as surely as plants after the harvest. She had not let herself think about that when a sale meant helping Tim, but now the full implications pained her heart.

Memories came to her, dozens of them, of happy times and sad ones. Of her older brother Ben announcing that he was buying into a bank where he would work in turn, stepping down in the world so they all could live better in the end. Of Tim as a child climbing that apple tree in the garden and pelting her with small fruit when she tried to follow. Of lying on that hill and feeling so dangerously free for an hour.

Of Kyle kissing her for the first time in an unexpected, bold reach across the formalities and differences that separated them.

"Other than the lien itself, it does not appear that any further steps have been taken. It just sits there, much as Lord Hayden's did. However, it also prevents any sale."

She turned to face him. He was standing, as was his clerk.

"If this new lien just sits there, perhaps the person who makes this claim can be convinced to remove it. As you can see from my brother's letter, his situation could become serious if I do not send him these funds."

Mr. Yardley was too polite to respond but his eyes

said it all. Tim in a serious situation would not sadden anyone but his closest relatives. "I think that it is unlikely that the lien will be withdrawn. They are not filed capriciously."

"I must try, nonetheless. I understand that this service does not appeal to you, sir. I will attempt to do it myself. Please write down the name of this creditor for me. I will write to him, or ask Lord Hayden to do so for me."

He hesitated. Then he looked at his clerk and nodded. The clerk picked up his pen, bent over his desk, and jotted.

The clerk folded the paper and brought it to her. She tucked it in her reticule and took her leave.

Once in the dry confinement of her carriage she plucked the paper out again. She pushed back the curtain for light and unfolded the note.

She immediately understood Mr. Yardley's ill ease and circuitous explanations.

She stared dumbfounded at the name of the person whose lien now interfered with the sale of that property.

Mr. Kyle Bradwell.

CHAPTER
EIGHTEEN

﹏

Kyle's visitor left with a signed agreement in hand but none too pleased by its terms. The first result had been assured from the moment the man walked in the door. The latter had resulted from an unexpected determination that gripped Kyle during the negotiations.

Normally he would have sacrificed a few pounds in exchange for a pleasant farewell. Today, however, he had not viewed this purveyor of timber with equanimity. The negotiations had become a game that Kyle was determined to win, not end in a draw.

He watched the door of his business offices close. The paper that had just walked out represented a lot of money. That timber would be coming from Norway. Maybe it had been a draw after all.

He slid out of his frock coat and laid it on a chair. He found it harder now to hide himself on the edges of this new world in which he lived and worked. A vitality had reclaimed him, one that did not like how he had been swallowing his natural character.

Rose had brought this about. He felt like himself

again when he was with her. Even in his own thoughts, in his reflections and plans, he had constructed walls and limitations these last years. In attempting to hide the fact that he did not belong, he had lost hold on who he was.

He stood over his desk and looked down on the paper that held the bones of the new agreement. He set it aside and glanced at a page of notes he had made this morning. They roughly charted extraordinary ideas. Daring. Audacious. The kind of ideas that had come in torrents when he was younger. He had not released that side of his character since his first year back from France.

Rose seemed to like the self he was. She appeared to approve of the hybrid man that past and present had created.

The notes faded and he saw only her. He remembered her this morning as dawn broke, her silken hair streaming over his arm and her warmth pulsing into him with her heartbeat. Her beauty mesmerized him as it always had, but it was not some distant woman now stealing his breath. It was not even the lovely lady who had traded her life and the rights to her body in a bid for redemption.

More images came. Erotic ones but also those in which desire played little role. Simple details had branded his brain. The curve of her face in the light of her Oxfordshire garden. Her hand lifting a fork. Little glimpses of beauty and grace popped into his mind all the time. Perhaps he had pressed the lumber seller with such determination because anything less forceful would have dissolved into daydreams about Roselyn.

She surprised him again and again. Not only in bed.
That was just a reflection of the other changes between
them. He had not expected much of anything in this
marriage, least of all from her. He certainly had not anticipated the joy that her company brought him.

She was calling on Alexia today. He wondered if she
had returned home yet.

If he went to her right now she would never let him
know if he interfered with her day. Maybe she would
even put her plans aside and lure him back into the raging desire and seismic fulfillment where he both lost
and rediscovered himself.

Perhaps—

A sound from the outer room disturbed his happy
thoughts. He walked over and opened the connecting
door.

Roselyn paced there, as if summoned by his contemplation of her. Her steps sounded in rhythmic thuds on
the wooden floor. She glanced at the scrivener's podium,
then at the door where he stood. She stopped walking
and just looked at him.

Something was wrong. It affected her posture and
the tilt of her head. It had sounded in those steps. The
sparking, brittle lights in her eyes made it clear that his
soft, sweet wife was very, very angry.

"I have not been here before," she announced, as if to
answer a challenge that he had no interest in making. "I
was in the City and thought that I would visit you."

"I am glad that you did. If I knew you were curious,
I would have brought you here before."

"Where is your clerk? Is he in there?"

"I do not use one. I write my own letters, and my solicitor ensures that any indentures are composed accurately."

The thin line of her mouth was too sardonic to be called a real smile. "They are useful in many ways, solicitors."

"Won't you come in? There are chairs in here."

She hesitated, then allowed him to usher her into his office.

She walked around, taking in the views from the windows and the measure of the chamber. Her slow, perceptive gaze noticed the jewel-toned carpet, the mahogany furniture, the tall cases for books and the big, shallow drawers for maps.

"It is very tasteful. Like a men's club, I would guess. Or a Mayfair library. Unexceptional but also unobjectionable. Like your coats."

He heard no sympathy in her assessment. This was not the woman in Teeslow who had comprehended better than he had the reasons behind the mold he had adopted. This was a woman who now implied those careful choices were deceptions and calculations. Since they partly were, he was not insulted.

He threw some fuel on the fire. "It is damp and you should warm yourself. Did you visit with Alexia today? Before you came to the City?"

She positioned herself by the fire. "Yes. She is full of plans for me and Irene. She is too good."

The fire cast a golden glow on her face. For a few seconds, while he watched the way that warmth brightened her eye and flushed her perfect skin, he forgot that her arrival was unusual and that she was angry about something.

She turned to face him fully. "I did not come here because I was curious about these chambers or your business affairs. I should have been. Just as I should have been more curious about your family and about your past. I have been guilty of a terrible self-absorption in my recent life, always seeing events in terms of me, not others. The truth is that I am so insignificant that even matters that touch on me are actually about other, more important things."

"While no event or action is isolated in its reason or result, you are wrong in saying that you are insignificant."

"I wonder."

She did. He saw skepticism in her gaze. She wondered about *him*.

"Kyle, I always assumed that all of Tim's victims, all the bank clients who had seen losses, were made whole. You said as much. Even your aunt and uncle."

"That is true. They all were."

"But not all of them received restitution from Lord Hayden, did they?"

"No, he was not bled by everyone."

"Bled? No one asked for that money from him."

"He bled all the same."

She absorbed that. Kyle knew they would not speak of it. The costs to Lord Hayden were an inconvenient, uncomfortable truth.

"I expect that most of those people were very angry, Kyle. Taking Lord Hayden's money would require that they give up that anger. It would have no anchor once they were repaid. Is that why you did not take it?"

So that was what this was about. "Did Alexia tell

you about this? That I would not take her husband's
money?"

"No."

But someone had. Or else Rose had figured it out
herself. He could not imagine how. "Pru and Harold
were the victims, not me. I was the trustee, however. I
could not accept Lord Hayden's offer. I do not understand how anyone could. It was not his crime."

"They could because they wanted their money back,
Kyle. The only cost of getting it was to release the anger
and to ignore the crime. What did you do instead?
Replace the funds for them? Once more invest your own
money in the trust?"

"I had a responsibility to them. My poor judgment in
banks caused the loss. Of course I ensured they did not
lose it."

"They would not have lost it if you had allowed Lord
Hayden to make up the loss. I think you did not because
then you would have no excuse for seeking revenge."

There was a good dose of truth in that. Kyle recognized it now. At the time he had not. In any event, Rose
was touching on matters that he could never explain in
ways she would accept or understand.

She walked up to him until she stood very close. She
peered into his eyes with a curious, questioning gaze.
She examined a stranger. "You are no Hayden Rothwell.
I daresay twenty thousand would make *you* blink. I
think much less would."

"I blinked long and hard, Rose. I am still blinking."

"Except that you found a way to cease blinking, I
think. If not today, then soon enough."

Her natural grace and poised demeanor barely held

in a fury that blazed through her, visible only in her tight expression and piercing, hot gaze.

He saw something else too. The subtle hardness that he had glimpsed when he first met Rose had returned. She had again donned the armor of pride that had allowed her to survive her family's ruin and her enforced poverty and isolation.

He reached for her, to draw her closer. To embrace her so that wherever this argument led, it did not take her too far away.

She pivoted and strode beyond his touch. "You are very good, Kyle. No wonder you have been successful. You admit to nothing. You do not speak at all, lest it put you at a disadvantage."

"I assume that you will explain what has unsettled you so much. I am waiting for you to tell me."

"Unsettled? *Unsettled?* That is a fine word for it." Her words sliced across the chamber. She closed her eyes briefly while she found her composure again. "I learned about my family's property in Oxfordshire today. I know that you have made a claim against it."

"How did you learn that?"

"How? I discover a duplicity that I never expected, and all you wonder is how?" She began pacing. Her fury flew. His own had begun rising with her revelation too.

"When did you do this, Kyle? After that first visit you made? You examined that house and sized up the land most thoroughly that day. You asked if it was a freehold. Stupid me, I thought you asked as a concerned friend. As my knight in shining armor. You were only calculating your potential gain."

"That is not true, damn it."

"You *knew* it was my brother's. Only I did not know that you were the one creditor who in fact had never truly been repaid. Dear heavens, you even checked the soil to see if it had more value as farms than turned into new estates—"

"*How* did you find out about this?"

She ignored him. Her eyes widened in shock. "Oh, my, I even gave you the name of another man who would buy it all if you could not be bothered to build those estates yourself. You misled me most ignobly. You used me."

That did it. He strode over and pulled her into his arms. She squirmed in resistance but he held her firmly. She glared up at him.

A memory came to him, of teeth bared to fend off an assault.

"Let me go, Kyle."

"Soon. You will listen to me first. Yes, I made a claim against that property."

His admission did nothing for her temper. She twisted for release, petulantly, like a confined cat.

He held her still. "I do not intend to take it. I never did. I made the claim so no one else could, either. And also so it could not be sold."

She froze. Her eyes met his.

"How did you learn about my lien, Rose?"

"The family solicitor informed me."

"He would only look into it if you asked. So you must have asked. Why? Were you thinking of selling it somehow, and going to Timothy anyway?" The very notion had his mind howling with primitive, ferocious assertions of eternal possession.

"Of course not." Realization cleared her surprised frown. "Is that why you did it? To make sure that I never could go to him? You warned I would not, whether we married or not."

"Short of asking your cousin for the money, it was the only way you might be able to find the funds for such a journey."

"I said I would not go to him. I married you, didn't I? I am not so dishonest or so stupid as to make a promise and a marriage and then run away to an uncertain future with my brother."

She seemed to find some inner calm from her logical explanation.

He did not. If she had not been trying to sell the land for her own purposes, that meant she had someone else's purposes in mind.

They looked in each other's eyes and it was all there—the joy of the last two weeks, and the knowledge that they would never be as free together again. He could tell that she knew his question was coming even before he asked it. He felt her body brace against his arms.

"You have received mail from him again, haven't you? He asked you to sell the land. That is why you spoke with the solicitor."

Her nod was not demure. Her gaze still held enough heat to challenge him.

She had disobeyed him. That was the least of the urgent conclusions that lined up with swordlike sharpness in his head.

Not only had Rose had contact with her brother, but also she had taken steps on his behalf that could be traced. If anyone wanted to name her as an accomplice, she had just given that person a piece of evidence to make the accusation more plausible.

Kyle emerged from his desperate assessment to find her looking at him with an expression of curiosity and worry. He instinctively held her tighter in reaction to the danger potentially waiting.

She misunderstood. Her face fell in astonishment, as if the embrace had become dangerous.

He released her and moved away. He looked out the window so he would not have to look at her. He did not want her to see anything else that might frighten her.

"Your carriage is back, Rose. The coachman is done walking the horses. You should go now, while there is still plenty of light. I will walk you down."

They did not speak on the way to the carriage. She walked beside him like a queen, her posture declaring her pride and position. Her eyes appeared a little moist when he handed her into the carriage, but her anger showed more clearly.

He would do what he could about both the tears and the anger soon. Right now he needed to find out if her disobedience had made her vulnerable.

He closed the door of the carriage and looked in the window. "Burn his letter when you get home. Tell no one else that you received it. If asked, lie. You never saw it. You do not know where he is. Do you understand? Do not disobey me this time."

Her distant expression melted. She suddenly appeared so sad and dismayed that he wanted to climb in there and soothe her.

"I cannot burn it. It contains a proxy for our solicitor, and he kept it."

Damnation. Kyle signaled the coachman to move, then walked in the direction of that solicitor's office, calculating what he needed to do now, and what he needed to learn, and whether the day might come when he would have to trade Timothy Longworth's neck for Roselyn's freedom.

CHAPTER
NINETEEN

~~

Rose did not see Kyle again that day. He had not returned to the house by the time she retired. She lay alone in her bed for hours, trying not to listen for the sounds of his step in the corridor or the dressing room next door.

She remained angry enough that she was certain she did not want him coming to her, but she also worried about their argument and his stormy reaction to that letter from Timothy.

Kyle's anger had been too extreme for the small disobedience. Too big, too fast, too focused. After a few hours of reflection she realized that he had not really been angry about the disobedience at all. His command at the end, and the way he strode away—his anger had been born of worry, not male pique with an errant wife.

If so, what worried him? Something important. The man she knew did not release his determination for small matters. So far she had mostly seen him do so regarding her brother. But if Kyle was bent on revenge, he would not have commanded her to burn the letter with the proof of Tim's current abode. Instead he would have insisted that she hand it over.

He had not done so. He had not even asked the name of that town from where the letter was sent.

She finally slept, fitfully. On rising the next morning she learned that Kyle had come home late but left again early. Unable to settle into anything that could distract her, she paced the house, then called for the carriage at midday. She had the coachman take her to Hyde Park. There she set off on a long walk.

That helped relieve her restlessness, but did nothing for the sick dread sitting in her stomach. Her entire spirit waited for bad news. She expected their next meeting to be more formal than any they had ever had. She wondered if she could live in a marriage full of practicalities and chilled reserve after briefly knowing more.

After an hour of aimless wandering, she turned and retraced her steps on the park paths. She saw a horse trotting toward her. The man in the saddle rode tall and straight. His garments, his command of the animal, his posture—everything appeared precisely correct.

As he neared she saw the blue eyes that never failed to compel her attention, and the depths that they revealed if one looked into them. She sensed the vitality that affected the air, and the way he controlled his strength lest it be squandered or used for ill purposes.

The knot in her stomach rose. She both feared this meeting and wanted it with impatient anticipation. They had parted so poorly yesterday.

Kyle pulled the horse up beside her and looked

down. He dismounted. "We need to talk about yesterday, Roselyn."

She wished his presence comforted her, but it really did not. She remembered walking beside him on the lane near Watlington the first time he called. Just like then, he fell into step with her and led his horse.

That had been a very pleasant stroll compared to this one. The echoes of yesterday shot like a million invisible arrows between them.

"Are you going to scold?" she asked. She wished he would, if it would remove the distance between them.

"Perhaps. First I am going to explain." He turned those blue eyes on her. "I should have earlier."

"Why didn't you?"

"If I had, you would have declined my proposal. You badly wanted to. You were looking for a reason and my explanation would have given you one. You would have lied to yourself that escaping this life for another on the Continent was the only future worth having. It was what you wanted to believe."

"How generous of you to save me from myself."

"I wanted you, Roselyn. I saved you for *myself*."

Wanted her. Wanted a thing of beauty, a possession forbidden by his birth. She could not blame him for that. She had known the motives behind that proposal.

"You were correct yesterday," Kyle said. "In part I did not take restitution from Lord Hayden because refusing it allowed me to hold on to the anger and justified a hunger for revenge. I called it justice, but I admit the anger made it something else. I told myself that at least I did not take his money and still seek revenge the way others did."

She stopped walking and looked at him. She prayed his eyes would reflect something to negate the implications of his last two words.

"Others?"

"At least eight that I know of. A small group of men who do not accept Lord Hayden's notions of justice. They have an agent following your brother on the Continent, with the intention of bringing him back to England."

The sick sensation inside her spread. It invaded her heart, making it heavy with dread. "I do not understand why they go to such efforts. To embark on such a quest when the loss has been rectified—" The full meaning of his revelation sliced into her. "An agent—Tim will never escape. He lacks that kind of guile—"

Her mind scrambled through thoughts too sad and desperate to speak. "You were right. If I had known about this, I could not have stayed here. I would have had to try to help him. I could have found him a safe place to live and a way to hide. He will never manage it himself."

"Then I am very glad that I did not tell you. You would have thrown away your life, and maybe even your freedom."

She gazed over the parkland, so empty now. So very cold. Her thoughts calmed enough to sort through them. "Who are these men who are so determined to snare my brother?"

"Norbury is one."

Dear heavens. But then, his use of her had already been an effort for a kind of revenge. He had said as much at that auction.

"Who else?"

"Prideful men. Lords. Men of finance. Merchants . . . The sort who could lose enough to matter. The kind who would care that Timothy played them for fools."

His sober, firm words made her heart beat hard. "Men who would still blink at losing twenty thousand, though. Men like you."

He met her gaze squarely. "Men like me."

"You astonish me. You proposed to me even while you sought to see my brother hanged? Did you intend to watch to see if you could learn his whereabouts from my mail and—"

"It was suggested. I told you to destroy all the mail, remember? Once we married I was out of it. However, that might have been a mistake."

"A mistake!" A horrible idea shot through her gathering dismay. "That solicitor. The letter. You went there after I left yesterday, didn't you? You learned the town's name, and his assumed name, and you have now given it to Norbury and the others—"

Kyle gripped her arms gently and forced her to look in his eyes. "No, I have not. But everything I have done since you left my City chambers yesterday has been to protect you. You. Not him. I do not seek his head, Rose. I do not want revenge or even justice anymore, because it would bring you pain. But if the choice is ever between you and him, I will not let you suffer when you are innocent and he is not."

She was beyond words. She did not know whether to weep or scream.

He took her in his arms and she was too lost to object.

Warmth flowed to her, and sympathy, and a subtle sadness that only made her frightened.

"There is more, isn't there?" she whispered. "You did not follow me today to confess. You came to warn me about something."

Kyle kept his arm around her back so she was close to him while they strolled forward. "I ask that you listen to me, darling. I will explain everything."

Rose remained shaky within his vague embrace. Her face went lax while she absorbed his tale of the men who wanted her brother. Kyle did not spare himself. Had he not thrown in with Norbury and the others at the start, he would have avoided the hellish decision that might face him soon.

"If I had not removed myself, I would have at least known how things stand," he explained. "Yesterday I sought out one of the others and learned easily enough, however."

Her lids lowered, as though one more blow would not surprise her now. "How do they stand?"

He hated telling her. Hated it. "They heard from Royds, their agent. The letter was written weeks ago. He was in Tuscany then. Royds knows Timothy is in the region and using the name Goddard."

"He will find him, you mean. Perhaps he already has."

Perhaps. The only good part of that discovery was it meant no one could demand that Rose give over the information herself or that her husband force it out of her, the way Norbury had wanted.

Still, the threat to accuse her of being an accomplice still hung there. There would be no gain from it now, most likely, unless Royds was frustrated in his attempts to track Longworth in all those small Tuscan towns.

"Why did you care so much about the solicitor and Tim's letter?" Her spirit had been bludgeoned, but her mind had not dulled. "If you were removed from it, if you did not want to know his name and town, why did you react so hard when you learned about it?"

He had come here to tell her everything. To give her the total honesty that she had requested the day she met him in Regent's Park. He gazed at her distress and weighed what total honesty really meant in a situation like this.

There may be no danger now. If Royds found Longworth on his own, no one would be threatening to name Rose as an accomplice.

"I saw him and demanded that he burn that letter. I said that I would not remove the lien, so the proxy is worthless. It is best destroyed, Rose, so no one knows that you received word of his whereabouts."

"Did he burn it?"

"I watched it go in the fire."

That seemed to reassure her. More than it probably ought, but she was too sad and unsettled to parse through the words and see the holes.

Yardley had indeed burned the letter, but only after Kyle himself had read it. And even with the letter gone, Yardley knew it had been written and sent to Roselyn Longworth. Solicitors were sworn to discretion in their clients' affairs, but if pressed there was no telling if

Yardley would keep his silence about the ongoing communication between Roselyn and her criminal brother.

A sword hung over Rose. She felt its edge aiming down.

A sad little ritual began her days. She would relinquish the comfort of Kyle's embrace when he left her near dawn. She would not sleep much after that. Finally she would go below where he read his mail and papers in the morning room, steeling herself with every step.

She performed the ritual the morning of the dinner party that she would attend at Alexia's. The notion of dressing for that party, of pretending gaiety and grace, made her nauseated.

She refused coffee or food. Kyle slid the papers toward her. "Nothing."

Her relief left her limp. She eyed his stack of mail. Nothing in any of that, either, she assumed.

"One day there will be something," she said.

"We do not know that for certain."

Of course they did.

Rose pictured Timothy wandering through that Italian town, his sandy hair marking him as English as surely as his language did, foolishly using the same assumed name that he had adopted upon fleeing. She had checked a map and discovered that Prato was not very big and not far at all from Florence.

Royds would most likely find Tim without any trouble at all.

When he did, and Tim was brought back and information laid down, and he was publicly named as a thief, and tried and found guilty—

"Do not dwell on it, darling."

She looked up. He knew where her thoughts were going.

It would affect him too. His tenuous position, maybe even his success with those estates in Kent, would be damaged by his association with such a big fraud. He never spoke of that. He acted as if it did not matter that his tainted prize of a wife might set him back by many, many years.

That pained her. A good deal of her heartsickness derived from picturing Kyle badly hurt by this marriage rather than helped.

"When do you think you will be leaving for Alexia's dinner?" he asked.

"Nine o'clock. Thereabouts. I do not really want to go."

"Once you are there you will enjoy it. You cannot sit in this house waiting, Rose. Since we cannot foresee the future, we should live as we want and expect the best."

There was truth in that advice. Only she was not sure this party was how she wanted to live her life, even if it was supposed to be.

"I will do my best to make Alexia proud." *And you too, Kyle.* For all the wanting that led him into this match, he had not had much cause for pride. "Perhaps, if we are going to expect the best, we could host our own dinner soon. One where we entertain some of your friends. I would not like us to forever live in separate circles and different worlds."

His expression altered slightly. For the smallest instant she thought she glimpsed surprise, even dismay.

"If you like, we can do that." He stood and leaned

over to kiss her. "I will be sure to be here to see you off. You will astonish them all, Rose, just as you have always astonished me."

"So, you are finally free to see your old friend Jean Pierre. Your lady goes her way, and you go yours, as married life was meant to be." Jean Pierre offered the slightly inebriated assessment while he lazily eyed the cards on the table in front of him.

Jean Pierre preferred *vingt-et-un* to the other options available in this gaming hell that they visited on occasion. He did not care for games of complete chance.

Neither did Kyle. He did not much care for this kind of gambling in any of its varieties, although he was not above losing or winning a few hundred. He frequented such places for other reasons.

Right now he watched the play while he conversed with his friend. The wins and losses did not interest him, but the players did. Not the ones who abandoned all rationality and played recklessly. His attention lingered on the men whose expressions revealed attention to the game, a weighing of options, and bold moves that could be justified as likely of success. It lingered even longer on the ones in that group whose clothes and demeanor marked them as gentlemen of wealth.

Kyle had met a good many future investors in his syndicates in gaming hells.

"I am free because my lady wife dines with her cousin," he explained.

"Then tomorrow I will be adrift and alone again. It is always so sad when a friend is hobbled."

"I am not hobbled. If I have not been available to go about town, it is because I prefer to spend my evenings with my bride."

"Now you make me feel more sorry for myself. Although I am happy that you find pleasure in her company and—" Jean Pierre's hand made an aimless gesture that managed to communicate the other things a husband might find pleasure in with his wife.

"From what I hear you have no reason to feel sorry for yourself. I do not think you would have been available most nights, either."

"Ah, you speak of Henrietta." Jean Pierre's brow puckered. "Hen, they call her. Like a barnyard animal. Such a stupid pet name. It is only because they are too lazy to say it all. Sometimes I do not understand you English." He shrugged in his vague, expressive way. "She is sweet if I keep her busy so she does not talk so much, but . . ." Another frown.

"Does the scent already fade, *mon ami*?" Jean Pierre rarely dallied long in any garden.

"No. Only . . . I think that I am being used most cleverly."

Kyle had to laugh. "I have met this woman. She is not clever."

"You do not understand. She too is being used." Jean Pierre gestured a dismissal to the dealer and turned his back on the cards. He sipped some wine. "Two weeks ago, a messenger arrives with a little note. This little note mentions that a certain box at a certain theater will not be used by a certain party, and offers me its use if I escort Henrietta and her daughter. Like a fool, I am flattered by the offer, by the note itself. Such fine paper it was. Such an impressive crest. Such an elevated man. That it reveals the marquess knows of my little seduction was not a concern. He is a man of the world, his aunt is mature, I am harmless—all is well."

"So you went, I assume."

"Like a king I sit there. I play my part. I scowl at young men who come to flirt with the girl. I know what is expected."

"How nice for you. And how generous of Easterbrook."

"I know that tone. You are correct. I have swallowed a hook. Five times now, I have found myself escorting my flower and her daughter in this very public way at these expensive diversions. The world now knows I am her lover. When it must end, now it will be awkward, so of course it will last longer than I want. The marquess has been most careless, I think to myself. Then I think about it more, and wonder if he wants her embarrassed, or perhaps just seeks to avoid the duty himself. No, I decide it is not that. I am being hooked for another reason."

"Easterbrook can be a very odd man. He may just want his aunt to enjoy her little affair. For a very long time."

Jean Pierre shook his head. "If so, why the girl? Always the girl is with us. It is part of the arrangements. So, only one question remains for Jean Pierre now. I am curious why I am being so used. What reason do you think?"

Kyle gave it half his mind. The other half noticed the arrival of a group of men. Merrily foxed, they entered too loud, too flushed, too arrogant. They were the four aristocratic members of the "hang Longworth" committee. Norbury was among them, acting like the young blood he was supposed to have had the sense to stop being a few years ago.

This den of gambling catered to anyone who could afford to lose a good deal of money, which meant it was haunted by lords among others. It was not the first time Kyle had seen Norbury here.

He turned his attention fully on Jean Pierre and ignored the new arrivals so he would not catch Norbury's eye. That could wait for another day.

"It sounds as if Easterbrook is indeed using you," he said. "It sounds as if he has found a way to rid himself of his aunt and cousin's presence in his house."

"You are the shrewd one. It took me a long time to see it all. Are you not now curious too?"

"No."

"Think. It is a very big house. If he does not want their company, he need only go to another chamber, another level, another wing. If he wants them completely gone..." A shrug.

Kyle shrugged back.

Jean Pierre tisked his tongue with exasperation. "He wants that big house empty for a reason. He is doing something there while they are gone that he does not want them to chance upon. There is a mystery here. I know it."

There was no mystery other than a man who preferred isolation. Explaining that to Jean Pierre would have to wait, however. One of Norbury's party had noticed Kyle, and the group sauntered over, beaming grins.

"We got him," Sir Robert Lillingston announced.

"Him?" Kyle asked, although he knew the answer. It was written on Norbury's smug face. No matter how Alexia's dinner party went tonight, Rose would be grieving soon.

He wanted to thrash these men who took such delight in something that would create misery for Rose. He hated that he had ever been one of them, no matter whether his motives had been just or prideful.

He managed to hide his reaction from everyone except Jean Pierre, who watched him with careful attention.

"Longworth," Norbury explained with relish. "You remember, don't you? Your wife's brother."

Kyle did not move, but Jean Pierre's hand came to rest on his arm anyway.

"Royds found him in Tuscany. It wasn't even hard. The fool thought he could hide in a small town, when he only stuck out there like the foreigner he was," Lillingston said.

"How long before he is brought back?" Kyle asked. How long before the worst part of this began.

"He is here now," Norbury said. "Royds found him fast, hauled him to the coast, and has him in hand outside London even as we speak. We four laid down information with the magistrate this afternoon. He'll be in Newgate soon."

They had laid down information already. They were foxed because they had been celebrating.

"Come and join us, Bradwell," Lillingston said.

"Yes, join us," Norbury said. "You were as indignant as the rest about that scoundrel's crimes. Raise a glass with us that he will finally pay, the way any poor miner would pay if he were a thief."

His arm flexed before his brain could stop it. Jean Pierre's hold tightened enough to restrain the impulse.

"My friend would never be so uncivilized as to toast the pending end of any man's life, least of all the brother of his wife," Jean Pierre said with scorn. "Go now, before I cease stopping him from smashing your drunken faces."

"Who the hell are you?" Norbury snarled. "French, eh? A French peasant, if Bradwell here is your friend."

Kyle stood for the fight that was coming, impatient for it, glad to have an excuse to release the horrible storm filling his head.

Jean Pierre stepped in front of him and faced Norbury. "Who am I? Let us just say that I am a man who knows all about chemicals. I can explain how there are poisons that cannot be detected, for example. Men much like you always find that topic most fascinating."

Norbury's sluggish mind slowly realized that he had just been threatened. Exuding disdain and hauteur as much as a foxed man could manage, he pivoted and walked away. His companions dragged after him.

Jean Pierre turned, but did not remove his body as a barrier. "*Merde*. Would you now please regain your rationality? It would have been four against one."

Norbury's departure had relieved the worst anger. Enough that the anticipation of Rose's sorrow now drenched Kyle.

"Four against one? Fine friend you are."

"This fine friend kept you from being most stupid

tonight. And this fine friend will not break his hands defending the name of a man who is a thief. His sister is your wife, but if he stole money her goodness does not change the truth of his badness."

No, it did not. Not for Jean Pierre. Not for anyone. Not even for Kyle Bradwell, when you got down to it.

CHAPTER
TWENTY

Rose understood the goal of the dinner party. She did nothing to interfere with it. However, she had her own goals too, and left Alexia's house believing they might also be realized.

The people sitting around that table had been among the most open-minded in society. Alexia had planned it that way. Rose had merely explored just what that meant while she conversed with them.

She did not hesitate to talk about Kyle. She waxed eloquent about his best qualities and his good character. Two of the gentlemen knew of Kyle's syndicates and expressed interest in meeting him. One spoke in vague, admirable terms about Kyle's honorable behavior toward her.

Three of the ladies mentioned that he was handsome in his way, and alluded to that compelling aura that he exuded. One of them expressed regrets that Kyle had not been able to attend the dinner.

While Rose rode home in her carriage, she assessed the night's success. It had been a victory for herself, that was undeniable. However, she was convinced that having Kyle by her side would not slow down her redemption. In fact, she suspected that he would only help.

He was a player in that scandal, after all. She sat at the table only because her marriage raised question marks about that whole night. A few lids had lowered when one of the gentlemen clumsily mentioned Norbury in passing while telling a story.

She walked up to her chambers calculating which of those dinner guests would agree to a more direct connection. If she hosted her own dinner, one with a democratic mix, who might accept? Her abigail helped her undress while a tentative guest list formed. M'sieur Lacroix was an interesting man, an intellectual, and no one would object to his presence. Lord Elliot and Lady Phaedra would probably come.

She sat at her dressing table and her maid brushed out her hair. She gazed in the looking glass. Her face showed a slight flush from the night's excitement.

She had enjoyed herself. She had laughed and talked and never felt out of place, or like a person tolerated for Alexia's sake but not really welcome.

This campaign might work. It actually might. She had never truly believed that before tonight.

She had never really believed that she deserved redemption.

That admission popped into her head, unbidden and unexpected. She looked in her own eyes and knew that it was true, though. She had accepted that the sins of her family demanded penance and that it was left to her to atone for everyone's, not only her own.

She drifted out of her reverie. Her maid was gone and the hairbrush rested on the dressing table.

"You were deep in thought, Rose. What absorbed you so much while you looked at yourself?"

She turned, startled. Kyle stood at the doorway that joined her dressing room to his. She could tell that he had been out tonight, but now his cravat was gone and his shirt opened at the neck.

"I was talking to myself," she said. "I was learning things from my reflection."

"Good things, I believe. You appeared content. Confident."

"Yes, good things, I think."

"I hope that means that the dinner was a success." He held out his hand. "Come and tell me about it."

She took his hand and he led her into his chamber. She sat on the bed and described the dinner while he lay on his side listening. His gaze reflected his total attention to her words.

The way that he shared her joy in the night touched her. Ever since their argument there had existed a subtle distance, a vague distraction. Right now, in their absorption with her little story, it disappeared.

That moved her to confide even further. "I truly did not expect such generosity from these guests. I did not believe they would be kind. Even with Alexia's plan, even with the way our marriage might confuse the view and rumor about that auction, I did not really think that I would ever be allowed to hold my head high again."

"I am glad that you realized that you were wrong. Is that what you were learning from your reflection tonight when I came upon you?"

"Yes. And more. I was realizing that I lost confidence in my right to hold my head up. My pride became a steel shell. It kept me standing, but inside was chaos and guilt about my family's sins. Even that affair—looking back, I barely recognize the woman who deceived herself so. It was not the Roselyn Longworth of two years ago, and not the Roselyn of today. She was a stranger, that woman, who saw only bleak choices, and who believed she deserved no better."

He turned thoughtful. His fingertips played at the hem of her nightdress where it flowed on the coverlet. "I took advantage in proposing when you had not yet reclaimed yourself."

"That is not true. Do not say that." He thought her last sentence referred to him too. His interpretation horrified her. "I had begun reclaiming myself before you proposed. Truly."

"I think that perhaps you had. However, if not, I do not regret pressing my advantage even if it was wrong to do so. I never will, Roselyn."

It was an odd declaration, and so honest that it flustered her. She decided to put off parsing through his words, and what they revealed about his motivations and calculations. Right now the look in his eyes commanded only the best interpretation.

She saw warmth in his gaze. It came from deep inside him and matched her own comfort and joy in this private moment of familial intimacy. Desire burned too, making her body thrill as surely as his hand did while it wandered up and down her bare leg. She saw something else too, however.

Pride. Not in himself, but in her. She had never noticed that before. Either it had not been in him, or she had been blind to it. "I am glad that you do not regret it, Kyle. I always thought your offer was a little foolish when you received little more than a pretty face in the bargain."

"I will not lie and say that your beauty never weighed in my want of you, or my pride in my wife. However, it is really not on the scale anymore." He seductively pulled the end of the ribbon that tied the top of her nightdress. "Which is not to say your beauty does not affect me anymore."

She giggled and pushed his hand away. He laughed and boldly caressed up her leg to her bottom. She scooted out of reach and rose up on her knees.

Joy made her heady and bold. She might have been dragging a cart for a year and now been freed of its yoke.

This was not like that day on the hill, either. She was not escaping the burden with a fantasy of becoming a different person. She was Roselyn Longworth, and this interesting, intelligent man, this unusual husband, found her character worthy of pride.

He still lay on the bed watching her, his hand poised to grab her if she came close. Sentiment drenched her joy, filling her heart until her eyes brimmed with tears.

She might not have found her way back on her own. She might have never figured out how to shed that heavy cart. Fate had been kind to her by sending this man to interfere in her life.

She lifted her nightdress and pulled it off so that she was naked. He looked a long while, so long that her body wanted to sway from the way his gaze alone aroused her. He rose up on one arm and reached for her.

She took his hand and moved closer, then pushed him back down. She straddled his hips and sat back on his thighs.

"I have taken much from you, Kyle. And you have given much, besides the redemption promised. I promise that the woman I am reclaiming is not as selfish and self-absorbed as the one you married."

He reached up to smooth down her body in two long, slow caresses. "Do not make me into a saint. I take at least as much as I give, I assure you."

"I wonder if that is true. I think that I will find out tonight." She began to unbutton his trousers.

He did not help while she undressed him. He allowed her to pull off his shirt before his cuffs had been loosened and only smiled with irresistible charm while she tried to rectify the problem.

"I expect that it gets easier with practice," she said while she burrowed through linen to find his wrists.

"You can practice as often as you want, Rose."

She already knew that. He enjoyed this, despite her clumsiness. It aroused him. A lot, from the evidence pressing against her cleft where she straddled him.

That pressure excited her too, and only impeded her progress. By the time she swung her leg away to strip off his lower garments, she throbbed down there with hot, vivid pulses.

She sat farther back on his legs once he was naked. He looked down his body at her, and at the engorged member rising so prominently between them.

"What now, Roselyn?"

She already wanted him, desperately. She wanted to move forward and rise up and take him into her body and experience that satisfying fullness and delicious climb to ecstasy.

"You tell me, Kyle."

Desire always hardened all of him—his limbs and jaw and mouth and entire body. Now his eyes darkened, and his vague smile was hard too.

"Touch me. Kiss me."

He did not mean his mouth or chest. Rose suddenly felt a tad less bold and a lot more ignorant.

He understood. There was no disappointment in how he smiled at her pause or in the way he reached to bring her up his body.

She leaned out of reach. She ran one finger up the length of his phallus, then circled the tip.

She had touched him before. There was no newness in this, except for the way she sat and looked at her hands and the way he reacted. She found that surprisingly exciting. The subtle flexes of his legs beneath her bottom and the astonishing sensitivity of his skin to her strokes sent pleasure spiraling down her body. She trembled and he had not even caressed her.

That more than anything made it easy to please him. He had been correct, that in giving pleasure he also took. She could not believe how much she took. So much that it seemed very natural, almost necessary to give him more. She did not even think much before she bent her head to kiss him.

She had heard of such things, but she did not know what she was supposed to do. She realized that her position was an awkward one and moved to kneel beside him. She could use her mouth more purposefully then. The low *yes* that whispered through his clenched teeth let her know when her explorations gave him special pleasure.

She almost reached a climax from the intense shudders that titillated her low and deep. When he lifted her she assumed it was so they would come together the way her body needed.

Instead he guided her high on the bed. "Kneel here."

Here was by his shoulders. His fingers gently stroked the source of her craving. She clutched the headboard for support when his head slid down. New caresses and kisses, those of tongue and lips, sent shocks through her.

Pleasure took over. Pleasure and screaming hungers. The excruciating sensations left her weak and helpless. She heard herself crying out, begging for him to stop and go on all in the same breath.

He managed to do both, somehow. She hung on the headboard while he brought her to a shattering climax. She hung longer while he allowed her to retreat halfway to sanity. Then he sent her back into madness.

Three times he did that. The last time she thought she would faint. She possessed no strength after that. No sense of self other than her essence desiring and hungering and being obliterated in release.

He moved her down, lifted her body gently, and entered the only part of her that was still alive. He held her on top of his chest, his arms wrapping her while he filled her. She emerged from her sated vagueness when he moved in her.

She gasped. The warmth of his mouth nuzzled her head. "Too soon?"

"No. I thought I would be numb to more. It seems not." She bent her knees under her body so she could feel him deeply.

He stroked slowly, fully, awakening yet again all the desire and need. More focused now. More physical and centered. The clouds closed in on her consciousness but she felt him clearly and totally. She tightened around him and moved in rhythm, joyed when his thrusts came harder.

It was different this time. The shudders centered on his pressure. They vibrated profoundly through her loins, increasing in pitch and speed but never leaving the spot where they joined. She could not bear it, could not believe the power of this pleasure. He grasped her hips and held her still so she would accept the ravishment of both her body and spirit.

The end was all darkness, all sensation. Even as she collapsed on him in exhaustion, the pleasure still flowed in perfect freedom, guiding her to another union, one of soulful peace.

When she woke the next day it was late. Mid-morning at least, from the light leaking through the drapes.

She sat up and saw Kyle sitting in a chair near the window, watching her. He had dressed already, but the chamber showed no signs of servants entering. No coffee or cleaning, no tending to the low embers of the fire.

His chair hugged the shadows. He noticed that she was awake and sat more upright, but did not speak.

"Why are you sitting there?" she asked.

"I was waiting for you to wake. I was enjoying watching you sleep."

"A long time, it appears. I seem to have slept away half the day. That is not like me, but I believe that I can be excused."

"Not so long. I did not rise until an hour ago myself."

"You too can be excused."

He did not pick up her playful cues about the night. Instead he stood. "I was not sleeping much."

He walked toward the bed and she saw what the shadows had hidden. For all the joy of the night, there was no happiness in him now. His sober expression alarmed her.

He sat on the edge of the bed and turned his body to look at her. "I need to tell you something. I hate doing so, but I do not want you to learn about it elsewhere."

Dread stretched its chilling fingers through her. "It is about my brother, isn't it?"

He nodded. "He has already been brought back to England. Information has been laid down."

She pulled the sheets up around her. "The one morning that I did not wake up worrying that such news would greet me is the morning that it does."

He caressed her face. She took comfort in his touch, but the dread would not retreat.

"It is in the papers?"

"No. Not yet."

"Then how did you learn of it?"

"I was told last night."

Last night. He had greeted her return with a smile and had listened to her talk of the party's success. An insignificant success, as he well knew, once her brother's capture was known.

"You hid this from me."

"There was nothing to be gained from your learning about it last night, except a few more hours of your unhappiness."

"I understand, Kyle. You wanted me to enjoy my freedom for a while before I returned to my prison of scandal. You fed me a delicious banquet before unhappiness made it hard for me to even sit to a meal."

"Something like that." He stood. His blue eyes reflected sympathy, but also determination. "We knew this day might come. You will survive this. I will make sure that you do. For now, however, you should retreat from the world until I learn how things stand. If anyone calls on you except your family, do not receive them. Put it out that you are ill."

"That will not be a lie. I am already sick at heart. Poor Tim."

The hardness entered him much as it always had when her brother's name came between them. "I promised that our marriage would spare you the worst of it, Roselyn, and I will make sure that you are protected. Whatever happens, remember that is my only duty and my only concern."

His determination soothed her. Comforted her. Worry about her brother receded while she surrendered to Kyle's aura of strength and confidence.

Memories from the night swarmed through her. Echoes of joy and pleasure pulsed inaudibly. He seemed to hear, though. The intimacy returned to the chamber and the air, despite the way he had girded himself for battling the gossip on her behalf.

"It must have been difficult for you to pretend last night that nothing was amiss, Kyle, especially since this will certainly affect you badly too. I am glad that you did, though. It was kind of you to spare me for a few hours."

"It was not hard at all, Rose. I was too captivated by a woman who had found her own happiness to think much about what waited once I left this bed." He cupped her chin in his hand and looked in her eyes. "And if we shared a banquet, it did not only feed my body, darling."

He bent down and kissed her, then strode from the chamber.

Kyle paused outside the bedroom. He listened for sounds from the other side of the door.

He did not hear the weeping that he expected to commence with his departure. The strength that she had mustered on hearing that the sword had fallen still sustained her.

She would weep soon enough, however. He tried not to picture the unhappiness waiting for her. He felt it for her, as if the misery flowed without barrier from her heart to his.

He could not spare her the sorrow over Timothy. He could only do his best to make sure that she remained enough removed from the proceedings so that she might pick up her life with some dignity after her brother hanged.

He went below and called for his horse. Before he left the house he sent a message to Lord Hayden, telling him that Longworth had been caught. It would not do for Lord Hayden to be questioned about those events and those payments without forewarning.

An hour later he entered a coffeehouse on the Strand. He caught the eye of a man playing chess at a large table. Bare acknowledgment nodded in his direction before another move was made.

He took a chair near the large window and waited. A half hour later Norbury lost his chess match. None too pleased, he rose and walked over to Kyle. He took another chair, ordered some coffee, and sat back while he gave Kyle a long inspection.

"It is wise that you came," Norbury said.

The message and summons had been waiting when Kyle woke this morning. It must have been written late last night. While passion had bonded two souls in one Mayfair house, in another house a man, no doubt still drunk and still angry from the argument in the gaming hell, had been plotting no good.

Kyle had not told Rose about that note. There truly were times when total honesty was not the best course.

"You need to apologize," Norbury said.

"To you? You insulted me and my wife. It would be wise for us to have only the most formal association in the future, not casual meetings in coffeehouses."

"I had the chess match arranged. I am not inclined to change my plan for such as you." Norbury stirred his coffee with ritualized precision. "The business with her brother needs to be discussed, or I would have gladly spoken to you in the future only through my solicitor."

"I have nothing to say about her brother."

"The hell you don't. We will be pressing to have the trial fast. You will have to give information at it."

Kyle gazed around the coffeehouse. These were democratic establishments for the most part, although this one catered to men of wealth and standing. It announced its preferred patronage through its divans and upholstered chairs, and the expensive cigars available for sale. Kyle much preferred the Kendal Coffee House on Fleet Street, where civil engineers held their meetings and men of affairs congregated.

"I will not give information. When I said that I was out of it, I meant thoroughly out of it."

"You will do as you are told unless you want that wife of yours in the dock too."

Kyle did not ask for an explanation. It would come soon enough. Norbury appeared too self-satisfied for it to have been an empty threat.

"A most interesting whisper came my way last week," Norbury said. "Lillingston was with his solicitor, and mentioned the matter of Longworth. His solicitor confided that Longworth's solicitor had heard from the man, and received a proxy to sell that land that Rothwell protected. Thinking to discover Longworth's lair, I visited Yardley myself."

Norbury waited for Kyle to pump him. Kyle refused to satisfy the man.

"He told me about that letter, and what it contained, and how it had been written to your wife. You read it before you made him burn it, so you know that she was intending to go to him. *You must bring me the money.* That is what he wrote."

"From the sale of the property. Nor was she going anywhere."

"Well, who is to say if it was only the proceeds of the sale? Yardley's recollection was not precise, and yours can't be trusted."

Would that be enough? People were inclined to think the worst. Along with Lord Hayden's restitution on behalf of a man out of the hangman's grip, and Rose's ill-fated affair with one of her brother's victims—this last piece, that letter, might make it enough.

"You were the only one not repaid," Norbury said. "It should not matter. The forgery alone should send him to the gallows, but juries can be peculiar at times. And Lord Hayden may bring influence to bear on the judges. You are the one victim not made whole, and no one can make the argument that you saw a type of justice already. You must testify. You will, or I will make sure that she is tried alongside him."

"I swear, you must be a bastard. It is impossible for a man like your father to have sired such as you."

"You would do well to remember my father's slipping hold on life before you forget your place and insult me so directly." Norbury's fist came down hard on the table. "You are too beguiled by that soiled dove to see the truth of it. Fine, be a besotted idiot. But you *will* speak at Longworth's trial."

Yes, he probably would. For a stupid man, Norbury had forged a snug net of steel ropes.

"Your tenacity regarding my wife's family borders on madness. Your pursuit of her brother is unseemly, despite all his crimes. You were repaid, after all. As for Roselyn, you compound your dishonorable behavior toward her by now threatening a woman you know is innocent."

"I know nothing of the kind. As for my interest in that family—no one makes a fool out of me without paying. No one."

Kyle left without another word. He strode out to the fresh air. He had just been warned, but it was not clear that Norbury even realized that he had revealed his intentions.

Years ago a collier's son had made a fool of Norbury. Last December he had done so again, and the Earl of Cottington's shield of protection would be gone soon.

CHAPTER
TWENTY-ONE

Kyle came to Rose that night but there was no passion. No pleasure or ecstasy, no joy or games. He just lay beside her, his arm embracing her while his heart beat out the minutes of the night into the ear she pressed to his chest.

He brought her peace as if he knew that was what she needed right now. She had spent the day trying to keep images of Timothy on the gallows out of her head, to little avail. Distractions did not last long before the swelling panic took hold again.

She did not know how long he held her like that, in a soothing silence and warmth. She wondered how long he would want to.

Right now, today, he sympathized with her sorrow. A week hence, or a month, would he still offer comfort? Would she continue to believe that he would have put justice aside if it meant seeing her spared?

Her raw emotions left her defenseless to his strength. She sensed its force most clearly tonight. It commanded that tranquility pervade the chamber so she would have a respite. It held the horrible images of Tim's future at bay.

That only meant others could invade her head. Those of Kyle suffering society's scorn because of his connection to an infamous thief. He had never really been burned by a scandal before. His role in the story about that auction had not reflected badly on him.

He knew nothing about how horrible it would be. He did not know what it was like when old friends abandoned you and heads turned away when you entered a shop or assembly.

It was not fair. His only crime had been to marry her. He would pay for that alliance, however.

She should have warned him more forcefully about that, when he offered this path to redemption. She should have seen that it might not work out the way he thought, and that instead of him saving her, her notorious family might damn him. She had been too willing to accept his optimistic view.

She tightened her embrace of him a little. It was a physical echo of the way emotion squeezed her heart. He kissed her crown in response.

"This is pleasant," she said. "The dark and the silence. Your warmth."

"Yes." He moved until he lay on top of her, his hips nested between her thighs. Braced on his forearms, his face hovering inches above her own, he traced her features, her jaw and nose, her eyes and lips, with his fingertips.

"I saw Lord Hayden late today. He had already learned more than I would have in a week. Timothy went before the magistrate this morning, and was sent to Newgate. The trial will be held soon. There are men pushing it forward fast."

Soon. Fast. Maybe that was for the best. For everyone except Timothy.

"Is it known that he is caught?"

"There were broadsides today. The papers will be full of it tomorrow."

"And the next day, and the next, until it is over. I stayed in this house today the way that you commanded, Kyle. However, I do not think that I can bear to do so for weeks. Nor do I think that I should. It will appear that I am hiding. Or that I am ashamed. His bad judgment is unfortunate, but I do not think that I should act as if his crime is mine."

She felt him gazing down at her in the dark.

"Are you sure that you want to face it, Rose? Are you confident that you can?"

Was she? Four months ago it would have been impossible to face the world and brave it out. Like a sacrificial lamb, she had taken Tim's sins on herself and accepted the scorn for him as hers as well.

She was not inclined to see it that way anymore. She was Mrs. Bradwell now, not Longworth's sister. A good man honored her with admiration and, yes, affection. Dread for Tim might rack her at times during the days ahead, and she would surely grieve, but Kyle had been correct this morning. She would survive this, because she would not allow her brother to make her a victim again.

More importantly, she would not let Tim do that to Kyle. And he might, if she hid away and did not face them all down.

"I am sure that I do not want to endure it. However, even more than my last scandal, I think that I must."

"You will not be able to defend him. There is no defense."

"I know that."

"It might not be too bad. Alexia will be by your side. And Lady Phaedra, and their husbands."

Oh, it would be bad. He did not know the half of it. Nor would he, either. She would not lay her misery at his feet every night.

"And you, Kyle. I think it will matter most if you are by my side."

She felt his sightless gaze intensify. Then he kissed her. There was no demand in the gentle way his lips touched hers. No expectation. She stirred anyway. Her heart filled.

"You need to know something, Rose. Lord Hayden will be speaking at the trial. He will validate the way he paid the victims, but in doing so he will be proving the accusations most thoroughly. He has no choice. He will be called, and he will have to go." He paused. "I too will be called, as one of the ones who saw losses."

"Losses that were not repaid in your case."

"Yes."

He seemed to brace for her reaction. Perhaps he expected an emotional one full of tears. Maybe he thought that she would push him away in anger.

She would not. Could not. But she also could not deny that her heart rebelled at the implications of that "yes." Of all the testimony at that trial, his would be the most damning.

"Must you?" she whispered.

"I fear that I must. If it stands between us afterward, or even now, I understand."

She wished that she could say it would not change anything, but she feared it might. Already a door in her spirit was closing, to protect a private, vulnerable spot from disappointment. Even the Roselyn who had found herself again, who knew Kyle was good, would be hard-pressed to feel no betrayal if her husband was the one to send her brother to the gallows.

"Why must you? For honor? For justice?" The words snapped more sharply than she intended. "We can leave London. If you are out of the court's jurisdiction, you will not have to speak."

"I do not give a damn about justice anymore, and my conscience would give my honor no argument in this matter, either. I just must do it. I ask you to accept that and to forgive me, but I know that you probably will not."

He moved back to her side, but the embrace was less peaceful now. She did not discourage him from staying. She accepted the comfort for what it still was. She tried not to dwell on what last night had promised it might have become.

The night before Timothy Longworth's trial, Kyle found himself part of a peculiar party, one taking place in full view of society at the Drury Lane theater.

It began simply enough. Jean Pierre once more received a note from Easterbrook inviting him to use the theater box. Jean Pierre suggested that Kyle come too and bring Roselyn, to distract her from the distress waiting to

engulf her. Rose had agreed that would be a perfect way
to show a brave face. At the appointed hour Kyle escorted
her into the very visible seats that Easterbrook kept at the
theater.

They were noticed, to be sure. Rose had her smile
ready and her dignity on full view. She proved that she
could brave it out with the best of them, but he recognized the little signs in her eyes that said the stares and
whispers pained her.

Soon, however, Rose ceased to be of much interest to
the crowd. The box door opened and Lord Elliot entered
with his unusual wife, Lady Phaedra.

"Bradwell. Aunt Hen," Lord Elliot said. "My brother
recommended tonight's play. I did not realize that the pit
would be treated to three of the most lovely women in
London all at once."

"Among the most scandalous too," Rose whispered
in Kyle's ear. "Hen's affair with your friend is quite the
on-dit, I am told, and Lady Phaedra is notoriously
outré."

"Then you will need less courage if you share the attention with them."

It heartened Kyle, Rose's decision to come here
tonight. She had spent the last week as if tomorrow held
no particular interest. Except when they were alone together.

Perhaps he imagined the small caution that had entered their dealings with each other. There was nothing
he could point to as evidence. No words or actions that
proved the intimacy had lessened by subtle increments.
It was just there, much as he had expected it to be once

he warned her about the trial. She would not be human if she did not resent the role that he would play.

The only question was whether in the future, when it was all over, they would ever breech the final formalities again, and know the secrets waiting in that total surrender of self that they had begun sharing that night in Teeslow.

Jean Pierre angled behind Henrietta and caught his eye. Kyle leaned toward him.

"It is a curiosity, no, that Lord Elliot joins us? Now there is no danger that he will visit the marquess." Jean Pierre's low voice carried nuances of drama.

"You are mad, my friend. All those chemicals, no doubt."

"Mad? Who is mad?" Henrietta asked, twisting to join their conversation.

"*C'est moi,*" Jean Pierre said. "Your beauty always does that to me."

Beaming from the flattery, she turned her attention back on the other boxes.

The door to the box opened again. Lord Hayden entered with his wife and Irene.

Caroline insisted that Irene sit in front so they could gossip and watch the crowd together. That required re-arrangements of the seating. Kyle found himself next to Jean Pierre in the back row this time.

"Almost full," his friend observed with a meaningful glance at the heads arrayed in front of them.

"Everyone seeks distraction, that is all. The worst ordeal waits tomorrow. We know Rome will burn and we are fiddling tonight."

"It burns for her only. For Lord Hayden there will be

flames, but small ones. Yet all are here. *He* arranged this. And once more that big house is empty of all but him and his servants." Jean Pierre tapped his nose.

Perhaps Easterbrook *had* arranged this. If so it had probably occupied his attention for a few minutes before he moved on. Kyle was grateful no matter how it had happened. Rose appeared to be enjoying herself. With all the other notables to notice, the world was not taking particular attention of her.

Halfway through the second act, the door opened one more time. Kyle heard the sound, then Jean Pierre's elbow jabbed him in the side.

He looked back. The marquess had condescended to grace them all with his presence. Polished and pressed and appearing the lord that he was, he took a position against the back wall.

"If he wanted to gather his family at the theater with him, why did he not just invite them all?" Jean Pierre whispered irritably. Easterbrook's arrival had quashed all speculation and hope for an interesting mystery tonight.

"I do not think that he intended to come. He does not appear all that happy to be here, either."

The marquess's gaze scanned the other boxes like a hawk. If he sought someone in particular, he must have been disappointed. He stepped forward, out of the shadows, toward the chairs.

His brothers noticed him. One could not miss the surprise in their eyes. The ladies rose in public deference to his title.

Rank has its privileges, and situating Easterbrook at

the front of the box caused a gentle commotion. The marquess took command.

"Caroline, you and your friend will sit in the back so I do not have to hear your giggles. Mr. Bradwell will thrash any young bloods who try to sneak in to flirt with you. Gentlemen, I am sure that you will not mind if I surround myself with these lovely ladies tonight. They are yours again when the play ends."

For the rest of the play, the marquess remained front and center, ostensibly absorbed in the action on the stage. Alexia had pride of place on his right side, a testament to his affection as much as to her role as the second brother's wife. Lady Phaedra sat on his left. Completing the row were Henrietta and Roselyn.

"You are right, there is no mystery and calculation with this man. He is just capricious and odd," Jean Pierre muttered.

Kyle had no interest in the marquess's impulses. He only cared about the beautiful blond woman sitting there in front, probably causing young men in the pit to lose their breath when they gazed at her.

The effect was the same no matter what Easterbrook's intention. A marquess had just greeted Mrs. Bradwell, whose brother went on trial for his life tomorrow, and had placed her chair near his. In the world she faced down tonight, that was all that mattered.

CHAPTER
TWENTY-TWO

〰

"H ayden would not allow Alexia to come. He feared
that she would not be able to withstand the excitement in her condition. She sends her love and her
prayers, Rose." Lady Phaedra settled into the chair beside Rose in the Old Bailey.

Lord Elliot took the seat beside her, and offered reassurances that everyone knew were lies.

Tim's situation was hopeless. The papers had been
full of the details of his crimes now that information had
been sworn. The names, the amounts, the audacity of it
all—she had learned more about her brother's sins than
any sister needed to know, but had also discovered how
much the world still did not comprehend.

This trial would go only one way, and quickly at that.
If she sat on the jury she would have to convict him too.

Only she did not sit there, but here, bracing herself to
watch, waiting to see his sandy head in front of all these
people once the current trial was completed.

She could not excuse him or defend him, but her
heart cried with grief anyway.

"You were very brave to come," Lord Elliot said. "I am sure that he will be grateful."

Who? Timothy? If he saw her, would it give him some comfort? She had not gone to him yet. There would be only one chance for such a visit, and she saved it for what would come after today. He would need her more then, although such a reunion and horrible parting would be hell for both of them.

Her gaze swept the men sitting below. It lit on Kyle. Perhaps Lord Elliot meant him, not Timothy. She doubted Kyle would be grateful, though. They would never be able to pretend he had not spoken today if she actually witnessed his words.

They had slowly, inexorably, stepped toward this day even as they tried to step around its implications. Kyle had become careful again. She had grown cautious once more. Veils of formality had fallen between them day by day, until she had to look hard to see the man who was no longer a stranger.

The last three nights they had slept apart. He had known that her terrible waiting could not be overcome. He had understood when she retired early, claiming exhaustion.

"Ah. There is Hayden," Lady Phaedra said.

Rose saw Lord Hayden pause by the door, then walk forward. He found a place next to Kyle. The current trial continued winding through its evidence and statements.

Lord Elliot reached over and placed his hand on her gloved fist. "My brother charged me to tell you that he will do what he can to see that your brother is spared. He asked that you understand that his words must be truthful, of course, but that his statement will have that goal."

"Lord Hayden has always been generous to my family. I would never question his motives now. Thank you, however, for warning me."

Lord Elliot frowned, and glanced at Phaedra. She shrugged. Rose was not inclined to explain. They would learn the truth soon enough.

There was only one thing that Lord Hayden could say that would mitigate the case against Timothy. He could tell everyone that Timothy had not been alone in taking all that money, and that the whole scheme had not even been his idea.

"Have you ever done this before?" Lord Hayden asked.

"Never," Kyle said.

"In your statement, speak only the facts. Simply and clearly, so the jury can understand. There may be questions. Answer only what is asked, nothing more." Lord Hayden glanced over sharply. "In giving that advice, I am assuming of course that you would rather he did not hang."

"Is there any chance that he won't?"

"One never knows. This judge has shown mercy before. If given cause, he might again."

They were not alone in waiting for one trial to end and the next to begin. A makeshift gallery above had been built, and not because of the poor pickpocket now facing justice. The fine hats up there sat on heads that slept on good linen. One perched atop Lady Phaedra's undressed fiery locks. A neat bonnet hid most of the blond hair and face of Roselyn.

More men arrived and jammed the space where Kyle

and Lord Hayden sat. Kyle saw Norbury and the other members of the "Hang Longworth" committee.

"A lot of witnesses," he said.

"A lot of victims," Lord Hayden replied.

"Will it help that you paid them back?"

"Restitution is often a condition of mercy. However, the last time this happened, the banker was executed for a single conviction on a forgery. I think, however, that his massive thievery really was the reason for his sentence."

The sickening irony was not lost on Kyle. "I should have taken your money too. I would not find myself the lone victim who was not repaid."

"If you had taken it, it would have changed nothing today, I assure you."

Bodies began shifting. The end of the trial created commotion as people left and others took their place. Lord Hayden tilted his head for some privacy. "Make your statement brief, with no supposition or elaboration. Tell only what you know for certain happened."

Rose almost wept when they brought Tim in. With his sandy hair ill-groomed, he appeared sickly and pale, and so terribly afraid. Not yet twenty-five years old, he looked too much like the boy he had recently been, and insubstantial in stature compared to the men who would judge him.

He failed to maintain his dignity. He gazed at the assembled witnesses and his jaw quivered. His eyes swept the gallery and he found her. She tried to smile, and raised her hand in a little wave. His expression crumbled. He had to look to the floor while he composed himself.

One by one the victims gave their information. One by one they told of funds disappearing, of dividend payments continued, of Timothy's confession and offer of repayment. Each one explained that the actual restitution had come from Lord Hayden Rothwell after he married Timothy's cousin Alexia.

Rose could see that the lack of real loss mattered to the jury, but not enough to absolve Tim. She watched the judge to see his reaction to this litany of financial penance.

"It is going better than I expected," Lady Phaedra whispered. "Since they were all repaid—"

"Not all of them were," Rose said. "Kyle was not."

Lady Phaedra's face fell. She whispered to her husband. Lord Elliot grew more sober.

Phaedra's glove came to rest on Rose's own. "I knew that this would be an ordeal, and that you would grieve, but I did not realize just how terrible this day would be for you, Roselyn."

Rose accepted the attempt at comfort. Her heart jumped, however, when Kyle's name rang out in the court.

Kyle's gaze met hers. She could see his regret, his apology. Then he walked forward and swore his oath.

His statement was brief. Astonishingly so. It sounded much like the others, a tale of a trust invested in the Funds, discovered to be empty due to embezzlement and forgery.

Missing this time was the part about getting the money back.

The prosecution counsel decided to make that clear. "Mr. Bradwell, was the trust repaid the money lost?"

"Yes, it is fully funded again."

Kyle's response caused consternation among the witnesses. Rose could see Norbury seething. Audible mutters of "perjury" erupted from that area of the chamber.

The prosecutor turned severe. "Mr. Bradwell, are you saying that Lord Hayden repaid this trust? I remind you that he will be speaking soon and that if you perjure yourself it will be quickly discovered."

Kyle faced the man down. "You did not ask me how it was repaid, or by whom, but whether it was at all. I answered truthfully. That trust is now fully funded to the same amount as before the theft."

"I see that you are a man of precision, sir. I therefore ask you now, precisely how was it refunded?"

"I replaced the money myself."

"Then you were the one from whom Mr. Longworth stole."

"The trust was not in my name. Mr. Longworth stole from my aunt and uncle, and they have been repaid. That was your question, and I have answered it. I cannot in good conscience hold him responsible for my reckless generosity in replacing the lost money with my own."

The jury found that amusing. The judge almost smiled too. The prosecutor all but snarled his next statement. "Whether you hold him responsible does not signify. The law does."

"Does it? A woman testified at the last trial that the man in the dock took her money. I think it likely that her husband replaced it so she could still buy the family dinner. However, he did not speak, even though the loss was ultimately his. In the case of this trust, I played the same role as that husband, or as Lord Hayden in the other stories that you heard today."

"He has a point," Lord Elliot muttered.

Yes, he did. It flustered the prosecuting counsel. "Your opinion of the law is not of interest, Mr. Bradwell. Allow me to ask again, more specifically. Were you repaid, by Lord Hayden or Mr. Longworth or anyone else connected to that family, for your own loss when you refunded that trust after the theft?"

"Yes."

The prosecutor threw up his hands and appealed to the judge. "My lord, we know he was not. He is lying."

"Are you lying, Mr. Bradwell?"

"I am answering the question truthfully."

"Lord Hayden admitted to the magistrate that you did not accept restitution from him."

"I was not asked if I received restitution. I was asked if anyone from Longworth's family repaid me. The loss was twenty thousand pounds. I have a lien on Longworth's property that is worth at least five thousand, for example."

"And the other fifteen?"

"Mr. Longworth's sister agreed to marry me. I consider the account balanced."

Rose had to smile, even if her eyes misted. He was trying hard to help Tim, and holding his own quite well.

The court erupted into talk and buzz. The prosecutor let the crowd have its say, then grinned. "You must think us all fools, sir. You marry a woman of no fortune and you ask us to believe that evens the accounts and her brother's debt to you?"

Kyle speared the man with a gaze so clear, so guileless, that the courtroom hushed. "Anyone who does not believe it has not met her. She is here, sitting up there two places from Lord Elliot Rothwell. Look at her, then tell me that she is not worth fifteen thousand pounds."

They looked. All of them. Hundreds of male eyes sought Elliot, then moved left to her. She felt her face flushing.

"Take off that bonnet. *Now,*" Lady Phaedra whispered.

Rose pulled the ribbons and slid the bonnet off. A memory came to her, of other eyes looking and judging her value for other reasons not so long ago.

Her gaze sought Kyle's, and his hers. She looked only at him so she would not see the others. He did this for her, to help her worthless brother. No matter what happened she would be grateful forever that he had tried.

His expression altered. It stunned her. His gaze did not communicate any acknowledgment of a little trick to save her brother's life. Instead his eyes were those of a man who truly looked on a woman of incomparable value.

He did not hide his admiration. His warmth. Others probably saw it. This public avowal of his affection and pride moved her. Humbled her. Honored her.

His gaze compelled her to the point where she ceased hearing the noise in the Old Bailey. In the silence that engulfed her she touched her lips in response to an invisible kiss and her heart spoke words of love that were long overdue.

"He does have a point, sir," the judge said. "A man could do worse with fifteen thousand pounds."

The jury laughed and nudged each other with

knowing nods. The prosecutor was not to be denied his conclusion. "She is most lovely, that is true. However, you were in fact not repaid at all."

"I disagree," Kyle said.

"Your agreement is not required. You may go."

Lord Hayden was sworn in next. He silenced the prosecutor's first question with a sharp gaze and upheld hand. "Before my statement, I would like to give evidence that bears on the information of the prior witnesses."

The judge nodded. The prosecutor shrugged.

"As the person who discovered the thefts and who examined all the bank records, I know the date when each theft occurred, and the amount and name of the account. Many of these other witnesses should never have been called because they have no standing in the matter. The losses they suffered happened before Timothy Longworth became a partner in that bank. He stole, that is true, but not from all of these people."

Shocked silence hung for a five count. Then voices rose in a roar of questions and shouts. The judge took steps to bring the noise down to where the prosecutor could be heard.

"It would be best if you explained yourself, Lord Hayden."

"When I made restitution last summer, it was not only to the victims of Timothy Longworth. It was also to those of the man from whom he inherited that partnership and learned both his trade and his criminal schemes. His brother, Benjamin. I did not reveal Benjamin's involvement for several reasons. Once repaid, no one cared who had stolen the money. Benjamin had been my friend, and I confess that sentiment influenced me too. However, if the length and depth of that fraud had become known, the bank would not have survived and many others would have suffered."

"Most admirable, sir. However, you are late now in revealing this."

"I owed Benjamin a debt of honor, and hoped his name might be spared."

"Of course. Yet you would be questioned. You had to know it would come out."

"I intended to answer much as Mr. Bradwell did. Without perjury, but without interpretation, either. However, Benjamin Longworth is dead, and after much thought I concluded that my debt died with him. His brother is a scoundrel to be sure, but he has sins enough without answering for his older brother's too."

"You are very certain regarding the earlier dates of the thefts?"

"Completely certain. Most of that money was gone before Benjamin Longworth went to fight in Greece."

The prosecutor insisted on quizzing Lord Hayden on which of the witnesses had in fact been Timothy's victims. Kyle decided that would take a good while. He slipped out of the Old Bailey for some air.

Many people milled there and the surprise revelations spread. That caused some confusion and arguments. With some luck it would cause some confusion among the jury too. Perhaps that was the real reason that Lord Hayden had delayed in revealing the total truth.

The weather mocked the sad events inside the

building. Unseasonably warm, it offered a taste of the season waiting to break. A cool breeze carried the scents of renewal to tease one's skin.

"I expect Lord Hayden's litany will take at least an hour."

He pivoted. Rose stood behind him with her bonnet in her hand.

"I expect so. He appears to have memorized those records."

"Alexia says he never forgets numbers. I suppose no man forgets paying out over one hundred thousand pounds."

She appeared calm enough. Composed. More than she had the last few days. Waiting for a bad thing to happen was worse than it actually happening in many cases.

"Did you know, Rose? That your older brother was part of it?"

She nodded. "Not the specifics of who took what from whom. Alexia confided the truth last summer after Tim was gone. Lord Hayden arranged for Tim to repay those people, only to then discover that there were more thefts. It devastated me when I learned that they both were bad, and I was not inclined to parse through the blame."

"I am relieved that he chose to make the distinction between their crimes today."

The barest smile curved her lips. Her eyes were sad but as clear as crystals. She gazed at him as if she could see right into his mind.

She embraced him and placed a careful kiss on his chest before releasing him. "I thank you, Kyle, for the way you spoke in there. Tim does not deserve the care that you took to do as little harm as possible. I fear that he will not understand how hard it must be to show kindness to someone who has only wronged you. He is too childish to know the sort of strength it takes to show mercy to someone whom you believe should hang."

"I did not do it for him, Roselyn."

"No. It was to spare me. To protect me. To honor me. I know that, and I will always be grateful." She glanced to the building and steeled her posture. "I must return, so that I am there when it ends. I do not want him to be alone for that."

"Of course."

She walked away. He strolled along the building's façade, delaying his own return. He would get back in time for the verdict and the sentence, though. He did not want *her* to be alone for that.

A little commotion broke into the street. Boys ran down carrying newly printed broadsides, shouting the news. Most of them announced the surprises in Longworth's trial. One, however, shouted less dramatic information.

Kyle walked over to the lad and bought the sheet. It bore a black border and a very brief story.

The Earl of Cottington was dead.

Rose walked beside Lord Hayden, trying not to retch from the smells within the prison. She carried a basket of necessities for Timothy, and also a few small luxuries. He did not deserve the latter, but she remembered how Alexia used to send her such things during the months of wearying practicality last year.

Alexia could not come with them, considering her

condition. Lord Hayden had forbidden Irene's company as well, and now Rose understood why. Newgate was a terrible place. They passed large cells where men and woman did things that no girl should see. From Lord Hayden's stern expression, she guessed that he thought no decent woman should be seeing them either.

Tim was in a small cell with only five other men. His accommodation in this more private abode had been Lord Hayden's doing. Hopefully it would be Lord Hayden's final time laying out money for a Longworth.

The turnkey moved the other prisoners out so she would not have to tolerate their interference.

Tim faced them once they were alone with him. His smile was a halfhearted, sad attempt. "It is good to see you, Rose. It was kind of you to come to the trial too."

"You are my brother, Timothy. Irene sends her love, as does Alexia. Alexia is going to have her child soon, and could not join me here. I wrote to you with the happy news but I doubt you received the letter."

"Is Irene well?"

"Most well. She lives with Alexia and Lord Hayden. She has been spared most of—well, most of it."

Tim had the decency to thank Lord Hayden for helping Irene. He then eyed Rose with less grace. "Your husband wouldn't come with you, I see."

"He has gone north, to the Earl of Cottington's funeral. But, no, I do not think he would have come anyway."

Tim's mouth twitched at her reference to the earl. "I expect Norbury is the new earl now. Good thing the verdict came down before that was widely known, or I'd be swinging for sure. Norbury wanted me dead and silent so I could never talk, and I'll laugh in his face that he failed. Not that what I face will be much better than dying."

"Do not talk like a fool," Lord Hayden snapped. "Transportation of fourteen years is not hanging. You will be alive. Eventually you will be free. You are young and can start over. You should thank God that the judge showed mercy."

"Mercy, hell. I'll die anyway, just slowly. They work men like slaves over there. I hear it takes half a year on a ship to even get there. I only borrowed some money, that's all. I was going to pay it back if you hadn't forced me to admit to it when you did. You could have said it was all Ben's doing in court too. They would have believed you."

Lord Hayden tensed enough that Rose thought he might hit Tim. "Except it was not all his doing. That would have been a lie."

Tim's face twisted in emotion and anger. "You are glad this happened. Glad they found me. Glad that Ben is dead. I know that you are."

Rose moved closer to calm her brother. "You are speaking foolishly. Lord Hayden helped you in there. He has helped us all along. But for the money that he laid out last summer, this would truly be a final farewell, Tim."

Tim's eyes misted but his petulance did not subside. Rose looked at Lord Hayden. "Could I be alone with him? For a half hour, no more?"

Lord Hayden seemed relieved by the suggestion. "I will be outside the door. If the turnkey gets impatient, I will hold him off."

She propped her basket on the little crude table that was the chamber's only furniture. "I brought you some things for your voyage and later. Do you still have the clothes that you had in Italy?"

Tim nodded, and watched as she set out her little gifts. She had packed practical items that one takes for granted, like scissors and pins. But she had also tucked in a tin of tea, a few sweets, and a bag of shillings. Also some paper and pens, so perhaps he would write if he could.

"No brandy?" he asked.

"No spirits, Tim. You would do well to stay away from them forever."

He shook his head in disgust. He paced away.

"Tim, what did you mean when you spoke of Norbury? You said that he wanted you dead so you could not talk."

He scratched his head, then gestured broadly to push the question away. "Nothing. It doesn't matter. I'm as good as dead this way."

"It may not matter, but I am still curious."

He came back and poked through the little gifts. "We spent some time in each other's company maybe four years back. We met while gaming, and he condescended to have me in his circle for some of his diversions on occasion." He opened the tea and sniffed. "He has this estate in Kent, not far from one of his father's. He has parties there."

"I am aware of those parties. Did you attend them?"

Tim flushed. "There was a bit of trouble at one. His lady friend and he had a row, and she left. So that night I was, um, sleeping, when I heard this woman scream. That was it, just once, but not a good scream . . . um, not the sort one might hear there, is what I mean." He got more red.

"I understand."

"Yes, well, it bothered me, so I went to see if someone was hurt and I heard it again. I followed it that time, I could tell it came from below, so I went there and I found him. He had a scullery maid in the library. She was no more than the age of a schoolgirl and he'd tied her up and, well—"

"Did he know you had seen this?"

"He wasn't noticing anything much when I looked in." He shrugged. "He had hurt her bad. She had the signs of blows, that was the first thing I saw, not that I stayed long. She tried to spit out the handkerchief he'd used to gag her. He noticed and hit her so hard I thought she went out."

Not that I stayed long. He had not tried to stop it. He had closed the door on that poor girl's suffering.

"If you left, and if he did not see you, why would you think he pursued you to silence you?"

His face fell. He flushed again.

"Timothy, were you so stupid as to approach Norbury? Did you tell him what you saw and ask for money to keep silent?"

"Not much. A damned pitiable amount, when things were bad last spring. He never even answered the letter. He knew I couldn't do it."

"I expect he did. But, of course, he could never be certain."

She pictured Norbury, weighing whether Timothy had the courage to either swear information against a viscount or pursue blackmail. Norbury would never be secure that a fit of bravery or a bad conscience would not inspire her brother at some point in the years ahead. Tim might not even have gone to a magistrate. He could have just written a letter to Norbury's father.

How convenient for Norbury when Tim's own crimes made him vulnerable. A hanged man is most silent.

She piled the gifts back in the basket. She set out the paper and ink and pen. "You will write that story down, Timothy. Right now."

"It won't matter, Rose. No one will believe the word of a convict, not against the man who swore information against him. It will look like nothing more than a story I concocted for revenge."

"You will write it anyway. Then you will write something else for me, as I dictate. If you do this for me, write these two letters, you will have committed two good acts, Tim. Two noble, honest ones to begin balancing out all the bad ones. It is a small beginning to reclaiming your soul and self-respect, brother."

CHAPTER
TWENTY-THREE

〜

K yle arrived late back in London. He entered the
house tired and low in spirits.

The house was silent. There was nothing different,
nothing special. Yet as he stood near the door his soul
exhaled the way it used to when he went back to
Teeslow during a school holiday. It was the emotion of a
person returning home after being gone.

Home. The sensation of comfort seemed novel, and
very pleasant. He had not really thought of any place as
home for some years now.

As he mounted the stairs, he noticed a glow at the
bottom of Rose's door. He had not expected her to be up
this late.

He went to his chamber and shed his frock coat.
Jordan had left everything ready should the master unexpectedly return. Kyle aimed for his dressing room,
but paused by the bed. A stack of letters rested there,
where they could not be missed.

He recognized the crest. He had seen it often before,
on letters sent by a man now dead. These were from a

different Earl of Cottington, however. Jordan, ever mindful of rank and title, had left them because he assumed they required immediate attention.

Kyle moved them to his writing table. Norbury could wait a while longer. In a day or two Kyle would read these letters and decide what to do about them.

He passed through the dressing rooms and entered Rose's chamber. She sat at her writing desk in a pink undressing gown and white lace cap, peering at a paper in the lamplight. She jotted, then scratched her chin with the pen's feather.

"Writing poetry, Rose?"

She startled, then threw down the pen and came to him. Her embrace was one of comfort as much as welcome.

Her feminine, living warmth made the best balm for heart and body. Just her scent helped the clouds of sorrow to thin.

"It was a grand affair, I expect," she said quietly.

"Very grand. Lots of sashes and ribbons and lords and ladies. Norbury arrived back north after me. He dallied here in London to celebrate his inheritance, no doubt. Once home, however, he played the grieving son to perfection."

"I think the symbolic son grieved more."

Probably. God knew he had grieved enough for a son of any kind. He had known, even as he grieved, that it was not Cottington alone that he mourned, but his boyhood and his youth and his roots that one by one would be severed in the years ahead like this one had been.

"Come and tell me all about it." She led him to her bed and made him sit beside her.

"I would rather not, if you do not mind." He did not want to explain that he had not really attended the funeral. He knew he would not have been welcomed. A confrontation was coming with the new earl and Kyle had not wanted it to mar the respect for the old one.

He had watched it all from a distance, looking down from a hilltop where he could spy the procession and the new tomb in the manor graveyard. He preferred it that way. He could be alone with his thoughts there.

"Of course. I understand." She patted his hand sympathetically, much the way a mother would.

He clutched her hand and raised it to his mouth. He pressed his lips to her skin. *Home.* "Did you see your brother?"

"Lord Hayden brought me."

"I suppose that was fitting."

"Sadly so. Tim is not much changed, I am sorry to say. No wiser. Still childish in his views. He may not survive what is coming."

"If he chooses to, he will. If he is your brother he cannot be too weak. He just needs to find the strength inside him, that is all."

"And if he doesn't—you are correct. It will be his choice."

"Let us speak of better things, Rose. Surely there have been normal, happier events these last days. A new bonnet, perhaps? News of Alexia? How is Henrietta faring?"

She laughed. It was a lovely sound of life. It affected him like a spring breeze.

"Alexia is well but quite uncomfortable. Irene is surviving the shock of learning about our brothers' crimes.

I do have a new bonnet, as it happens, and we have been invited to a party."

"A party. Now that is blessedly normal for London. Who is giving it?"

"Lady Phaedra and Lord Elliot, so it may not be so normal after all. It will be in Easterbrook's house. It is to honor the painter, Mr. Turner. She knows him, it turns out. Anyone who is anyone will be there, along with her old circles who are said to be very interesting people. Artists and such. She was very specific that you were to come."

"I look forward to it. The most proper and the eccentrics all in one place. I wonder if the marquess will make an appearance himself. He should enjoy it."

"Maybe I will ask him and find out. I am going to try to call on him tomorrow next. I must give him the earl's message. Alexia promised to use her influence to have me received."

Kyle looked around Rose's chamber, so full of the touches and details that spoke her presence in his world. He slid his arm around her back and pressed a kiss to her temple.

"It is good to be back, Rose. I should have stopped at an inn, but I forced the coachman to push on. I walked in the door and immediately felt at peace. It has been a long time since I entered any place and felt that way."

"It is a good house. The sort that becomes more comfortable with time and familiarity."

"It was not the building, but because you were here."

"I suppose people become more comfortable with familiarity too, Kyle. That is what it means to be married."

Perhaps, but it had not been comfort that he experienced the last fifty miles. Instead, a building anticipation occupied him. He thought of nothing except being with her, talking to her, lying with her. Loving her.

She made him rise, and folded down the sheets. "It is late and you are tired. Sleep here with me."

He took her arm and turned her into his embrace. He plucked at her lace cap. It rose gently off her crown.

It was late, but not too late. He was tired, but not that tired.

"I told you that he would not receive you. It is always like this. He doesn't even pretend that he is out of the house. He just sends down the same message. *Not today, thank you.*" Henrietta shook her head in dismay at her nephew's rudeness. "You would do better to write him a letter. That is what I do. I write a letter, post it, then it comes right back to this house and goes up to him with his other mail. That is a fine kettle of fish, isn't it?"

"I cannot communicate this in a letter. I am obliged to speak to him."

"If you had waited until I arrived, Henrietta, we might have had better luck," Alexia said. "I was not very late."

Alexia had breezed in right after Hen decided to take matters into her own hands. Now the rejection had come, and Rose would have to wait for another day.

"Do as I said. Write him a letter. I believe that he even reads them."

"I think I shall, but I wish to avoid the time it must

travel to and fro if it is posted. May I?" Rose gestured to the library's writing table.

"By all means. Now, Alexia, tell me who has accepted Phaedra's invitation. I have heard that she is friends with some extraordinary people."

While Alexia gave a report, Rose jotted her note. She folded it and called for a footman to deliver it.

"There are those who think she should make it a masked ball, so those who are dying to attend but think they should not can still come," Hen said.

"Phaedra would never countenance such cowardly behavior," Alexia said.

"If she wants the best of the best—"

"She is inviting the best of the best for your sake and mine. If they choose not to attend, it will not signify to her."

Hen smiled vaguely while she tried to accommodate the idea that such matters would not signify to someone, even Lady Phaedra.

The footman returned. "The marquess will receive you in the drawing room, Mrs. Bradwell."

Hen's eyes widened in surprise, then narrowed in annoyance. Rose followed the footman to the drawing room.

She waited a good while. Long enough that she wondered if he had changed his mind. Maybe he intended to put her in her place by letting her just sit for hours. Considering her note, there would be a type of justice in that.

Finally, however, he entered the chamber, looking distracted and vague and barely allowing a corner of his mind to attend on where he was.

She curtsied. "Thank you for receiving me."

"Since you threatened to take up residence in the library until I did, I had no choice. Aunt Hen and her daughter are quite enough feminine intrusion on this house, thank you."

"That was bad of me, I know. But I would like to discharge this duty quickly. It would not do to give you a man's dying words a year hence."

He angled his head back and gave her a good inspection. "That you were so charged is odd, since I barely knew the man, but speak you must and speak you will. I am listening."

Her mouth felt a little dry. "He insisted that I use his exact words. Please keep that in mind—"

"Speak them, Mrs. Bradwell."

She fixed her gaze on the carpet twenty feet away. "He said to tell you that you shirk your duties most shamefully. It is time that you got out in the world and stopped indulging your bent for eccentricity. You must marry and sire an heir and take your place in the government. He said that your family has too much intelligence to waste it and that your life is not yours to live as you like and that is the damned truth of it."

She heard no cursing. No anger. She snuck a look at him.

Nothing. No reaction at all. He had just been scolded from beyond the grave, taken to task like a schoolboy, insulted in a way, and he did not care.

"Now I know why he told you to wait until he was dead."

"I dreaded this obligation because it was a very rude message. However, I decided that the charge would be useful because it might enable me to see you privately. It is my hope that you will spare me a little more of your time."

He thought that over. He gestured to a settee. "A little more will not matter, I suppose."

She sat down. He did not. She wished he would. He just stood ten feet away, his hands clasped behind his back, with half of his attention waiting to hear what else she had to say.

"Lord Easterbrook, I have an odd question to ask you. Did you pay my husband to marry me?"

Rather more of his attention gathered on her. "Why do you think anyone did? You are a beautiful woman. That was reason enough for him, I am sure."

"Thank you for the compliment, but with an intelligent man a woman's beauty only goes so far."

"If you think there was more to it, why not ask him?"

"Because it does not signify anymore in matters between him and me. I ask for other reasons." And because Kyle wanted her to believe he had not profited too much other than in having her herself. No matter what she learned here today, she would allow that little illusion to stand.

"No doubt Hayden interfered if anyone did. Why would you ever think it was me?"

"Lord Hayden says he did not and he does not lie. Lord Elliot has been too absorbed by his recent marriage to much notice my situation. Your aunt Henrietta would be a most odd angel of mercy to a fallen woman. I think it was you because there is really no one left."

He strolled over to a table near the window and absently jostled the top of a bejewelled gold box there. "I will admit that I might have encouraged him a little. It would be indiscreet to explain how."

"Why?"

"It had nothing to do with you. Alexia, however, has brought my brother more happiness than he probably deserves. I appreciate that, and I am moved to make her happy if I can." He paused. "She seems to inspire me."

"To kindness?"

"No, not to kindness, Mrs. Bradwell. To optimism."

It was not the motive she had hoped to hear. She stood. "I see. I had thought that perhaps . . . well, good day. Thank you for receiving me."

She reached the door before he spoke again. "What had you thought?"

"That perhaps you cared about fairness and justice. That you had interfered to right a wrong."

That appeared to amuse him. "And if I had?"

"I would have asked your advice on a matter of that nature."

"Fascinating. People rarely ask me for advice. I can't think of the last time it happened." He appeared genuinely charmed by the extraordinary nature of her suggestion. "I can claim no experience in giving advice as a result, but the novelty of the notion diverts me. If you still want to ask, I will do my best."

Rose extracted Tim's letter from her reticule. "Norbury's interest in my brother was not just about money, or pride, or justice. Tim told me the truth, and I had him write it down."

Easterbrook took the letter and read it. "Have you shown this to your husband?"

"No. That alliance will be strained enough with the

death of the earl, and already is full of bad blood. After the business with me, if Kyle saw this, he might . . ."

"Misunderstand that business with you? Think there was more than you admit? Call Norbury out?"

"Something like that."

Easterbrook scanned the letter again. "It is the word of a criminal. Questionable at best. Useless in the least."

"Timothy believed that it would be useless too, which meant he had no reason to lie. I do not think it was the first time Norbury misused a woman, either. The village where my husband grew up—when they were boys, something happened back then. It involved Kyle's aunt. And all those house parties—"

"Willing women, he would say." Lord Easterbrook peered at the letter with an expression of distaste. "Although there are limits to what any woman would will, let alone a girl. Still, there is nothing to be done in the law. There is no one to swear information."

"There is the girl, if she can be found. There is Kyle's aunt. There is even my husband."

"That was years ago. He was a boy. His aunt did not speak then, and he may not even know for certain himself now."

"I think that he does know."

"Mrs. Bradwell, we are talking about an earl. The other peers would never convict him in a public trial in the House of Lords. I doubt it would even get that far."

"You mean that they will weigh his words more heavily than those of common women wronged long ago." It was always such. Even as Norbury, he had been out of reach. Now that he was the Earl of Cottington, he was totally safe.

Perhaps there would be another way someday. She strode the few yards between them and held out her hand for the letter.

He held it up and away from her reach. "I will keep this, Mrs. Bradwell. It might only get you and your husband into trouble."

"I have erred in coming to you. It was poor judgment on my part. I forgot that the peers reserve a special justice for their own."

He did not respond before she left, with her hands now lacking even the slim evidence that Tim had provided of Norbury's depravity.

Rose admired her husband from across the ballroom. He looked extremely handsome tonight. His new frock coat, of the deepest blue, made his eyes even more vivid. Its lines hugged his body in a fashionable silhouette, revealing his taut strength and fine form. Most amazing was his waistcoat. Subdued but in no way staid, it sported a weave of silver mixed with touches of sapphire.

He held his own over there, talking to some artist friend of Phaedra's. Kyle's time in Paris made him attractive company to that element of tonight's ensemble.

Others noticed him. The ladies in particular responded to this tall, broad-shouldered man, so handsome in his way, with the deepest blue eyes and a vitality that seemed to alter the air around him. He was not containing that very well tonight.

"You do not have to worry about him, Rose." Lady Phaedra spoke at her ear. Rose startled. She had not noticed Phaedra approach.

"No, I do not. He is very at ease. Very comfortable."

No one had to worry about Lady Phaedra tonight, either. She had dressed her hair into a fiery crown styled in the latest fashion. Her mint green dinner dress showed off her snowy skin. She had set aside her eccentricities for the night. Rose suspected that was part of the bid to have her mix of guests appear more acceptable. To show up in black gauze would tilt the balance decidedly one way.

"I was not referring to his social grace, Rose. I thought that perhaps you were jealous about the feminine attention directed at him."

"I know that I do not have to worry about that, either." She did know that. Knew it so well that jealousy had not even entered her mind. "It is not his lack of appeal that makes me confident, of course."

"Since he is demonstrating enormous appeal, that goes without saying. However, if you are secure that is very good. Then you can accept invitations that are made for the wrong reasons, and use them to a benefit not intended by the hostesses. From the looks of things, some such invitations will come your way soon."

One lady had decided to approach Kyle and the artist for those wrong reasons. Kyle chatted with her amiably and did not seem to notice her rising color when he turned those blue eyes on her.

He saw Rose watching him. He eased away from the artist and flirt and walked over. "There will be much envy in town when the season starts, Lady Phaedra. Word of this assembly will make many regret that they did not open their houses a little earlier."

"This date made the list of my friends easier to assemble. I did not have to pick and choose to avoid a crush. As for the others, Elliot said I must invite any peers who are in town, along with their wives, since his brother never entertains on his own. Fortunately, Norbury has not shown even though he had the poor taste to accept."

Kyle did not blink at Norbury's name. Instead he surveyed the crowd from his superior vantage point. "Where is Lord Elliot? I have not seen him since we arrived."

"His eldest brother cajoled him into smoking. Easterbrook barely stayed ten minutes before finding excuses to escape." Phaedra's own survey raised a frown. "Oh, dear, Sarah Rowton is boring Mr. Turner silly. He looks as if he will fall asleep on his feet. I must go and save him."

She left Rose and Kyle to do her duty.

"She looks especially lovely tonight," Kyle said. "But not nearly as lovely as you, Rose. You outshine every woman here."

She felt herself blush under his gaze. "It is a little like coming out, what with the circumstances of the last months and my exile. I feel as if I have one foot still in the schoolroom and don't really belong here."

"No one would know you were not at complete ease. They see only grace and poise, I promise. Nor were you prettier the first time you came out, I am sure."

"Actually, I never did officially. We were in Oxfordshire then, and there was no money. Oh, how I resented that at the time. Living there instead of London, it felt as if my life was being stolen from me. For a year or so I hated that house. Now I find that I yearn to visit it. Is that odd, Kyle? Not long ago it was a prison and yet I am nostalgic."

"It has always been your home, Rose. Perhaps it was never a prison, but a sanctuary. Do you need one again?"

"I could use a respite and some time in a quiet place to mourn the loss of my brother. I am sure that I will never see him again."

Kyle took her hand and tucked it around his arm. "Then we will go there. Now, however, we will take a turn through this fine ballroom. You expressed curiosity about my friends once. Lady Phaedra had Henrietta wheedle some names out of Jean Pierre and a few are here. I want you to meet them so I can puff with pride that you are mine."

Rose dazzled them all, of course. Kyle knew that she would. Her elegance, her poise, and her goodness made the result inevitable. She listened earnestly to all the conversations with these friends of his whom she had never met before.

She would never know that Mr. Hamilton, the banker, had cursed her family when Kyle told him of the match. Hamilton knew the Longworth brothers rather too well.

Nor would she ever learn that Mrs. Caldwell, whose husband designed bridges for nations far and wide, had let it be known that the scandalous Roselyn Longworth would never sit at her table even if respectably married to her husband's friend.

He knew that they would come around once they met her, just as Pru and Harold had. An invitation to an assembly where they mingled with lords and ladies and luminaries in the arts probably helped soften their views too. Drinking punch out of a marquess's cups no doubt put a different light on everything.

Had Jean Pierre not supplied names to Hen, the meetings might never have happened. Kyle had assumed they never would. He was prepared to reduce these friendships to formal business associations.

Rose appeared to like his friends, however. If she wanted to accept Mrs. Caldwell's invitation now, he would not let resentment over past prejudices interfere. Rose could probably use all the friends she could get. The war was not over, even if it looked to be going well.

He escorted Rose from the corner and crossed the room after these new alliances were forged. Rose spied Alexia just as someone else spied them.

Kyle saw a tawny head turn and narrow eyes focus. Norbury had shown up after all.

"Why don't you go talk with Alexia, Rose. I am going to try to find Lord Elliot. He spoke of rowing some morning next week."

She walked away just as Norbury aimed toward Kyle. Kyle turned and headed to the wall, so that whatever happened did not occur right in the middle of the chamber.

Norbury was in fine form when he stationed himself in front of his quarry. "You have not answered my letters. I bid you to call, but you did not."

"I have been too busy to call, and am not inclined to do your bidding in any case. I have had nothing to write in response to your letters. I could not even understand the first one, the accusations were so irrational."

"You understood them well enough."

Yes, he had. That first letter had been the drunken ravings of a man pouring out resentments about a father now dead. The mixture of hatred, regret, and grief had been too raw, too revealing, to have been written when sober, least of all to Kyle Bradwell.

On the other hand, to whom else could Norbury write such things? Not the men who joined his orgies. Those men would not care about a son's momentary despair that his dreams of his father's death had come true. Nor would they have understood the allusions to the questionable parentage of the two men facing each other right now.

Kyle wondered if Norbury even remembered what was in that letter, or the bizarre, bitter accusation that they were brothers in fact. The other letters, coldly sane and sober in their venom, Norbury probably could recite word for word.

"I've things to say to you, Kyle. You *will* hear them."

"Perhaps we should go elsewhere, then. The library should offer some privacy."

Fortunately the library was empty. The accusations began before the door had closed.

"You tried to get that bastard off. You made it sound like you had been repaid."

"Don't you want to sit? Those high chairs facing the fire look comfortable."

"Damnation, explain yourself."

It appeared they would have this out in the middle of the room, circling each other like two pugilists eyeing each other for good blows.

That suited Kyle just fine.

"I told the truth in court. Nothing more or less."

"You lied. You said you had been repaid with that marriage to his sister. To my whore."

Kyle's fist connected with Norbury's face. Norbury staggered, wide-eyed.

"I warned you," Kyle said. Icy anger claimed him. Its chilling danger waited.

"Warned me? Warned *me*!" Norbury held his face where the blow had landed. "How dare you! I will have you on a ship alongside that thief, and your soiled dove with you. My father cannot protect you now. You are just another parvenu who clawed his way to a spot near his betters that he has no right to have."

"You will do nothing to me. If I am asked to explain that blow, I will tell the jury about the way you insulted my wife, now and before we married. I will show them that raving letter in which you impugned my mother's virtue. I will tell them about other things, from long ago. How this is not the first time I thrashed you, and why I did before."

Norbury stilled. He appeared cautious at first, but his face turned mean. "Your family was compensated more than enough."

"Hardly. Be glad I did not kill you after I learned the truth."

"She asked for it. Your aunt was a pretty thing back then, not worn out like now. She flirted all the time. She invited us all—"

Kyle hit him again. This time Norbury fell. A trickle of blood formed beneath his nose.

He sat up and found his handkerchief. He blotted and expressed astonishment at the blood. "You are mad!"

"I don't feel the least mad."

Norbury scrambled to his feet. "You are too much trouble, and it is time to be rid of you. I know about that report you wrote on the mine. How dare you interfere with how men use their property? I was going to give you the chance to recant it, but now I will not. I am glad he is dead, and my association with you can end." His eyes glinted. A nasty sneer formed. "I will not be allowing that property in Kent to be used. It is mine now. It doesn't matter what papers were signed. My solicitor will tie it up so long that you will be dead before it is cleared."

Kyle glared at him and absorbed this blow that required no fist. It should smart more than it did. Instead he experienced only relief that after today he would never have to see this man again.

A small sound came from his right. He glanced over to see a hand setting a wineglass on the floor beside one of the high-backed chairs.

They were not alone in the library after all.

A dark head rose as a man stood. Easterbrook turned, his expression bland and bored. "You should make sure that you are alone before you discuss private matters, Norbury."

"And you should make yourself known before listening to them!"

"I did not have a chance to make myself known. You began blustering immediately and have not stopped since."

Another man rose from the other chair. Lord Elliot had overheard too.

"Is that a bruise forming there, Norbury?" Lord Elliot asked. "I thought that I heard the sounds of fisticuffs, but when there were no returning blows I assumed that I was wrong."

"No doubt Norbury feared hurting Bradwell if he responded with his fists," the marquess drawled.

Norbury sneered. "I seem to have witnesses, Bradwell. You attacked me, and I will be laying down information."

"What a ridiculous drama that would be. I would not be pleased to be drawn into something so common," Easterbrook said. "Why not just settle it here and now? Elliot and I will make sure you don't kill him, Norbury. We will stop you before it goes too far."

Norbury's frown froze. He appeared to be thinking hard behind his coldly glinting eyes.

Lord Elliot walked past them and secured the door. "I will take your coats."

Kyle shed his and handed it over. Norbury hesitated.

"You really should answer his challenge," Lord Elliot said. "A gentleman has no choice in such a situation. Nor do you really want to lay down information on such a minor matter. That would require us to repeat to a magistrate everything that we heard. That business about Bradwell's aunt might be interpreted as an admission of guilt."

Norbury flushed. He relinquished his coats.

The marquess strolled over, casually moving some light furniture so it was out of the way.

Lord Elliot set the coats down on a divan and took up a position behind Kyle. "Queensberry rules, of course."

"Must I?"

" 'Fraid so."

Norbury lifted his fists and grinned. "He doesn't know Queensberry rules. They aren't used by his sort."

"I know them. It just takes longer to thrash a man with them, and inflicts more pain in the end. Under the circumstances, I don't mind."

It still did not take very long. Norbury was neither quick nor strong, and his practice did not help him much. *For Rose. For Pru. For the others I do not know.* Kyle's mind chanted his purpose with each hard punch to Norbury's body. In ten minutes Norbury was on the floor again, unconscious and more punished than he appeared.

Kyle gazed down on him. The ice in him had turned to a cold fire that wanted to burn on and on. His fists would not unclench.

The marquess placed a hand on his shoulder. "I understand that you want more, but that will have to be enough. Prop him against the wall, Elliot. He'll come around soon enough."

Alexia could not stand too long without tiring, so Rose accompanied her in search of a quiet place to rest. They tried the library door only to find it locked.

"That is odd." Alexia jostled the latch again.

The door moved this time, swaying in. The opening framed three tall, dark men standing right beyond the jambs, mere inches from Rose's nose. She peered up at the marquess, Lord Elliot, and Kyle in turn. Kyle appeared a little flushed, and a bit angry, and very hard.

She and Alexia seemed to have interrupted an argument.

"The door was locked," she said.

"Was it?" Lord Elliot asked innocently.

A moan sounded behind them. She angled her head one way and Alexia angled the other, to see into the chamber.

"Who . . . Is that someone on the floor over there?" Alexia asked. "Is someone ill?"

"That is just the Earl of Cottington," Lord Elliot said. "He is still celebrating his inheritance with unseemly enthusiasm, and I fear he is in his cups. I am on my way to call for his coachman to come help him home. Discreetly, so the other guests don't gossip about his condition."

Rose squinted at Norbury. He did not look drunk at all. He looked—

A broad male chest in a deep blue coat suddenly cut off her view. Her gaze traveled up until she looked into amazing eyes.

"Kyle, did you thrash him? *Again?*"

"He and I merely had a conversation that was long overdue."

Kyle took Rose's arm and guided her away from the door, toward the ballroom. His expression captivated her. Not gloating. Not smug. Not even satisfied. He appeared a man contented that he had completed a piece of work that needed doing, much as he had after he fixed her garden gate.

Easterbrook strolled behind them, escorting Alexia. With one sharp glance he commanded a comfortable chair in the ballroom to empty of its current rump.

He settled Alexia down and fussed over her comfort. "You are looking a little pale. You need some refreshment."

"I will bring some punch," Kyle said. He walked off to do so.

Rose sidled closer to the marquess. "Did he thrash him good?"

"Thoroughly."

"I am glad. That is not very ladylike, but it is the truth."

Easterbrook glanced to Alexia, whose attention had been claimed by the arrival of a friend. "Mrs. Bradwell, you might tell your husband about our conversation when you called on me, if you have not already. If he starts to wonder if meting today's punishment was worth what it will cost him, your brother's tale might give him heart."

Cost him? "I fear that he will only thrash him again if he knows about that child." The real fear was that Kyle would kill him.

"They will not cross paths in the future."

"I do not believe that can be avoided."

Lord Easterbrook watched Kyle returning with the punch. "I spoke with an influential group of peers yesterday. I explained the new earl's long history of bad behavior, and showed your brother's letter. Their conclusion was the same as mine."

"Since that means they agreed that Norbury would never even be judged, let alone punished, my husband will surely cross his path in the future."

"I did not say he would never be judged or punished, Mrs. Bradwell. I said he would never be convicted in a public trial. The mere threat of one can be a powerful weapon, however."

"I do not understand."

"Several bishops will be calling on Norbury while he recovers from today's beating. They will bear the tidings of a jury's sentence, a very private one. Unless he is stupid and requires stronger persuasion, I predict that he will soon retire permanently to his country estate in Kent, where he will only entertain vicars and their wives in the future."

"I do not think anything will stop him. Even in Kent, even alone, he will do as he pleases."

"A very special valet and housekeeper have been chosen for him. It will be much like the close confinement of old—all the luxury but none of the freedom. Trust me, he has been stopped as of this day."

Kyle passed them with a quizzical expression, as if he found her long conversation with Easterbrook curious.

"May I tell my husband this news that you confide?" Rose asked.

"Certainly, although I think he feels much vindication already. He threw his fists as if he intended to even the score."

The marquess strolled in the direction of Alexia, and Rose fell into step. "Thank you for troubling yourself with this matter, Lord Easterbrook."

"It was my duty to my station after you brought the sordid history to my attention, Mrs. Bradwell. As you said, the peers reserve a special justice for their own."

CHAPTER TWENTY-FOUR

~

Rose loved the country in spring. She loved the smells of the earth warming and plants resurrecting their growth. Even the chilled air promised more warmth later in the day.

She loved the coziness of lying with Kyle in her bed, snug beneath the covers. The breeze cooled their bodies even while passion kept them hot.

"You are too beautiful," he muttered. He gently kissed the hard tip of her breast, so sensitive this morning to the air and his touch and his tongue. "I ache whenever I see you."

She playfully wrapped her hand around the source of that ache. His eyes darkened from azure to the deepest sapphire. "If you ache, I can soothe you."

He let her, while he ensured that she ached too. His mouth and caresses made her float in blissful surrender. She knew the ecstasy very well now. Her spirit released all cares and worries, all defenses and excuses, and finally all separateness when they joined like this.

His hand, so strong and masculine, caressed down

her body. His kiss found her ear. "It is not only my body that aches, Rose. Your caress soothes my heart too, if only for a while. Even your smile does."

"I am sorry if your heart aches, Kyle. I am sorry if anything brings you any pain."

"You misunderstand, darling. The ache is a good one, of love and yearning. You warned me that you were beyond romantic illusions, but I never promised you I would not love you anyway."

She touched his hand, stopping its seductive stimulation. She held him, his breath on her neck and his heart beating against her own.

"I said that I would never lie to myself about that again, Kyle. But the truth is not a lie, and I know you would never say such a thing if it were not true. We could have made a good and reasonable marriage without love, but it is better that we love each other, I think."

He rose up on his forearms and looked down at her through the strands of his mussed hair. Her confidence still wavered when he looked at her like this, so intensely and deeply.

"I did not expect to hear a declaration in turn, Rose. I was prepared to never hear it."

Yet he spoke of love anyway, anticipating no reciprocation. That made her heart ache, in the good way he described. "I know that you would never speak lightly of loving, Kyle. I know that I can trust you. I have felt your love, and seen it, so I did not need words, either." She traced the hard line of his jaw with her fingertip. "I am glad that you did say it, though. And that I did. It is, I realize now, the final surrender of the past, and to the future, and of my heart."

He kissed her deeply, masterfully. He moved on top

of her and bent her knees high and looked down at her exposed body while his careful caresses drove her to madness. Pleasure coursed through her in tight waves of exquisite sensation until she begged for him, loudly and without shame.

He rose up on his arms, his strength hovering above her frail, insane helplessness. His head dipped so he could watch the way he entered her. She did too, seeing in the clear light of day how she absorbed him again and again while he entered and withdrew in slow strokes.

It could not go on like that forever, much as she relished the profound sensation. His eyes closed and his head rose and he thrust harder, faster. The power spun her into darkness.

She lost herself as she always did now. Lost herself in the physical and spiritual yearning. In the purity of his energy and presence that banished all other thoughts and aches but those about him. He brought her to fulfillment and crossed that glorious threshold with her, still bound together body and soul.

She held him to her body afterward, enjoying the contentment and security that their declarations had added to their union. She savored the perfection while the day brightened beyond her curtains, and the breeze drifted in, carrying the smells and signs of renewal.

"The day is fair. Let us take a long walk."

Kyle posed the suggestion while Rose dried the pan in which she had cooked some eggs. She had done for them because they had come here alone, to be away from all the cares in London.

She loved spring, but fair days and warmth also meant mud. She put on her half-boots, grabbed a wrap, and followed him out to the garden.

They strolled out the far gate and onto the field beyond. In the distance she could see the hill on which she had lain that day when she dreamed of joining Timothy.

Today, with Kyle by her side, she could not even remember what perversion of the spirit had led her to think that joining Tim would be a good thing to do. Her heart had been too quick to tell itself lies not so long ago.

"I need to explain something to you, Rose. It is not happy news, I am afraid," Kyle said.

She stopped walking and stared at him. His tone produced a sickly pang of foreboding in her heart. "What is it?"

"I am about to launch you into another scandal."

"I do not believe that you are capable of creating a scandal."

"Oh, I am. One that you have known before. I am ruined, darling." He tried to speak normally, but she heard too much careful kindness in his voice.

He might worry about how she would react, but he did not appear sad about it himself, or even especially concerned. He might have looked at his boots after walking across this field and noticed that he had stepped in some manure. Unfortunate, but easily remedied.

"How ruined?" She almost gagged on the word. It had heralded so much unhappiness in her life.

"Totally. Norbury has withdrawn his property from our estate development. His father signed papers, but his solicitor can tie matters up indefinitely. In the meantime, I have timber arriving that must be paid, and other supplies on credit. The other investors will see losses but survive. I, however—"

"You were already blinking before this happened, and you will not survive. Will it mean debtors' prison?"

"That will depend on the generosity of my creditors. There is little to be gained in that for them." He lifted her chin with his fingertips. "Do not worry for me. I will come back eventually. It will take some years, however, and the opportunities may not be in London."

He embraced her shoulders with his arm, and they continued their walk.

"You are provided for," he said. "You will not have to ration fuel and bread again. You can continue your little war for respectability. There is your settlement from the marriage, and another trust that will provide an income of three hundred a year."

"What trust?"

"I established one for you soon after we wed."

"You were blinking hard but you put money into a trust? That was not wise, Kyle. You should have kept that money."

"If I had foreseen current developments, I might have, but I do not regret that I did not."

How could he be so calm about this? Ruin was not a minor thing. It was not some manure on one's boot at all, but more like having one's leg cut off. Yet he displayed no regret that his impulse to settle too much of his fortune on her had left him facing disaster now.

Panic welled inside her. His creditors might not be generous but instead vindictive. She could not bear the thought of him in debtors' prison. Her heart beat heavily from the implications of the way he spoke of her secure future. It sounded as if he did not expect or want to have her with him if the opportunities were far from London.

"We will both live on that income you arranged, of course, so perhaps it was wise after all," she said. "In fact, we should find a way to break the trust so that you can use the funds to avoid this ruin."

"No. Even if the courts permitted that, I would not do it."

She thought that she knew one reason why he had established that trust soon after they wed. That money must have been the encouragement he received from Easterbrook. It had been a reckless gesture to give it to her. Also a romantic one, long before she believed this marriage had a chance for such sentiments.

"It seems to me that if all those supplies are ordered that you would do well to use them to build something," she said.

"There can be no land development without land, Rose. Trust me, the property in Kent, and the funds already paid to Cottington's estate, will not be available for years even if I go to court and prevail."

"Then you must find other land."

"That takes money too. Even if the arrangement is similar to that with Cottington, payments are made up front."

"Perhaps Lord Hayden would loan—"

"No, Rose. I will not be in debt to your relatives."

Of course not. It had been stupid to even suggest it. He would have little left except his pride soon.

She looked ahead at the hill, then around at the fallow fields. One of her earliest childhood memories was of walking this path that she trod now, with her two brothers by her side. In her entire life nothing had changed in this landscape except the seasons.

Through everything, through her grief over deaths and loss, through the poverty after her father's debts and again after Tim's ruin, this property had served as testimony to her place in the world, no matter how poorly she might eat. The drawing room might hold only two chairs and a small table, but it was the place where her ancestors had hosted assemblies for the entire county.

Her throat burned. Nostalgia wanted to drown her. The emotion was not enough to keep her silent, however. She stopped walking and caught Kyle's arm so he stopped too.

"Why not use this land, Kyle? Put the timber and supplies to work here. It would be inadequate repayment for what my brothers did, but something at least."

"When I said in court that I had already been repaid, I meant it, Rose." His smile charmed her but also proved that she had not swayed him. "It is your family home, darling. Your sanctuary. And it still belongs to your brother, who will return one day."

He took her hand and urged her forward with him, into the breeze.

"Actually, Kyle, it belongs to me now, not my brother. Timothy wrote a letter to our solicitor, giving him a proxy to transfer the property to my name. If his last letter regarding the property's disposition would stand scrutiny, this one will as well."

They reached the top of the hill before he responded. "When did your brother write this letter?"

"While in prison, when I saw him before he was transported. I had Lord Hayden and the turnkey witness it."

"Why would he do such a thing?"

"I told him to. I feared he might do something fool-ish during the years away and lose it. I also thought it might be useful to have that letter, and this property, as security. It appears that I was correct."

He shook his head. "If it is yours, all the more reason why I cannot do it."

"Heavens, but you can be a stubborn man." She stepped close to him and let him see her vexation with his inconvenient nobility. "You are my husband. We are one, in pleasure and in love and in ruin. I will not attend parties while you go to debtors' prison or struggle for years to rebuild your fortune. If you will not use this land and you will not break the trust, then we will pledge my income against your debts and live here on what else we can scrape together."

"You will not live like that. I forbid it. You have en-dured that once and I will not allow it again."

"I will, no matter what you think to allow. I will find a way to pledge the income. I will save every shilling of it and carry it to the creditors myself."

A scowl began forming but did not get very far. He looked down at her long and hard.

"Please, Kyle," she urged. "Think of this property as my gift to you, if you must. Think of it as my dowry. Think of me as one of your syndicate investors if necessary."

"I would have to sell the land. Do you understand that? Leaseholds will not be enough. I will have to take the land through that lien while it is still in Tim's name. Once it is yours, as your husband I can use your real property but not sell it."

"Then use the lien to take it."

He paced away and narrowed his eyes on the rolling land. "We could spare your house and the field behind it, I think. This hill too. The rest should be enough."

She went to him and embraced him from behind. She rested her face against his strong back. "If it is not enough, we will sell the house and field too."

He turned in her arms and looked down. "Are you very sure about this? It will never be the same, even if the house is spared. You are sacrificing something that—"

"I am very sure. Please do not argue against it anymore, or speak of sacrifice. If you love me, if you honor me, you will not."

He did not argue. He did not even speak. He only kissed her as sweetly as he ever had. Her heart lightened with relief.

"Then it is decided. Yes?" she whispered.

"We will settle with the tenants at once, and find them other farms," he said.

He held her tightly. His breath warmed her hair and his kiss pressed her crown. "You move me, Roselyn," he muttered, his voice ragged with emotion. "You always have. First with your beauty, then with your goodness and passion, and now with your love. You make my heart burn and ache and fill with pride. Of all the good fortune that has come my way, you were fate's greatest gift."

She tilted her head so her lips could meet his. His warmth and love flowed into her. More warmth than she ever expected. More love than she had dared believe she deserved.

She nestled against him while they looked out from the hilltop. She melted into him until his embrace alone kept her standing.

ABOUT
THE AUTHOR

MADELINE HUNTER has published sixteen nationally bestselling historical romances. More than two million copies of her books are in print in the U.S., and her books have also been translated into nine languages. She is a five-time RITA finalist, and won the long historical RITA in 2003. Madeline holds a Ph.D. in art history, which she teaches at the college level. She currently lives in Pennsylvania with her husband and two sons. She can be contacted through her website: www.MadelineHunter.com.

If you loved *Secrets of Surrender,* stay tuned for the next scintillating novel in Madeline Hunter's Rothwell Brothers series.

THE

SINS

OF

LORD EASTERBROOK

By Madeline Hunter

Coming from Dell in 2009

The Sins of Lord Easterbrook
on sale in 2009

CHAPTER ONE

Leona paced back and forth in her opulent prison, simmering with vexation.

It was difficult to maintain one's dignity when one had been hauled off the street like so much lost baggage. Leona hoped that she had managed anyway.

She had spent the short ride to Grosvenor Square ignoring her captor and treating him like the lackey he was. Only once did she almost lose her temper, when she perceived that her young abductor found her pose of hauteur amusing.

A seed of worry sent out a vine to wind through her anger. While scathing scolds formed in half her mind, the other half assessed the implications of this insult. This lord's treatment of her reflected his view of her lowly status. He had concluded that she deserved no better.

When others learned about this lack of courtesy, they would imitate it. Nothing, not her mother's blood or her letters of introduction, would help her cause now.

Her plans here in London would be more difficult after today, and some of them might be nigh impossible.

She stopped walking. Her gaze took in the apple-green silk bed hangings and drapes, and the elegant, fine-boned mahogany furniture. She noted the exquisite watercolor paintings lending rainbow hues to the cream-colored walls. Then she saw nothing at all of her surroundings, but only the mental image of her brother, Gaspar, smiling as his boat pulled away after he had transferred her to the ship at Whampoa.

Gaspar had appeared so young to her that day. Far younger than his twenty-two years. Perhaps his unquestioning trust caused him to look juvenile. He had agreed to risk everything on this journey. His patrimony and his future were at stake, but he had handed the fate of both to her.

His image faded, and she again saw the luxury surrounding her. Her heart still beat heavily, but no longer due to insulted pride. Calm determination had replaced anger.

Her father had taught her that if one viewed adversity from a different angle, one could often see an opportunity hidden within it.

If one looked at this development from a different angle, one might say that she had just obtained an audience with one of the highest titles in the realm. A man of such consequence could be very useful. She might want to slap Easterbrook's face, but it would be wiser to win him over.

She walked to the dressing table and bent to see her reflection in the looking glass. Not really pretty, but hopefully pretty enough.

She removed her bonnet and set it on the table. She pinched her cheeks to make them flush.

"Primping for me, Miss Montgomery?"

The voice startled her. Her gaze shifted from her own reflection to that of the room behind her.

She saw high black boots and snug breeches in the shadows near the door. She dipped her head until the white billows of a shirt came into view, then the ends of very dark hair. The man who had intruded appeared to be a servant, and a lowly one at that, if he worked in such informal garb.

Only he wasn't a servant. His confidence clothed him in nobility more than any garments could. His body stood in lithe relaxation, exuding assumptions regarding his rights in this chamber, and in the world outside its walls.

She straightened and sought the kind of poise that might impress such a man. She turned to greet him with calm grace.

"Are you Lord Easterbrook?"

"I am."

"Your invitation was unexpected, Lord Easterbrook, but I am delighted to meet you all the same." She made a little curtsy.

He appeared to be waiting for something more. She could not imagine what it might be. Her smile began to feel odd and stretched.

Goodness, he looked for all the world like a pirate, now that she saw him from head to toe. The boots were high-quality, but his general appearance was not fashionable. His hair fell in long, lazy waves to well past his shoulders. They framed a face that, from what she could see, was younger than she had expected, and handsome enough to make his lack of coats and cravat romantic rather than crude. His dishabille was an insult, as had been her abduction and her entry up the servant's stairs, but she could not afford to dwell on that now.

He finally made a cursory bow. "Please forgive the rude way that you were brought here. My only excuse was my impatience to see you alone."

He walked toward her, and the light from the windows found him. It made the black boots blacker and the white shirt whiter. His face also became distinct. Dark eyes appeared hawkish in their intense focus on her. An unexpected elegance softened the strong bones of his face. His wide mouth curved into a vague smile that could easily turn hard.

A strange sensation stirred in her. It carried dark, deep caution, but not without a thrilling note. The way his body moved in his stride...the tone of his voice...those eyes...

Suddenly her mind saw him with short hair and more proper garments and a younger, less severe face. Her confusion crystallized into shock. She squinted at him, peering hard.

"Edmund?"

CHAPTER TWO

He enjoyed her astonishment. It amused him.

Maybe she would slap Easterbrook after all.

Just how big a scoundrel are you?

A very big one, it seemed.

"I always guessed that you had deceived us. I did not realize the depths of it, however." Her voice snapped with her anger. She felt a fool in more ways than she could list. Humiliation almost buried the girlish elation at seeing him again. Almost.

His amusement disappeared. "You know why I could not reveal who I was when I arrived in Macao."

She knew, but there might be more to his deception than what he alluded to. The potential implications of his true identity, to the past and future, to her plans here in England, jumbled together in her mind. They evoked a chaos of emotions, but nostalgia threatened to submerge every other reaction. She struggled to hold it at bay.

An awkwardness settled between them, one created by distance and time and the questions shouting in her mind. The silence made it worse. His proximity made it excruciating.

What a sight he was. That long hair made him look like a Tartar. The years had hardened him in all kinds of ways too. Echoes of his youthful brooding still spoke to her, but Easterbrook exuded none of the soulful pain that Edmund had carried.

"You have changed," she said.

"So have you." His appreciative gaze indicated that he found her changes pleasing.

He had always been too obvious about that. He had never had the courtesy seven years ago to pretend there was no attraction between them. He had deliberately made her blush and fluster. He still did, even if she refused to show her reactions. She warmed all over, as if he caressed her body with his gaze.

Her heart beat rapidly. The memories broke free. They flowed and an old, secret wistfulness soaked her.

It all came back. All of it, as if she were nineteen again and her womanhood was blossoming under the wayward traveler's seductive attention. Only she was not nineteen now, and the traveler had not been what he claimed, but a marquess. That changed everything about their friendship back then. It meant that he had toyed with her most ignobly.

Fury spiked fast and hot, and she surrendered to it. "You unforgivable bastard."

He reached out and rested two fingertips on her lips. "Such language. What would Branca say?"

Her lips pulsed beneath his touch. A terrible, wonderful shiver slid down to her heart.

She turned her head to break the contact. "Branca is dead," she said. "Two years now."

"I am sorry. She was a good duenna, even if I found her inconvenient."

She could not believe that he referred to his cynical pursuit so casually. "My father is also deceased. He died the year after you left Macao."

"I know. Word came to me through the Company."

"Yes, I imagine a marquess can get whatever he wants from them. Is that how you traveled back then? Other men might have to pay their way or work for their berth. I expect a marquess need merely present himself to the captain of an East India Company ship to obtain passage."

He shrugged, as if such privileges were of little account. "I was surprised to hear that you are using the name Montgomery. You did not marry Pedro after all."

"When the financial condition of my father's trading house became apparent upon his death, Pedro withdrew the proposal. Everyone understood."

"You must have been disappointed."

"Saving the business from total failure occupied me. I was able to preserve it for my brother. After he reached his majority and was allowed into Canton, it improved significantly."

He smiled. For that brief moment he looked much like Edmund, whose rare smiles made her heart rise with both joy and relief. "I think, Leona, that the trading house improved under your own hand. Your father relied on you, and I suspect that your brother does too."

"My brother has proven most capable. I do help him when I can, of course. In fact, that is why I am in London. I intend to meet with shippers and traders based here, and convince them to forge associations with Montgomery and Tavares for their intercoastal trade in the East."

He assessed her again, with a gaze both curious and admiring. She clung to her pose of friendly but casual interest.

His dark, deep-set eyes showed humor and warmth and disconcerting familiarity. His countenance subtly shifted from handsome to beautiful as his thoughts allowed the softening elegance to have its way.

Her instincts reacted the same way that they had when he watched her in Macao. She sensed something emanating from him, something both dark and dangerously alluring. His aura became possessively invasive. His attention tried to compel her to explore a mystery that would be her undoing.

Her inexperience had sent her running seven years ago whenever that power sought to absorb her. Now here she was, a grown woman who had seen the world, and she still wanted to hide.

Instead, she retreated within herself. She pulled walls around her soul so that it would be safe.

Immediately, his softness disappeared. His gaze turned searching, as if he was trying to see through that barrier.

"So you traveled all the way to England to serve as your brother's agent? You came for no other reason?"

He was very close to her. Too close. She had to look up to see his face. "There was no other reason to come."

"Wasn't there?"

"None at all."

"I think that there was."

"Goodness—do you think I journeyed all this way to find *you*?" She feigned astonishment. "Of course, if I had known your true identity, I would have. I daresay you can arrange introductions in a day that it will take me weeks to obtain. If I had known that Edmund was

really Easterbrook, I would have sought you out immediately upon arriving in London."

He responded with a lazy, devastating smile designed to
disarm her. She could feel his aura sliding around her in
a curious caress, seeking any gaps in her defenses. "You
would have done no such thing. Whether I was Edmund or
Easterbrook, you would have run away and hid from me, no
matter what benefit I might bring to your missions here."

"Hid from you? Why would I do that?"

"Because I frighten you. I terrified the girl, and I still
alarm the woman."

He guessed her reaction so confidently that it irritated her. She squared her shoulders. "You are a little
peculiar, and you are somewhat rude, and you have been
insulting today, and you were too brooding then, but
you have never been frightening."

He abruptly stepped closer. She almost jumped out
of her skin.

He laughed quietly. "See?"

She stood her ground, facing him down almost nose-
to-nose. "Startled is not the same as frightened, Lord
Easterbrook."

"You would never have sought me out here in
London, because you were relieved that I had to leave
Macao. You could not get me on that ship fast enough."

"There was no choice but to get you on that ship, or
have you forgotten that?"

"There was unfinished business between us, and you
were not sorry to escape the reckoning. You were too innocent and unawake to understand that you wanted me
as much as I wanted you."

"You are wrong, but that is all in the past anyway. I
am no longer an ignorant girl, and you are no longer
Edmund. Those two differences change everything."

"Actually, Leona, I have learned since entering this chamber that time, place and names change some things not at all."

No, they did not. Damn it. Damn him.

He loomed over her, close enough to subtly dominate her. Near enough that he might hear the stunning way her heart beat.

The hard curve of his mouth matched the arrogant confidence in his eyes. He could tell that she was too much affected by him. He knew that he could still turn her into the nineteen-year-old girl who was promised to a fiancé who did not excite her nearly as much as the handsome stranger taking hospitality in her father's home.

However, one thing *had* changed. As a woman, she understood his appeal in ways the girl had not. She recognized her response to his mysterious allure for the sexual arousal that it was. She worried that he knew that too.

She tried to move away. He caught her arm, stopping her. He pulled her toward him. His boldness stunned her.

His hand touched her face, commanding her to be still. His gaze demanded obedience. Her thoughts spun into incoherent objections when he tilted her head back.

His warm, dry lips touched hers and lingered, then began proving that he could still mesmerize her.

Warmth. Intimacy so immediate and deep that it seemed unnatural. Sly, sensual shivers and expanding wonder and astonishment. The years fell away, and she was being kissed for the first time ever by a reckless young man with a dark, chaotic spirit—a dangerous man who offered adventures of the body and heart that she dared not accept.

The kiss banished suspicions while it lasted. Youthful emotions refreshed her like a coastal breeze. Arousal tingled at her breasts and tightened her womb and teased one devilish spot very low in her body. Low, long waves of pleasure lapped through her.

She restrained herself from showing how powerfully he stirred her. One sigh or gasp and they would probably end up on that apple-green bed. She did not fight him, however. The sensations so stimulated her that she lacked the strength for that.

"You are an enigma, Leona," he muttered. His hand remained on her cheek and his breath warmed her ear. "You always were. Perhaps that is the fascination."

"We all are enigmas to each other, I suppose."

"Very few people are to me."

She gently lifted his hand off her arm. She stepped away and pulled her composure together.

"Lord Easterbrook, since you arranged this unexpected reunion, perhaps you will agree to aid me in my mission. Out of sentiment for our old friendship in Macao, that is."

He scowled at the way she picked up the threads of their conversation, as if nothing of note had just happened. "That depends on the kind of aid that you request, Leona."

"I would like to be introduced to your brother, Lord Hayden Rothwell."

"What do you want with Hayden?"

"I have been told that he is likely to know the traders and investors whom I came to London to meet."

He shrugged, as if bored by such a simple petition. "I will arrange for you to meet him if you wish."

"That is kind of you. I am very grateful. Now, while seeing old friends is always pleasant, this unexpected visit has delayed my day's plans. Am I allowed to leave? Are we done?"

His attention sharpened on her. He did not care for the way she dismissed the meeting, and him. "We are nowhere near done, Leona."

"To my mind we are entirely done, Lord Easterbrook. Please accept my decision about that."

A tense silence passed, no more than ten seconds, she guessed. In that brief span he appeared to be making a decision. Their intimate surroundings, the bed and pillows and sensual fabrics, ceased being mere background and turned into visual arguments for why it would be pleasant not to be entirely done after all.

She wished that she could summon anger or outrage or pride to shore up her defenses. She wished she could claim that the kiss had not tempted her. In truth, a little whirlwind spun in her heart now, and her body ached from the intense desire pulling between them with tantalizing tugs.

"You were always allowed to leave," he finally said. "There is no guard outside the door."

"I will continue with my afternoon's excursion, then. Good day to you, Lord Easterbrook."

She grabbed her bonnet and strode to the door on legs that barely allowed her to walk.

"Leona."

His quiet address stopped her after she had opened the door. The resonance of his tone sent a treacherous thrill down the center of her body.

"Leona, it appears that you are no longer so innocent and unawake."

She looked back at him. He was far too dashing in his shirtsleeves and open collar and high boots. Stronger than she remembered. More arrogant too. There had been poignant moments when Edmund was vulnerable in ways that she suspected Easterbrook never was.

"That is a peculiar farewell, Lord Easterbrook. Maybe I will run and hide like you predicted."

"I am not worried about that. Your missions will keep you nearby. And this time, Leona, before any ship takes one of us away, I will have you."